TO BRIE OR NOT TO BRIE

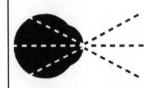

**This Large Print Book carries the
Seal of Approval of N.A.V.H.**

A CHEESE SHOP MYSTERY

To Brie or Not to Brie

Avery Aames

WHEELER PUBLISHING
A part of Gale, Cengage Learning

GALE
CENGAGE Learning·

Detroit • New York • San Francisco • New Haven, Conn • Waterville, Maine • London

GALE
CENGAGE Learning·

Wheeler Publishing Large Print Cozy Mystery.
The text of this Large Print edition is unabridged.
Other aspects of the book may vary from the original edition.
Set in 16 pt. Plantin.

LIBRARY OF CONGRESS CATALOGING-IN-PUBLICATION DATA

Aames, Avery.
 To Brie or Not to Brie / Avery Aames. — Large Print edition.
  pages cm. — (A Cheese Shop Mystery) (Wheeler Publishing Large Print Cozy Mystery)
  ISBN 978-1-4104-6116-2 (softcover) — ISBN 1-4104-6116-5 (softcover) 1. Cheese shops—Ohio—Fiction. 2. Caterers and catering—Ohio—Fiction. 3. Murder—Investigation—Fiction. 4. Ohio—Fiction. 5. Large type books. I. Title.
 PS3601.A215T63 2013
 813'.6—dc23   2013020171

Published in 2013 by arrangement with The Berkley Publishing Group, a division of Penguin Group (USA)

Printed in the United States of America
2 3 4 5 6   24 23 22 21 20

To my sister, Kimberley.
You are my dear friend.
I am blessed to have you in my life.

ACKNOWLEDGEMENTS

Let us be grateful to the people who make us happy; they are the charming gardeners who make our souls blossom.
— MARCEL PROUST

There is no possible way to acknowledge all those who have helped me along the road to publishing and the road to life — family, friends, teachers, and more. I'll do my best.

First and foremost, thank you to my family for loving me and understanding that a creative person is sometimes crazy. Thanks to my first readers: my husband, Chuck; Krista Davis; and Janet Bolin. Thanks to good pals Kate Carlisle and Hannah Dennison for supporting me and listening to me wax "not poetic." Thanks to my brainstormers at Plothatchers. Thanks to my blog mates on Mystery Lovers Kitchen and Killer Characters. Thanks to Jenn McKinlay, Julie Hyzy, Cleo Coyle, Lorraine Bartlett, Hank Phillippi Ryan, and Jamie Freveletti for your savvy advice. And thanks to the Sisters in Crime Guppies, a superb online group.

Thanks to those who have helped make the Cheese Shop Mysteries sparkle: my fabulous editor, Kate Seaver; Katherine Pelz; Laura Perry; and Kayleigh Clark. I appreciate all your insight and enthusiasm. To my artist, Teresa Fasolino, wow. You amaze me. Thank you to my publisher, Berkley Prime Crime, for wanting books about a cheese shop and for granting me the opportunity.

Thank you to my business team, including Kim Lionetti, P.J. Nunn, Lindsey LeBret, and Sheridan Stancliff. And thanks to my cheese consultant, Marcella Wright. Your tasty knowledge is so helpful.

Last but not least, thank you librarians, teachers, fans, and/or readers. Thank you for loving the written word, and thank you for sharing the world of a cheese monger at Fromagerie Bessette with your friends.

Say cheese!

CHAPTER 1

"Charlotte Erin Bessette, you're a goner." A blissful moan escaped my lips. Had I died and gone to heaven? I took another bite of the ciabatta, spinach, and goat cheese crostini — one of many appetizers sitting on the granite counter in The Cheese Shop kitchen — and sighed again. Adding minced sun-dried tomatoes to the recipe had done the trick.

I downed the remainder of the scrumptious morsel and eyed the array that I had started at six A.M. The jalapeños packed with mascarpone and seasoned with Cajun spices had nearly seared the roof of my mouth, but the ricotta-stuffed mushrooms were a good balance. All in all, the experiment was a success. I had at least ten winning choices for the taste testing.

As I collected cartons of cream to use in the desserts I planned to make, I paused. Did I smell smoke?

I tore out of the walk-in refrigerator. Flames not only licked upward from the sauté pan on the stove, they spiraled from the twenty-five-pound bag of flour beside it.

"Fire!" I yelled to no one. I was alone in the shop. Lured by the ciabatta crostini, I had forgotten that I was frying shallots for one more dish. "Shoot, shoot, shoot." I hadn't patted the shallots dry enough. Water must have boiled a spit of oil out of the pan, which caught fire and nailed the flour bag.

"You dope, Charlotte." I knew what danger lurked in a kitchen. That would teach me to multitask. Why did I always think I could do everything . . . at once? Wonder Woman I was not, though, at the age of seven, I had liked her costume so much that I begged and pleaded to wear it for Halloween. What girl hadn't?

I dumped the cartons of cream on the counter, swooped to the stove, grabbed a lid, and threw it onto the sauté pan to douse the flame. Then I switched off the gas beneath the burner, snatched one of the oven mitts, and batted the bag of flour. I quenched the fire, but smoke coiled toward the ceiling, and the fire alarm began to bleat.

"Dang." I chucked the oven mitt, hoisted one of the wicker stools that nestled under the counter, placed it beneath the alarm, and climbed on.

"*Sacre bleu,*" a woman yelled from the front of the shop. Rebecca galloped into the kitchen. "Charlotte, I smell smoke." She skidded on her heels. "What are you doing?"

"What does it look like?" I teetered on tiptoe, the hem of my pumpkin-colored sweater rising up my midriff, the heels of my loafers loose. "I'm trying to hit the red button." I jabbed at the darned thing with my index finger but missed my target. The smoke alarm began to howl like a banshee.

"You can't turn it off that way." My young assistant covered her ears. "You have to remove the battery."

Swell. Out of spite, I poked at the red button one more time before unclipping the alarm case, which came loose but remained fixed to the ceiling by its wires. I plucked at the battery, breaking a nail in the process — *double swell* — and removed the battery from its slot.

Just as the siren stopped blaring, I felt something give way beneath my feet. "Oh, no." The seat of the wicker chair burst. I let rip with a yelp, lost my grip on the alarm, and careened heels-first through the seat's hoop. The wicker and rubber matting on the floor cushioned my landing; the underside of my bare arms scraped the rim. I would have black-and-blue bruises, but at least I hadn't broken skin, or worse, my neck.

Rebecca rushed to help, her ponytail flapping behind her, her pencil skirt preventing her lanky legs from making long strides. "Are you all right? Are you hurt?"

"Only my ego."

"What were you thinking? We have a ladder."

"Do you see it nearby?" I said. "No, you do not. I didn't have time. I had an emergency."

"Impulsive," she muttered.

"Proactive," I countered.

"Okay, okay." Rebecca offered a hand to help me out of my confinement.

Spurning her goodwill, I snuggled my feet into my loafers and, balancing both palms on the broken chair's hoop, slipped one leg out, followed by the other. I brushed bits of wicker from my clothes and tugged the hem of my sweater over my chinos. After a stunned second, I burst into giggles.

Rebecca covered her mouth with the back of her hand and sniggered. When she regained control of herself, she said, "What kind of quiche are you making — let me rephrase that — *were* you making?"

"I wasn't." Each day at Fromagerie Bessette — what the locals liked to call The Cheese Shop — we made a different quiche to sell to our customers, but I had finished the dozen long before I had started in on the wedding menu. Every October, when daylight savings ended, my inner clock went cuckoo. For weeks, I had been waking before dawn. "I was testing out wedding appetizers."

"*Bien sûr.* But, of course."

I smiled. Ever since she had started working at the shop, Rebecca practiced her French. She loved the way my grandparents, who had owned the place before ceding it to my cousin and me, settled into their native tongue. To date, I think she had learned close to a hundred phrases.

"How is the menu coming?" she asked.

"Pretty well, except for one." The shallots — now ruined — were intended to go into a radicchio marmalade that would garnish a filo dough turnover, filled with breast of turkey and smoked Gouda.

I headed to the kitchen sink to freshen up.

"Why are there ice cream fixings on the counter?" Rebecca trailed me.

"I'm planning on trying out a few new desserts." I wasn't a caterer — I was a cheese shop owner — but when my best

13

friend had asked me to come up with an eclectic menu for her wedding, I promised I would do my best.

"Maybe you should have waited until you had more hands to help."

I frowned. The last thing I wanted after a kitchen fiasco was sage advice from a twenty-something who was ten years younger than me. Wonder Woman wouldn't take it, would she?

"I wasn't expecting you," I said as I rinsed my hands and patted them dry on a fluffy white-and-gold-striped towel. "It's your day off, isn't it? I thought you were spending it with your fiancé and his parents. You were going on a tour of Amish country."

"Speaking of desserts," she said, ineptly changing subjects, "remind me to show you an all-cheese wedding cake that I saw on the Internet."

I glanced over my shoulder. Was there trouble brewing in Romance Land? Was that why she had come to work? "Are you okay?"

"The cake was so cool," she went on, fluttering her fingers to describe the shape. "Wheels upon wheels of assorted cheeses. Cheddar, Smoked Gouda, Cashel Blue, and Ashgrove Double Gloucester, all topped with a wedding couple carved out of cheese."

I raised an eyebrow and pursed my lips, my standard look when demanding an answer to a question.

"I'm fine," she assured me. "Really."

She didn't seem to have been crying. Maybe I was making more of her sudden arrival at the shop than I ought. I turned back to the sun-shaped mirror over the sink and assessed the damage the shock and awe of a kitchen fire had done to my appearance. Thanks to nerves, my short feathery hair had gone as flat as a pancake. I tweaked it but to no avail. Giving up, I dabbed perspiration off my face with the tip of the towel and walked back to the main shop.

I fetched a container of Brie from the glass cheese case, set it on the wooden counter, and cut it in half with a carving knife.

Rebecca scooted to my side and tapped the cheese counter with the tips of her hot pink fingernails. "Okay, truth? I don't want to go on the tour. Ever."

"Why?"

"Because I'm afraid I'll run into Papa. He was so shut down the last time we saw each other."

Her Amish father had been as cordial as a bale of straw. He had come to town to bring Rebecca her grandmother's shawl. They had exchanged few words. Anger and disappointment could run deep for the elders of a clan when someone like Rebecca left the fold.

"Was I nuts not to go?" she asked.

"Sometimes you have to protect your heart."

"That's what I told my future in-laws. They seemed to understand. Do you think they understood?"

"I'm sure they did."

"Let's not talk about me anymore." Rebecca clapped her hands. "I'm here. What can I do to help?"

I loved her no-pity-parties attitude. The day I took ownership of Fromagerie Bessette from my grandparents I had hired Rebecca. She had helped me through all the renovations. Together we had decided where the wooden display barrels would stand and what jams and other accoutrements would sit on the many shelves around the spacious room, and she had been instrumental in helping me decide on our color scheme of Tuscany gold and burgundy. I don't know what I would have done without her.

I pointed. "Open some windows and let in the fresh air."

"I'm on it." She scurried to the rear of the shop and cranked open the window beside the exit door, then flew to the front door

16

and propped it open with the cheese-shaped doorstop. "Next?"

"Fetch some blueberries from the refrigerator."

Her gaze went from the cartons of cream in the kitchen to the Brie sitting on the cheese counter. "Are you planning to make Brie blueberry ice cream?"

I nodded. "I've been collaborating with the owner of the Igloo Ice Cream Parlor. He's a wizard with flavors."

"And he's willing to share a recipe?" Rebecca whistled.

"Actually, it's my recipe," I said as I rewrapped the remaining Brie. "He —"

"Mystery and magic abound ever since he took ownership, don't you think?" Rebecca's eyes widened; her face flushed.

"Magic?"

"And he's very secretive. He's in and out of town all the time. What's up with that?"

"I don't have a clue." And, to be honest, I hadn't paid attention.

"He's so dishy handsome. He reminds me of Houdini, with that thick black hair and those ebony eyes."

I pushed the Brie to one side. "Rebecca Zook, if I didn't know you better, I'd say you had a crush."

"Oh, no." She crossed her heart. "I'm

committed to my man. He is the best, sweetest —"

"Who's the sweetest?" Umberto Urso, our chief of police, appeared in the opened doorway.

"Not you," I teased.

"I am, too. My mother tells me so."

"She's sparing your feelings."

Urso removed his broad-brimmed hat before sauntering into the shop; otherwise, he was so tall he would have scraped the top on the upper edge of the door. As he moved toward the counter, he smoothed the front of his snug-fitting brown uniform. Had he lost a pound or two? He seemed robust and happy. He perched on one of the ladder-back chairs by the tasting counter and sniffed. "What did you burn?"

"Nothing."

"Don't kid a kidder. I'm guessing onions."

"Shallots."

"Ah, one of my favorite smells." He swatted the Genoa and Cervelat salami hanging on the silver S-hook. The group swayed to and fro. "Hey, I heard you set a wedding date."

"You heard wrong." The love of my life and I had been discussing dates. We hadn't settled on one yet. He had suggested November; I had proposed June, mainly be-

18

cause I didn't want to steal my best friend's thunder and get married too soon after she tied the knot. "Are you here for your usual?" In addition to cheeses and the occasional quiche, we offered sandwiches, made fresh every morning. Urso preferred a Jarlsberg with maple-infused ham on a torpedo-shaped roll. Over the last six months, I couldn't remember a day when he had missed ordering one.

He stopped the salami from swinging. "Actually, I'm going to take two of your heroes made with prosciutto, Morbier, and pesto."

Knock me over with a feather.

"Two." Rebecca winked. "Planning a picnic, Chief?"

"The weather is perfect for it," I said. Autumn in Ohio was one of the most beautiful seasons. I loved the vistas of amber hills and the trees turning burnt orange and gold.

"So who's the girl?" Rebecca asked.

"Girl?" I echoed.

"Picnic means date," Rebecca explained.

I ogled Urso. He avoided making eye contact, but his mouth quirked up ever so slightly.

"C'mon, who is she?" Rebecca pressed. She had no compunction when it came to

19

Urso. She ribbed him mercilessly, as if he were her older brother. And he took it. I could banter with him only so far before he turned disagreeable.

He ran the rim of his hat brim through his fingers. "Mine to know," he said, his voice cagey.

"Will she be your plus-one at the wedding?" I said. A select group of the town's residents were invited.

"We'll have to see." He chuckled.

Not eager to pry further for fear he would think I was interested — which I most definitely was not — I grabbed a pair of the requested sandwiches from the glass case, stowed them and a pair of napkins in one of our glossy gold bags, and beckoned Urso to the cash register.

As he paid for his purchase, a group of tourists wearing purple T-shirts, with *Stomping the Grapes* inscribed in cursive writing on the front, crowded into the shop.

Behind them marched Prudence Hart, Providence's self-appointed diva. "Charlotte!" She booted the cheese-shaped wedge from beneath the door and slammed the door shut. The picture display windows rattled with a vengeance. Wagging a bony finger, Prudence made a beeline for me. The mustard-colored sheath she wore matched her dour expression. I swear, I couldn't remember Prudence ever smiling. "You won't believe what I . . . I . . ." she sputtered.

Oh, dear. I hoped she wasn't going to do what she had done during a previous visit to the shop — pass out. I didn't have any brown paper lunch bags on hand.

". . . what I" — Prudence drew in a deep breath, tapped on her toothpick-thin leg as if to regulate the intake, and exhaled — "what I heard."

"What?" Rebecca said.

I prodded her not to encourage Prudence. The woman was an uptight authoritarian who rarely came into Fromagerie Bessette unless to spread rumors or make a fuss.

"The Harvest Moon Ranch has been sold," Prudence blurted.

"Oh, no," I said. That was the site for my pal's wedding. It was a charming red ranch north of the city, with a gazebo and barn and acres of lush grounds. Would the sale cause a postponement?

"Oh, yes," Prudence went on. "I was going to buy it."

I didn't believe her for a second. She was forever blustering about purchasing this and that. She considered herself a real estate mogul in the making. So far she hadn't

21

purchased a thing other than her dress shop, which was situated catty-corner from Fromagerie Bessette.

"Who bought it?" Rebecca said.

"That divorcée," Prudence hissed, the word as distasteful as wolfsbane.

I didn't have a clue who she meant.

"She snatched it out from under me. Why I should —" Prudence gestured as if wringing someone's neck but stopped when she spotted Urso, his head tilted, his steely gaze blazing at her. She blanched. "Oh, Chief, I didn't see you there."

How had she missed him? He was almost as large as a grizzly bear.

"I didn't mean . . ." Prudence hesitated. "What I should have said . . . I'll have my attorney speak to her attorney and —"

The door to The Cheese Shop swept open. The grape-leaf-shaped chimes jingled.

With murder in her eyes, Prudence bolted toward the woman who entered. "You-u-u-u!"

CHAPTER 2

Tyanne Taylor, one of my part-timers, entered the shop, her cheeks burnished pink. The rose-colored tank dress she wore hugged her toned body in all the right places.

"You!" Prudence stopped in front of Tyanne and extended a finger like a sword. "You stole it."

Tyanne threw back her shoulders and finger-combed her highlighted hair. "I did nothing of the sort."

"Right from under my nose," Prudence persisted. "I was counting on the ranch to carry me into retirement. Why, I have half a mind to —"

"— to beat the stew out of me?" Tyanne planted a fist on her hip and smirked.

Prudence peered over her shoulder at Urso, who hadn't budged from his spot near the register, but he looked primed. She gulped and refocused on Tyanne. "I have half a mind to tell you a thing or two more, but I don't have the time. Good day." She swept past Tyanne and out of the store.

Rebecca wiggled her pinky at me. "What's that biblical proverb? 'Don't count your chickens until they're hatched.' "

I was pretty certain the saying hadn't come from the Bible but kept mum. No sense stirring the pot.

"I'm worried about what Prudence might do," Rebecca added.

"Don't be. Prudence will find something else to protest."

"Why is she always so prickly?"

I shrugged. Some said it was because Prudence let the man of her dreams get away. Others said she was such a miser that she wouldn't share a dime with another soul. Perhaps, like an uncared-for cheese, she had developed a hard, distasteful rind.

Urso chortled. "I guess the crisis has been averted. Be seeing you." He lumbered out of the shop.

Tyanne hurried toward the counter. "Charlotte, sugar, you'll never guess what I did," she said with a drawl.

I wasn't dense. After Prudence's tirade, I was pretty sure I could figure it out.

"I bought the Harvest Moon Ranch. I'm so-o-o-o excited," she continued. That was an understatement. She needed gravity boots to anchor her to the ground. "And I've taken a partner."

My mouth fell open. The latter statement held all sorts of connotations. Recently Tyanne had finalized her divorce. Had she found a soul mate so quickly?

"A partner?" I repeated.

"Business partner. A *silent* business partner. But don't worry your pretty head," Tyanne said. "I'm still going to work part-time at Fromagerie Bessette. With two of my sisters having moved here, I've got all sorts of seconds, minutes, and hours on my hands."

Tyanne's older sisters had left New Orleans and had arrived in Providence about two months ago. The eldest loved spending time with Tyanne's children; the one that was a year older than Tyanne had taken over the beauty salon and had turned it into a new hot spot in town.

"I'm going to do destination weddings," Tyanne went on. "I know, I know." She put up her palms to hold us at bay. "The Harvest Moon Ranch was doing weddings before, but nothing like I imagine. People from all over will come to Providence to get hitched."

"I'll bet that was what Prudence had in

mind," Rebecca said.

"Prudence-Schmudence," Tyanne said. "She has no vision. And don't let her snow you. She did not make a bid on the ranch. I heard about it going up for sale and snatched it up before anyone could offer a counterbid."

"Where did you get the money?" I asked.

Tyanne giggled and leaned forward to impart her secret. "Sugar, I told you. I have a silent business partner. Plus, I've been saving for a rainy day. My two-timing husband had no idea. A cookie jar is a magical thing." She slipped behind the counter and grabbed both of my arms. "Isn't this the yummiest idea? I close the deal in two days, all cash. And guess what? My first event will be Meredith and Matthew's wedding."

My best friend was marrying my sweet cousin.

"I've already met with Meredith," Tyanne went on, hands painting the air. "She's mighty relieved that she has me as her wedding planner. To tell the truth, she was overwhelmed having to do it all herself. The previous owners weren't offering a lick of help. But I'm on the case. Now" — Tyanne tapped her watch — "I need you for a maid of honor dress fitting next door. Got a half hour? Meredith is already there."

With longing, I eyed the Brie sitting on the cheese counter. After the fiasco with the shallots, I had wanted to make a successful dessert. On the other hand, I couldn't wait to see my dress. Ice cream would have to wait.

Rebecca nudged me. "Go on. I'll defend the fort."

Entering the colorful Sew Inspired Quilt Shoppe always took me back to childhood memories of my grandmother and me sewing. In addition to being mayor of our fine city, my grandmother ran the Providence Playhouse. Often she brought home swatches of fabrics, and we pieced together costumes for a production. I would never forget the variety of textiles she gathered: nubby wools, cool cottons, and jerseys in wild, exotic patterns. A color palette, she advised me, helped convey a mood on stage.

Freckles, Sew Inspired's owner, felt the same as I did about color. As a tribute to autumn, she had redecorated in warm rusts and golds. In the display window, she had spread silk leaves on the floor and draped the mannequins with mustard-colored crinkle knits. In the shop, handmade brown-toned quilts adorned the walls; each told a story about the history of Ohio.

"This way." Tyanne led me beyond the racks of thread, lace, ribbons, and buttons. "We're doing the fittings in the back. Oh, did I tell you that Amy and Clair are here, too?"

Amy and Clair were my nieces — well, not actually my nieces. Their father, Matthew, was my cousin, but long story short, I called his girls my nieces for simplicity's sake, and they liked it. We all had the same last name: Bessette.

"And their mother?" I asked tentatively.

"Lucky us." Tyanne batted my arm. "She's busy at her shop. Follow me behind the luscious curtain."

Sew Inspired Quilt Shoppe wasn't set up as a boutique. People didn't normally come to the store for dress fittings, but Meredith had insisted Freckles — Providence's expert with a needle — design the wedding attire. Beyond the velvet curtain at the rear of the shop stood a stockroom.

Tyanne pulled back the curtain and gestured for me to enter first. Floor-to-ceiling cubbyholes held more fabrics and more accessories. Freckles, who was button-sized with the most adorable grin and a penchant for the color orange, approached me. She held her arms wide for a hug.

I reciprocated. Though I barely reached

five-foot-three, my chin hovered above the top of her head. "Where are your girls?" I asked.

"Super Dad has them for the day. They're studying the changing leaves. Doesn't that sound fun?" Freckles and her daughters, a homeschooled thirteen-year-old and a surprise one-year-old, played and studied in the stockroom. "And now for our fun." She pushed up the sleeves of her orange V-neck sweater and clapped her hands. "Amy and Clair, it's time. Come out, please."

My preteen nieces popped from behind a pair of rattan dressing screens and ran toward me. Each did a twirl.

"Wow!" I said.

Freckles had created a pair of frothy cornflower blue dresses draped with toile. Clair revolved like a ballerina in a jewel box. Amy, closer in height to her sister than she was a few months ago, whipped around with fervor, her dark chin-length hair fluting out with abandon.

"Wow!" I repeated.

"Is that all you can say, Aunt Charlotte?" Clair stopped twirling and searched my face with intensity. She was such a serious soul.

"Yes," I said. "I mean, no, you look delicious, like spun sugar."

Clair poked her sister. "I told you our

dresses were beautiful."

I noticed Amy's mouth was turned down in a frown. "You don't like the dresses, sweetheart?" I glanced at Freckles, who waved off any insecurity about hearing an opinion.

"They're a little girlie." Amy was our tomboy. Like me, she loved cheese, and like my grandmother, she adored singing and acting, but recently she had turned to sports. Running, leaping, and jumping encompassed most of the hours of her day, probably because her latest crush — Tyanne's son — was a jock.

"You are both stunning." I gripped their hands. "You should be very proud. Where's Meredith?"

"With Edy. Over there." Amy pointed toward a third rattan screen.

"Edy Delaney?" I whispered to Freckles. Edy was the alterationist at La Chic Boutique.

"I stole her away from Prudence," Freckles confided with a guilty giggle. "She said Prudence cut her salary by twenty percent. Even a single girl's got to eat. And she's got talent."

Tyanne nudged me. "What's wrong, sugar? Your nose is all scrunched up. Don't you like Edy?"

How could I admit, without spurring rumors, that I hadn't trusted Edy since high school? I hated saying anything bad about someone.

"C'mon," Tyanne said. " 'Fess up."

"She's —"

"Charlotte." Meredith stepped from behind the screen and climbed onto a platform in front of a three-way mirror. "Look at me."

My heart caught in my chest and all thoughts of Edy's cheating on the tenth-grade chemistry test flew out the window because Meredith, my best friend since I could remember, reminded me of a Disney princess, right down to her tawny blond hair, which was twisted into elegant curls, and her sun-kissed skin, which glowed with ethereal hope.

"Wow," I said.

"There she goes again." Amy punched Clair, who tittered.

Freckles had designed a satin wedding dress that was breathtakingly dramatic. The neckline scooped from shoulder to shoulder, exposing a demure hint of décolletage. The bodice fit Meredith's slim frame like a glove. The skirt, starting from a dropped hip line, layered out in tiers upon tiers of shimmering white to the floor. A pair of glass slippers wouldn't have been out of place.

"Edy," Meredith called. "I think we need to shorten the hem."

Edy Delaney emerged from the fitting room. Though tall and long-limbed, at first glance she reminded me of a human pincushion. She was clad in signature black — stretchy T-shirt, jeans, and boots — and clenched long pearl-studded pins between her teeth. Her short hair stuck out with spiky defiance, as if she had poked her finger into a light socket. A black pincushion, clinging to her wrist, completed the ensemble. Without saying a word of hello, she crouched beside Meredith and gazed at the mirror and back at the dress, pinning as needed.

Tyanne leaned into me. "Why don't you like her? I mean, besides her *Girl with the Dragon Tattoo* getup and the fact that she towers over you?"

"You can tell us," Freckles whispered. "Is it that she cheated back in school?"

I gaped at the pair of them, both eager for gossip, their mouths hanging open, their eyes alert. Had my princessy pal spilled the beans?

"Meredith didn't tell me," Freckles added. "Edy did. I like her. She's got energy, and her Goth style? It's been drawing in scads of new customers. She's a novelty." Freckles giggled, as she often did. "I'm not averse to a boom in business."

A breeze billowed into the room, kicking up flecks of thread and dust.

"Someone entered the shop. I'll be right back." Freckles headed toward the curtain.

Before she reached it, Prudence Hart stomped into the stockroom, followed by her equally tall and reed-thin pal, Iris Isherwood. Poor Iris. Behind her back, members of the Providence Garden Society snickered about her lack of style. She had taken to wearing floral dresses at all times. No one was sure if she was advertising her name or her flower business.

"I found you at last," Prudence said.

"At last," Iris echoed while brushing lint off the peacock blue tote bag inscribed with her company name and slogan: *Iris's Flowers. Growing Stronger.*

"What's going on?" Meredith said from the platform.

Edy tugged on the base of the dress to keep Meredith in place.

"Nothing, sugar," Tyanne said. "I've got this. Don't you worry your pretty head." She directed Freckles to shuttle Meredith and the twins behind their screens and marched toward Prudence. "Let's talk out in the shop."

"No." Prudence folded her arms across her chest.

"Yes, let's," Iris said, uncharacteristically taking the lead. I couldn't remember her ever having an opinion, let alone a backbone, not even when chairing the garden society meetings. She hoisted the strap of her tote over her shoulder with a grunt — what did she carry in that thing, gardening tools? — and said, "C'mon, Pru."

Prudence didn't seem to have heard, not because she was staring daggers at Tyanne; she was glowering at me. What was up with that?

"C'mon, Pru," Iris repeated. By nature, Iris was a fixer, though a tad zealous and somewhat misguided. She was always tweaking things — her garden, her neighbor's garden, the church garden. She pulled her friend by the forearm.

Begrudgingly, Prudence moved.

"Who else wants to come with us?" Self-consciously Iris plucked her shaggy wheat-toned hair, which reminded me of a dandelion, so feathery and sparse that it all might blow away in a strong wind.

"Me." Edy loped past them and held open the curtain. "Charlotte, Tyanne, are you coming?"

She certainly seemed keen on leaving the

stockroom. Did she want to keep her ears tuned to whatever Prudence might have to say about her former employee?

"While we're here, Pru" — Iris pushed through the curtain — "we can look at a couple of quilts to hang on the walls of your shop. Redecorating will cheer you up."

As we followed them out of the stockroom, Tyanne whispered, "If that's all it took, I'd buy Prudence the quilts myself."

I would have laughed, but Prudence whirled around by the cash register and glared at me as if she wanted to squash me like an ant.

"What?" I said, instinctively on the defensive.

Tyanne said, "Lookie here, Prudence, if you want to talk to me about the Harvest Moon Ranch deal —"

"She doesn't." Iris sagged, her Pollyanna essence fizzling. "She wants to discuss that thing your grandmother is doing, Charlotte. I tried to talk her out of it."

"What thing?" I asked.

"That production of *Hamlet*."

"Production?" Prudence sniped. "That spectacle, you mean."

Here we go. Providence Playhouse offered a variety of works. The theater had garnered all sorts of awards. However, for the first time in years, my grandmother had chosen to do a classic.

"She's putting it on in the Village Green," Prudence said. "Of all the nerve. With a Renaissance theme, no less."

"No less," Iris echoed, retreating to her comfort zone of passive friend.

"Won't it be fun?" I said, trying to defuse Prudence's fury. "She'll enlighten people about the times. There will be a winepress and pretend sword fights and —"

"It will draw the riffraff of Ohio," Prudence snapped.

"Oh, button it, sugar," Tyanne said.

Prudence spun around and stabbed a finger at Tyanne. "You can't talk to me like that."

"I may and I did." Tyanne mirrored the finger-pointing. "Having a highly respected Shakespearean play in our park will educate our townsfolk. And to a man, they like being educated. So, I repeat, button it."

I had never seen Tyanne so forceful. The transformation was electric. Divorce counseling had been good for her.

"You . . . You . . ." Prudence laid her hand upon her own chest. "Me. I was going to be the destination-wedding planner in town. Not you."

"Aha," Tyanne said. "The truth will out."

"What is that supposed to mean?"

"You didn't come in here to attack Charlotte about her grandmother's plans." Tyanne planted her hands on her hips. "You knew I was here. It's me you wanted to confront. I purchased the ranch."

"It was supposed to be mine." Prudence stamped her foot.

"Except you couldn't buy it." Edy butted through Tyanne and me, hand slicing the air. "Because" — her voice grew shrill — "you're under water with the loans on your boutique."

The group fell silent. Prudence's eyes simmered with unbridled anger, no longer directed at me but at Edy. If looks could kill.

"Is it true, Pru?" Iris laid a hand on her friend's arm. "Are you suffering financial woes?"

Prudence's face flushed. Strawberry-shaped blotches emerged on her cheeks.

"Don't be embarrassed," Iris went on. "Everyone in town is afflicted. Me, the hardware store, everyone."

"Not everyone," Tyanne said, her voice a little too cheery.

Prudence flinched. We all did. Talk about rubbing salt into the wound.

Prudence reared back her head, her mouth

opened, and her nostrils flared. She looked like a bull ready to attack anyone who entered its arena. "I am not, nor will I ever, suffer financial woes. Do you hear me?"

I surveyed the shop to make sure no one nearby was wearing anything close to a red cape. I nearly choked when a woman in scarlet sashayed through the front door.

CHAPTER 3

Sylvie, the twins' mother and my cousin's ex-wife, marched into Sew Inspired Quilt Shoppe outfitted in a fire-engine red flapper dress and ridiculously high red espadrilles. In addition, she had accented her ice-white hair with red stripes.

Prudence snarled.

"Where is she?" Sylvie shouted, never one for decorum. "Where is that floozy who stole my husband?" She continued in her British accent, her words clipped with precision. "And now she wants to steal my girlie-girls."

"Mercy," Tyanne said.

I moved in front of the knot of women formed by Prudence, Tyanne, Iris, and Edy. "Hold on, Sylvie," I said, my tone firm. "Meredith did not steal anyone. You left." A few years ago, Sylvie walked out on Matthew and the twins and returned to merry old England to live off Mumsie and Dad.

When that didn't work quite as she expected, she returned to Providence, determined to prove that she could be a good mother. And I had to admit, she was devoted to her girls. But her transformation hadn't won back Matthew's heart.

"What's going on?" Meredith emerged through the curtain at the rear of the shop. She had changed into a honey-colored sheath and had swept her hair into a ponytail. "Oh, it's you."

"How dare you act all high-and-mighty," Sylvie said.

Meredith inhaled deeply. I could tell she was tamping down her anger. "Sylvie Bessette, get over here, now." After the divorce, Sylvie hadn't reverted to her maiden name. To spite my cousin, no doubt. Meredith indicated a spot next to her, ordering her rival as she would one of her fourth-grade students.

"You know perfectly well that I have dresses in my boutique," Sylvie said. "You could have purchased the girls' wedding attire from me. They did not need handmade dresses." She sniffed. "People will think we're paupers. Amy, Clair, come out here."

The girls, who hadn't changed clothes yet, obeyed.

Sylvie gasped. "You look so . . . froufrou."

"Sylvie." I edged to her side. "They look beautiful, and you know it. Go apologize."

"But —"

"Do it," I whispered in her ear. "Be the bigger person."

With a hiss of defeat, Sylvie traipsed to the girls, the bangles and beads on the hem of her dress spanking her legs as she moved.

As everyone watched her swoon over her girls' garments, I spotted the love of my life, Jordan Pace. He was peering through the display window, hand shielding his eyes from the glare. As always, my heart did a little skip at the sight of him. What wasn't to love about a guy who looked like a cowboy movie star — the good guy, not the villain — not to mention, he could whip up a mean lasagna and knew how to make a scrumptious double-cream cheese. *Heart be still.* I waved, and a grin spread across his face, creating a dimple that streaked his cheeks. Oh, yeah, I was toast.

He strode into the shop with a bit of a swagger and stopped beside an iron blanket rack draped with quilts. I hurried to meet him.

"Hey, gorgeous." Jordan raised his hand and gestured to the gold engagement band on his finger.

Discreetly, I flashed mine as well. We had

gone for simple tokens of our love, with an inscription on the insides of both: *To hold, forever,* sealed with our initials. He ran a finger along my jawline that sent a tingle to my toes. I kissed him primly on the lips, though we both lingered longer than primness might allow. As we did, our fingertips touched and electricity shot through me.

"Do you have time for dinner tonight?" Jordan continued. "My place."

His *place* was a sprawling farm north of town, set amid rolling hills, with hundreds of cattle, and the most exquisite man-made caves to cure his cheeses. We would eat on the porch of his ranch house, looking out at the tall grass glistening in the moonlight. Heaven.

A shiver of lust ran down my spine. I was just about to say, "Yes, yes, and triple yes," when his sister, Jacky, tall, dark, and leggy like Jordan, entered pushing a stroller carrying her baby girl, who was a raven-haired beauty like her mother.

"Hi, Charlotte," Jacky said, adding a nod.

Baby Cecily said, "Cha-cha," which had become a new word in her vocabulary about a week ago. I nearly melted every time I heard her utter my name.

"May I hold her?" I loved babies, but years ago, after my engagement to an ex-fiancé I snarkily referred to as Creep Chef fizzled and the idea of finding another man that I could love for the rest of my life seemed hopeless — until now — I had put aside the dream of becoming a mother. I cared for the twins as if they were my own, and I convinced myself that would be enough. But as I kissed Cecily's silky cheek and smelled the soft scent of her skin, a tremor of desire swept through me. I didn't dare glance at Jordan lest I reveal my innermost thoughts and scare him away. Though I was pretty sure he wanted children, I had never asked.

"How is she liking the Mommy and Me class you're in, Jacky?" I asked, keeping the conversation light.

"She loves it."

"You look radiant."

"It's the weather. I love it here. It suits me . . . us." She caressed Cecily's cheek with her knuckles. "I only wish . . ." Her voice trailed off; her gaze turned guarded.

"Wish what?" I said.

"I —" She glanced beyond me.

I turned to look. A few feet away, Prudence had cornered Edy by a stand of silk fabrics. They stood nose to nose. She was jabbing her finger into Edy's chest.

"Don't mind them," I said. "Prudence is mad that Edy left La Chic Boutique to work here. But back to you. What do you hope?"

"Let's go outside to talk."

"Is something wrong?"

Jacky reached for Cecily, who squirmed and groped for the iron rack of quilts behind me. She caught hold. The rack tumbled to the floor. I stooped, with Cecily tucked firmly in my arms, to right the display. Jacky squatted to help. So did Jordan.

"Jacky's been having dreams," Jordan whispered.

"Nightmares," Jacky said, her voice as low as her brother's.

"About?" I asked.

"Him," Jordan said.

"Giacomo?" Jacky had moved to Providence and changed her identity to flee an abusive husband.

"He won't stop looking for me," Jacky said. They had not formally divorced. "He'll find me. Find Cecily." She stacked quilts in her arms.

"No, he won't," I said. After the last beating, Jordan had whisked his sister out of her house and brought her to Providence. He bought her a home, set her up in business, and promised her she would never have to fight off her sumo-wrestler-sized husband again. She was free of her previous life. Free. "Jordan, reassure her. Your sister is off his radar."

Jordan opened his mouth, but Jacky cut him off. "You know I'm right. Giacomo's a Capriotti. He can find anybody if he searches —"

Edy gagged.

Still crouched, we all turned our heads.

Prudence had hold of Edy's collar. With no effort at decorum, Prudence yelled, "You listen to me."

Edy batted Prudence's hand away. "You're mad."

"Darned straight I'm mad," Prudence said.

Jacky offered a swap — quilts for the baby. I handed over Cecily, took the quilts, and rose to a stand. As I looped the quilts over the rack's rails, I whispered, "Jordan is right. You shouldn't worry."

"But what about the dreams, Jordan?" Jacky said, her skin pale with fear. "You know Mom was psychic."

Jordan screwed up his mouth.

Baby Cecily started to cry. "Shh, there." Jacky drew the baby's head into her chest. "What if I'm psychic, too? The dreams are so vivid. Oh, if only William were here."

William was the man who had given Jacky the courage to leave her husband. She had been prepared to file for divorce, but then her husband found out about the affair and hurt her. Sadly, William died in an unrelated car accident.

Jacky tucked Cecily into the stroller. "I'm sorry, Charlotte, I shouldn't have dragged you into this soap opera." Pushing the stroller, she raced from the quilt shop.

Jordan seemed torn, his gaze darting from me to Jacky.

I said, "Go. She needs you."

He pecked me on the cheek and hurried after his sister.

The instant he exited the shop, Edy rushed to my side. "Charlotte." She mouthed: *Help.*

Prudence clung to her like an angry shadow. "Edy Delaney, I'm not done talking to you yet."

"I'm done listening," Edy squawked. "I had every right to switch jobs."

"But not to spread rumors about me."

Iris joined our group. "Speaking of rumors, what was that about?" She pointed at the doorway, indicating that she wanted to know what had sent Jacky running from the shop.

"Nothing," I said, my tone carefree. "Hormones," I added, a standard answer for women.

"Hormones, my foot," Iris said. "I'll bet

she learned something about that new boyfriend of hers."

"Which new boyfriend?" Edy asked.

"She's not dating anyone," I said. Jacky and Urso had broken up months ago.

"She is, too." Iris toyed with her shaggy hairdo, delaying the moment of revelation. "Hugo Hunter."

"The owner of the Igloo?" Edy sounded as surprised as I felt.

When had Jacky started dating the ice cream maker? I flashed back to my earlier conversation with Rebecca, when she said Hugo was so mysterious he reminded her of Houdini. A shiver of apprehension ran down my spine. Was Jacky having nightmares about her estranged husband because of something Hugo had said to her? Did Hugo know about her past life?

"What do you think Jacky learned about Hugo?" Edy asked.

Iris lowered her voice. "He has a past. She should be warned."

"You're just bitter," Edy said.

"I'm what? Why you . . ." Iris raised a fist.

I flinched. I didn't like Edy much, but I didn't want her to wind up with a bloody nose. Not in Sew Inspired Quilt Shoppe. I said, "Edy, come to the fitting room with me."

"Don't you want to know why Iris is bitter?" Edy said.

No, I didn't. Not really.

"Don't say a word." Iris waggled her fist. Her eyes flared with conviction.

Prudence snagged her friend's arm. "Iris, don't rise to the bait." She pulled; Iris resisted. "Iris, let's leave." After further struggle, Prudence, who was taller and heavier, if that were possible for someone so thin, won the tug-of-war.

When they exited and the door closed, I said to Edy, "Are you nuts? Taking on not only Prudence but her best buddy, too?"

"That woman makes me so mad."

"Iris?"

"Heck, no. I mean Prudence. Iris is a pushover. Getting left at the altar didn't do her any favors. Didn't you notice that silly slogan on her tote? *Growing Stronger.*" Edy snorted. "Wishful thinking."

"Iris was left at the altar?" I said. Perhaps that was why Iris and Prudence were such good pals. They had bonded over lost relationships. "Wait a sec. She has a teenage daughter."

"Adopted."

"Really?"

"Maybe dating that sweet dog groomer will perk her up."

I gaped. "Iris is dating the owner of Tail-waggers?" How had I missed so many secrets? Usually Fromagerie Bessette was the place in town to gather the news.

CHAPTER 4

Days passed before I was able to find enough time to experiment with ice cream flavors, but it was well worth the wait. Mid-afternoon on Friday, while a couple of male tourists wearing *Stomping the Grapes* T-shirts browsed the shelves, Rebecca and I stood at the cheese counter in Fromagerie Bessette, spoons in hand, four china bowls of ice cream in front of us.

"Is it okay to taste right here while we have customers?" Rebecca asked.

"They're not even looking our way. Go ahead," I said, eager for her responses.

She dipped her spoon into one, savored the bite, and then moved on to the next. I followed, relishing the flavors: Brie and blueberry as well as Brie with strawberry, Cheddar apple, and simply cinnamon. For each, I had used a vanilla ice cream base that Hugo Hunter had divined, substituting mascarpone cheese for part of the cream.

"I like the cinnamon," Rebecca said. "It's got a zip to it."

"I do, too" — I took another taste of each — "but I think the Brie and blueberry is the best."

"You're right." Rebecca nodded. "The nutmeg blends perfectly with the tartness of the berries and the richness of the Brie."

The inspiration for adding nutmeg — a minor inspiration at best — had come to me in the middle of the night.

"Charlotte." Matthew, my handsome cousin who was not only the twins' father but also the groom-to-be, emerged from the wine annex that abutted The Cheese Shop, and loped toward me. The cream color of his shirt set off his bronzed skin. He paused at the door leading to the kitchen. "I'm going downstairs." His eyes sparkled with zeal. He was excited about the wedding — that was a given — but he was also keyed up about the cheese and wine cellar beneath the shop. We had finished construction less than a month ago. We wanted a storage site to age wines and cheeses to their proper maturity. We intended to offer special, top-of-the-line tastings below. He said, "Need anything?"

"Yes, I want you to taste this." I held out a spoonful of the Brie blueberry ice cream.

He downed the bite and licked his lips. "Delicious. Meredith will love it." He turned to go.

"Wait. You didn't taste the others."

"I don't have time. I've got to make sure the cellar is prepared." Matthew and Meredith had decided to have their rehearsal dinner catered in the wine annex. After dessert, Matthew would show all of the out-of-town wedding guests the cellar. The room was so new that Matthew was still moving around bottles of wine and wheels of cheese to get the right *look* — Old World European. "I've got a lot to do. The clock is ticking." He scanned the shop. "Not bursting with business, are we?"

"We were an hour ago," I said. "It ebbs and flows."

"Sometimes we only have browsers," Rebecca said.

As if feeling our eyes on them, the pair of tourists slunk out of the shop without buying anything. As they exited, the twins entered.

"Hi, Daddy. Hi, Rebecca. Hi, Aunt Charlotte," they sang in unison.

Grandmère Bernadette, my seventy-plus grandmother who was a spitfire of a woman, entered behind them. Her burgundy peasant blouse and matching corduroy skirt flounced as she moved. *"Bonjour."*

Rocket, the shaggy Briard that the twins' mother had bestowed upon them — and therefore me, seeing as they lived under my roof — barked from the sidewalk.

"Hush," Grandmère said.

As the door swung closed, Rocket whimpered. He didn't like being leashed to the parking meter. He adored snippets of cheese and probably felt he deserved a romp in the shop, not to mention that he knew my Ragdoll cat was enjoying a relaxing snooze in the office.

The twins scampered to the cheese counter.

Amy, who had Grandmère's chugalug energy, spoke first. "We packed more of our clothes, Aunt Charlotte. The foyer at the house is crowded."

The week after the honeymoon, Matthew, Amy, and Clair were moving into Meredith's house. Though they would only be living a few blocks away, every time I heard someone attach a strip of cellophane tape to a box, my heart wrenched. I was going to miss hearing the twins' cheery voices and seeing their bright smiles on a daily basis.

"Can you believe it?" Amy went on. "The wedding is almost here."

"I heard your dresses are beautiful," Rebecca said.

"They are," I said. Mine was a work in progress. At the fitting, Tyanne hadn't liked the way it had fallen on my hips. However, we had agreed that the pale gold color was a nice match with my skin tone and complemented the highlights in my blond hair.

"They're pretty, I guess," Amy said, not enthusiastically but almost. I hinted that Tyanne's son might like to see her in the dress. She pooh-poohed that notion.

"Did you hear we're going to get our hair styled at Tip to Toe?" Clair said with such fervor it surprised me. I wouldn't have thought she cared about a hairdo. Her stick-straight, light-gold hair hung to her shoulders and fell forward like a curtain. More than once I had needed to push strands behind her ears so I could see her adorable face.

"Actually, I'm going with you," I said, then turned to my grandmother. "What have you got in your hand?"

She flapped a ream of purple paper. "Flyers. We're having a footrace to raise money for the cause."

"Which cause?"

"The animal rescue shelter." My mouth must have fallen open because Grandmère said, "Do not look so surprised." In the past, she wasn't necessarily the most pet-enthusiastic person on the planet. Was she going through a shift? Granted, she had warmed to my two pets. What wasn't to love? Rocket nuzzled her whenever he had the chance, and Rags was the most interactive cat in the world. "The Providence Cares Foundation saves so many, but resources are low," she went on.

I didn't know how many animals the foundation had saved over the years, but it had to number in the hundreds — perhaps thousands. Rags and Rocket were both rescued animals.

"Do you ever stop?" I asked. "Mayor, theater manager, and now rescued animals enthusiast?"

Grandmère patted the flyers. "We are calling the race *Stomping the Grapes.*"

"You're sure getting the word out," Rebecca said. "There were a couple of tourists in here a bit ago wearing T-shirts with the logo."

"Ah, yes, the T-shirts." Grandmère beamed. "They have been a big hit."

"Do you remember the guys, Charlotte?" Rebecca twirled a hand as if conjuring up the image for me. "Mutt and Jeff. The short guy with the icky skin reminded me of an evil actor. He had the same hooded eyes, don't you think? And the other guy, the tall guy, had saggy jowls."

"Jowls?" I hadn't noticed. Was my eyesight going? "I thought he was pretty handsome."

"Nah, he had a wattle" — she tapped the underside of her chin — "like a turkey. Neither of them bought a thing. If you'd served him at the cheese counter, you would have spotted it."

"So far we have over fifty entrants," Grandmère went on as she handed everyone a flyer. "The race will be held at the Bozzuto Winery." The Bozzuto family, who owned the oldest farmstead in Providence, made light and fruity wines as well as the most delectable natural sodas. Matthew said their chenin blanc was one of the best he had ever tasted. It was elegant and crisp — nothing like the old syrupy sweet chenin blancs that we used to down in college.

"Can we join in?" Amy said. "I love to run."

"Can I walk?" Clair asked.

I grinned. She would probably want to carry a book and read at the same time. "Yes, of course you can participate."

"Entrants are encouraged to get sponsors," Grandmère said to the girls.

"How do we that?" Amy raised a skeptical eyebrow.

Grandmère pulled an entry form from her purse. "See the numbers by each line? Ask someone to donate a dime or a quarter for every hundred yards you walk. Write their names down. All the money will go to the rescue fund. Turn your form in to the Tourist Information Center."

"We can do that," Amy said.

"Good girl." Grandmère patted Amy's cheek as if she were an obedient pup. "But homework first."

Amy groaned. She wasn't the best of students.

"Can we take Rags with us?" Clair asked. She adored my Ragdoll.

"Fine." Grandmère waved for them to hurry. "Now, get packing."

Packing! I eeked.

"What's wrong?" Rebecca said.

"I nearly forgot that I had promised to help Octavia set up her bookstore."

"Go," she said. "I'll manage here."

Octavia Tibble — dedicated librarian, Realtor, and new ecstatic bookshop owner — had done a fabulous makeover on All Booked Up. She had ripped out the carpet, laid hardwood floors, and placed hand-woven rugs everywhere. She had covered all the wing-back chairs in deep blue and had set Tiffany lamps beside each. She had converted a little nook into a tea-and-scone café, and lastly, she had decorated each aisle according to its reading genre. Pictures of fairies and Harry Potter floated above Fantasy. Cutouts of Sherlockian hats and magnifying glasses adorned the shelves in Mystery. All she had left to do was add inventory and remove items that belonged to Anabelle Rossi, the previous owner, and she was set to open.

Stacks of unpacked boxes stood in front of the oak checkout counter. Anabelle's boxes nestled behind it. Bottled water sat beside the register.

"Did you think I'd forgotten?" I said as I entered the shop and made a beeline toward Octavia, who stood bending over a box.

"You? Not for a second. You're like an elephant. You never forget."

Without waiting for instruction, I dipped into a box of books, devouring titles and making a mental list of which books I wanted on my bedside table. With the preparations for the wedding and packing up the twins' things, I hadn't found much time to read lately, but I couldn't go without a good read for too long.

"Whewie." Octavia rose to her full height, brushed her beaded cornrows over her shoulder, and dusted off her jeans and holey T-shirt. "This is backbreaking. And dirty."

I had to laugh. I couldn't remember seeing my friend in anything other than a business suit or a costume — the latter because she loved to dress up to read to the kids at the library. A head taller than I, she held herself like a queen and usually moved with effortless grace. Not now.

"Is anybody else coming to help?" I asked.

"Just you and little old me."

"You're not old."

"I've got years on you. Years."

"And don't forget me." Anabelle popped up from behind the counter. With her saucer-shaped eyes, timid smile, and dark ponytail that trailed down her back, she reminded me of a lemur. The caramel-colored knit cap and fluffy sweater she wore enhanced the furry image. "I'm here to help."

Octavia chuckled. "You? You're no help at all. You've been packing your own stuff for hours. What do you have crammed in that cupboard anyway?" She peeked over the counter. "Are those dolls in that box?"

Anabelle blushed. "I'm a collector."

"Honey, you are a hoarder."

"They're my babies, and they're antiques. I've picked them up everywhere I've lived."

59

Octavia eyed me. "Six states in her twenty-plus years. She's rootless."

"I'm a world traveler," Anabelle said.

"I repeat, rootless." Octavia snatched a bottle of water and cracked open the top. She swigged down half of it and set the bottle on the counter.

Anabelle toyed with the scalloped collar of her sweater. "How did I accumulate so much stuff?"

"We all do," I said, thinking of the twins' things. How many toys and craft projects had I packed over the past few weeks?

"Anabelle has nearly as many boyfriends as dolls," Octavia went on. "What was the last count, twenty, thirty?"

"Ten." Anabelle sniffed. "Don't make fun simply because I was making eyes at some guy before Charlotte came in."

"Making eyes?" Octavia did a side-to-side Egyptian goddess move with her head, something that, when I was a teen, I had tried numerous times in front of the mirror to master but couldn't. Attitude was not always a God-given talent. "Honey, you were waving your finger at that man just begging for an engagement ring."

Anabelle sputtered. "I did no such thing. I just met the man. He and his brother are new in town, or did you miss that tidbit?"

She reached over the counter and flicked Octavia's arm. "Don't listen to her, Charlotte. I was totally professional. I told him we weren't open for business yet, and to come back."

We returned to emptying or packing boxes.

After a moment, Anabelle appeared from behind the counter again and said, "He was hunky, though, wasn't he, girlfriend?"

" 'Girlfriend'? Who are you calling 'girlfriend'?" Octavia offered a mocking grin, and then a small frown creased her forehead. I recognized the look. She was going to be sorry when Anabelle left town. She delighted in having someone her daughter's age to watch over.

"C'mon, he was hunky. Chiseled face." Anabelle drew an image with her fingertips. "Did you hear him say he was an investor?"

Instinctively, I cringed. Investors with dishonorable motives had recently come and gone in Providence. I wasn't eager for more to appear.

"He also said he was checking out the college."

Providence Liberal Arts College — or PLAC, a project Meredith had championed — had just started its first year of education with a full freshman class.

Octavia jutted a finger at Anabelle. "That means he's too old for you. He probably has kids near your age."

Anabelle clucked her tongue, dismissing Octavia, and then turned to me. "Hey, Charlotte, he wants to see your grandmother's production of *Hamlet.* Isn't that cool? He's a Shakespeare buff." Clearly smitten, Anabelle flipped her hair in a flirty way. "I'd like to date an educated man at least once in my life."

Octavia huffed. "Do I need to remind you that you are scheduled to move in a week?"

"So it would be a fling. Big deal." Anabelle had owned All Booked Up for three years, and as far as I knew had planned to remain forever, but when she learned that her father, who lived in Chicago, was ailing, she put the store up for sale. "Ooh, what if Mr. Hunky visits me in Chicago? He said he travels. A lot."

"Anabelle Rossi," Octavia said, gripping the young woman's shoulders. "You have got to keep your head on straight. Pack your dolls, put away your girlish fantasies, and keep your eye on the target. Your daddy needs you. Not this man, one in a string of how many? Forty?"

"Ten."

"Humph. Now, do us a favor and fetch a

couple more bottles of water from the storage room."

Anabelle left on the errand.

"That girl." Octavia heaved a sigh and continued unpacking books.

"What's got you so bugged?" I asked.

"I'm worried, that's all. Anabelle is young and impressionable. She collects dolls, for heaven's sake. She's not ready to date some . . . some" — she waved a hand — "lothario."

"And that's what this guy seemed like to you?"

"He didn't look nice. And his brother, the one with the bad skin? I've seen the likes of him in a few horror movies. The guy could use a year of facials, if you ask me. And nobody that walks into a shop and leaves empty-handed without buying a thing is okay in my book."

"They sound like the same guys who were in Fromagerie Bessette a while ago."

"Cheapskates."

"But Octavia, you're not open for business yet."

"A minor detail." She swatted the air, and then returned to her chore. She opened another box and winked. "At last. I finally found the mysteries." With glee, she withdrew not just any mysteries but collectors' copies by Arthur Conan Doyle, Agatha Christie, and more — a semi-dusty taste of bibliophile heaven.

An hour later, I returned to Fromagerie Bessette. I found Rebecca preparing an order for Jordan's sister, Jacky, who was cooing to Cecily and setting her into a stroller.

"Mmm," I said as I joined Rebecca behind the counter. "How I love the aroma of Bayley Hazen Blue." The Jasper Hill Farm cheese resonated with flavors of nuts and licorice. I glanced into the wine annex, which was empty. "Where's Matthew?"

"Around." Rebecca twirled her hand. "Walking on air. Humming. That man is happier than I've ever seen him. It's so sweet."

"Yes, it is."

Jacky rose to her willowy height. "Hi, Charlotte."

"Hi. Don't you look great, and isn't Cecily growing fast?" I wiggled my fingers at the baby and blew a strawberry at her. She mimicked me. "You're going to love the Bayley Hazen Blue."

"I buy it whenever I can."

"One of my favorite quickie snacks is putting a wedge of the blue cheese on a cracker with a sliver of fresh fruit."

"Sounds tasty."

Cecily gurgled, and Jacky immediately bent over to see if something was wrong, ending our conversation.

Rebecca hitched her chin. "Look who else is here."

Hugo Hunter, the owner of the Igloo Ice Cream Parlor, stood by the mustard remoulade display. He anchored back his unruly dark curls as he studied the labels.

"I'm telling you, he looks like Houdini," Rebecca continued, sotto voce.

As if sensing we were discussing him, Hugo swiveled his head. On other occasions, I had thought he resembled Elvis, with that swoop of hair and devil-may-care grin, but maybe Rebecca was right. He had Houdini's haunting eyes.

"He and Jacky are having dinner together," Rebecca added. "At Jacky's place."

"Is there any gossip you don't glean?" I teased.

"He's good with the baby. He was holding her earlier and tickling her chin."

A guy that was good with infants was worth his weight in gold, right?

"Speaking of gossip, did you pick up any at the bookstore?" Rebecca asked.

"Like what?"

"Anything."

I propped my hand against my hip. "Rebecca Zook, are you bored because your lover man is out of town? Don't you have enough to keep your overly active mind busy?"

"No, I don't. C'mon, a nugget. Feed me." She wrapped the deeply veined blue cheese in our special paper, affixed a cheese information label, and set the purchase into one of our gold bags.

"I learned that Anabelle is hot for a tourist," I said.

"Which one?"

"I think it's one of the men that were in here earlier. Mutt and Jeff. The ones that didn't buy any cheese."

"The bad-skin guy?"

"No, the other one who appeared to have lost all the weight. They're brothers."

Jacky snapped her head up and gazed at me, her eyes tense and alert.

I was about to ask what was wrong when Hugo approached the counter.

"Charlotte, how did the Brie ice cream turn out?" he said. With his rich baritone voice, I could imagine him addressing an audience, and I wondered if he had done some kind of acting or orating prior to settling in Providence. Perhaps he had been a magician. With his muscular body, I could see him trying to escape from a water torture cell.

"Great, delicious," I said. "By the way, I've been meaning to give you this." I fetched a copy of the Brie blueberry ice cream recipe that I had tucked beside the register and handed it to Hugo. "You should offer it on your menu."

"Am I allowed to make it before the big day?" He winked.

"I don't see why not."

"In that case, let me buy five pounds of Brie."

As he paid for his purchase, Rebecca whispered, "Back to Anabelle. Tell me about the tourist she's interested in."

At the mention of the tourist again, I searched for Jacky. She had turned the stroller around and was heading toward the exit. Anxiety swept through me. Why had she reacted so strongly when I had mentioned the tourists before, and why wasn't she sticking around to fill me in?

CHAPTER 5

Later that night, I stood at the sink in my grandparents' kitchen washing pots and pans, my mouth watering even though I had finished a big meal. The lingering aromas would make the most dedicated dieter hungry. Remnants of the feast of roast beef, Yorkshire pudding, and the most delectable string beans known to man, brined in salt and drenched in butter, sat on the counter. Clair, who had to follow a strict celiac diet, had consumed the entire gluten-free Yorkshire pudding popover I had made for her.

Jordan snuggled behind me and wrapped an arm around my waist. "I need some fresh air. Care to join me?" He breathed a sigh on the back of my neck. "It's beautiful out. The temperature is unseasonably warm. The sky is a dusky, romantic orange."

I swiveled to meet him, my chest brushing his ever so slightly. "I'm a little busy."

He assessed the stacks of dishes. "I'll

help." He rolled up his sleeves, grabbed a dish towel, and began drying what I washed. Each time his shoulder, his hip, or his arm touched mine, I hungered with desire.

"Jacky was in the shop with Hugo Hunter today," I said, doing my best to push aside sexy thoughts and keep the conversation lighthearted. "How long have they been going out?"

"Are you hoping for a little town gossip, sweetheart?" he joked.

"Gossip? Me?"

"Yes, you." Jordan flicked the tail of the towel at my legs.

I laughed. "She hasn't mentioned word one about their relationship at our girls' night out." Once a week, a bunch of girlfriends and I got together for a yoga class or a self-defense class or dinner.

"They've been dating for two or three weeks," Jordan said.

"That long?"

"Some people can keep secrets." Jordan had moved to Providence a few years back, and until last year, his reason for moving had been a mystery to me, but once the puzzle was solved to my satisfaction, he proposed and our romance soared.

"No, no, no." Grandmère, carrying wine and water glasses, waltzed into the kitchen, followed by my friend Delilah, owner of the local diner, former Broadway dancer, and current director of *Hamlet.*

"But we need them." Delilah spanked the back of her hand against the palm of her other hand.

"Gaslights are not in keeping with the times," Grandmère countered.

"Then torches." Delilah swooped her curly hair over her shoulders and planted her hands on her hips. "If we don't have lights, people will bump into each other." After her rousing success with the play she had written for Providence Playhouse a season ago, Delilah was granted the opportunity to direct again. My grandmother claimed she hired Delilah because she, Grandmère, was losing her touch as a director, but I knew better. She wanted to foster Delilah's talent. Delilah had dreamed up the brilliant idea of making *Hamlet* an open-air production in the Village Square.

"Fine," Grandmère conceded. "How are the costumes coming along?"

Pépère pushed through the swinging door. "*Mon amie,* please. It is Matthew and Meredith's night. No more discussion about the play."

Since Delilah had arrived at the house, Grandmère and she had talked nonstop about the production.

Grandmère tsked. "It will be their night a week from Sunday. The play is imminent."

Pépère huffed. "You should not have scheduled *Hamlet* for this time."

"I could not change the calendar, Étienne. You know that." Grandmère patted my grandfather's cheek and gave him a *not to worry* look. "It is only two nights. It will not infringe on their festivities."

"Bah," he said.

"Bah, yourself." Unwilling to argue longer, Grandmère turned her gaze to me. "*Chérie,* will you put up a pot of coffee?" My grandmother was a whiz when it came to cooking, but she couldn't brew a decent cup of java no matter how many times we went over the proportions.

"Hey, Charlotte." Delilah's eyes sparkled with curiosity. "I saw Jacky walking with Hugo Hunter today. What's up with that?"

I glanced at Jordan, who shrugged *No comment.* At times he could be so cagey that it drove me insane.

"No, no, no," my grandmother said. "No gossip." She prodded Delilah out of the kitchen. "We will need wigs."

"*Impénitente,*" Pépère muttered as he followed them out.

I couldn't disagree. My grandmother was

incorrigible.

Before the swinging door closed, Rebecca hurried in. "How can I help?"

No matter what the occasion, Rebecca was invited. My grandparents hadn't adopted her, but they might as well have. She basked in their affection.

"Take the desserts to the table," I said. Before washing the dishes, I had set a tray of delectables on the counter. Though our family often had gatherings for no reason at all, tonight we had come together to do yet one more tasting for the wedding.

"Jordan, have you tried the ice cream?" Rebecca asked. *"Tout de suite."* She kissed her fingertips.

"You mean, *très doux*," I said. "*Tout de suite* means 'right away.' "

"Are you sure? I heard someone on *NCIS* say *tout de suite*." When not working, Rebecca was a mystery reruns junkie, on television or on the Internet. She loved the problem-solving aspect.

I grinned. "Whoever said it was making a joke."

"Harrumph."

"The tartlets look fabulous," Jordan said. "Rebecca, did you have a hand in those?"

I could have kissed him full-on. He had a way of making a woman feel ultra-special.

"I did," she said, her French mistake all but forgotten. "I suggested a dash of almond flavoring."

In addition to a cake, Meredith and Matthew wanted an assortment of finger-food-type desserts. Rebecca and I had spent a good two hours putting the treats together. Mini pumpkin cheesecakes, mascarpone fruit tarts, and the pièce de résistance, Brie blueberry ice cream tucked into a white chocolate candy shell.

All chatter in the dining room stopped as Rebecca, Jordan, and I entered with the goodies, and a chorus of "Ooh," followed. A few months ago, Grandmère had redecorated the dining room, removing the flocked paper and painting the walls a luscious pearl color. The effect had made the space bright and conducive to conversation.

"You've outdone yourself," Meredith said, looking cheery in a peach-colored sundress and a matching grosgrain ribbon that she had laced through her hair.

Matthew sat beside her, his hand wrapped around hers. "Bravo."

"Let's taste them first." I had experimented with the recipes for a few of the items. Though I liked the flavors, I wasn't certain everyone would, the twins in particular. "All are gluten-free," I said to Clair.

"Even the tarts?" she asked. She was our sweet-tooth girl. Amy preferred salty foods.

"You bet." Although I hadn't come upon a gluten-free sourdough bread recipe that would rival real sourdough, most other things I could make. Pie dough was one of the easiest. If made with sweet rice flour and xanthan gum, the dough was pliable and cooked up crisp. Sometimes I left out the gum and added an extra egg white. Weather conditions made a big difference in the texture.

"Are you sure?" Clair said.

"Absolutely." I served up individual plates, each set with a trio of the confections, and said, "Dig in."

Matthew leaned over as I took my seat beside him. "I heard about my ex-wife's outburst at Sew Inspired Quilt Shoppe. I'm shocked she hasn't made a surprise appearance tonight."

I smirked. "She wouldn't dare. No matter how bad she is, she still wants Grandmère's approval. An out-of-sorts mayor can make things difficult for a small business owner."

Grandmère, who was positioned at the head of the table, sat taller. "Did I hear my name mentioned?" Octavia said I had the memory of an elephant; my grandmother had elephant ears.

"No," I said, putting an end to that discussion. Talking about Sylvie would not enhance the evening's festivities. "Enjoy."

"Étienne, eat." Grandmère fluttered her hand at my grandfather. He hadn't taken a bite of the desserts, and he adored ice cream. He visited the Igloo Ice Cream Parlor at least once a week. He was the one who had talked me into collaborating with Hugo on a recipe.

"Forgive me, *mon amie,* but I am not hungry." Pépère rose from his chair. He teetered.

I reached out to steady him. "Are you all right? You look a little pale."

A man of staunch character, he did not suffer people fussing over him. He waved me off. "I am fine, *chérie.* I worked too long in the garage. It is the heat." For fun, my grandfather built birdhouses. Many of his creations adorned his yard as well as mine. "Or perhaps it is all this talk about the food. My waistline" — he patted his bulging stomach — "is not getting smaller, no matter how hard I try."

"You know what it takes," Grandmère said.

"*Oui, mon amie.* Less food and an extra dose of exercise." Pépère rolled his eyes at her, though I spotted the gleam in them.

My grandmother and he were the most adorable couple I knew. They loved each other unconditionally. I hoped that Jordan and I, after forty years, would be as devoted.

As my grandfather squeezed my grandmother's hand, a shriek cut the air. It wasn't the cat. Matthew and the twins had taken Rags and Rocket home before we sat down to dinner. I shot a look at Jordan. His sister, Jacky, lived next door.

Jordan leaped to his feet and bolted from the room.

I hurried after him but pivoted at the door and pointed at the twins. "You stay here."

"Aww," they chimed.

"Matthew, Meredith."

"On it," they said as a team.

With my heart doing a jig, I tore out the kitchen and down the driveway.

Jordan passed through a hole in the boxwood hedge that created a border between properties. Jacky raced to him. She cradled Cecily in her left arm. Using her right, she painted a story.

I sidled through the hedge and joined them.

Thick hair flopping, Hugo sprinted to us carrying a flashlight in his hand. He stopped, out of breath, a foot behind Jacky. "No one's lurking in the bushes," he said.

"You're sure?" Jordan asked.

"I'm not crazy. I saw someone." Jacky's breath was jagged, her eyes pinpoints of fear. "I think . . . I'm not sure . . . I think it was *him*."

"Him, who?" Hugo asked.

Jacky's gaze flew from Jordan to me and back to her brother.

Jordan said, "Hugo, this is a private family matter."

Hugo straightened his shoulders. "Whatever the secret is, I should know it, too. I'm in love with Jacky."

"You're what?" Jacky gaped.

Hugo squeezed her shoulder and let his hand rest there. "You heard me."

He certainly was impulsive. Could he know that he was in love in three weeks' time? Yes, I reminded myself. I had fallen hard for Jordan in less time than that. Perhaps a minute. And yet something about Hugo made me wary. I recalled what Rebecca had said in the shop. He was a man of mystery. Like Houdini. Disappearing from town and reappearing whenever it suited him. Had he moved to Providence with some ulterior motive? He had arrived not long after Jacky had moved here. Had her husband sent Hugo to track down Jacky and keep an eye on her? I pushed that notion away, having once before thought Jacky was being stalked and the guy turned out to be nothing more than a man hired to work at the honeybee farm.

I scanned the shadows at Jacky's house. Was someone waiting for an opportunity to strike when all of us weren't hovering about? I didn't spot a hint of movement.

"Don't worry," Hugo said. "I can see in your eyes that you love me, too. You don't have to say the words back to me. I'm a patient man."

Why did his words sound rehearsed?

"I repeat," Hugo pressed, "him who?"

"My husband," Jacky said.

"You're married?"

"I was . . . I am . . . It's too hard to explain."

The notion that Jacky's husband might be skulking about made my heart pound. The man had a gun. He had never used it on Jacky, but he had threatened her with it.

"Okay," Hugo said. "You'll tell me at another time. Right now, breathe and tell us what you think you saw." Hugo inhaled and swirled his hand in front of his chest, directing Jacky to do the same. He gazed at her with his mesmerizing cobalt eyes, and she obeyed. How could she resist? I was working hard to keep myself in check.

"I thought I was seeing things earlier in the day," Jacky said. "I went out for a walk, pushing Cecily in the stroller. There were two men hanging outside the bookshop. They were arguing. One of them reminded me of Giacomo — my husband — but he had lost so much weight."

I flinched. Could she be referring to one of the tourists that had come into the shop earlier? The one Rebecca had said had a wattle? The one Anabelle had called hunky?

"I didn't want to stare. I made a U-turn. They didn't see me," Jacky went on. "But then I was in Fromagerie Bessette, and I overheard you, Charlotte, talking about a guy with bad skin, and I knew you meant Vinnie."

"Giacomo's jerk of a brother," Jordan explained.

As if Giacomo, a wife abuser, wasn't jerk enough. If only I had put two and two together, I could have alerted Jacky. I glanced again at the perimeter of her house. I didn't see any movement. No flash of metal.

Jacky gripped Jordan's hand. "My nightmare is coming true, Jordan. He's found me. I've got to get out of town. He'll take Cecily."

"Wait a sec," Hugo said. "You told me

Cecily's father's name was William."

"It is. *Was.* It's a long story. See, I was leaving Giacomo. William was my lover. He died in a car accident. A drunk driver hit him. He . . . that's not what's important," Jacky cried. "Giacomo will think she's his, don't you see?"

"Because you're still married."

"In name only." Jacky turned to Jordan. "What will I do?"

Jordan's jaw ticked with tension. "I'll stay with you."

"No, I will," Hugo said, his voice commanding. "I'm trained in combat."

CHAPTER 6

When Jacky grew calm and almost giddy with relief that her estranged husband was nowhere in the vicinity, she told Jordan to leave her in Hugo's care. Not one to hover, Jordan agreed. We finished cleaning up after the meal at my grandparents' house, and a short while later, headed to Jordan's farm.

To shake off tension, we decided to take a walk. The air felt warmer than usual for October. A harvest moon cast a shimmering golden glow on the hills. As we strolled along the road, our hands entwined, a breath of breeze caressed our faces, and I worked hard to make my mind relax. So much was going on in my life, with the wedding and the twins moving out. Jacky's distress had magnified everything for me.

I broke the silence. "What do you think about Jacky dating Hugo?"

"Nothing to think."

"What about the fact that he was trained

in combat? Doesn't that worry you?"

"No. It probably means he served in the army." Jordan turned to me. "I don't want to talk about Jacky anymore tonight. Or Hugo. Or anybody else. I just want to talk about us." He gazed at me with those bedroom eyes. "I want you to move in with me."

I gulped. I wasn't a prude. I had stayed the night with him and intended to stay again tonight, but move in? "Before we get married?"

He offered a lopsided grin. "Ohio is advanced enough to see that we're committed, heart and soul. We'll get that legal certificate when you finally pick a wedding date." He ran a knuckle along my jawline. "C'mon, say yes."

"What will I do with my house?"

"We'll put it on the market. There are lots of people, like Hugo, moving into town. Your grandmother's *Come to Providence for the Good Life* campaign is working. Sales are on the rise."

I loved my little Victorian house. I had put sweat and tears into it. I adored the latticework, the veranda, the quaint rose garden, and the antique but updated kitchen. I supposed I could keep it and rent it out, but did I want to be a landlord?

"What about the twins? It's their home, too."

Jordan chuckled. "Darling, you shouldn't be worried about the girls. They've got a new life ahead of them."

"What will I do with Rocket and Rags?"

"Isn't Rocket moving with the girls?"

"Matthew isn't sure there's enough room, and the poor mutt is attached to Rags."

"Fine, they'll move in with us. The more the merrier." Jordan owned a couple of dogs and cats. Only the cheese caves and processing facilities were off-limits to them.

"The twins will be heartbroken without them. I can't imagine —"

Jordan released my hand and gripped my shoulders. "Are you trying to back out of marrying me?"

"No."

"Good, because I won't have it." He kissed me with so much passion that electricity zipped to my toes.

When we broke apart, I found myself gasping for breath.

Jordan ran his palm along my hair. "Did that calm you down?"

"Sure did. Can we do it — ?" Movement to my right caught my eye. "Will you look at that? Is that your neighbor, the confirmed bachelor, walking with a woman?"

The thickset man twirled his equally thickset girlfriend under his arm, and then the two embraced while doing a quickstep and hooting like lovesick teenagers.

"That old sneak," Jordan said. "I'd noticed that he had cleaned up his truck."

I grinned. "People will go to great lengths for love."

"Hmm, sounds like a lead-in for a song." Full voice, Jordan belted out, " 'What a day this has been, what a rare mood I'm in. Yes, it's almost like being in love.' "

I was surprised that he knew the lyric to a beautiful standard from the musical *Brigadoon.* What stunned me even more was the timbre of his voice. I had never heard him sing. I cocked my head and lasered him with my gaze. "Okay, confession time. Back in high school, were you a Broadway wannabe?"

"Broadway *almost,*" he said. "I thought I had the chops."

My mouth snapped shut in shock. He had wanted to be a singer? What else didn't I know about him? *Stop it, Charlotte. You know enough.* I knew where he came from, what he had done in his previous life — he had been a topnotch chef — what food he liked, and what books and movies he enjoyed. The rest was going to be a learning experience, one I anticipated with pleasure.

I winked at him. "Wait until I tell Grand-mère."

"You wouldn't dare."

"She needs dashing leading men for her musicals." I raced ahead, yelling, "Grand-mère!" She couldn't hear me, miles away, but I continued to shout.

Jordan tore after me. He tried to nab me, but I eluded his grasp and dashed off.

"Think of the press you'll get." I swiped a hand in front of me. "Jordan Pace, local star." That was the last thing he wanted. No one from his past knew where he lived . . . and shouldn't.

"Charlotte."

"Catch me if you can."

Laughing myself silly — it didn't take much — I sprinted all the way to the main house at Pace Hill Farm. When Jordan caught me, he hauled me into the barn and tossed me onto a pile of hay. Talk about acting like lovesick teenagers.

Later that night, after we showered Jordan's Chocolate Labs with lots of love, we settled into the cane chairs on Jordan's porch for a nightcap and a small tasting of one of his farm's cheeses that he had named Pace Perfect. It reminded me of Fromage d'Affinois, a double-cream cheese with an edible white rind. Paired with a slice of a crisp heirloom apple, the velvety cheese tasted like ambrosia.

An owl's hoot cut the peaceful hush, and I felt the urge to discuss Jacky and her nightmare and the possibility that her husband really had come to Providence, but I couldn't find my tongue because of the way Jordan had responded earlier when I had broached the subject.

"Want another sip of port?" I said, instead.

"Sure." Jordan started to rise.

I waved for him to sit. "Don't budge. I'll get it."

I picked up the cut-crystal aperitif glasses and went into the living room that abutted the porch. Jordan had decorated the room with some of the most unusual and rustic antique pieces I had ever seen, including a coffee table made out of a trunk with brass fittings, camel leather armchairs, and my favorite, a claw-foot oak hutch, its shelves filled with rare books and collectibles that Jordan had amassed as a kid — framed stamps and butterflies and fishing lures.

Jordan kept liquor in the lower portion of the cabinet. We had finished off a bottle of tawny port, but I discovered a reserve stock behind a stand of liquor bottles. As I scrounged through the left hutch drawer looking for a wine bottle foil cutter, I drummed up a spot of courage and said, "Do you think there's any rationale for Jacky's dream?"

I heard Jordan shift in his chair; the cane creaked. I peeked around the corner and spied him rubbing his finger along the arm of the chair. Was he lost in thought or ticked off?

"She said she's psychic," I went on.

"Doesn't every woman think she's clairvoyant?" he said. I couldn't tell by his tone if he was teasing or serious. He didn't glance in my direction.

Resuming my search for the foil cutter, I pushed aside a pair of marble-inlay boxes, signed baseball cards sealed in Plexiglas, and a glass box filled with what looked like uncut gems. Why all these valuable items weren't stored in a locked safe was beyond me. "What if it was her husband outside her place?"

"It wasn't."

"How can you be so sure?"

"Because he would have barged through the door and dragged her out by the hair."

That image tightened my throat. I swallowed hard then continued. "Tourists came into the store. Two guys. One —"

"Charlotte, drop it," Jordan barked. "I mean it."

Miffed by his *see no evil, hear no evil* attitude, I rummaged loudly through the treasure trove drawer. I dug beneath a pile of old photographs. "Don't you have one?"

"One what?" Jordan said.

"I'm looking for a —" My hand landed on something that felt like a chain. I pulled it from beneath the photos and saw two silver rectangular-shaped charms attached to it. Dog tags. The name on the top tag read: *Pierce, Jake.* Was that Jordan's real name?

Jordan materialized in the doorway. "What are you looking for?"

Like a kid caught with her hand in the proverbial cookie jar, I dropped the tags and smothered them with the photographs. I hadn't intentionally snooped, and yet my heart was thrumming. "A foil cutter," I said.

"Wrong drawer." Jordan nudged me aside, closed the left drawer, and opened the right one. He retrieved the foil cutter and bounced it in his palm. "Let me do the honors, but" — his mouth turned up on one side and carved a dimple in his handsome cheek — "we're only having another drink if we keep the conversation light."

He would get no argument from me.

■ ■ ■ ■

The next morning, wanting to get a jump on the day, I woke early. I kissed Jordan on the cheek. He pulled me into a warm, luscious bear hug, whispered, "Have a good day," and quickly fell back to sleep. Quietly I slipped out of bed, dodged the Calicos nestled on the floor at the foot of the bed, got dressed, and hurried to the kitchen. While nibbling the remaining Pace Perfect cheese and sliced apples, I scribbled a note: *I love you, call me later.*

As I climbed into my Escort, a cock crowed. A frizzle of fear spiraled down my back. I flashed on an English class discussion about the opening scene in *Hamlet*. Had Shakespeare employed the cock's crow to set time, or had he meant it to be an omen of evil things to come?

Was I overreacting?

Eager to shake off bad vibes, I focused on work. For two hours, I experimented at Fromagerie Bessette with more wedding dinner recipes. Meredith and Matthew had agreed on two carving stations, one for beef and one for roast turkey, but neither could decide on the side dishes. I had suggested a savory herb quiche, mashed potatoes with

Cheddar, and popovers loaded with Parmesan stuffing. The kitchen smelled luscious. Almost nothing whetted my appetite more than the aroma of garlic and onions. Quick study that I was, I didn't leave anything burning on the stove this time. I arranged all the food on platters and placed the platters on the carving board behind the cheese counter.

In the early afternoon, Rebecca returned from her lunch break and slung an apron over her checkered sheath. "Ooh, do I smell rosemary?" She leaned over the platter of mashed potatoes and inhaled deeply.

"And basil," I said. "Taste."

I handed her a spoon. She dug in.

"I love the mashed potatoes, and the quiche is seasoned to perfection," Rebecca said like a veteran *Top Chef* judge, "but I think the stuffing could use a little more Parmesan." She quirked her mouth. "I always like more Parmesan. By the by, did you see Sylvie?" She set her spoon in the sink and collected her long hair into a clip. "She's outside her shop wearing a sandwich-board sign and not much else. What is that woman thinking?"

She isn't, I wanted to say, but held my tongue. Sylvie had one mind-set. Whatever was good for her was the right thing to do.

She didn't think about the consequences.

"She's parading in front of Under Wraps announcing discounted facials," Rebecca went on. "Does she think that will draw bees to honey? And please" — she slapped her thigh — "explain to me why on earth she has a day spa in her dress boutique?"

"Because she wants to outdo Prudence."

"She might have a shot."

"What do you mean?"

Rebecca fetched a wheel of Manchego from the display case, removed its plastic wrap, and started to reface it with a sharp knife. I admired her style. She could prepare all the cheeses we stowed in the case in less than an hour. "You heard what Edy said. Prudence's business is struggling."

I waggled a finger. "Don't go spreading rumors."

"It's not a rumor," Rebecca said. "I was at the grocery store. I saw Prudence in the bank next door."

Although the area around the Village Green consisted of small boutique shops at the center of town, Providence also had a more generic section near the elementary school. Providence Grocers, Providence Savings and Loan, and more.

"She was arguing with a loan officer," Rebecca said.

Grandmère pushed through the front door while tugging on the strap of the crocheted bag she had slung crosswise over her chest.

"There you have it." Rebecca spread her palms.

"Have what?" Grandmère asked, stopping beside me.

"Prudence is struggling financially," Rebecca answered.

I growled. "We don't know that for a fact." I eyed my grandmother. "What are you doing here?" I peered out the front window. "Where's Pépère?" Saturday was his day to help in the shop.

"*Je suis désolée.* He is under the weather."

I felt a nervous tug on my stomach. My grandfather was never sick. He had the constitution of an ox. And yet, last night, he had looked pale and tired. Now my grandmother appeared the same.

"*T'inquiète pas,*" Grandmère said.

"I'm not worried."

"Then why do you frown?" She petted my arm. "I am here to assist, *chérie.*"

Over the past year, I couldn't remember more than a handful of days when Grandmère had helped me in the shop. She had resisted Matthew and me taking over the place, but in the end, I think she was relieved. She had enough to tend to, with her mayoral duties and managing the theater.

"Should I take Pépère some soup?" I asked.

Grandmère shook her head. "He is not interested in eating today."

Another ripple of concern coursed through me. A day my grandfather didn't want to eat was a red-letter day.

"Where shall I begin?" Bent on ending the discussion, my grandmother slung an apron over her purse and clothing and swept past me. "Are there shelves to be dusted? Jars to be cleaned? Do I see more wedding food to taste test?"

"Yes, I —"

"Charlotte." Delilah rushed into the shop, her breathing staccato and face stark white. "He" — she hiccuped — "he died."

My grandmother whirled around. Her hand flew to her chest. Did she think my grandfather had sneaked out of the house, gone to the diner, and dropped dead? *No way.*

Heart catching in my throat, I said, "Who died?"

"That man."

Not my grandfather. Delilah would never have called him *that man.*

"Which man?" I hurried to her and gripped her hands to calm her.

"The man who was in the diner yesterday. The tourist."

"Still not enough information." For an observant playwright and a woman who could recite every item on an extensive menu, including daily specials, Delilah was coming up woefully short on details.

"He's dead in the cooler at the Igloo."

"What was he doing there?"

"I don't know." Delilah wheezed. "I. Don't. Know."

Worried that she might hyperventilate, I wrangled her onto a ladder-back chair by the tasting counter and said, "How did he die?"

"He was murdered."

Rebecca, my grandmother, and I gasped. Another murder had occurred in our fair town? What was this world coming to?

When I found my breath again, I said, "Start at the top. Which tourist?"

"The tall one with the . . ." She patted the skin beneath her chin.

"The wattle?" Rebecca said.

Delilah nodded. "He's . . . . There's a crowd. I have to get back to work. Charlotte, you should find out what's going on."

"Why me?"

"Because you'll get the real scoop from Chief Urso. He'll talk to you."

"Not always."

"Just find out what's going on. Keep rumors from starting. Rumors aren't good for the town."

"She is right, *chérie,*" my grandmother said. "Go. I will tend to the customers."

Judging by how many people on the street and sidewalks were running east toward the ice cream store, she wouldn't have much to do.

"And *chérie,*" Grandmère whispered, bidding me to her side. "Do not tell your grandfather about the murder. I do not want him to get sicker."

CHAPTER 7

A crime scene worked like a magnet. Saturday was always a busy day in Providence, but more people than I had seen in weeks crowded the sidewalks and spilled into the street. A couple of waiters stood outside La Bella Ristorante. A few women hovered by the bay window at All Booked Up, looking in the direction of the Igloo Ice Cream Parlor.

Rebecca and I elbowed our way to a cluster of locals who had gathered in front of the store, among them Edy, who looked as pale as a corpse bride. Where had she found a black maxi-length vintage dress? Upon awakening, had she sensed something dire in the air and dressed for the occasion? And what was with the silver studs piercing her upper lip and side of her nose? All I could think was ouch, ouch, ouch.

Stop it, Charlotte. You're being mean.

I peered around her into the Igloo, one of

Providence's favorite hangouts, a shop that embraced Old World charm. Its name was etched into the window in sepia ink. The antique décor and fixtures inside were dark bronze. The floor was patterned with black-and-white one-inch octagonal tiles set in a checkerboard pattern. Locals and tourists often took photographs of the scrolled, twenty-by-six-foot mirror hanging behind the aged oak ice cream counter. The yoga studio, which was located above the ice cream shop, looked dark. The owner always traveled during October.

"Is Chief Urso in the shop?" I asked. I didn't see anyone milling about inside.

Edy said, "He's in the back with the Igloo staff and the coroner. The scuttlebutt is the guy was killed after closing."

"My baby." Iris zigzagged through the crowd, arms jutting forward.

I dodged in front of her. "Iris, stop."

"But she's in there." She stabbed a finger at the Igloo. "My baby. He's probably grilling her right now." Iris's *baby* was one of the two high school seniors that the Igloo had hired as servers. Everyone referred to them as the Scoops. They had wrists of steel.

I said, "Calm down, Iris, I'm sure she's fine. Chief Urso is probably asking the standard questions. 'Where were you last night?' "

"In my orchid garden," Iris said.

"Not you. Your daughter. The chief will want to know what your daughter did after work. What she did this morning. When she arrived to prep the store." The Igloo Ice Cream Parlor didn't open until four P.M. and remained open until midnight.

"Oh, there's . . ." Iris pointed to her right. "He'll know how to fix this."

She hurried through the swarm of bystanders toward a man who was hard to miss — Stratton Walpole, the local dog groomer and star of *Hamlet,* who was as sturdy as an oak tree, though he was thinning on top and a little too old for the role, in my humble opinion. My grandmother said he had given the best reading and added that a wig and makeup would mask his drawbacks. As if prepared to go to rehearsal, Stratton and a few buddies carried Renaissance costumes. When Iris joined him, he slipped his muscular arm around her shoulders.

Beyond them, I saw Hugo Hunter hotfooting it toward us, pumping his arms like a professional athlete.

I pressed through the crowd and edged toward the front door. Rebecca followed.

Hugo staggered toward me. Drenched in

perspiration, he rested his hands on his thighs. "My car broke down. I ran . . . Is Chief Urso inside?" His gaze darted to the front door and back to me. "The chief called me. Said my employees found a body when they came on their shift. Said a tourist was murdered in the freezer after closing." His voice rasped with anxiety. "Why would someone do that? In my store?" He ran his fingers through his hair, drew in a deep breath, and pushed open the front door.

Through the picture window, I caught sight of the Scoops and Urso. All were emerging from the rear of the store. The Scoops grabbed their things from behind the counter and raced out of the store.

Iris flew to her daughter, gripped her shoulders, and asked who died. When her daughter muttered, "Capriotti," my insides clenched. Had I heard her right? Was Jacky's estranged husband, Giacomo Capriotti, lying dead inside? I gazed back into the Igloo.

Hugo headed for the rear of the store. Urso stopped him and put a hand on his chest. Hugo resisted. He tried to see over Urso's shoulder. Urso gripped his elbow and steered him to a stool by the counter. Urso asked a question. Hugo shook his head. Urso asked something else. In explanation, Hugo tapped his watch, then spoke some more, his mouth and hands working in conjunction.

Knowing I would get nothing from watching their silent play, I pivoted, searching for Iris and her daughter. I wanted details to relate to Jordan and Jacky, but the Isherwoods were gone.

Rebecca poked me. "Charlotte, the chief is coming out. Get ready."

"To do what?"

"Grill him." She shoved me into Urso as he emerged through the front door.

I skidded to a halt and tilted back my head. The sun's glare hit my eyes. I shielded them so I could assess Urso's face.

His eyes grew dark, his mouth tight. "What are you doing here, Charlotte?"

"What do you think?" I said — a snappy retort, if ever there was one — glad that the words *I'm here to grill you* hadn't escaped my lips.

He huffed, then held up his hands like Moses ready to part the Red Sea. "Folks." The crowd hushed. "Please go back to your jobs or homes or whatever you were doing. This is police business."

A grumbling murmur swept through the throng.

"Who died?" A heavyset man's voice rose

above the others.

"I heard it was an out-of-towner," someone yelled from far back in the crowd.

"Did Hugo Hunter do it?" Stratton asked, his voice resonant.

"I will not comment," Urso said.

I gripped Urso's elbow and cleared my throat. "Chief, is the victim's name Giacomo Capriotti?"

Urso snapped a hard look over his shoulder. If I were a gnat and his gaze a laser, I would have been zapped. "Where did you hear that?"

Rather than get Iris's daughter in trouble, I glanced at the deputy who lingered by the front door. He was a true blue cop, but he was no palace guard.

"He doesn't know squat," Urso said. "Where did you get your information?"

My shoulders sagged. "One of the Scoops."

He gave me a cold, hard look. "Do you know the victim?"

I inhaled.

Rebecca gasped. "You do, don't you? Who is he?"

I kept mum.

Urso's eyes narrowed to slits of distrust. "Charlotte." He reminded me of my grandfather, when I said the dog ate my homework. We didn't have a dog at the time. Pépère had been hurt that I hadn't trusted him with the truth.

I wriggled with guilt. Should I tell Urso what I knew, or should I protect Jacky and Jordan until I talked to both of them?

"Charlotte," Urso hissed.

"I know *of* him," I blurted. "Hugo told me the man was killed in the freezer. Is that true?"

"How did he die, Chief?" Rebecca said.

Urso shook his head. "Uh-uh, Miss Zook. I'm not giving out any information until Charlotte tells me everything she's got." He tapped his foot, waiting.

"What's that on your shoe, Chief?" Rebecca pointed.

Urso glanced down. "Ice cream cone crumbs."

"Was the freezer a mess?" she asked.

Urso remained stoic.

"Was there a struggle? Will the killer have bruises?"

"Miss Zook, you can give up trying to coax something out of me." Urso's mouth quirked up on the right. "I repeat, you won't get another word out of me until Charlotte spills what she's got."

I opened my hands. "But I don't know anything."

"You do, too." Edy wedged between Rebecca and me. Had she followed us to listen in? "Giacomo Capriotti is Jacky's husband. I overheard you and Jordan talking at Sew Inspired Quilt Shoppe the other day."

She'd heard us? At the bridesmaids' dresses fitting? We had been whispering. Gack.

No fonder of her now than I had been in high school, I craned my neck and glowered at her. Her eyes wavered. A niggling suspicion crept into my brain. "You're hiding something," I said.

"Don't be ridiculous."

"You are. Your eyes are" — I jutted an accusatory finger — "cutting left and right."

"Oh, for Pete's sake." Edy blinked rapidly. "They are not."

"What did you do?"

"Nothing."

I tried in vain to figure out how Jacky's husband had located her. What would have made a guy in New Jersey contemplate coming to Providence, Ohio? I said, "Did you call him, Edy?"

"No."

"Did you tell him where he could find Jacky? You had days to track him down."

"Why would I do that?"

"Maybe you need money. Maybe you

asked him to pay you for the information."

"I do not need cash. I have a steady job at Sew Inspired Quilt Shoppe, or have you forgotten? And I like Jacky." She twitched her nose with smug satisfaction. "Try again."

"How else would Giacomo Capriotti have tracked her down?" I demanded.

"Maybe Prudence contacted him. She overheard, too. She —"

"Ladies, enough," Urso snapped, glaring from me to Edy and back to me. "Charlotte, who is Giacomo Capriotti?"

I turned my back on traitorous Edy. "Jacky Peterson was married. Is married," I revised. "To Capriotti. But he beat her. He threatened her at gunpoint."

"Was he shot?" Rebecca asked. "Did he bring a gun with him? Did he and his killer struggle for control?"

"He wasn't shot," Urso said. "Go on, Charlotte."

"Fearing for her life, Jacky relocated to Providence. Jordan helped her change her name and set her up in business." I cocked my head. "I guess she didn't tell you all this when you were dating her."

Urso's face turned sour. Bringing up his failed relationship with Jacky wasn't smart on my part.

"Did Jacky kill him?" Edy asked.

"No way," I hissed, wishing Urso would disappear so I could throttle her. "She did not kill her husband."

"She's got motive," Edy said. "She was abused."

"She's not capable of murder."

"Abused women lash out at —"

"Stop it, Edy," I yelled. "You do not know everything, no matter what you might think."

"What about Jordan?" she demanded, not cowed by me in the slightest. "Tell her about the eyewitness, Chief."

"What eyewitness?" I asked.

Edy smiled smugly. "Late last night, Anabelle was at the bookshop, and she saw someone tall running from the scene of the crime."

"How did you know about — ?" Urso sighed. "Don't tell me, the Scoops told you. I knew I should've kept those girls inside longer."

"And threatened them with obstruction of justice," Rebecca added.

Urso shot her a hard look.

"Jordan is tall," Edy said.

"You're tall, too," Rebecca countered.

"Not as tall as he is."

"Jordan didn't do this," I shrieked. "And

Anabelle is so short that even I would seem tall to her." Except, I noted, that Anabelle always wore high-heeled shoes — wedges, boots, and even sandals with three-inch soles. "Urso, Jordan did not kill Giacomo Capriotti."

Urso rubbed his chin as if, despite my plea, he were considering the possibility.

"Jordan seems like the protective type to me," Edy said.

I whirled on her. "That's enough, Edy Delaney, do you hear me? Neither Jordan nor Jacky killed anyone."

Edy gave me an *oh, really* glance, and I fought hard to stifle the urge to pop her in the nose. She was fast becoming my Least Favorite Person in Providence, a title that, up until now, I had bestowed upon Sylvie and/or Prudence, depending on the day. Edy must have sensed my desire — maybe she saw my fisted hands — because she huffed, turned on her heel, and threw over her shoulder, "If you need me, Chief, you know where to find me."

"Chief, when does the coroner think the murder occurred?" Rebecca asked.

"Sometime after the shop closed, most likely between twelve and two A.M."

Relief swept over me. "Jordan is cleared," I said. "He was with me all night."

Urso stiffened. He couldn't still be hoping that I would throw over Jordan for him, could he?

I pressed on. "Jacky is innocent, too. She was at her house with Hugo Hunter. He must have told you that when you questioned him a bit ago." I didn't offer that Jacky suspected her husband had returned to town and had been lurking around her house. Urso didn't need to add malice aforethought into the equation. I said, "How did Giacomo Capriotti die?"

Urso kept mute.

Rebecca flicked his arm. "C'mon, Chief, it's your turn to spill. The truth is going to get out anyway. If he wasn't shot, what happened?"

Urso screwed up his mouth then exhaled. "Someone bashed the victim's head with a five-gallon container of Brie and blueberry ice cream."

"Oh, Lord." I covered my mouth. If I hadn't given Hugo the recipe for the ice cream . . . *Don't be ridiculous, Charlotte. Giacomo Capriotti would still be dead. The killer would have used some other weapon.*

"Why was he in the Igloo?" I said.

"Got me," Urso replied.

"Did Hugo give a reason?"

"Nope."

Rebecca cleared her throat. "It sounds like an impulsive murder, Chief. Otherwise, the killer would have brought a gun."

"You don't know that he didn't, Miss Zook," Urso said. "Don't go theorizing."

Rebecca had a habit. Some would say it was good; others, including our revered chief of police, would call it bad. Rebecca adored crime shows. She watched as many cop and detective episodes on television as she could, and when she missed one, she would watch the rerun or stream it on her computer. This slapdash education convinced her that she was as good as any professional detective. By the look on Urso's face, he would beg to differ.

"Where were the Scoops after the shop closed?" I asked.

"Both were at a study group until two A.M." Urso said. "They woke up after noon and slogged into the shop an hour ago. They discovered the body together."

Iris would be thrilled. Her daughter was exonerated.

"At least you know it wasn't Jordan or Jacky or Hugo," I said.

"Look" — Urso scratched his chin — "I'm doing my best. I promise you I will solve this crime, and our town can get back to business as usual. Now, if you don't mind,

I'm going to A Wheel Good Time."

"To do what?" I asked.

"I'd like to have a chat with Miss Peterson," Urso said.

Uh-oh. He hadn't referred to Jacky by her first name. Whenever Urso reverted to using formal names, it spelled trouble.

"Urso, you know her. Very well."

"She's strong, Charlotte," Urso said. "With all the pottery work and lifting the baby, hoisting a five-gallon container of ice cream would be easy."

"She didn't do this. And she has an alibi . . . Hugo."

"People fall asleep."

He had a point. Jordan had slept like a baby while I wrestled all night with images of a stalker lurking outside Jacky's house. But Jacky did not kill her husband. I felt it in my bones. "Chief —"

Urso pushed past me and directed his deputy to keep the lookie-loos off the sidewalk and away from the ice cream shop, and then he marched down Hope Street toward Jacky's pottery shop.

Not willing to let Jacky suffer Urso's interrogation alone, I followed.

So did Rebecca. "Did you find any forensic evidence, Chief?" she asked as we passed Mystic Moon Candle Boutique.

I cut a look in her direction.

"Hair fibers?" she went on, ignoring my second silent plea to cease with the questions. "Footprints? Was there a fight? Was there tissue under his fingernails?"

Urso worked his tongue inside his mouth.

I whispered, "Rebecca, stop."

She winked. "Sorry, I can't help myself. Once a TV junkie, always a TV junkie."

I grabbed her arm in front of Sew Inspired Quilt Shoppe and said, "I mean it. Don't harangue him." I appreciated her pluckiness, but unwilling to get on Urso's bad side, I ordered her to return to the shop and relieve Grandmère.

She protested, but I insisted. Like a chastened puppy, she lowered her head and scurried past us.

I drew alongside Urso and said, "U-ey, talk to me."

Umberto Urso and I had grown up together. Many of us called him by his nickname U-ey, created because of the two capital *U*s that started his names. He didn't appreciate when we used it in formal situations, but now was different, wasn't it? Just the two of us. No crowds. He growled under his breath. I pressed on, despite his warning grunt.

"C'mon, it's me," I said. "Share. Maybe I

110

can help."

"Charlotte, we are not *CSI*. What we found is inconclusive."

"Meaning you found something."

He raked the nape of his neck with his fingertips. "We found black hair."

"Hair. That's something."

"It's nothing. Hugo's hair is dark."

So was one of the Scoops' — not Iris's daughter. And Jacky and Jordan both had dark hair, but they were innocent.

"Anything else?" I asked.

"Nothing. Not a darned thing." After a long moment, he said, "For your information, I did guess that Jacky was hiding her identity. I never figured out why. How stupid am I?"

"You're not," I said. "They went to great lengths."

"Is Jordan hiding his identity, too?" He held up a finger. "You don't need to answer. Of course he is. Otherwise, Jacky's husband would have found her sooner."

I leaped in front of him to make him halt in his tracks. "There's another guy that Giacomo Capriotti was traveling with. Anabelle said it was his brother."

"Anabelle?"

"She met them in All Booked Up. She didn't catch their names. They came into

Fromagerie Bessette, too. I had no idea who they were. Jacky thought she saw her husband arguing with his brother on the street the other day, but he looked so different — so much thinner — that she wasn't sure if . . ." I wagged my hand. "That doesn't matter. What if Giacomo's brother killed him?"

"What does the brother look like?"

"He's tan and thin and he's got pockmarked skin. You've got to track him down. I didn't see him in the crowd outside the Igloo, but somebody might have. A killer likes to come back to the scene of the crime, right? If he was there, someone can point you in the right direction."

"Is he tall?"

"Tall enough. Anabelle . . ." I twirled a finger.

"Got it. She's short. She doesn't have perspective." Urso sidestepped me and continued west on Hope Street.

"Wait," I said. "Where are you going?"

"To the pottery shop. I want to hear Jacky's alibi from her."

CHAPTER 8

A Wheel Good Time was located next door to Fromagerie Bessette. Urso entered the pottery store at a fast clip. In the nick of time, I caught the glass door before it smacked me in the face. So much for gallantry. The scent of freshly baked, hand-glazed pottery hung in the air. A gaggle of teenage girls sat on stools around a rectangular table at the front of the shop. Each girl had a round unfinished bowl in front of her. A tray of paints, brushes, and jars of water to cleanse their tools sat in the middle of the table.

Jacky hovered beside Cecily's stroller in the back. She rose as Urso approached, brushed her hair over her shoulders, and smoothed the front of her paint-splattered smock. A thin sheen of perspiration clung to her flushed face. Cecily lay in the stroller, sound asleep, a crocheted blanket tucked about her teensy body.

"Umberto." Jacky gave a little nod. "To what do I owe the pleasure?"

"Where were you last night?" he said, all business.

"At home." She raised a worried eyebrow. "Why?"

"Alone?"

"Hugo was with me until eleven." She folded her arms across her chest. "He left to attend to some business."

"He left?" I blurted, remembering how Hugo had sworn to stay with her and defend her, if necessary. "He didn't spend the night?"

"It's way too early in our relationship for that."

"Where did he go?" Urso asked.

"Urso," I cut in. "Hugo lied about his alibi."

"Charlotte, hold off." He stared at Jacky. "You don't know where he went?"

"I'm not his keeper. I assume he went to close his store."

Urso shifted his weight. Was Hugo now his number one suspect, or was he considering Jacky, since she didn't have anyone who could vouch for her whereabouts?

Jacky cleared her throat. "I repeat, why are you asking?"

"You haven't heard," Urso said.

"Heard what?"

"Your husband came to town."

"My husband? How do you know about — ?" She cut a quick glance at me then lifted her chin and scowled at Urso. "You were always curious, Umberto. Yes, I'm married, but I don't consider myself married. I didn't tell you because —"

"He's dead," Urso said. "Murdered."

Jacky sucked in air. She clutched the bib of her smock so fiercely that her knuckles turned white. "How? When?" No way could she have manufactured her shock. She hadn't a clue. Urso had to realize that, but his shoulders remained as taut as steel. Did he think she was acting? "Was he killed last night? Is that why you're asking all these questions? I was home."

"You knew he was in town," Urso said.

Jacky shot me another look. "Did you tell him I believed Giacomo was lurking outside my house?"

I shook my head. "When I found out it was Giacomo who was killed, I told Urso that you thought you had seen him outside the bookstore. That's all."

In my defense, Urso said, "I had to pry it out of her."

Jacky's gaze softened. At least she knew I was able to keep a secret. Up to a point.

Score one for the home team. Slowly I released the breath I was holding.

Urso waited for an answer.

"I wasn't sure it was really him by the bookstore." Jacky shuddered. "I thought if I didn't say it out loud, then it wouldn't be true."

But she had said the words out loud — to Jordan and me.

"I worried that if he found me, he might hurt Cecily. She's not his daughter. She's . . . It's a long story."

Urso slipped his hands into his pockets and immediately looked less stern. Did they teach that move in cop school? "If you were fearful, why didn't you come to me?" Did I detect concern in his voice? TLC was better than reproach any day.

"We broke up," Jacky said softly. She had cared deeply about Urso. Being the romantic that I am, I had secretly hoped they would find their way back to each other.

"Let's review last night," Urso said. "After Hugo departed, did you go out?"

"No. I would never leave Cecily alone, and I certainly wouldn't have taken her with me. The air was too cool." Cecily murmured. Jacky bent over the stroller and ran a finger down the girl's cheek. Cecily settled down, and Jacky rose and folded her arms across her chest. "She's got a cold. She was colicky. She's not sleeping well at night. She's —"

The front door flew open. "You!" a man bellowed.

I spun around. Giacomo's brother stormed inside. The tweenies screeched. A couple of them slid off their stools and clustered in the corner.

The man's sinewy arms jutted from his rolled-up sleeves and his fists were pumping. A bantam rooster at a cockfight couldn't have looked scrappier.

"That's him," I said. "The brother."

"Vinnie," Jacky whispered.

As he approached, Vinnie whacked raw pottery off tables. The items crashed to the ground and broke into pieces.

Urso jerked his hands out of his pockets, hovered his right hand over his pistol, and positioned himself in front of Jacky. "Sir, stop right there."

I edged to Urso's side to form a blockade.

"She killed him," Vinnie said. "Jessica killed him."

"I'm no longer Jessica," Jacky said. "I've changed my name."

"I don't give a dang what you call yourself, woman. You killed him."

"No, I didn't."

"You left him." Vinnie had a screechy

voice, like nails on a chalkboard. "It nearly broke his heart. He came to apologize, and he's dead. Murdered."

I said, "I'm sure Chief Urso —"

Vinnie whirled on me. "Who are you?"

I scooched back; my knees clacked together. "A fr-friend," I sputtered.

"Shut up, blondie." He glared at Urso. His gaze took in Urso's uniform and then Urso's hand hovering over the gun. "Are you the police?"

"Chief of police," Urso said, his tone steady, though his fingers flicked with tension.

"Arrest her." Vinnie shot his forefinger at Jacky. "She's heir to fifty percent of my brother's estate."

"No, arrest him." Jacky mirrored the accusatory gesture. "He hated Giacomo. Always did. What were you arguing with him about the other day? Money?" She flapped her hand. "Vinnie's a gambler. He would be in jail or dead if Giacomo didn't always bail him out."

"Liar."

"Buffoon."

"Do you inherit the other fifty percent?" Jacky said.

"No."

"Are you sure about that?"

Vinnie stuffed a hand in his pocket. "My brother has . . . *had* a foundation."

"Urso." I snapped my fingers softly to catch his attention and whispered, "Vinnie might be the person Anabelle saw running from the scene."

"Him?" Urso said. "He can't be more than five-six."

"Remember, she's —"

"— short. Got it. Point made." Urso held up his hands. "Okay, folks, that's enough." He hooked a thumb at the tweenies. "Young ladies, take a walk around the block. Get some fresh air."

The girls couldn't race out of the shop fast enough. The gossip at Providence Junior High would be rampant tomorrow.

Urso turned back to Jacky and — what was Vinnie? Her former, estranged, ex? — brother-in-law. "Tell me about the argument with your brother, Mr. Capriotti."

"What's your name?" Vinnie demanded.

"Chief Urso."

Vinnie snorted. "Urso, as in bear? Because you look like a bear."

Urso's mouth turned grim. He didn't take kindly to anyone making fun of his family name.

As if realizing his faux pas, Vinnie sucked his lips into his face and grew quiet.

Urso said, "The argument. I want details."

"We weren't arguing exactly. I mean, yeah, we raised our voices. Giacomo always bossed me." Vinnie stroked the side of his face. "I wanted to get a facial."

Sylvie's aesthetician would have a field day with his damaged skin.

"He told me I was a wuss," Vinnie went on, "but I wouldn't kill him because of that."

Behind us, Cecily started to cry. Jacky swiveled to calm her.

Vinnie tipped to the right to catch a peek. "Is that a brat?" Before Urso could react, Vinnie darted past him. He shoved Jacky out of the way and lunged with both hands at the baby.

Urso nabbed him by the collar of his shirt and yanked him backward. "Hands off, Rumplestiltskin."

"Is that my brother's baby?" Vinnie snarled, struggling to get free of Urso's hold. "You witch. You kept the baby a secret."

Jacky snatched Cecily from the stroller and clutched her to her chest. Cecily continued to wail. "She's not Giacomo's."

"Prove it."

"She's beautiful," Jacky sniped, "and he was a swine."

Vinnie swung a fist at her but missed making contact, thanks to Urso's firm grip. "She's not getting a dime of my brother's money, do you hear me?"

Urso tugged him backward a few more feet. "Okay, that's it, pal. You're coming with me to the precinct." He nodded to Jacky. "Don't leave town. We're not finished."

As Urso steered Vinnie out the exit, Jacky sidled up to me. "Urso thinks I'm guilty."

"No, he doesn't."

"If I'm still in Giacomo's will —" She paused. "He was wealthy, Charlotte. That's motive."

"Did you know you were his heir?"

She nodded. "New Jersey is a common-law state. There's no community property, but there are laws preventing a wife from being disinherited." She sighed. "But I thought when I abandoned Giacomo, he would have figured out a way to circumvent the law. I had left him for good. He knew that."

Did he? According to Vinnie, Giacomo had come to Providence to apologize to Jacky.

Cecily wailed. Tears pooling in her eyes, Jacky rocked her baby and cooed to her. Soon the only sound in the shop was the ticking of the clock over the kiln.

I said, "Who do you think killed Gia-como?"

"Vinnie."

"I don't know. He was pretty adamant about his innocence."

"He was also a hack actor at one time. A hack can fake anger. I'm telling you, Charlotte, he hated Giacomo. They had knock-down, drag-out fights."

"What if Vinnie didn't do it? Who else might you suspect?"

Jacky sighed. "I guess someone could have followed Giacomo from New Jersey. A disgruntled client, maybe." Her husband had been a lawyer — a defense attorney. He had managed a dangerous clientele. But would any have followed him from New Jersey to Ohio?

"Do you think someone in town might have known him?" I asked.

"I can't imagine how. He'd never been to Ohio. That's why I thought I was safe here." Jacky started to quiver. She set Cecily back in her stroller, tightened the safety belt, and then settled onto a stool by the kiln. "I was relieved to hear he was dead. Is that wrong of me?"

"No. He abused you. You feared for your life."

She laid a hand over her heart. "What if

Vinnie wants to kill me or Cecily? If I were out of the picture, Cecily would inherit. If we both died, wouldn't the other inheritor, i.e., Vinnie, get everything? You know, because of right of survivorship or whatever that's called."

"That makes sense, except Vinnie denied that he was named in Giacomo's will."

"I don't believe him. No matter how much they fought, Giacomo loved Vinnie. He would have provided for him. He suffered the ultimate big brother complex. And Giacomo never donated to foundations. Never. Vinnie's lying."

"I'll make sure Urso is aware. In the meantime" — my thoughts returned to the onset of Urso's brief interrogation before Vinnie so rudely dismantled it — "let's discuss Hugo. He lied about his alibi and told Urso he was with you. Why would he do that unless he wanted to cover his tracks?"

"I don't know." She sighed. "To protect me? I can't imagine him as a killer."

"He recently moved to town. What do you know about him?"

"He's nice. Kind. Funny. And he's creative. He's always telling Cecily big, grandiose stories. A simple *Cinderella* won't do."

"But what do you know about him? Where

did he come from?"

"I've never asked." She covered her mouth. "Isn't that amazing?"

It was. Curiosity dominated my life. With Jordan and Jacky's history, I fantasized that every new person who moved to Providence was running from his or her past. "Do you think Hugo might have killed your husband to protect you?"

"No, it's not possible. How would he have known where to find Giacomo?"

"Maybe he didn't have to. Maybe Giacomo found him."

"What do you mean?"

"Urso didn't tell you, but Giacomo was found dead in the Igloo Ice Cream Parlor."

"Oh, heavens." Jacky's hand flew across her mouth. She stifled a scream. After a long tense moment, she lowered her hand. Lips quivering, she whispered, "He couldn't . . . Not Hugo." She shook her head. "Giacomo must have threatened him. He has a gun. A Beretta. Did they struggle? Did Hugo turn Giacomo's gun against him?"

"There was no gun," I said. At least Urso said there wasn't one, but perhaps he had found evidence of a gun and was being coy. If there had been a gun involved, where was it now? Had Giacomo brought it to the

Igloo? Had the killer — whoever he or she was — taken it?

CHAPTER 9

When I returned to Fromagerie Bessette, Rebecca was behind the cheese counter catering to a long line of customers, many of whom were wearing *Stomping the Grapes* T-shirts.

I slung on an apron, edged beside Rebecca, and took note of the patron number on the wall.

"What did you find out?" Rebecca whispered.

"Later." I called, "Seventeen."

A woman I recognized from Café au Lait waved her fleshy arm. "That's me." She ordered a pound of our daily special, Mahon — a creamy Spanish cow's cheese, with the teensiest of holes and nutty flavor — and a tomato, olive, and oregano quiche.

As I filled her order, Matthew drew near carrying a tray of wineglasses. "I'm heading to the cellar. Cover for me in the annex."

"You're not slipping down there for a nip

or two, are you?" I teased.

"Ha-ha." He threw me a rakish glance. "You have unearthed my secret." Matthew was one of the most temperate people I knew. He liked wine; he never overindulged.

"Are you excited about the big day, Matthew?" Rebecca asked.

He grinned. "The wedding is ten days away. Ask me in seven." He whistled the opening bars of "Wedding March" by Mendelssohn as he disappeared.

Four more customers requested Mahon cheese. At my suggestion, they also purchased a Chalk Hill sauvignon gris, a fragrant white wine with flavors of tangerine and melons. The two paired perfectly.

When the shop was empty of customers, Rebecca pivoted and leveled me with a look. "So-o-o?" She tapped her foot as she dragged the word out.

"What?" I said.

"You know what. I heard the racket next door. What happened?"

I told her how Vinnie had come into A Wheel Good Time and how Jacky had accused him of killing his brother. "He's a gambler."

"I knew it. He seemed reckless to me. Murder is always about" — Rebecca rubbed her thumb and finger together — "money."

"Or sex or politics or revenge."

She clucked her tongue. "Find the motive, find the killer. We should —"

I held up a hand. "No, we shouldn't."

"But who will? You said yourself that Urso suspects Jacky, and you know he suspects Jordan, too. You're not a reliable alibi."

"I am, too."

"You're in love with Jordan. You'd lie to save him."

Would I? I couldn't imagine keeping quiet, knowing I was with someone who could commit murder. No, I would tell the truth, so help me God. Besides, Jordan didn't kill Giacomo Capriotti. But how about Jacky? Was Rebecca right that we had to investigate? Maybe I should find out more about Hugo Hunter.

I grabbed a towel and started wiping down the counters. "Urso is a good policeman. He will get the job done."

Rebecca harrumphed. "In what alternate universe do you live? He's only got two deputies."

"Two capable deputies." He had added one to the force a few months ago.

"And a big community — growing bigger by the day — to patrol."

"Solving this murder will be his number one priority, I promise you." I swabbed harder, in big swooping circles. "Besides, what do we know about Giacomo Capriotti? Where would we start?"

"While you were gone, I did a little research."

The front door of the shop opened, and Jordan, wearing his standard crisp white shirt and jeans, sauntered in. A cool breeze followed him inside.

Welcoming the fresh air and the end to my debate with Rebecca, I tossed the white towel into a bin, cut around the register, and weaved through the display barrels to greet the love of my life. As I neared, I tensed. He looked grim and discouraged. Why would I have expected anything else? He must have learned that his sister was a suspect in a murder.

"Hey, sweetheart," he said, his gaze flat.

Though I wanted to wrap my arms around his neck and kiss him passionately, I held back. "You've heard."

He nodded.

"Have you seen Jacky?" I asked.

"She's ragged."

"Urso thinks she might be guilty. I'm worried that he —"

"Shh." Jordan drew a finger along my arm and clutched my hand. "I know what Urso thinks. He's wrong. I told Jacky to close up shop. Now that the word is out, customers will understand."

"She was scared when I saw her earlier."

"She should be," Rebecca said as she sidled up with a feather duster in her hand. "Urso's gunning for her. And there might be other people after her, too."

"What do you mean?" I said. "What other people?"

Rebecca waved the duster. "I was trying to tell you a second ago. While you were out, I researched the Capriotti family on the Internet. I found an article that implied the Capriottis have Mafia ties."

"Not this segment of the family," Jordan said, his jaw tense. "It's all legit."

"But if Vinnie's a gambler, he might have messed around with the wrong folks, you know, thugs." Rebecca swished the duster across a display of crackers and jams. "If Urso lets Vinnie go, Vinnie might alert the thugs to Jacky's whereabouts."

"Why would they harm her?" I asked.

Rebecca rolled her eyes as if I was the dumbest student in the classroom. "Because if she's Giacomo Capriotti's heir, they might dun her to repay Vinnie's debts."

"I'm sure Urso will hold Vinnie if he has cause," I said.

"Sure as rain, which we have had none of

in weeks," Rebecca said snidely. "Jordan, you could investigate. You're Jacky's brother."

"I know Vinnie very well," Jordan said. "Married twice, a couple of kids. He's a lot of hot air."

"Hot air can explode," Rebecca said. "Just look at the *Hindenburg.*"

"That was filled with hydrogen," I said.

"Pfft." Rebecca blew her bangs upward. I was obviously not on her level of understanding. When I frowned at her, she gave me a single shoulder shrug and used her duster as a point maker. "I saw that Vinnie guy. He's got beady eyes. You can't trust gamblers. If they need money, they take it, no matter the consequences. They're born losers. They're the horse that finishes last."

I smirked. "What television show provided that theory?"

"Actually, I've branched out. Thanks to your suggestion, I've been watching the American Film Institute's top-rated movies. In the sports category, there's this flick called *The Hustler* with Paul Newman. Know it?"

I nodded. I had viewed it about ten times. I adored Paul Newman movies. So did Pépère. Thinking of him made me wonder if he was feeling better. Maybe I would take him soup later.

"Paul Newman was magic with a pool cue." Rebecca flipped the duster around and mimed a pool shot with the handle. "Speaking of magic, while we're trying to come up with suspects other than Jacky, let's not rule out Hugo 'Houdini' Hunter, as a suspect."

"Houdini?" Jordan said.

"Rebecca thinks Hugo looks like Houdini — you know, dark and mysterious."

"He doesn't have an alibi." Rebecca sashayed back to the cheese counter. "He told Urso he was with Jacky, but Jacky said he left around eleven. She figured he went back to the Igloo. What if he killed Giacomo to protect Jacky?"

"Don't jump to conclusions," I warned. "Hugo could be blameless. Vinnie may have set him up."

"How so?" Rebecca said.

"Maybe he knew that Hugo and Jacky were dating each other, and he killed his brother in the Igloo specifically to frame Hugo."

"How would he have gotten inside?" Rebecca said like an experienced interrogator.

"Maybe the door was left open."

"Flimsy," she said.

"But possible. There are nights I've left

the front door of The Cheese Shop unlocked." I didn't add that I knew Rebecca had done the same. I turned to Jordan. "Rebecca is right, however. We have to come up with a list of possible suspects."

"Not you," Jordan said. "Me."

"But —"

He touched my lips with a fingertip. "Sweetheart, I know you can't help yourself, but this time, let me investigate. Jacky's my sister."

"And she's Charlotte's future sister-in-law," Rebecca said. "She's got to help."

Jordan released my hand. "Let me see what I can find out first. I'll have a chat with Urso." He kissed my cheek, whispered, "I love you," and headed for the door, a hint of a swagger returning to his gait.

As he exited, I spotted Anabelle trotting along the sidewalk, hair tucked into another knit cap, her camel sweater, skirt and boot combination trendy. She carried a stack of boxes. They tilted in the breeze. If I didn't hurry, the upper box, its top flaps open, would tumble to the ground.

"Want some help?" I yelled as I dashed out of the shop and across the street.

Anabelle turned her head, her saucer-shaped eyes wide. "Sure do." She motioned with her chin. "My Chevy Malibu is over

133

there. The green one."

I removed the top box from her stack. Her collectible dolls peeked up at me. "Why did you park so far from the bookshop?"

"Why do you think?" She waited for traffic to clear on the two-way street before stepping onto the pavement. "Tourists don't simply take up the parking spaces on the street. They use the area behind All Booked Up, as well. They're ruthless. Our meager police force won't do anything about ticketing. The guys are overworked as it is." She set her load of boxes on the hood and fished in her oversized tote bag. "Listen to me having a pity party. Silly, isn't it? Guess I won't have much longer to grouse about Providence traffic. I'll have Chicago's unruly tourists to deal with." Her voice caught. "I don't want to leave Providence, Charlotte. I was actually building a life here. I'm tired of moving, but what can I do? My dad needs me." She withdrew a set of keys and pressed two icons on the key chain. The car doors unlocked, and the trunk popped open. With a small grunt, she lifted the boxes off the hood of the car. "Say, did you hear about the murder?"

"Yes, terrible."

"And to think I was interested in that man."

I had forgotten. When I had helped Octavia unpack boxes at All Booked Up, Anabelle had mentioned being attracted to the newcomer.

"How fleeting life's possibilities are," Anabelle said.

Her words hit home. I needed to jump on the bandwagon and set a wedding date with Jordan. The sooner the better.

"The victim's brother came into the bookshop a little while ago," Anabelle went on. "He was distraught. His hands were shaking. His name's Vinnie, I found out. Vincent, actually." She stowed the boxes in her trunk, rearranging and shoving until they fit. She took the box of dolls from me and set it on the passenger seat. Under her breath, she said, "There, there, Mommy's right here," and I bit back a smile. Octavia had made fun about Anabelle and her dolls the other day. I wouldn't follow suit.

Anabelle stood up and slammed the door. "What a contrast Vinnie was to how he was before. When he came into the shop with his brother, he flirted with me even though he could tell I liked his brother better." She returned to the trunk, slapped it shut, and slotted four quarters into the parking meter. "But this time, he was a mess, poor guy. He asked me if I knew anything about the investigation."

I said, "I heard that you saw someone tall running from the scene."

"It was late. I'm not certain what I saw."

"Were you wearing high heels?"

"What do you think?" She blushed. "Flats and I have never been friends. My father says I've got a Napoleon complex."

"What did you tell Vinnie?"

"That people were talking about him and his brother, but they weren't saying much. You know how it is. They're gossiping and starting rumors. I hate rumors." She made the statement with such vehemence that I wondered what rumors had been said about her over the years. Was that why she had moved so often? "He said his brother was carrying a wad of cash. He wanted to know if the police found the money on him."

"Did they?"

She chuckled. "Yeah, like the police would release that information. You've got Urso's ear. I saw you walk off with him at the crime scene. Did he tell you what he discovered?"

I shook my head, though I found it interesting that she had been watching Urso and me.

She leaned toward me. "Vinnie confided something else, Charlotte. I'm wondering if I should tell Chief Urso."

"You should mention anything pertinent to the case."

"How do I know if it's pertinent?"

"Tell me, and I'll let you know," I said, assuring myself that I was helping with the case in a way Urso could appreciate. Jordan might have gone to talk to Urso, but I was gaining clues.

"Vinnie said" — Anabelle glimpsed left and right — "that some woman telephoned his brother in New Jersey and gave him Jacky's location."

I flashed on the moment when I had accused Edy of calling Giacomo Capriotti to tell him that Jacky lived in Providence. She swore that she hadn't contacted him. In her defense, she claimed Prudence had overheard the conversation between Jacky, Jordan, and me, too. But why, I reasoned, would Prudence have contacted Capriotti? I could see her ratting out someone like Sylvie, whose business was in competition with hers, but I couldn't see Prudence ratting out my future sister-in-law. Jacky was one of the few people in town that Prudence liked.

No, I thought, returning to my previous theory. Edy was the culprit. She had been a liar in high school. She was lying now. Leopards didn't change their spots. She was

the one who had called Giacomo Capriotti.
But how would this information help
Jacky's case?

CHAPTER 10

After closing shop, I headed to the Country Kitchen with the twins, Meredith, Matthew, and Tyanne for a quick bite.

Delilah caught my arm as I entered the diner. "I heard what happened," she said sotto voce. She looked fresh in her red gingham waitress costume, her dark curls secured by a red bow. Men around the diner ogled her. She paid them no mind; she never did.

I glanced at the members of my group as they squeezed into a cheery red booth. Meredith sat beside Clair, who nudged Amy toward the window. Matthew slid in before Tyanne, who left room for me. I said to Delilah, "I can't talk now."

"I've heard the scuttlebutt," Delilah said. "You know Jacky didn't do this."

I nodded. I did know. I felt it deep in my heart.

"She isn't capable of committing murder.

Do something," Delilah pleaded. She was a member of our girls'-night-out events. "I adore Jacky. We all do. Talk to Urso."

In the hours since Jordan had left The Cheese Shop, I hadn't heard back from him. How had his conversation gone with Urso? Had he convinced Urso that Jacky was not guilty? I curbed the itch to call him. He would fill me in soon.

"Let's discuss this after I eat," I said to Delilah, then I slid into the booth and picked up a menu.

She pulled an order pad from her apron pocket. "Who wants today's special? It's a delectable grilled cheese sandwich made with Doux de Montagne cheese, crisp bacon, onions, and grapes."

"Grapes?" I said, intrigued.

"The sweetness of the grapes mixed with the salty bacon is divine," she said. For the past two years, Delilah had been testing out all sorts of grilled cheese recipes. She was campaigning for the National Grilled Cheese Challenge to wind up in Providence. So far, it hadn't come to pass.

I eyed the twins, who were battling for control of the knob on the tabletop jukebox. Whichever song they selected would play throughout the restaurant. On the way into the place, they had dismissed my playful suggestion of "Chapel of Love," in honor of the wedding. I said, "Girls, does grilled cheese sound good?"

"Sure," they said in unison, not looking up.

"How about the rest of you?" I asked.

None of them answered. We had come to the diner to finalize wedding plans — food, flowers, timing. Tyanne held open a blue leather album filled with pages of floral possibilities. Matthew and Meredith seemed riveted.

I set the menu in the holder near the jukebox. "Delilah, can you make Clair's and my grilled cheese sandwiches gluten-free?"

"You know I can." She made a notation on her pad.

"Great." I twirled a finger, including the table with the gesture. "A round of the special for all of us and a couple of cones of fries." The Country Kitchen made the best fries, super-thin and crisp, all fried in a separate pot of oil so Clair didn't have to worry about cross-contamination from other fried foods that were flour-coated. The fries came in a paper cone set into a silver wire holder. Very cute and retro. "And a pitcher of Bozzuto root beer."

Amy stopped spinning the jukebox knob.

"When are the waiters going to sing?" she asked.

"As soon as you select something upbeat," I replied. The diner was incredibly quiet for a Saturday night. Someone had selected a dirge of a song from the jukebox list. Perhaps the pall of a murder had subdued everyone.

"We can't decide," Clair said. "It's between two."

"Heads or tails?" I pulled a quarter from my purse, caught it, and covered it on the back of my left hand.

"Heads," Amy chirped. She always answered first.

I revealed the coin. "Tails it is. Clair, pick."

"This is for Rocket." Clair reached over Amy, twisted the knob on the jukebox, double-checked the number, and pressed a button for Elvis Presley's "Hound Dog."

I didn't have the heart to tell her the song wasn't about a dog. "It'll take a minute or two to crank up."

"I'm going to miss Rocket." Clair's eyes grew teary.

That caught Meredith's attention.

"Hey, I know." Amy spanked the table. "What if we make Rocket a show dog? We could train him and groom him and spend loads of time with him."

Meredith swiveled in the booth. "Girls, I was talking to your father earlier today. We decided Rocket can move in with us."

"Yay," Amy cried.

"Then I'll miss Rags," Clair said. "And so will Rocket."

"C'mon, Clair-bear. Don't be sad." Meredith stroked Clair's hair. "You're only going to be a few blocks away. You can see Rags every day."

Like an invasive vine, angst wrapped its way around my heart and squeezed. Would the girls see Rags often enough if I moved in with Jordan? It would be hard to set up visits without someone driving the twins to the farm. Guilt made me blurt: "I'll get you a new cat."

"You will?" Amy said.

I glanced at Meredith for a visual okay. She shrugged *What can you do?* and mouthed *Deal.*

"Yes," I said.

"Can we get a Ragdoll like Rags?" Clair said.

"Can we get two cats?" Amy asked. "I like tabbies, too."

"One," Meredith said. "We don't want Rocket to feel outnumbered."

"Two, please," Clair and Amy cried in unison.

"We'll see," Meredith said. "Won't we, Matthew?"

If either of them caved now, they would have a hard time saying no to the twins in the future. I know; I was one of the worst offenders, having just offered a cat without checking with either of them first. *Bad Charlotte.* Though Matthew and Meredith adored the girls and wanted their new life with them to be packed full of adventures and good memories, I silently willed them to hold firm.

"I'm not sure —" Matthew flinched.

Had Meredith given him a gentle kick under the table? I bit back a laugh.

"We'll see," he said, amending his statement.

"Here we are." Delilah set white paper doilies on the table and placed a beverage on top of each. "Back in a bit."

I took a sip of my frothy root beer and turned to Matthew. "Any floral decisions?" I asked, thrilled to change the subject.

He swiveled the album to face me. The page was filled with pictures of sweet williams, lilies of the valley, and hyacinth. "What do you think?" His face radiated with hope and joy.

"I'm noting a white theme."

Meredith giggled. "Isn't it beautiful? Iris

Isherwood suggested using hyacinth, white narcissi, and pine-needle rosemary for the sprays that will be on the ends of the rows of chairs as well as for the vases that will stand on the buffet. I'll carry white Ecuadorian roses. It sounds elegant, don't you think?"

I agreed. "So you've decided to use Iris as your florist?"

"We have two bids," Tyanne said. "Iris's suggestions are the best. And get this, sugar? She cut her rate by half, which makes her the most affordable. She said it's because she likes Matthew and Meredith so much."

Or she needs the business, I thought cynically. Would there come a day in our country's iffy economy when I would have to cut my prices at The Cheese Shop? Our daily specials, usually at discount, did sell out first.

"Show me the rest of the album," I said.

"Take a look at the bridal bouquets," Meredith suggested. "They're on page . . ." She turned to Tyanne for the answer.

". . . seven." Tyanne flipped the cellophane-enclosed pages slowly, giving me time to drink in the displays on each.

I was astounded by the plethora of white flowers: dahlias, asters, anemones, gladiolas, and more. I had only reached page nine of twenty when our meals arrived. I said, "I'll check out the bouquets after we eat, okay? What color ribbons?"

"Cobalt blue," Meredith said.

"Her favorite color," Matthew added.

"And yours." She nudged him.

Tyanne closed the album and wedged it behind her on the banquette.

"Gluten-free for you," Delilah said, placing a red-rimmed plate in front of Clair. "And one for your aunt."

Clair shot me a look of thanks. Because she had to eat a special diet, she often felt alienated. She appreciated when I joined her. The Country Kitchen, thanks to my suggestion, used the same brand of bread mix that I used at home.

"I'll be back in a sec with the fries," Delilah said. "Do you want grated Parmesan cheese?"

"You bet," I said. Grated Parmesan added all sorts of flavor to the most modest of dishes; french fries was one of them.

I took a bite of my sandwich and hummed with pleasure. The cheese oozed from the sides of the sandwich. The grapes popped in my mouth. Eager to serve Jordan this sensual meal soon, I logged the recipe into my brain.

The Elvis-shaped chimes over the diner's

front door jingled. As if picking up on my mental vibrations, Jordan entered. He spotted me and made a beeline for our booth.

When he arrived, I noted the pinch of worry around his eyes. A jolt of concern coursed through me. I excused myself from the table, and we moved to the counter.

"What happened?" I said.

"Urso released Vinnie Capriotti."

"Oh, no." Dreadful thoughts collided in my brain. What if Jacky's theory was true, and both she and Vinnie were Giacomo's heirs? What if there was a clause of survivorship? Vinnie might attack Jacky and Cecily. And what was Jacky's fate vis-à-vis jail? Urso had let Vinnie go. Maybe Rebecca was right. Urso was *gunning for* Jacky. "Do you think Urso believes Jacky killed Giacomo?"

"He said he doesn't have enough evidence to hold anybody."

I brushed Jordan's forearm with my fingertips. His muscles rippled with tension. "That's good news for her, isn't it?"

"Not good enough. A killer is on the loose."

Again, I flashed on Vinnie, not because he might kill Jacky to inherit all of his brother's money, but because of another notion. What if Vinnie, in retaliation for his brother's

147

murder, lashed out at someone Jacky adored . . . her brother, for instance? My fear reached my mouth. "Vinnie knows where you live," I whispered, looking around to see if anyone was listening to us. No one was. "What if he tells the people who are searching for you where to find you? He's got to be silenced."

Jordan raised an eyebrow.

I fluttered a hand. "Not *silenced* silenced, but maybe we could pay him to keep quiet."

He grabbed my shoulders. Matching my low tone, he said, "Charlotte, don't you realize that Vinnie is like a horse who will keep coming back to the trough for more water?"

"You mean if we give him money, he'll want more. Yes, of course, it's just —"

"Don't do anything. Vinnie doesn't know about my . . . situation."

"Are you sure?"

"Positive."

Jordan's secret identity had nothing to do with Jacky's. He had moved to Providence as part of the Witness Security Program. The reason was simple. He had been a chef and owner of a fancy restaurant in upstate New York. One night, when he went outside for a breath of fresh air, he saw two men attack a third man. Without thinking, he sprang to the third man's defense. The attackers had knives. Being a chef, Jordan knew how to use one. He wrestled one of the knives away. The struggle turned bloody. The third man died. Jordan stabbed and killed one of the two attackers, but the other got away. When he met with the police, he found out the attackers were the linchpins of a gambling ring. He entered the WITSEC program to testify against the surviving attacker. Knowing how to make cheese gave Jordan a real chance to start over in Providence.

I said, "Can we ask Urso to hold Vinnie indefinitely? What if we convince him that you and Jacky aren't safe if Vinnie is free?"

"Charlotte —"

"We could say he's obstructing justice or threatening you."

"But he's not threatening us."

"Yes, he is. His presence, alone, is menacing." I gazed into Jordan's eyes. "I see what you're thinking. You're wondering if you and Jacky will have to leave Providence and start over again."

"I am not."

"You're wondering if WITSEC can protect you now." My breathing became staccato. I felt like something was squeezing the air out of my lungs. And then I sensed someone staring at me. I caught Delilah, cones of french fries in hand, watching us. She tilted her head as if to ask what was going on. I jerked my chin — a gesture that meant *move away*. She frowned, then proceeded to take the french fries to the table.

"Please, sweetheart, calm down." Jordan pulled my hand to his mouth and kissed my palm. His breath was warm, reassuring. Why didn't I feel at peace? "I didn't come here to rile you," he said. "I simply wanted to keep you informed. Don't worry about Vinnie. He's not a threat."

"Unless he's a killer."

"If he is, Urso will figure it out." A year ago, Jordan wouldn't have given Urso an iota of credit. I was glad that they had become allies over time, but was his trust misplaced now?

"Did you ask Urso about Hugo Hunter?" I said, recalling Rebecca's insistence that I drum up other suspects. I didn't know Hugo well enough to care to protect him, and he had lied about his alibi.

"Urso is following up."

"That sounds vague."

"Urso isn't always forthcoming. We're civilians, remember?" Jordan squeezed my hand. His touch sent a sizzle of desire through me, and I wondered if people on the brink of war experienced the same desperate hunger.

"Try not to worry," Jordan went on. "Urso's a good man. I'm sure he has it handled. In the meantime, I'm going over to Jacky's to watch Cecily and give my sister a much-needed rest. I'll call you when I leave. Is ten too late?"

"No." Pent-up energy would keep me reading until at least midnight.

As I watched him stride from the diner, Delilah sidled up to me and whispered, "You can't sit back."

"What are you talking about?"

She tugged on her earlobe. She *knew something.* "Why didn't you tell me Jordan was in a WITSEC program?"

Panic zipped through me. She couldn't have overheard us. We had spoken so softly. "He isn't," I said.

"I can read lips, you know. I played Helen Keller during high school, or did you forget? Remember how much research I did for that role? I learned the entire ASL alphabet and over fifty words to sign."

I clasped my friend's wrist. "No one knows. Not Meredith, not Rebecca, not my grandmother, and not Urso. You can't tell a soul."

"I won't."

"Promise."

She touched the tip of her index finger to her chin then flattened her palm against her other hand. "By the way, that's the ASL sign for promise."

I released her.

"But you have to do something about this thing with Jacky," Delilah went on.

"Jordan said Urso has it under control."

"Sweetie." Her tone dripped sarcasm. "Urso and Jacky broke up. Jacky is your lover boy's sister. Urso used to have a crush on you. He still might. You do the math." She tapped her foot.

"Is that the ASL sign for impatient?" I said.

Delilah glowered at me. "You have to find out more about this Vinnie guy. You have to break him, get him to confess to the murder, eliminate the competition."

Who was she kidding? As petite as I was, I couldn't frighten Vinnie. I didn't own a gun. And I sure as shooting wasn't going to hire someone to eliminate him. "No. Double no. Triple no. If Jordan says Urso has it handled, he has it handled."

As she hummed her disapproval, I prayed Jordan was right.

CHAPTER 11

I loved Sundays. Occasionally I asked Rebecca to open Fromagerie Bessette so I could attend church. Often I asked her to open the shop so I could make pancakes for the girls or while away a stolen moment with the Sunday crossword puzzle. Today I had put her in charge for the whole day because I wanted to spend it paying attention to last-minute preparations for a wedding that was one week away.

Standing on the knoll of the Harvest Moon Ranch, looking out at Providence to the south and nothing but farmland to the east, north, and west, I set aside the worry about Jordan and Jacky's situation, which had kept me up half the night, and I focused on my purpose for being in such an idyllic location — Matthew and Meredith's blessed event. A hint of afternoon breeze swept across the grassy hills and tickled my legs. Birds trilled merrily at the dozens of bird feeders set out on the lawn between the red ranch house and the barn.

Amy skipped to my side and yelled, "Clair, look, that's Kindred Creek."

Clair arrived at a leisurely pace, looking like a true intellectual with her hair wound into a nub of a ponytail, a pair of binoculars slung around her neck, and a book about Ohio's birds tucked under her arm.

Amy pointed at the winding river at the base of the hill. The Nature Preserve lay just beyond.

"Wow," Clair said. "It's so vast."

"Where's Providence Liberal Arts College from here?" Amy asked me.

I gestured to the right. What a change had come over that property in less than a year, thanks to Meredith's deft guidance. The mansion had been revitalized, and the once-dead vineyard was flourishing.

Clair lifted the binoculars to her eyes and peered through them. "Ooh, I think I see a family of Prairie Warblers in the vines."

"Big whoop," Amy said. "I'd be more excited if you saw a pack of boys."

I elbowed her.

Amy grinned an elfin smile. "Hey, is that Mum?"

Sylvie crested the hill and pranced toward us with her arms spread wide. Who had invited her? I had to stifle a laugh. She looked like Maria in *The Sound of Music,* floppy sun hat bouncing with abandon, frilly blue-green dirndl skirt fluting out. The leather suitcase she carried looked ages old. As she drew near and opened her mouth, I expected her to break out singing, "The hills are alive with the sound of music . . ."

"Hello, my girlie-girls," she cried.

The twins sprinted to her and hugged her. For all her faults, Sylvie did love her daughters.

"Look what Mumsie has brought you." Sylvie heaved the suitcase on the ground. It landed with a thud.

Amy knelt down, popped it open, and yanked out matching pale green dirndl outfits, complete with leather lace-up bodices. "What are these?" She fingered the outfits as if they were road kill.

"Aren't they perfect?" Sylvie said.

"For what?" Amy scrunched up her nose.

"For the wedding."

"But we have dresses," Clair said.

"Not the right dresses."

"We'll look stupid in these," Amy said. Like her mother, tact was not her strong suit.

"You will not." Sylvie smoothed the leather bodice of her getup. "You will look like little girls and not . . ." She twirled a hand.

"Beautiful princesses?" I said, offering my two cents.

"Tosh." Sylvie shot me a snooty look. "They do not dwell in England. They live in Ohio."

I squared my shoulders. "That doesn't mean you have to dress them in old-fashioned costumes."

Amy, the lesser girlie-girl of the two, said, "Mum, we like our wedding dresses."

My mouth fell open. I propped it back up with my knuckles.

"But —" Sylvie huffed. "They're not appropriate."

"Because they didn't come from your store?" I said.

"Speaking of which, whatever are you wearing, Charlotte?" Sylvie assessed me, head to toe, curling her lip when she reached the hem of my Bermuda shorts. "Denim is out, or didn't you know? And the white shirt with rolled up sleeves? *Très passé.*"

"Sylvie!" Grandmère chugged toward us, arms pumping, gaze smoldering. "What are you doing here?"

"Charlotte invited me."

"Chérie?" Grandmère turned to me.

I lasered Sylvie with my best *liar, liar, pants*

on fire gaze, but she didn't balk. Rather than buckle myself — a weak habit that I was eager to break — I concocted my own set of battle conditions. "Yes, I did invite Sylvie, because she said how delighted she was about the wedding plans, and she couldn't wait to see the twins in their bridesmaids' dresses. And guess what, Sylvie? You're in luck." I held up a gleeful finger. "Girls, the dresses are here. I hung them in the bridal dressing room inside the house. Go put them on. Your mother will be so thrilled." I petted Sylvie's arm. "Won't you, Sylvie, love?"

Amy dropped the dirndl outfits like stones and dashed away. Clair loped after her.

Grandmère eyed the pale green dresses and the old suitcase. "What are those?"

"Play outfits for the girls," I said. "When they want to pretend they're part of the von Trapp family singers. Sylvie brought them. Isn't she ever so much fun?" I added an extra cube of sugar to my tone and winked at Sylvie.

She muttered something I couldn't quite make out, but I was pretty sure it rhymed with *witch.*

"Charlotte," Tyanne called.

I shielded my eyes from the sun and gazed down the knoll. Tyanne, wearing a stylish

157

ecru linen suit, beckoned us to the white birdhouse gazebo. Matthew and Meredith paced inside the gazebo, chins tilted upward as they took in the space. Iris, dressed in a balloon of a floral dress that nearly swallowed her whole, her company tote slung over her shoulder, hovered outside the gazebo. She examined the vines of white roses that weaved up the latticework, and the lavender, hosta, and variegated pittosporum bushes that surrounded the base. By the look on her face, she must have learned that she was the final pick for wedding floral consultant. Her mouth was turned up in a confident grin.

"We're coming." I slipped my hand around Grandmère's elbow and escorted her down the knoll to the gazebo. Over my shoulder, I said, "Leave the suitcase, Sylvie, and join us. You can see for yourself all the wonderful choices Matthew and Meredith have made."

Grumbling, Sylvie followed.

I snuggled my grandmother. "How's Pépère? How is he feeling?"

"He is still under the weather, but it is nothing. Do not worry."

"I'll make him some soup. I'll put in all of his favorite things. Onions, kale, and legumes."

"Please, *chérie.* You have so much to worry about. You take care of yours" — she patted my arm — "and I will take care of mine."

"Nonsense. It's not a bother." I had all the ingredients in my kitchen at home and, for me, cooking was therapy. Seeing stacks of moving boxes in my foyer growing larger by the day was definitely making me feel sick at heart. Maybe downing soup would help me drown my own sorrows.

"Gather 'round, everyone," Tyanne said. "We wanted to walk you through the plan."

Big blue organza bows were tied around the railing of the gazebo. An empty six-foot-tall white rattan birdcage was situated to the right. A sample white chair and spray of flowers stood beyond that.

Tyanne painted imaginary pictures with her hands. "I'll set out rows of white chairs. Meredith, you said the guest list was an intimate fifty, so there won't be a ton of chairs, but they'll be well spaced and elegant. The altar will stand inside the gazebo. A white carpet will run between the chairs to the altar. Sprays of white flowers with blue ribbons will adorn the aisle chairs, as well as the gazebo columns. I'll have the buffet and dining tables set up by the dining hall."

"Perfect," Meredith said.

"We'll have a tent ready, if necessary," Tyanne went on, "although the weather forecast is sunny, sunny, sunny. A young man in a white suit will stand beside the birdcage, which will be filled with Indigo Buntings. They're blue birds, to match your color theme, and they sing in pairs. Their warble is incredible. I thought they would be a good metaphor for your love."

"Spare us," Sylvie said.

Tyanne moved to the side of the gazebo. "Meredith wanted a string quartet to play Beatles' music. I love that idea. We'll station them here."

" 'Love, love me do,' " Matthew sang as he slung his arm around Meredith's waist and squeezed. She giggled her delight.

Sylvie coughed into her hand. I shot her a stern look and jabbed an index finger to hush. Like a disgruntled teenager, she hiked a single shoulder.

"At the end of the ceremony, on my cue, the bird master will release the Buntings," Tyanne said. "They're indigenous, so no harm will come to them. And Iris has suggestions for the most marvelous table flower arrangements, as you already know."

Iris flourished the blue album that I had previewed last night at the diner.

Tyanne folded her hands in front of her. "What do y'all think?"

Meredith said, "I love everything. Don't you, Matthew?" If she had clouds for feet, she couldn't float any higher off the ground.

Matthew said, "I do."

Meredith tapped his lips. "Remember those words, mister."

"Oh, please, kill me now," Sylvie muttered.

I flicked her hip with my fingertips. "If you don't like it, leave."

"And miss the fun?" She smirked. "Never."

Amy raced through the dining hall door. "Look at us!" she cried.

Clair burst through after her and skipped toward us. Their midi-length bridesmaids' dresses flounced around their calves. "How do we look?

"Tell them," I ordered Sylvie.

She cocked a defiant hip. "Tell them what, love?"

"How beautiful they are."

"I did at Sew Inspired Quilt Shoppe."

"Do it again. Now," I hissed under my breath. "If you don't, I'll tell them that little tidbit about you at eighteen that you shared with me after a few too many martinis. It involved a missing brassiere, if I recall."

"Oh, my darling girlie-girls," Sylvie gushed as she ran toward them, arms outstretched. "Princess Kate has nothing on you two."

"Really, Mum?" the girls said in unison.

"Absolutely."

Problem solved, for the moment. I clapped my hands. "Everyone, inside for the tasting."

In addition to hearing Tyanne's summation of the wedding plans, one of the other reasons I had come to Harvest Moon Ranch was so I could explore the kitchen layout. Before today, I had never been inside the main building. Although Tyanne had hired a caterer to do the actual cooking and serving of the wedding appetizers and meal, I had wanted a look-see at the kitchen so I could be mentally prepared for snags. Guests shouldn't go hungry; glasses shouldn't go empty. I had arrived earlier than the others and set out cheese platters. To my delight, the kitchen faced the backyard. Transportation of food to the buffet tables would be a breeze. From inside, big plate-glass windows provided a perfect view of the wedding site, and from outside, I could peer into the kitchen all the way to the walk-in refrigerator. Nothing would go amiss.

CHAPTER 12

In keeping with the red ranch theme, the Harvest Moon Ranch kitchen was set in a horseshoe shape and was decorated with red-flecked Amazon Star granite and white cabinetry. Platters of cheeses with dipping sauces and crackers on trays sat on the island. Bejeweled spreaders rested beside the sauces. White porcelain labels jutted from each of the cheeses to help identify them. Cocktail napkins stood in a stack at the center of the island.

"This way, y'all." Tyanne herded everyone into the kitchen. The crowd circled the island as if it were a dining table without chairs.

I pulled a packet of comment cards and pencils from my purse and started handing them out. When I reached Sylvie, I said, "Oh, my, I must have run out. But then I wasn't expecting you, was I?"

She growled at me.

I snickered. "My cat Rags can be scarier than that, love." Discreetly, I brandished a cat claw, then addressed the group. "Try to taste everything. Write me a note about what works and what doesn't. Matthew brought some bottles of a sauvignon blanc from the Bozzuto Winery. It has a luscious floral aroma and flavors of white peach and cloves. Girls, I made homemade apple juice for you." Ohio apples in October tasted like nectar of the gods.

"Charlotte." Tyanne held up a snack made of cheese, cracker, and topping. "The spicy lemon curd is delicious with this Dorset Drum cheese. Mm-mm good."

"I'll second that," Iris said. "I've never liked lemon anything, but this is divine, and I adore the presentation."

The Dorset Drum English Farmhouse Cheddar was hand-dipped in black wax and as small as a child's tom-tom. Pépère had introduced me to its sweet, tangy goodness.

Matthew and Meredith sidled to me. "What is Sylvie doing here?" Meredith asked.

"Long story," I said. "Smile and don't let her get to you."

"Not an easy task." Meredith slathered apple butter on a cracker, added a slice of the Bellwether Farms San Andreas cheese, which was a sheep's cheese as smooth and creamy as an Italian Pecorino — *pecora* meant female sheep in Italian. She downed it in one bite and sighed with delight. "Oh, yum. Now, tell me, how difficult was it for you the other day at the fitting?"

"What do you mean?"

"With Edy Delaney telling you what looked good on you." She elbowed me. "C'mon, admit it. That had to gall you. I'll never forget how Mr. Burger ordered the two of you to the front of the tenth-grade science class and failed both of you on that test. Like you would ever cheat."

"I heard that story," Matthew said. "Edy was mean-spirited."

I waved a hand. "It's water under the bridge." But thinking about Edy made me reconsider the scenario that had come in a flash to me the other day. Had Edy contacted Giacomo Capriotti and told him where to find Jacky? Had she asked him to pay her for the information? She said she wasn't hurting financially, but she was a liar and a cheat. I felt I should press Urso to dig a little deeper, but how could I do so without sounding petty? And what if it wasn't Edy who had called Giacomo? Who else might gain from luring him to Providence? Jacky, his heir, would, but I couldn't believe she had called him. She had a career, a life, and anonymity. She didn't need his money and the heartache that would go with his reappearance. I wiped the theory from my mind.

"Charlotte." Iris joined us.

"Congratulations on getting the gig," I said, drawn back to the moment at hand.

"Thank you. I'm thrilled, if you couldn't tell." The smile still hadn't left her face. "I was walking by All Booked Up yesterday. I know it's not open yet, but Octavia let me in. She has done a great job reinventing the place, hasn't she? I knew right where to go to find a historical romance. Have you visited?"

"I helped her unpack boxes."

"Anabelle looks a little forlorn about the whole move, poor thing."

"That's because she doesn't want to leave town."

Iris downed a morsel of cheese then licked her fingertips and wiped them on a cocktail napkin. "Isn't she the one who saw someone running from the scene of the murder?"

"So she says."

"She claimed the person was tall."

"Which isn't saying much." Again I wondered about Anabelle's account. She was inches shorter than I was, and she was a head shorter than Iris and Edy and just about everyone else standing at the counter, other than my grandmother and the twins. How tall was tall? Vinnie tall? Hugo Hunter tall?

"*Chérie,*" Grandmère cut in. "This herb aspic is lovely with the Tomme de Bordeaux."

"Thanks." For the aspic, I had combined tomato juice, rosemary, and basil. It balanced well with the juniper-encrusted cheese. "What do you think of the crackers?" I had chosen a basic butter cracker for all. Even Clair's gluten-free crackers were simple. I wanted guests to be drawn to the flavors of the cheeses and accoutrements and not the crackers.

"Perfect and understated," my grandmother said. "By the way, you look happy and vibrant, *chérie,* which warms my heart." She petted my face. "Now, let us get the twins involved."

"Use the round, gluten-free crackers for Clair, Grandmère." I pointed with my index finger to a separate plate.

"*Oui.* Amy, Clair, come taste." She made up a portion of cheese and aspic for each of the girls.

The twins swooped around the island and came to a stop by Grandmère.

"Girls," Sylvie said. "Before you eat, change out of your dresses."

Amy and Clair glimpsed from their mother to me, their faces studies in confusion. Normally I was the one to remind them about napkins and not spilling. Sylvie . . . well, she was a little more cavalier. However, looking at the twins' faces, I couldn't help remembering when I was a little girl and how I would put on my Halloween costume the moment I purchased it and wore it day and night until Thanksgiving. I gazed at Matthew.

"Forget it, Sylvie," Matthew said. "Girls, don't worry about spilling. We can dry clean them."

"But —" Sylvie sputtered.

"We'll be careful, Mum," Clair rushed to say.

"Promise," Amy added.

Sylvie looked stricken that Matthew had usurped her authority. I offered a supportive smile, but she ignored me.

Amy ate her morsel in one bite. Clair nibbled the edges of her cracker before eating the center. Both finished with a sweet moan of appreciation. Neither made a mess.

After wiping off her fingers, Amy said, "Can we play outside?"

Sylvie opened her mouth to speak, but

168

Matthew jumped in. "Yes, you may. Meredith and I will come with you." He called over his shoulder, "Great job, Charlotte."

As the foursome exited through the screen door, Tyanne said, "Don't they look deliriously happy?"

Sylvie muttered, "Delirious, anyway," and then her mouth curved up in a malicious sneer and she zeroed in on Tyanne. "So, Miss Wedding Planner, what are you doing about the ceremony? Will it go on for ever-so-long and drip with boredom?"

Tyanne thinned her lips. "Not long at all. Pastor Hildegard is preparing a seven-minute ceremony that he believes is perfect for this occasion."

"Seven minutes?" Sylvie said. "Ridiculous."

"He believes a crowd gets restless after seven minutes."

"Whatever." Sylvie snorted. "The marriage won't last longer than seven minutes."

Tyanne flinched. "Ooh, you are impossible. Why, I . . ." She sputtered, then spun on her heel and stormed out of the house.

"Sylvie, Sylvie, Sylvie." Iris smacked the counter. "Why must you alienate everyone?"

I whispered, "Don't, Iris."

"She has no right." Iris shot a finger at Sylvie.

"I'm so scared." Sylvie fluttered both hands in the air. "Iris, please, you're about as terrifying as a moth. Holster that finger."

Not surrendering, Iris said, "A wedding ceremony is a cherished thing. It is a matter to be determined between husbands and wives, not ex-wives."

Sylvie clucked her tongue. "Get off your high horse, love. You're just siding with the happy couple because they hired you. You don't believe all this drivel."

Iris's hands formed into claws.

"Sylvie," Grandmère said. "Take it back."

"No."

Iris said, "Why you —"

I grabbed Iris's shoulders. "Don't let her provoke you."

"I'm so provocative." Sylvie chortled. "Say, Iris, how's that salve working out that I gave you? If you want more free samples of that sixty-dollar-an-ounce goop for those burns, you'd better be nice to me."

"Burns?" I glanced at Iris.

Iris flushed crimson. "I'm so stupid. I was making boiled eggs for my orchids."

"You've lost me."

"Eggshells are good for fertilizer. It's the cheapest way to get calcium to the roots," Iris explained. "I forgot to use a pot holder and lifted the pot" — she mimed the ac-

170

tion, wrists inward. "Stupid, right?"

"Pathetic," Sylvie said.

"Sylvie, that is enough." Grandmère marched around the counter to face Sylvie. "You must change."

"I like my outfit, love, thank you very much." Sylvie fluffed her outlandish skirt.

"No, you must change your ways." Grandmère thumped Sylvie's chest. "You have a nasty disposition that will rub off on my great-granddaughters, and I will not stand for it."

"Oh, tosh, Bernadette." Sylvie swatted the air. "If I must change, so must you. You're a driven, controlling woman. How many projects do you have going? There's talk that you'll drop dead of exhaustion. What kind of example is that for my girlie-girls?"

Grandmère fumed; her coconut brown eyes turned dark. She grabbed a bejeweled cheese-and-sauce spreader.

"Charlotte," Iris whispered, her voice catching. "Do something."

Visions of a food fight, or worse, zinged before my eyes.

I turned to my cousin's ex-wife, palms open in a pleading gesture. "Sylvie, please."

Sylvie's gaze twinkled with wicked victory. "Fine, I'll be the bigger person. I won't speak about the wedding anymore. Happy,

Grandmère Bernadette? Now put down that knife or people in town will wonder about you, with your" — she cleared her throat — "reputation." She was alluding to the past, when my grandmother was wrongfully suspected of murder.

My grandmother muttered, *"Sorcière,"* and left the kitchen, letting the screen door slam on her exit.

Sylvie cackled, then turned her attention to the others standing around the counter. "Who wants a little local gossip?"

Iris raised a hand. So did I. Anything to change the subject to something neutral.

Sylvie shimmied with delight. "Speaking of the fabulous restorative creams that I offer at my boutique and day spa, do you know that man, Vinnie Capriotti, the brother of the victim?" Her segue was clumsy, but I let it pass. "He's coming in for a facial. He's my first male customer. If I succeed with his terrible skin, who knows what opportunities will arise?"

Vinnie had said his brother called him a wuss for wanting to get a facial. Had the slur enraged him enough to want to kill his brother? Or was there something deeper at the root of their relationship? Cain slew Abel because God loved Abel more. Had Vinnie been jealous of his brother's success?

Had he tagged along on the trip to Providence so he could get his brother alone and slay him? If so, why kill him in the Igloo, and why use a vat of ice cream?

Sylvie continued. "And get this, Anabelle is dating him. She's over the moon."

I gaped. She had to be wrong. Sylvie often said things that weren't true. I remembered a conversation where she swore her history was colored with encounters with royalty. But that didn't matter now. Anabelle did. She was a nice girl who would not deign to date somebody as low as Vinnie Capriotti. Besides, she had been interested in his brother. Could she switch loyalties that quickly? I exchanged a glance with Iris, who looked as fretful as I did.

Iris tapped the counter with her finger. "I heard the man got kicked out of the Victoriana Inn." She scooped lemon curd onto a cracker and topped it with a piece of Manchego cheese, a piquant Spanish sheep's cheese that was Don Quixote's favorite. "The inn's manager sent him packing for disorderly conduct."

"How disorderly?" I asked.

"He tossed his spa cuisine dinner at the fireplace."

Sylvie chuckled. "I'd have tossed it, too.

Have you seen how skimpy the portions are?"

"He hurled a Waterford crystal goblet right after," Iris continued. "Smashed it to smithereens. Now he's living in a car."

"Why is he staying in town?" Sylvie said. "Didn't Chief Urso set him free?"

"I imagine he wants to see his brother's murder solved," Iris said.

Sylvie folded her arms across her ample chest. "You of all people understand that, don't you, Charlotte? Isn't that how you felt when your grandmother was in a scrape with the law?"

I gritted my teeth and white-knuckled the counter. Heaven forbid Sylvie get a verbal rise out of me.

Iris said, "I saw Vinnie entering church this morning. Do you think he was looking for solace?"

I would bet he was seeking more than that. Absolution came to mind.

CHAPTER 13

Monday morning, while Rebecca mopped The Cheese Shop floors and I inventoried the items on the display cases, Urso entered. He strode to the cheese counter and surveyed the freshly made sandwiches.

" 'Morning, ladies," Urso said, trying to sound chipper, though his tone was as lackluster as his eyes and his shoulders slumped ever so slightly. I had to keep reminding myself that at one time he had dated Jacky. Investigating this particular crime and suspecting her to be guilty of murder had to be eating at him.

"Good morning." I set my pad and pencil beside the register and moved behind the counter. "What'll it be?"

"That focaccia sandwich looks good," he said.

"Really? That's not your usual."

"It's what I want."

"Well, good for you for taking a risk. It's

one of my new creations." I added a merry lilt to my tone — ever the cheerleader. "Grilled mushrooms and onions with Mortadella salami and Jarlsberg cheese. Best if broiled. You can heat it in the toaster oven at the precinct. Remove the top half and put the bottom half with all the ingredients under the broiler for about three minutes. The Jarlsberg will melt like a dream."

"I'll take two," he said.

Two again. He wasn't putting on weight. Did he have another lunch date?

Rebecca stopped mopping. I could almost see her curiosity feelers wiggling. I waved her to back off. I was not going to press Urso for details about his love life. For all I knew, that was why he seemed forlorn this morning, and it had nothing to do with his failure to solve the recent murder. Maybe he hoped to woo his ladylove with a scrumptious meal.

He shifted feet as I packed his lunch. After a moment, he said, "About Jacky —"

"Don't arrest her," I pleaded. "She's innocent."

Urso sighed. "What if her husband had threatened to take her back to New Jersey by force?"

"Via the Igloo?" Rebecca quipped. "That doesn't make sense."

Urso scowled. "What about the inheritance she'll get? I'm guessing it's sizable."

I sliced the air with my hand. "She doesn't need the money, U-ey. Get it through your head. Either Vinnie or the person who telephoned Giacomo Capriotti killed him."

Urso cocked his head. "What are you talking about? Someone called him?"

"Vinnie revealed to Anabelle that a woman called his brother and told him where to find Jacky."

"That girl is dialed in," Rebecca said.

I didn't remind Urso that I had proposed that same theory to him outside the crime scene. "Maybe the caller demanded payment for insider information, but Giacomo reneged. Vinnie said his brother was carrying a lot of money. Did you find a wad of cash on him?"

Urso hedged. "You know I can't —"

I folded my arms. Rebecca coughed her impatience.

"No, I didn't find any cash," Urso admitted. "But Vinnie could have made that up."

"How much did he say his brother was carrying?" Rebecca asked.

"I don't know." How much was a wad? A thousand? Twenty thousand? More?

"If you ask me," Rebecca continued, "Vinnie could have fabricated the story about a woman calling his brother, too."

I agreed. "He's a sly one."

"If you don't watch out, Chief, he'll slip through the cracks. What if he stands to inherit from his brother's death, too?"

"Jacky thinks he might," I said.

"Bingo." Rebecca spanked the cutting-board-style counter. "In that case, he wouldn't mind seeing his sister-in-law hanged for the crime. He'd get the whole nut."

"Yep. Jacky called it a survivorship clause."

Urso, who had been following our theorizing like a tennis line judge, said, "Wouldn't Cecily inherit Jacky's portion?"

"Yes," I said, "unless Giacomo inserted a clause that prevented such a grant. Cecily wasn't his child."

"He could do that?" Rebecca said.

"Jacky said he was savvy enough to do so." I eyed Urso. "Have you spoken to Capriotti's estate attorney?"

"I've got a call in to him."

"He hasn't returned your call? You're the authority."

"He's a one-man office and he's on vacation."

Rebecca snorted. "Giacomo Capriotti used a small firm for his estate planning? Doesn't that seem suspicious? With his wealth?"

Urso said, "Miss Zook, do you know how psychiatrists define paranoia? Y-O-U."

"Oho. Very funny."

Urso jammed his hands into his pockets. "Look, I don't know what to think right now, but don't worry, I'm doing my job, and for your information, Vinnie's not leaving town anytime soon."

"Why not?" Rebecca asked. "Let me guess. He's sticking around until the case is solved." Her words echoed what I had said to Iris and Sylvie in the Harvest Moon Ranch kitchen. "I can tell by the way you're glaring at me that I'm right, Chief, aren't I? Ha!" She plunked her mop into the bucket of vinegar-laced water. Water sloshed out and splattered her bare calves and sandals. "Solved, my foot. He's sticking around so he can keep an eye on you" — she jutted a finger at Urso — "to make sure you don't nail him for the deed. You watch. He'll throw in some red herrings simply to confuse you."

Urso's nostrils flared with annoyance.

"If you don't think Vincent Capriotti is your best suspect, what about Hugo Hunter?" Rebecca said, switching gears. "Did you corroborate his alibi after he left Jacky's house?"

"He was home," Urso said, "talking on the telephone to his mother."

"In the wee hours of the night?"

"She lives in California."

"Did you check his phone records?"

Urso sighed. So did I. Of course Urso had. He was nothing if not thorough.

Rebecca said, "If you ask me —"

"I didn't ask, Miss Zook." Urso jerked his hands from his pockets and stabbed a finger at her. "I didn't ask you a darned thing. I didn't ask for your opinion. I don't want it."

Nonplussed, she continued. "But if you did, I'd say you have some digging to do on good old Hugo."

"That's it! Miss Zook, you are going to be the death of me. No more. Not another word." Urso paid for his purchase, snatched the bag of sandwiches from me, and marched out of the shop. The grape-leaf-shaped chimes clanged. The door slammed shut.

I glowered at my pain-in-the-police's-butt assistant.

"I know, I know," she said. "I will catch more bees with honey. But he makes me so . . ." She threw up her hands.

I shook my head. There was no reasoning with either of them, but one thing was clear.

Urso seriously considered Jacky a suspect, and if I didn't figure out who really killed her despicable husband, Urso might arrest her.

A short while later, I left Rebecca in charge of the shop, and after setting a carton of Pépère's favorite soup into a wicker basket, I went to visit him. Grandmère, her face riddled with exhaustion, met me at the door. I thought of what Sylvie had said at the ranch the day before. Was my grandmother running herself ragged? Was there any way I could convince her to slow down? Who was I to talk?

I stepped into the entryway. A spray of lavender and white roses stood on the antique foyer table giving off a divine scent.

Grandmère peered at the basket I carried. "What have you brought?"

"Homemade chicken bean soup." I lifted the checkerboard cloth that I had nestled on top of the soup.

"*T'es douce, chérie,* so sweet, but I told you that you did not have to cook."

"But I did, so there." I pecked her cheek. "Now, I need a bowl, a spoon, and a napkin, and I want to chat with him."

"*Oui, oui,* but no talk that is strenuous." She shook an admonishing finger. "Nothing of the events of this week, and please, nothing of Sylvie showing up at the ranch. That woman sends him into a snit."

She sends you into a snit, too, I mused as I slipped my fingers around hers and squeezed playfully. "I won't speak of anything except how lovely the weather is. I also brought him a book." I patted the leather bag that I had slung over my shoulder. "A culinary mystery. *Pies and Prejudice* by Ellery Adams. You know how he loves pies."

"And . . . ?" She tilted her head.

"And what?"

"Did you sneak in some cheese?" Grandmère held out her hand like a schoolmarm, ready to search my purse or the hamper for contraband.

"No."

"A sliver of Brie?" She tapped her foot. "A wedge of Camembert?"

"No," I repeated. I wasn't lying and yet my cheeks flushed with warmth because old habits died hard; I was one of my grandfather's best suppliers. "Not a slice." To prove my innocence, I handed her the hamper and pried open my purse. "Check."

She did and chuckled. "Forgive me, *mon amie,* I worry so. I will return to my rehearsal."

"What rehearsal?"

She shuffled toward the kitchen and pushed open the swinging door. "We have been cast out of the park for the afternoon to make space for the farmers' market."

I followed. "Yes, but why have a rehearsal here? Why not the theater?"

"Because we are a few days away from opening. We must rehearse in the open air to use our vocal instruments properly." She set the hamper with the soup on the tile counter and fetched a bowl from a cupboard. "Everyone is out back. All have taken off work. It is *très bon, non?*" She swept a hand. "Listen."

The crank windows above the sink hung open. A mournful drone filled the air.

I peeked over the arty glass roosters that perched on the sill in front of the center window and caught sight of five actors on the lawn. Four were robed in Renaissance costumes; a fifth was covered in a white sheet. Delilah, clad in her red-checked waitress garb, paced in front of them while flailing her arms.

"That's it," she said, her voice loud enough to carry over the actors' drone. "Arms up. Come on, up, up, up!" She was guiding the group through a movement exercise while they moaned in unison. "All right, let's start where we left off. Ghost, speak."

" 'Revenge his foul and most unnatural murder,' " said the actor quoting Shakespeare while hidden by the sheet.

" 'Murder?' " replied Stratton Walpole, the bald, oaktree-sized dog groomer who was playing Hamlet.

"Come on, Stratton, louder," Delilah shouted. "Let the lines resonate from your belly." She believed that loosening one's abdomen and deep breathing before a rehearsal or a performance were vital.

Stratton bellowed the line again. " 'Murder?' "

"Much better," Delilah said. "Now do the lines from act two, scene two, and breathe." She raised her arms up over her head. The actors followed suit.

" 'O, what a rogue and peasant slave am I!' " Stratton said. " 'Is it not monstrous that this player here, But in a fiction, in a dream of passion, Could force his soul so to his whole conceit . . .' "

The words resounded like a tuning fork in my mind. Had Vinnie Capriotti become a monster in a play of his own making? Had he accompanied his brother to Providence so that he, as I'd divined before, could slay him like Cain slew Abel?

"Move on to act three, scene three." Delilah liked to jump around in the script when rehearsing her actors so they would be fully prepared if others went up on their lines during a performance. "Flap your arms."

A chorus of mourning doves flew to the telephone wire beyond the fence and lined up, as if preparing to observe the rehearsal.

Stratton powered his arms like an oversized whooping crane. " 'A villain kills my father, and for that, I, his sole son, do this same villain send to heaven.' "

Hearing those words made me readjust my theory about Vinnie. What if he weren't guilty? He could be sticking around Providence to take matters into his own hands. Did he intend to send the villain who had slain his brother to his death? Other than Jacky, whom might he suspect? Anabelle was *dialed in,* Rebecca said. Did Vinnie suspect her? Was that why he was paying her so much attention?

Someone applauded. The sound startled the birds. As they flew away, my gaze was drawn to the far end of the yard where Iris sat on a bench watching the rehearsal.

"What's she doing here?" I asked.

"Ahh." Grandmère tapped her heart. "Love is in the air. She wants to watch her beau."

I had to admit that Iris looked almost chic in a snug coral dress, and she had styled her hair with gel. Was her trendy makeover an effort to entice Stratton, or was she just feeling good about herself because of her newly found success?

Delilah said, "Excellent. We're done with movement. Grab your props. Be ready in five."

The cast clapped heartily then broke to rummage through their respective duffel bags. A few retrieved scripts; others fetched wigs and hats.

"Are you enjoying working with Delilah?" I asked.

Grandmère beamed. "She is a kindred spirit. I love her work ethic. But enough talk of the theater." She swatted my behind. "Fill a bowl with soup and visit your Pépère, and remember . . ."

". . . only speak of the weather. Got it."

A minute later, I hustled down the hallway carrying a wooden bed tray that I had arranged with a bowl of steaming soup, saltines, a napkin, a spoon, and a glass of ice water. As a last thought, I had added a tiny vase holding an orange gerbera daisy. I knocked on Pépère's bedroom door.

"Entrez," he said in a whisper.

He sat in bed with three pillows behind

his back and a burgundy quilt that I had given my grandparents draped over his legs. *"Chérie."* He set the magazine he was reading on the maple bedside table and anchored the pair of reading glasses on top of his head. "What a surprise."

"You look pretty good." I carried in the tray. "Hungry?"

"Absolument. I have a cold, that is all. 'Feed a cold; starve a fever.' "

I set the tray over his legs and wiggled it closer to him. "Grandmère seems to think you are fragile."

"Bah." He scoffed. "She cares too much. It is her way." He beckoned me close and kissed my cheek.

"Do you want to watch TV?"

"It is on the blink."

I glanced at the television, saw the plug hanging idly on the floor, and smiled. My grandmother had unplugged it to keep Pépère from hearing the current news. I wouldn't reveal her ploy. "I brought a book," I said. "A mystery." I pulled the paperback from my purse and set it on the tray.

He scanned the title. "I love pie. I wish you had brought some of that, too."

"Soup is better for you."

He took a bite of soup and licked his lips.

"Mm. *Délicieux.* My favorite. You spoil me."

"I try."

He sipped another spoonful, then said, "How is Jordan?"

"Fine."

"And the rest of your friends?"

I thought of Jacky, fretful and on edge. "Great," I lied. I wouldn't worry him. I had promised.

He eyed the purse slung over my shoulder and tickled my rib cage. "Did you bring me something else in that magic purse of yours? Perhaps a sliver of something?"

I wriggled away. "I didn't."

He pouted. "*Ma petite,* you let me down."

"Better you than Grandmère. I knew she'd search me on the way in."

"Did she? *Coquine.*"

"Yes, she is a rascal."

He laughed heartily. We spent the next hour discussing the weather and books. True to my promise, I didn't offer a whiff of news of the murder or Jacky's plight.

On my way out, Delilah raced up to me. "Hey, I was hoping to see you before you ran off. Explain something to me."

"Not about *Hamlet.* I'm not an expert." At a young age, Grandmère had me reading Shakespeare, but Hamlet's debate with himself continued to baffle me. He should have been a man of action. Why had he gotten mired in doubt and denial?

"No, silly. It's that Vinnie guy."

My ears perked up. "What about him?"

"I've seen him hanging outside Jacky's shop."

Mindful of my grandmother's warning not to alert my grandfather, I steered Delilah to the foyer. "Hanging how?"

She mimed the action, stoop-shouldered, hands in pockets, chin lowered but gaze alert. "I'm worried, Charlotte. He creeps me out. What can he possibly hope to get from stalking Jacky?"

An admission? A slipup? An opportunity to attack and get rid of his fellow heir — even though he continued to protest that he wasn't an heir?

CHAPTER 14

When I returned to Fromagerie Bessette, I was pleased to see Tyanne standing behind the counter tending to customers. "Slow day for wedding planning?" I said as I passed.

"I'm not as flush with business as I'd hoped, sugar, but I will be. You watch." She greeted the next customer, which to my surprise was Prudence. "What'll it be, Miss Hart?"

Prudence, dressed in a prune-colored sheath that made her skin appear sallower than normal, fidgeted as if she were in the store under protest. I couldn't understand why the woman was putting herself through the personal torture of buying cheese until Iris emerged from the wine annex carrying two bottles of McKinlay pinot noir.

"How are we doing, Pru?" she said.

Prudence snarled, which made me smile. Had Iris threatened to disown her friend if she hadn't accompanied her to the shop?

I shrugged into an apron and moved to Iris. "Good choice of wine."

"A tag on the display case said it received a ninety-one rating."

"It's one of Matthew's favorites, with strong undertones of plum and minerals."

"I'm not much of a wine drinker, but Stratton is."

"You two are getting quite close. I saw you watching him at rehearsal earlier."

Iris beamed. "Isn't he excellent?"

"He's certainly enthusiastic." The word *ham* came to mind, but a few days before opening wasn't always the best time to judge a person's performance, especially when Delilah's energetic exercises might have colored my opinion.

"And he's dedicated, a rare find," Iris added.

I wondered if she was talking about his acting or his ability to be devoted to her.

Iris set the wine by the register. "Pick a cheese, any cheese, Pru."

Prudence hissed something murderous between her teeth. The word *die* was loud enough for all to hear.

"Don't mind her, Charlotte." Iris leaned closer to the register, girl to girl, but she didn't lower her voice. "I suggested that she have a soirée at La Chic Boutique. Needless to say, she's a tad resistant. But with all the tourists who are coming into town to see *Hamlet,* I thought that a party might spark her social life."

Except one of those tourists was dead and his brother was hardly dating material, which steered my mind back to Anabelle. What did she see in Vinnie? Money? Maybe he had bragged to her about his possible inheritance.

"Social life, pfft." Prudence joined Iris at the register and flicked her hand at her like she was an intrusive bug.

Iris giggled, something I couldn't recall her doing before. "Prudence is mad because I suggested she date Stratton's acting buddy, you know, the high school history teacher. She thinks he's too old and bald. I told her bald is sexy. Stratton's bald, you know," she said, stating the obvious. "Right, Pru?"

Prudence sucked in air. Her face started to turn beet red. She reminded me of a kid trying to hold her breath for too long. If she released the air, she might fly around the room backward like a spent balloon.

"Prudence wants me to fully vet the teacher," Iris went on ignoring her friend's mini-tantrum. "But, really, is anyone ever fully vetted?"

My thoughts caromed to Hugo. Jacky

hadn't vetted him. None of us had. What did any of us know about him? He was nearly as mysterious as Jordan, and yet Jordan turned out to be not only a delicious man but also a kind, upstanding citizen. Had Hugo really called his mother and talked to her long enough to establish an alibi? I didn't know any man who talked to his mother for hours on end. Had Urso seen a telephone record yet? Although I realized I had telephone calls on the brain, I couldn't help going one step further with my theory. What if Hugo, upon learning of Jacky's secret identity, had pretended to be a woman and had called Giacomo Capriotti? I recalled thinking that his voice was resonant, as if he were trained to address large crowds. Was he also trained to disguise his voice? But what did he have to gain by luring Giacomo to Providence?

"I've paid," Prudence announced yanking me back to business. "Let's go."

Tyanne handed Iris the gold Fromagerie Bessette bag filled with their purchases.

Iris peeked inside. "What did you choose, Pru? Ah, Pace Perfect double-cream. I love that cheese. Did you get the cocktail napkins I recommended?"

"Yes."

"And the rosemary crackers?"

Prudence huffed, and I smiled to myself, tickled that the town's diva had found a bossy match in Iris.

As they exited, Rebecca entered the store through the rear door, her arms loaded with herbs from the garden out back.

At the same time, Tyanne rounded the register and joined me. "Sugar, Rebecca said you needed my help in the office."

"I did, did I?" I appraised my sweet assistant.

She raised her chin and strutted toward the kitchen. "Yes, you did."

"What help do I need?" I followed, and Tyanne trailed me.

"I was talking with Delilah this morning," Rebecca said over her shoulder. "She came in for some Grafton Clothbound Cave Aged Cheddar to take to the diner."

"Don't tell me. She's making more grilled cheese sandwiches?"

"You got it."

The Cheddar was a firm cheese with a whisper of almond flavors, and it melted beautifully. If I were making a grilled cheese with it, I would add bold flavors like jalapeños and black pepper to the sandwich.

Rebecca tossed the herbs into the sink, turned on a sprayer to rinse them, and tumbled them with her fingers. "Delilah thinks you should investigate Vinnie Capriotti."

"I know. I just ran into her. She was conducting a rehearsal at my grandmother's house."

"Then she must have told you that you need some dirt on Vinnie to keep him quiet about Jordan."

Tyanne's gaze zipped from Rebecca to me. "Why would you need him to keep quiet about Jordan?"

Rebecca slapped her hand across her mouth. Water splattered her face. "Oops."

My neck and chest flushed so hot that I thought I might hoot like a boiling teapot. That Delilah. Why hadn't she mentioned to me that she had blabbed to Rebecca about Jordan being in a WITSEC program? I didn't need to be blindsided. To how many others had she revealed Jordan's secret?

"I'm waiting." Tyanne folded her arms and tapped a foot. If I had learned anything about her in the past two years, it was that she didn't like being in the dark about anything. Not her husband's affair. Not her kids' grades or schoolyard scrapes. Nothing.

"Anabelle," Rebecca blurted.

"What about her?" Tyanne remained resolute.

"Um . . ." Rebecca glanced upward and

then sideways as she scrambled to cover her blunder. "Anabelle saw a tall person running from the scene of the crime."

"So I heard," Tyanne said.

"Urso thinks it might have been Jordan."

I had to give Rebecca credit; she was quick. I joined her charade. "But it wasn't Jordan, of course, because he was with me. I told Delilah that I was worried that Vinnie would convince Urso it was Jordan . . ."

". . . so Delilah suggested we get the dirt on Vinnie," Rebecca said, continuing the lie. "Something to convince him to keep quiet."

"Blackmail?" Tyanne said.

The word left a bitter taste in my mouth, but I nodded.

"Delilah thought we could find something online," Rebecca added.

"I'll help." Like an eager student, Tyanne waved her hand overhead. "I'd love to learn how to do an in-depth Internet search, you know, maybe using Deep Web or Dig It. I've been doing all the blog posts and newsletters. I think I'm ready." She grabbed my wrist and dragged me from the kitchen to the office. "By the way, I saw Vinnie on the street, loitering outside the pottery shop. I didn't like the look of him."

Rags meowed a greeting from his spot on

the office chair. Rocket perked up in his tiger-striped pillow and gave a single "Arf."

Tyanne snagged a treat for each of them from the lower drawer of the desk, then nudged Rags out of the chair and plunked herself down. "Ready," she said, hands poised over the keyboard.

Rags did a figure eight around my ankles, his curiosity piqued by Tyanne's fervent behavior.

"Relax, pal," I said. "Tyanne is going to help me."

For the next three minutes, I instructed Tyanne on how I would go about researching Vinnie Capriotti, birth name Vincent. She picked up the steps quickly. I gave her a pad and pen and asked her to write down any web links she thought might be important. I didn't really know what I would do with the information once I had it, but getting Tyanne focused on something other than Jordan's past was important at this point in time.

"Another thing," Tyanne said. "Did I hear right? Jacky is the heir to her husband's fortune?"

"It's unconfirmed."

"Might Vinnie Capriotti want to harm her so he inherits her portion? He's an heir, too, right?"

"The jury is out." When would Urso have a conversation with Giacomo Capriotti's estate attorney? Would he confide in me when he had?

"I remember," Tyanne continued, "when my grandfather died, how my uncles harangued my father. They told him he had better toe the line, *or else.*"

"*Or else* what?"

"*Or else* he might meet his Maker a tad early." Tyanne blew out a long hiss. "Money makes people do the vilest things."

"It does," I said, her words reigniting my concern. Jacky and Cecily could be in danger.

"Don't you worry your pretty head." Tyanne pointed at the computer. "I'll find out all I can from this box. Go on, now. Back to work." She shooed me away.

I returned to the kitchen, rested my hand on the granite counter, and tapped an imaginary rivet into the floor with my toe.

Rebecca looked up from the sink. "What?" she said, lips parted.

"You know what."

"Actually I don't. Delilah didn't tell me anything. Granted . . ." She let the word dangle.

I waited for her limp explanation.

". . . having watched all the detective

shows that I do" — she plopped the herbs into a white-matte-glazed colander and shook out the water — "I'm guessing I know what's up, but Delilah didn't say a word to me. Not a word."

Forcing myself to keep cool, I said, "What have you guessed?"

"Jordan is running from the law. He's got warrants out for his arrest because he stole a lot of money, and that's how he could afford to buy the farm."

All the tension melted from my shoulders. "You're not even warm."

"He's a foreign millionaire, hiding from the press?" Her voice lilted upward.

"No," I said, wanting to slug myself. If I hadn't overreacted earlier, I could have kept a cap on everything. Rebecca would have been none the wiser, and Tyanne wouldn't have become curious. *Rats.*

"Is he in the WITSEC program? You know, ready to testify at some big trial?"

"Where do you get these ideas?" I returned to the cheese counter. She followed and, in between customers, she pelted me with more questions. In the course of an hour, I didn't give her one clue, and I never outright lied. I was very pleased with myself.

When The Cheese Shop emptied of customers, Rebecca said, "Charlotte, you're driving me nuts. You're as stoic as a sphinx."

Remaining mum, I refaced a block of Beemster XO cheese — XO for extra old. It was one of my favorites and tasted like butterscotch.

"Have you seen the Beemster guy lately?" Rebecca said, trying to draw me out. "You haven't gone up in his hot air balloon yet, have you? So far, he's only made a flyby over Providence, right?"

Beemster USA was a co-op of several hundred dairy farmers. The guy who managed the concern was a charmer and loved to pilot his hot air balloon around the country.

"You're mad at me, aren't you?" Rebecca went on. "That's why you're not talking."

I wrapped the cheese in the saran-like cheese guard — a necessity since cheeses kept together in a cheese case might commingle, if not kept airtight, and their molds might jump to another cheese — and I replaced it in the cheese case.

"I don't blame you," she said. "But I won't blab anything else. Promise."

I spun to face her. "You almost revealed something to Tyanne, and it would have been a rumor. I don't want you circulating rumors. Got me?"

"Yes, ma'am. Forgive me?"

I grinned. I could never stay angry with her.

An hour later, when the shop had filled and cleared again of customers, Rebecca sidled up to me at the counter and said, "What's taking Tyanne so long?"

I had forgotten that I had given my other assistant a task. I tiptoed to the office and found Tyanne leaning back in the chair, Rags tucked against her chest. Tears streaked Tyanne's cheeks.

I hurried to her. "What's wrong?"

"I" — she hiccuped — "I got sidetracked. Nothing was coming up for Vincent Capriotti that seemed noteworthy, so I made a detour and . . ." She indicated the computer screen.

On the main page was a picture of her ex-husband and a lusty woman — the woman with whom he had the affair — at a celebration in New Orleans. After Tyanne divorced him, he and his paramour returned to his hometown. So much for being around to see his kids on a daily or weekly basis.

"They're getting married." Tyanne sobbed. "Look at the honker of a ring."

The woman wore a piece of jewelry large enough to choke a frog. "There's no accounting for taste," I whispered.

"You're telling me." Tyanne sniffed back

more tears. "Big fake breasts go right along with big fake gems. *Fake is as fake does,* my mother used to say."

"Charlotte." Rebecca appeared in the doorway.

"Not now," I said.

"Charlotte, it's important." Rebecca beckoned me to her.

Tyanne fluttered her fingertips. "Don't worry about me, sugar. I'm a steel magnolia. I will get through this, won't I, fella?" she said to Rags. The cat purred his support and nuzzled her with his head.

I met Rebecca at the door. "What's so important?"

"Vinnie's out there."

"Vincent Capriotti?" Tyanne swiveled in the chair. "He's in The Cheese Shop?"

"No," Rebecca said. "He parked on the street. He's walking west."

"Ooh, Charlotte, have I got an idea." Tyanne picked up the phone. "Didn't Sylvie say that Vinnie was going to be the first man to have a facial at Under Wraps?"

"Yes. What are you doing?"

She held up a finger then said into the receiver, "Hey, Sylvie, sugar, it's me, Tyanne. Why, yes, I did want to talk to you about the wedding plans. Input is always welcome."

I frowned. What kind of input did Sylvie want to offer?

Tyanne winked at me, a signal not to worry. "But, first, I'm calling to get the scoop from you. Did that man with the bad skin come into your shop?" She listened. "Vinnie, that's right. He did? Oh, he's there right now?" She nodded to Rebecca and me and turned her attention back to Sylvie. "Indeed, you are. Very clever. Why, just the other day you were saying how you had him wrapped around your pinky. Yes, indeed-y, I could learn a thing or two from you." Tyanne eyed me and mouthed: *Not.* "Yes, let's meet at Café au Lait tomorrow. What time?" She nodded. "Perfect. 'Bye now. *Ciao.*" She hung up and swiveled in her chair. "Vinnie Capriotti has gone in for a facial. He'll be there for an hour and a half."

"What was that about you having coffee with Sylvie?" I asked.

Tyanne screwed up her mouth. "Sylvie wants to talk privately about the food you've got on the wedding menu."

"Of all the gall."

"Relax, sugar. I'll cancel the coffee. I was just talking fluff. Nothing's going to change on the menu. Now, focus on the task at hand. You must investigate Vinnie's car."

"What?" I gasped.

Rebecca clapped while bouncing like a jack-in-the-box. "She's right. You need to investigate. All you have to do is peek in the car."

"And look for what?"

"Anything, sugar." Tyanne rose from the chair and set Rags back on the seat. She snuggled his neck, thanked him for the hugs, and prodded Rebecca and me back to the shop. "Anything that will get Urso to switch his suspicions away from Jacky."

"The truth might be a good idea," I muttered.

"Vinnie is a gambler," Rebecca said. "Maybe you'll find a large IOU."

"Or a ledger revealing what debts he owes," Tyanne offered.

"Or his brother's last will and testament, naming Vinnie his heir, too." Rebecca paused for effect. "His *sole* heir."

I nixed that idea. Would the guy be stupid enough to travel around with something so incriminating?

"Maybe you'll find a gun," Rebecca said.

I gaped at her. What if Giacomo Capriotti had come to the Igloo with the gun Jacky said he carried? What if Vinnie met him, they argued, and the gun flew free. What if Vinnie retrieved the gun and hid it in his car? Would that evidence convince Urso that

Vinnie was guilty?

Except Giacomo wasn't killed with a gun. He was killed with a container of ice cream.

CHAPTER 15

"Hold it." I ground in my heels by the cash register and opened my arms, palms up, a weak gesture in the face of the defiant stares of Rebecca and Tyanne. "Why must I be the one to investigate?"

"Because —" Rebecca paused as a woman in a *Stomping the Grapes* T-shirt entered The Cheese Shop.

In unison, we welcomed her. Like most newcomers, she gave a silent nod and, as if drawn by a magnet, ambled toward the cheese counter.

I said, "Let me know if you need any help."

The woman scrutinized the cheese in the case with downright awe. "How about a taste of that Stravecchio?" she said. "It looks like Parmesan. Is that what it tastes like?"

I moved behind the counter and lifted a wedge of the buttery cheese from the case. "It's similar but not as salty." I set the cheese on the wood counter, removed the saran, shaved off a slice, and offered it to her. "It's nutty and nuanced with rich caramel flavors."

The woman slipped the piece into her mouth and cooed. "Mmm, delightful."

Rebecca sidled up to the woman. "If you like that, you might want to pick up a jar of Quail Ridge honey to go with it." She pointed to shelves on the far side of the shop.

As if Rebecca had cast a magical spell over her, the woman walked, trancelike, toward the crackers and other accoutrements.

Rebecca hooked a finger at Tyanne, and the two hurried around the register and drew me into a huddle.

"Go to Vinnie's car, Charlotte," Rebecca continued. "We'll take care of her." She indicated the customer. "Peek inside the car."

"Why me?"

"Because you're the one who checks out cars on the street."

My hand flew to my chest. "I do not."

"Yes, you do, sugar." Tyanne tittered. "You're always making sure they have money in their meters. Why, I've even seen you remove a parking ticket from the windshield and give it to Chief Urso to handle."

Okay, so I didn't like it when our deputies acted like rookies and ticketed everyone who violated the hourly limit; I wanted tourists to feel they had plenty of time to browse and shop in Providence. So did Urso. But I didn't peer through car windows.

"What if I don't see any IOUs or ledgers inside the car?" I asked.

Rebecca smirked. "Maybe you'll see a compromising picture. One he'll bargain for."

The thought made me cringe. "Why on earth would Vinnie carry something like that around?"

"Men do these things," Rebecca answered, as if she had been a woman of the world her entire life and not a mere two-plus years.

"Not men I know," I argued. "Is this another idea you picked up from a cockamamie TV show?"

Tyanne cackled.

Rebecca shot her a caustic look. "They are not cockamamie shows. They're packed with good tips. I saw this *Law & Order* episode" — she rubbed her chin with thumb and forefinger — "or maybe it was on *Castle,* it doesn't matter. In the show, the detective scrounged around a bad guy's car and found an address book."

"That's breaking and entering," Tyanne said.

Rebecca raised a scornful eyebrow. "Boy, are you green. It's done all the time."

"It is? You mean . . . ?" Tyanne gaped. She looked to me for confirmation. "Have you?"

I couldn't deny it. I had. Sure, at the time, I had broken and entered with what I had perceived as cause, but a lawyer would have had a tough time clearing me based on my personal opinion.

"Maybe an address book would provide a list of Vinnie's personal contacts," Rebecca went on. "If we figure out who he owes money to, we can —"

"— threaten him with exposure," Tyanne said, finishing the thought.

It was my turn to gawk. "You've got to be kidding."

"Honey, in the Bible Belt, they say an eye for an eye."

Maybe they did, but I knew a lot of Bible Belt people who didn't resort to outright vengeance.

"Now mosey on out there" — Rebecca prodded me — "and peek into his car. It's the blue Firebird."

"Go on, sugar." Tyanne whisked her hand like a broom.

I glanced at the customer, who was peering from one jar of honey to the next while silently incanting: *Eeny, meeny, miny, mo.*

"I told you, we'll handle her," Rebecca said. "Go."

I didn't resist. I had to admit, I was as curious as they were. What if I did find something incriminating? If confronted with the evidence, would Vinnie fold like a bad poker player? Would he leave Providence and allow Jacky and Jordan to live in peace? I had to try.

Vinnie's 1970 royal blue Firebird stood near the Country Kitchen diner. The front of the car was filthy, the grille splattered with bugs. We had a car wash facility at the edge of town, but he hadn't made use of it. However, he had squeegeed the windows. I could see inside. A whole ton of junk sat piled on the passenger seat and the coupe back seat. More was wedged into every spot in between. Papers, books, newspapers, wadded-up fast-food bags, a camera, a couple of duffel bags. Had Giacomo Capriotti driven with Vinnie to Providence in this mess? From all I had heard from Jacky, I couldn't believe he had. He was a limousine kind of guy. Maybe he had decided to travel incognito. If so, where was his stuff? In the trunk? I caught a glint of metal. Not a gun, but almost as good. It was the hasp of a black leather book, which was poking from beneath a sheaf of newspapers. Would I find an IOU, a ledger, or last will and testament tucked inside the book?

The driver's door was locked; the passenger door wasn't. People were pretty trusting in Providence. All I had to do was open the door. Get in, get out. Adrenaline zipping through me, I stole to the sidewalk and looked left and right. The coast was clear. As I reached for the door handle, I heard a familiar voice.

"After you, milady," Urso said.

I snapped to attention and shoved my hands in my pockets. A kid kicking a tin can down the street couldn't have looked any more innocent.

Urso, in uniform, emerged from the diner, balancing a to-go tray with two sodas on the palm of one hand while holding the front door open with the other.

"Milady?" Edy giggled as she swept past him, the skirt of her all-black bohemian outfit swirling in the breeze. "How quaint. I like this Shakespeare thing." Coyly, she batted Urso's arm and then plucked at her spiky hair while her eyelids fluttered at warp speed.

My stomach did a flip-flop. Was she his current flame? Not that I was upset. I wasn't. I wanted him to date. I hoped he would fall in love and get married and have a family. But not with Edy. She wasn't his type and, at least to me, she was possibly a suspect in Giacomo Capriotti's murder.

Stop it, Charlotte. What did she have to gain from killing him? She said she didn't need money.

I recalled the cash that Giacomo Capriotti was supposedly carrying on his person. Was it hidden in Vinnie's Firebird? Had he killed his brother to get the money? With Urso nearby, I couldn't find out.

I slapped on a game face and hustled toward them. "Fancy seeing you here," I said to Urso, acknowledging Edy with a nod. "Got a hot date?" Inwardly, I groaned. Why did I sound so lame? Why was I trying so hard?

Edy widened her baby blues. "We're having a hot *lunch.*"

"At the precinct," Urso said quickly, his tone a tad defensive. "We're heating up those sandwiches like you suggested."

Edy slipped her hand around Urso's elbow. "It's not very romantic, I'll admit, but U-ey's on call."

I gaped. U-ey? Urso let her call him U-ey?

"Uh-oh." Edy patted her hip. "Someone's buzzing me." She pulled her cell phone from her jacket pocket and glanced at the read-out. "It's my employer. I have to take this. Excuse me." She moved out of earshot.

Urso cocked his head. "What were you doing, Charlotte?"

"When?" I said, sounding guiltier than a fox in a henhouse, to quote Tyanne.

"You were checking out Mr. Capriotti's car."

"I wasn't."

He narrowed his eyes; his eyebrows merged into one thick line. "I'm not a fool."

"You never have been." I stood a little taller, although in his shadow, I felt about as big as a midge.

"Charlotte, confess. You were snooping."

"I wasn't."

"You think I'm not doing my job."

I tsked. "Don't be paranoid."

"You'll do anything to keep a friend or loved one out of jail."

He had me there. I said, "You're wrong about Jacky."

"Am I?" He switched the to-go beverages to the other hand. "Give me another suspect."

"Hugo Hunter," I blurted.

"Why?"

"Because he wanted to protect Jacky."

"He's got an alibi. Try again."

213

I shifted feet and jutted a finger, the only weapon in my flimsy arsenal. "Vinnie Capriotti."

"We've been through this."

"Have you heard from the estate attorney?"

"Not yet."

"Or Anabelle," I said, not sure why her name came up.

"Why Anabelle?" Urso glowered at me like I was a witness perjuring myself on the stand.

"Because she liked Giacomo. A lot. Octavia told me that Anabelle was flirting like she wanted an engagement ring from Giacomo."

"Did they date?"

"I don't think so, but have you ever seen *Fatal Attraction*?" My cheeks flushed with heat. *Bad, Charlotte. Toss another local under the bus, while you're at it.* On the other hand, why did Anabelle know so much? She was the eyewitness who claimed to have spied someone running from the scene of the crime. She knew about the phone call to Giacomo and the wad of money he was carrying. Was that true or false? She had a sketchy, transient past, moving from town to town.

"U-ey," Edy returned, shaking her cell

phone. "Crisis averted. Are you ready?" She gave me a sly grin as if daring me to say something.

What was up with that? Was she dating him, hoping to tick me off? I grinned back. She would not — *would not* — get the better of me. I had no interest in Urso.

"C'mon, I'm starved." Edy snuggled into Urso and tugged him toward Cherry Orchard Street. Urso didn't resist.

As they rounded the corner and disappeared from view, a rush of restless energy welled within me. I returned to Vinnie's car and grasped the passenger-door handle. The sooner I got answers, the faster I could be done with suspecting everybody and her mother.

"What the heck are you doing?" a man barked.

Thinking it was Urso, I whipped around, my cheeks burning with guilty embarrassment.

I was shocked to see Vinnie charging me, his face thick with green goo, shoulders bare, raggedy jeans drooping over a pair of spa sandals. A terry cloth sarong with Under Wraps emblazoned in red flapped open over his scrappy torso. He brandished a fist. Though he looked cartoonish, I backed up. In my panic, I stumbled over a crack in the sidewalk and banged into a parking meter. *Very slick.*

Vinnie drew near enough for me to smell his minty facial masque. "You were trying to break into my car, blondie."

"No. I —"

A car alarm bleated across the street.

"I was coming out of the diner," I said. "And . . . and . . ."

Another alarm started to wail.

". . . and I heard a blaring sound, and I thought someone might have damaged your car, and —"

"Liar."

"I thought it was your car. I swear. Guess I was wrong." I searched for the source of the noise. Out of the corner of my eye, I spied Tyanne and Rebecca standing inches outside the front door of The Cheese Shop, each aiming key chains with car openers. A wave of relief swept over me. They had been keeping watch over me. I sidestepped the parking meter with every intention of skirting around Vinnie's Firebird and dashing across the street, but before I moved a foot, Vinnie snagged the hem of my red crewneck sweater and yanked me toward him.

"Uh-uh, you're not going anywhere. Don't think I can't see those two broads over there. You were searching, and I caught you red-handed." With me in tow, he cranked open the door of his car, rummaged through the glove compartment one-handed, and grasped something. I spied a shiny silver object at the back of the compartment. Was it a gun? Was he going for it?

"Don't," I rasped.

"Don't what?" He snatched a wallet, slammed the compartment, and swiveled his icicle-worthy gaze in my direction. "What were you hoping to find?" He wasn't addressing me. He was thinking out loud. He returned his gaze to the mess in his car and zeroed in on the passenger seat. He glanced at me and back at the seat. "Aha." He fetched the leather book from beneath the newspaper, then he backed out of the car and stood to his full height, which was a couple of inches taller than me. Brandishing the items, he said, "Were you trying to get your hands on this?"

"I told you, I wasn't looking in your car."

"Yeah, and pigs fly," he hissed. "Were you hoping to find a list of my known associates?" Though Jordan swore that Vinnie wasn't Mafia, he sounded like it. "Nice try. Listen up, blondie. If you keep poking around, you might find your pal Jacky doesn't feel so good one day."

"Did you just threaten my friend's life?"

"No, I didn't. Got me?"

"Oh, I got you, all right," I said, emboldened by the fact that Tyanne and Rebecca were still keeping watch. "Loud and clear." As a ruse, I glanced over Vinnie's shoulder and hitched my chin as a *hello* at an imaginary person, then I eyeballed Vinnie's hand clutching my sweater.

Vinnie swiveled his head. His hold on me loosened. I wrested free.

He whirled around, his gaze fierce. "Before you run off, blondie, one last thing." He shook the book in his hand, which I realized was an address book, complete with gold alphabetical tabs. "I haven't called any of the folks in this little beauty yet, but I will if I have to. So you tell Jacky that if she wants to stay off the radar with all the nice folks in New Jersey, she might consider paying me a little cash. Keeping a person's whereabouts secret doesn't come cheap."

Jordan's comment about the horse coming to the trough flew into my head. I gritted my teeth. "Why should she worry about people in New Jersey knowing where she lives? Her abusive husband is dead."

"Because money is like a magnet, and she'll be the one rolling in dough. My brother had a lot of angry clients." He held a finger to his mouth and whispered, "Shh."

The sound sent a shiver through me. "Where should she contact you?" I sputtered.

"I'll let her know." He chomped his teeth as if he meant to bite me.

I recoiled.

"Have a good day, blondie."

As he strutted away with the tails of his terry cloth wrap flapping like angry snakes, I heard him snickering, and I wondered how my plan to find some tidbit that might coerce him to leave town had made such a major U-turn.

CHAPTER 16

After closing the shop and taking Rags and Rocket home, I headed to Timothy O'Shea's Irish Pub for girls' night out. The pub was busy; it usually was on Monday nights, but not because of the music. The musicians were given Mondays off because every television screen over the old oak bar was tuned to *Monday Night Football.*

As I headed toward the banquette where Meredith, Tyanne, and Rebecca were sitting, I caught the score. The Cleveland Browns were up by seven.

"You're late, Charlotte," my friends said in unison like a Greek chorus. They had already ordered cocktails, including a glass of sauvignon blanc for me.

I snuggled onto the leather seat beside Meredith and clinked glasses, then said with the others, "To gossip." The Musketeers had nothing on our camaraderie.

"Where are Delilah, Jacky, and Freckles?" I asked.

"Can't make it. Life's hectic," Meredith said. "Now, Charlotte, what's this I hear about an altercation with Vinnie?" Her mouth turned down in a frown.

"I didn't tell her everything," Rebecca blurted. "Just up to the point where Vinnie caught you."

I set down my wineglass and sketched the story in fifty words or less, keeping my tone light. "There I was." I shot my hands up and plastered myself against the back of the banquette. "Vinnie's nose nearly touching mine. I swear my knees were knocking. All because these two" — I indicated Tyanne and Rebecca, who both looked chagrined — "prodded me to action." I didn't add the bit about Vinnie's not-so-subtle request for hush money. I was still trying to figure out what to do about that.

Meredith poked my ribs. "You take too many risks."

"It was daylight," I said. "Besides, I'm tough."

"And we were ready to defend her," Rebecca chimed in.

Meredith said, "Oh, yeah, like you could defend her. You're about as big as a bantam rooster." She turned her focus to Tyanne.

"And you're a southern belle. You wouldn't hurt a fly."

"Sugar, you are mightily mistaken," Tyanne said, chin raised. "My sisters know how ferocious I am." She boxed the air with her fists.

"Your husband does, too," Rebecca said. "That's why he split town."

Tyanne grinned. "Better believe it."

Meredith shook her head. "Charlotte, did you at least call Urso and tell him Vinnie threatened you?"

"I left a message and gave him the basics." Not that Urso had returned the call. After the face-off on the sidewalk, I hadn't expected him to. He was never happy when I was a snoop.

"Here we are." Our waitress set a combo platter filled with mini goat cheese pizzas, tamale cakes with salsa verde, and Parmesan-and-rosemary-stuffed potatoes in the center of the table.

Rebecca said, "We ordered for you. Hope you don't mind."

What was to mind? I was salivating. When had I eaten last? I dove into the stuffed potatoes first. The crispy crust popped as I bit into it; the rest melted in my mouth.

As the waitress sashayed away and Tyanne and Rebecca struck up a conversation about the football game, Meredith elbowed me. "Psst. Look who walked in."

Iris and Prudence entered the pub, followed by Stratton and his history teacher buddy. Prudence wore a boxy suit and clutched a purse under her arm. Everything about her, from her tight jaw to tense shoulders, screamed: *Keep away.* Iris, on the other hand, radiated confidence. She had blown her shaggy hair smooth; her tawny brown silk sweater and trousers were stylish and formfitting.

Meredith elbowed me again.

"Cut that out," I said. My ribs were starting to ache.

"Didn't you just say you were tough?" she teased.

I glowered at her.

She chortled and made a *gotcha* face. We had been friends since elementary school. Some childish behavior never died. "What did you poke me for this time?" I said.

"Anabelle is sitting at the bar talking to Tim."

The owner of the pub was one of the friendliest people on earth. Whenever he was bartending, he would let any patron bend his ear for a minimum of five minutes.

"So?" I said. "She has every right to be here."

"She's checking her watch."

"I repeat, so?"

Meredith leaned forward. "I think she's waiting for Vinnie to show up."

"Oh, yeah, without a doubt." Rebecca dragged her gaze from the TVs and back to us, her fervor matching Meredith's. "Frilly blouse, full makeup. Yep, she's on a date."

"Do you think he stood her up?" Meredith asked. "She looks forlorn."

I said, "She'll be forlorn when she discovers what the inside of his car looks like. It's a rat's nest."

"Charlotte, twelve o'clock," Meredith said, gesturing toward the front door again. At least she hadn't poked me this time. "Mr. Handsome just walked in with his sis and her boyfriend."

Jacky, Jordan, and Hugo approached the attractive hostess, who held up a hand and mouthed: *five minutes.*

As Jordan continued to chat with the hostess, Jacky and Hugo headed to the bar. Each sat on a stool. With sleight of hand, Hugo pulled something shiny from behind Jacky's ear. It shimmered in the glow of the pendant lights hanging over the bar. Jacky laughed. In all the time I had known her, I had never seen her so at ease. She seemed totally into Hugo and not at all anxious that he might

224

have killed her husband. I felt the urge to ask her whether Hugo had regular conversations with his mother in the "wee hours of the night," as Rebecca had noted, or whether he had fabricated his alibi, but how could I question his character without driving a wedge into Jacky's relationship either with him or with me?

Let it go, Charlotte, I told myself. Jacky had good instincts, other than having married her abusive-now-dead husband. She could tell if Hugo was a nice guy or not. At least I hoped she could.

Jordan joined them but remained standing and surveyed the pub. When he caught me looking his way, he crooked a finger. A flutter of desire bubbled inside me, and I wondered if I would ever grow tired of his come-hither gestures.

"What do you think?" Tyanne said, drawing me back to the conversation at the table.

"About what?" I said.

"Where did you go?" Meredith teased in a singsong voice while toying with her hair. "Is someone having a crush moment?"

It was my turn to elbow her. "It's not a crush. It's full-on love."

Meredith fanned herself. "Heart be still."

"You're a fine one to talk," I said. "You soon-to-be-brides can't keep your feet on the ground, either."

"Can, too." Meredith stamped her feet beneath the table.

Tyanne giggled. "C'mon, you two. What I was asking was, what do you think about Anabelle and Vinnie dating? My sister said Anabelle was in the Tip to Toe Salon on Saturday, and she couldn't stop talking about the new man in her life."

"Uh-oh." Rebecca aimed a finger at me. "You should call Octavia."

"Why?"

"She'll get Anabelle in line. She's like a mother hen to her. She'll warn her that Vinnie could be a murderer."

I wondered whether I, at Anabelle's age, would have wanted all these people butting into my personal affairs. Of course I wouldn't have, and yet people had talked. After all, a good-for-nothing crêpe chef had dumped me.

I caught Jordan looking my way. He hooked a finger at me again, his face grim. So much for a come-hither glance. I excused myself from my friends.

Tyanne said, "You tell her, sugar," obviously thinking I was heading to Anabelle to set her straight.

I drew near to Jordan.

"Hello, gorgeous," he said.

"Hey." I stroked his arm, then slipped my hand into his. "You didn't call me Saturday night after visiting Jacky."

"We had a crisis at the farm Sunday and today. A couple of cows got sick."

"I'm so sorry. How's Jacky?"

"She's hanging in. I was at her place until after midnight." With his free hand, he ran a finger across my cheek and tucked a hair behind my ear. I shivered with desire. Sotto voce, he said, "Now what's this I heard about your confrontation with Vinnie?"

I gulped. How had he heard? Trying to play dumb, I said, "What confrontation?"

"Outside the Country Kitchen."

I pulled my hand free. "How — ?"

"Tim told me. He heard it from Anabelle."

I shot a look at Anabelle, who waved a pinky greeting. How had she known about my mini-clash? Had she been keeping an eye on me? Why? Now that she no longer ran the bookshop, was that how she stayed tuned in to local gossip? I turned my gaze back to my fiancé. "It was . . ." I was about to say nothing, but thought better of it. Honesty was the best policy where Jordan was concerned. "He demanded hush money."

"For what?"

"To keep quiet about where Jacky is. He intimated that there are others in New Jersey who might want to harm her."

"He's full of beans."

"He has an address book. He said he would contact all those people and tell them where to find Jacky unless she paid him to keep quiet."

Jordan sighed. "He must really be hurting for instant cash."

The notion made me wonder again what had happened to his brother's wad of cash. I assumed Vinnie had stolen it, but if he hadn't, who had?

"I'm worried about you, Charlotte. You're a little too eager and a little too inquisitive." Jordan cupped my neck, his hand warm and comforting. "I need you to stand down."

My insides tensed. There were those words again. Less than a year ago, I thought I had learned everything about Jordan's past, but there was something hanging in the wind. Something intangible. I loved him and wanted to trust everything he told me about his past, but he needed to explain the language he used and those dog tags hidden in the hutch in his living room.

"What's wrong?" he said. "You shivered."

Keeping my voice as steady as possible, I said, "You use those phrases that make me suspect that at one time you were more than a restaurateur in upstate New York."

He dropped his hand to his side. His lips drew thin.

"What is the rest of your backstory?" I said. "There's something . . . I don't think it's dangerous, but it's private and almost sad. The other night —"

Jordan held up a palm. "Let's not talk here."

"Then when? Where?" I rarely picked a battle, but I needed answers.

"Come with me." He gripped my elbow and steered me out of the restaurant.

The evening breeze was cool and stimulating. The scent of smoke from fires in chimneys permeated the air. Children's happy screaming voices resounded from the Village Square as the children enjoyed their final moments of play before dinner and bedtime.

Jordan pressed me up against the wood siding — not to kiss me, but to speak quietly. The exterior lights on the pub cast a golden glow on his face, but they didn't soften his intense gaze. "What do you want to know?"

My breathing grew short, peppery. I didn't fear for my life. I feared the truth. Would my world fall down around me with whatever Jordan was about to reveal? It was serious, that much was certain. But I had to know. "Were you a cop?"

"No."

"You say things like *stand down.*"

"It's an expression."

"You know jujitsu and karate."

"Which I learned in the army."

"Were you Special Forces? Were you a spy?"

His eyes crinkled, and he smiled the smile that melted my heart. "I'm too heavy-footed to be a spy."

Ha! He was as fleet and stealthy as a tiger. I had seen him catch a quail bare-handed.

I jutted a finger at his nose. "Tell me about the dog tags I found hidden beneath the photographs in the claw-foot oak hutch."

He released me, jammed his hands into his jeans pockets, and heaved a sigh. "I thought you'd stumbled upon them, but I wasn't sure. They're not mine."

I searched his face. "Why do you keep them then?"

He drew a heavy breath and closed his eyes for a brief second. When he opened them again, his gaze landed on me. "They're my brother's tags."

"You have a brother?"

"I *had* a brother . . . a younger brother."

His eyes grew moist, his cheeks flushed. The emotions he held back made my breath catch in my chest, but I didn't say a word lest I disturb the tenuous moment. "We went to war together. He didn't come back."

What could I say? Nothing that would matter. I drew Jordan into my arms and stroked his back. Before I knew it, he was clutching me as though there were no tomorrow. He sobbed into my shoulder once. Only once. After a long moment, he pressed away from me and cupped my fingertips in his.

I said, "Why didn't you tell me before?"

"Because you would have wanted to know his name. You would have researched him on the Internet. You like to do that."

My cheeks warmed with embarrassment.

"That search would have led back to me. All it takes is one weak link to draw people to my location."

"Like Vinnie."

"Don't worry about him."

"But I do. He's violent." I blurted everything that Vinnie said to me outside his car. "He wants money. Hush money."

Needless to say, Jordan, like Meredith, wasn't happy that I had taken the risk. "Charlotte, Charlotte, Charlotte." He had said the same to me nights before, but then my name was uttered in the throes of passion. Now, he was talking through clenched teeth. "I need you to back off. I'll handle Vinnie."

Something in those words jolted me to my core. "You can't —"

"Legally," he said, cutting me off. "I will handle him legally. I will never operate outside the law."

"You're going to pay him off?"

"I'll do something. I repeat, legal." He kissed my eyelids and then my ear. He nibbled gently as he ran an idle finger up my back and stopped to work a knot out of my neck muscles.

Every fiber of me tingled with anticipation. But now wasn't the time or the place to give in to lust. Besides, a question burned inside my mind. I stopped his hand from working its magic and held it against my chest. "You have to answer one more thing. Your last name is Pierce. What's your real first name?"

"James Jordan Pierce. You can call me Jordan."

CHAPTER 17

Brimming with energy, I rose the next morning before the cock crowed. In a little less than an hour, I showered, changed, did a few chores, and fixed breakfast. When the twins settled at the table for a batch of gluten-free pancakes topped with shredded Havarti and a dollop of homemade apricot jam, I drizzled maple syrup on their pancakes. While we ate, we discussed homework and the upcoming *Stomping the Grapes* footrace. As I did dishes, Matthew scooted in, grabbed a granola bar, and whooshed the girls off to school. Clair would do arts and crafts, and Amy would romp around the playground until first bell.

At The Cheese Shop, I plunged into my daily routines, making quiches and the day's sandwiches. Rebecca appeared an hour after me and immediately started arranging the cheeses in the display case.

"Incoming." Matthew tramped into the

kitchen with a tripod easel looped over one shoulder and a box of wineglasses tucked under his other arm. He headed toward the cellar door and tried to toe it open.

"When did you get here?" I hurried to help. "I didn't see you arrive."

"I'm sneaky."

"Aren't you a busy beaver?" I slipped the box from his grasp. I wasn't worried about product damage as much as I worried about him breaking his neck as he descended the stairs carrying awkward items. He was acting a little crazed, of late. I chalked it up to pre-wedding jitters. "What's the easel for?"

"I'm going to post a chart of all the wines, their attributes, and the regions they come from," he said. "A separate chart column will pair the wines with cheeses." My cousin was nothing if not thorough.

"Perhaps you should make the rehearsal dinner a little more simple, you know, with the move, and well, everything."

He shot me a cockeyed grin. "This coming from the multitasker who woke early to pack the girls' bathroom items, walk the dog and cat, make a gourmet breakfast, and then opened the store and infused it with these fabulous aromas."

"Why, thank you for the compliment."

"I mean it, Charlotte. My stomach is

grumbling for a taste of the Swiss chard and nutmeg quiche."

"I'll save you a slice." I opened the cellar door and gestured for him to descend first. "Rebecca," I called over my shoulder. "Tyanne is coming in for a quick hour this morning. Have her spruce up the display barrels. I'll be back in a second."

"Okay," she answered.

I followed Matthew downstairs, drinking in the briny aroma and inhaling the moisture as I neared the basement floor. No single cave system was right for every cheese maker or cheese shop owner. Thanks to Jordan's design, our cellar was the perfect size to house all the wines and wheels of cheese we wanted to age. We had fitted the cellar with white brick walls and dozens of wood racks. Wheels of cheeses ordered from nearly every state in America sat on the shelves; some needed a tad longer to mature before we could sell them.

"Set the glasses on the buffet table over there." Matthew gestured toward the alcove, an eight-foot round niche. We had commissioned a local artist to paint a faux window with a view of Providence. Below the painting stood a rustic buffet. In the center of the alcove, Matthew had placed a mosaic table and six chairs. I reflected fondly on the intimate meal of cheese, salami, and champagne that Jordan and I had shared the night we finished the cellar's construction.

"By the way," Matthew said, his conversational tone turning strained. "Meredith tells me you've been nosing around. You're trying to find out who killed Giacomo Capriotti."

I set the box of glasses on the rustic wooden counter. "C'mon. Don't you start razzing me like your future bride."

"Meredith is worried. Heck, I'm worried."

"You needn't be."

"Isn't Urso doing his job?"

"He thinks Jacky might be guilty of the crime, but she's not."

"Are you sure?"

"Of course I'm sure."

As Matthew unfolded the easel and hooked its legs in place, I filled him in on my aborted search of Vinnie Capriotti's car, the leather address book that Vinnie had shaken in my face, and Vinnie's demand for hush money. Then I shared my feelings about Hugo's iffy alibi, Anabelle's flimsy eyewitness account, and Edy's possible connection to the murder via an anonymous call.

"Are those your only suspects?" Matthew asked.

"Edy swears Prudence overheard the conversation about Jacky's husband, too, but why would she have called him? What did she have to gain?"

"Maybe she blackmailed him. From what I hear, Prudence is a little low on cash."

"So is everyone in town." My thoughts returned to Edy. How much was Freckles paying her? Enough to keep her outfitted in her expensive bohemian clothes and jewelry?

"Chérie," my grandmother called from the top of the stairs. "Are you below?"

"Oui," I said. "I'm coming up." I kissed Matthew on the cheek. "Don't worry about me. I promise I'll be careful. And don't stay in the cellar too long. With all the hours you've spent down here, I'm afraid you'll become one with the environment."

He chuckled.

As I rounded the corner from the kitchen into the main shop, I spotted Grandmère waiting at the cheese counter, her arm looped through Pépère's. She wore a hand-made shirred midi dress in warm autumn tones and looked absolutely glowing.

"Look who is up and about," Grandmère

said, her tone cheerier than I had heard in days.

To my delight, my grandfather's skin looked robust. Whatever sickness he had suffered had passed. I skirted the register and kissed him, *la bise,* with a quick peck to each cheek. "You look *merveilleux,*" I said. He did. Absolutely marvelous. His eyes sparkled with good humor.

"Charlotte, a little assistance," Rebecca cried, voice muffled. She stood bent over, half of her reaching into the cheese case. "Tyanne's otherwise occupied."

"What's going on?" I asked.

Rebecca extricated herself from the case and motioned at the knot of local actors huddling around Tyanne near the honey display. From what I could hear, she was instructing them about the benefits of the gooey goodness. Stratton and his history teacher buddy seemed the most enraptured.

"Your grandmother has brought the gang for lunch," Rebecca continued. "And we have a group of tourists roaming the wine annex, too."

Grandmère eyed me. "I am serving a picnic on the set. You have enough sandwiches for all, *non, chérie*?"

I nodded.

"I will help." Pépère released Grandmère,

238

fetched an apron, and shuffled to the front of the cheese counter.

"Do not exert yourself, Étienne," my grandmother said.

"*C'est rien.*" Looking revitalized, he clapped his hands. "*Mes amis,* gather around. Make your choices." He peered at the sandwiches in the case, each of which was affixed with a detailed label. "We are offering basil pesto, roast chicken, and mozzarella on homemade focaccia; Swiss and salami with chutney mustard and grilled onions on French bread; and my personal favorite, Tomme de Crayeuse, ham, and sweet pickle relish on an onion roll. What will it be?"

The actors swarmed him, all talking at once.

To escape the din of their chatter, I clutched my grandmother's elbow and steered her to the archway between the shop and the wine annex. "Why aren't you rehearsing at night?"

"We are, but the play is lacking oomph. I asked the cast if they could rehearse during the day. Many could. I bribed them with lunch, of course." She winked. "Let me also have a sampling of cheeses and salami. For the crew. They are hard at work, sawing and building."

"Mon dieu," Pépère's voice sliced the air.

I spun around. My grandfather's face was bright red, his eyes pinpoints of angst. My grandmother and I raced to him.

She gripped his shoulder. "Étienne, sit."

He shook her off, jammed his fists on his hips, and stared daggers at her. "Why did you not tell me, Bernadette?"

"Tell you what?"

"Why did you not tell me about *le meurtre?* A man is dead?"

The actors, who must have spilled the beans, were as mute as mimes.

"Jacky's husband was killed," I said.

"Oui, oui. I know that much. Why would you keep me in the dark, *mon amie?"* Pépère asked. My grandmother reached to caress his cheek. He gripped her wrist. "Speak."

"I worried about your heart," she said.

"My heart is fine."

"But you are getting —"

"Stop." He released her and held up both palms. "Do not say it. Do not say *older.* I am not getting older; I am getting wiser. Is this not what Americans say?" His mouth curled into a smile.

Grandmère released a tense breath and threw her arms around his neck. "The French say it, too, you old fool."

"Wise," he insisted. "I am a *wise* fool."

He peeled her arms away and held both of her hands in his. "Now, from the beginning. What happened?"

Grandmère filled him in with the sketchy details. That Giacomo Capriotti, Jacky's husband, was found bludgeoned to death in the Igloo.

"Jacky was married?" Pépère said. "I had no clue."

"*Bien sûr.* She had a baby."

"But not with him," I said. "It's complicated."

"Many women have babies on their own nowadays," Pépère said. "It has become a custom." He ogled me, as if willing me to have one on the spot.

A ripple of giggles fluttered through me. My neck and face flushed with warmth. We had never had this conversation. He didn't expect me to respond, did he?

Grandmère grabbed his chin and swiveled it back so his focus remained on her. "Do not be a goose. Charlotte will become a mother in time."

Pépère shrugged. I breathed a sigh of relief, off the hook for now.

"Jacky's husband was rumored to be a nasty man," Grandmère went on.

"Not rumored. He beat Jacky," I cut in, unable to keep the truth hidden any longer.

The actors let out a collective gasp.

Rebecca clacked a knife on the cheese counter. "So that's why she moved here and changed her name."

I nodded. I hadn't brought it up in our conversations about the crime, but with her astute sleuthing skills, I had just assumed she had figured out that much on her own.

Stratton said, "An abuser deserves to die, right, guys?" He turned to the other actors for support. To a man, they agreed.

Pépère said, "When did this murder occur?"

Muttered responses told him sometime between midnight and two A.M. on Friday night.

"The night we had the wedding tasting at your house," I said. "You weren't feeling well."

"Who does Chief Urso think is guilty?" Pépère looked to me for the answer.

"Jacky," I said.

"Ah, but no," Pépère said. "*C'est impossible.* I saw her pacing at all hours with the baby."

"Étienne, do not lie," Grandmère said.

"I do not lie about such things." He raked his silver hair. "I was up all night. I had a stomachache. A fever. When you slept, *mon amie,* I crept out of bed. I roamed the

242

backyard to keep cool. The night air, it was so crisp. I saw Jacky."

"Really?" I hooted with glee. "That means Jacky has an alibi. I knew it. She didn't do it."

"She walked to and fro," Pépère continued. "The baby was colicky. We had similar nights with your mother, Charlotte. Remember, Bernadette?"

"*Oui,*" Grandmère said. "She was quite vocal. But Étienne, why did you not wake me?" She sounded heartbroken.

He sighed. "You are driving yourself crazy with all that you do. The play, your mayoral duties, and the race to raise money for the rescued animals. I worry that you do not get your rest." He drew her to him.

Grandmère cooed, "*Je t'adore,*" and snuggled closer while poking him gently in the stomach.

As the actors talked among themselves, I turned to Rebecca. "Watch the shop. I'm going to tell Jacky the good news, and then I'll track down Urso." I flew out of the shop with virtual wings on my loafers.

CHAPTER 18

Zinging with good vibes, I hurried to A Wheel Good Time. During school hours, the shop wasn't busy. A pair of women sat at a table dabbing paint on matching bowls. A mother and toddler nestled beside a counter filled with coffee mugs, teapots, vases, and more, searching for an item to paint. "Margaritaville" played through speakers. I zigzagged through the shop as Jimmy Buffett crooned, "Some people claim that there's a woman to blame, but I know it's nobody's fault."

In seconds, I found Jacky at the rear of the shop, bent over a turntable, working a palette knife beneath a clay vase. Her creations never failed to impress me, the current one broad at the base with grooves tooled around the narrow neck. Her gaze met mine as I rushed toward her. "Great news," I cried. "My grandfather can corroborate your alibi on the night of the murder."

"But I thought you convinced Urso that I wasn't . . ." She paused. "Don't be naïve, Jacky," she whispered to herself then raised her gaze to meet mine. Sorrow flooded her eyes. "Of course he thought I was guilty. Everyone does." With a heartfelt sigh, she lifted the vase, wiped her palette knife on her apron, and shuffled to a workstation. She set the vase on the shelf beside other items that were ready to be fired in the kiln. "Tell me what your grandfather said."

I explained that Pépère hadn't felt well, and he had gone outside often through the night. "He saw you and Cecily pacing. He didn't come forward until now because Grandmère kept the news about the murder and everything else from him. But now, thanks to him, you're cleared. Completely."

The colorful hand-glazed clock over the kiln chimed once for the quarter hour. It resounded like a good omen, and yet Jacky heaved another sigh.

She swiveled away from me, but not before I noticed tears pooling in her eyes. "Time is so precious," she said.

"Yes, it is." I laid a hand on her shoulder.

She patted my hand and nestled onto a stool beside the counter. She touched the seat of another stool, indicating I should sit. "Did I ever tell you about the day that I first met Giacomo?"

She hadn't. I knew only snippets of her past life from things Jordan felt he could reveal.

"Time stopped," she said. "I couldn't breathe. He was so handsome, so charismatic. Never in my life had a man professed love to me so quickly. Starry-eyed, I didn't look beyond the surface. A few short months later, I met his cruel side. He had addictions — to food, to liquor, to women. He had affairs from the day we got married."

"I didn't know."

"None lasted a long time. He quickly grew tired of the women, so I tolerated the missteps. But when he began to blame me for his shortcomings . . ." Jacky toyed with the ring on her right hand then released it and laid her hand on the counter. "All of the women looked like me: dark hair, dark eyes, but they were younger."

How much younger could they be? Jacky was in her thirties, like me.

"He told me once that, in every affair, he was trying to relive our first moment. He wanted magic. But I knew better. He was searching for a younger model, end of story. I was no longer good enough for him. I was too logical, too disciplined, and too old. He told me more times than I could count that he had made a mistake marrying me. He wanted someone reckless, someone who could make him feel like a kid again."

I flashed on Anabelle with her dark hair and dark eyes. Given her past, she might qualify as reckless. She had been drawn to Giacomo. Did he arrive in town and instantly fall in lust? Had he wooed her? I didn't think they had dated, but maybe they had. Had something gone terribly wrong on a date? Maybe that was why she claimed to have seen a tall man running from the scene. She killed him and needed to steer Urso away from thinking she was the murderer. Was hers the dark hair that Urso had found at the crime scene?

" 'The course of true love never did run smooth,' " Jacky whispered.

"Shakespeare," I said, recognizing the quote. *A Midsummer Night's Dream.*"

A single tear trickled down Jacky's cheek. She swiped it away with her fingertip. "I could have tolerated the affairs, you know. But three years into the marriage, when Giacomo hit me after an affair gone awry, I knew the beatings would continue. I had to leave."

"Do you think he could have made a play

for someone in town?"

"Like whom?"

"Anabelle. I remember the day he arrived, I was in All Booked Up, and Anabelle was swooning over this stranger she had met. He beguiled her. What if she threw herself at him, but he tired of her, and, angry at his rejection, she lashed out?"

"She's so small," Jacky said. "Could she have hefted the ice cream container?"

"I've seen her lift sizable cartons of books."

"Why would they have met in the freezer at the Igloo? How did they get inside?"

Both were good questions.

"Perhaps they went for a late-night walk," I said. "Your husband would have wanted to keep a low profile. Maybe they found the Igloo unlocked, and they sneaked in. They grew passionate, but then something happened. Giacomo told her that their future was not to be, and Anabelle attacked."

Jacky fingered her throat. "Maybe. I don't know."

"Did you know Anabelle's dating Vinnie now?"

"So soon? He's barely been here a week. Giacomo's only been dead . . ." Jacky scrunched her mouth as if she had bitten into something sour. "If that's the case, something's off about that girl."

"Maybe she's more calculating than we think. Maybe she turned her affections to Vinnie to make it seem like she was never interested in Giacomo."

Jacky anchored a loose strand of hair behind her ear.

"May I use the telephone?" I said, having run out of Fromagerie Bessette without my purse or my cell phone. "I've got to touch base with Urso and let him know that you're cleared."

She pointed to the cherry red phone on the desk behind the counter. "Please."

As I strode to the telephone, Jacky placed her elbow on the counter and cradled her forehead between her thumb and fingertips. She sniffled as I dialed. The precinct line was busy. I dialed again and received a recording to be patient; someone would be with me shortly. Patience was not my virtue.

I hung up and said, "I've got to go. I've got to track Urso down." I gave Jacky a squeeze, advised her to be brave, and hurried to the front door.

On my way outside, a woman yelled, "Charlotte, stop!"

Octavia dashed out of Fromagerie Bessette and tore up the sidewalk toward me while fanning herself with a floral paper fan. Her ankle-length sundress swished as she jogged.

"What's up?" I said, wishing I could borrow the fan. The warmth in the air stunned me. Ohio experienced heat waves in October, but none nearly as hot as this.

"I'm so glad I found you." Breathing as hard as if she had run a marathon, Octavia clutched my elbow and urged me to halt. "I've been doing a little investigating. Great news about Jacky, by the way. Rebecca informed me."

"I'm on my way to tell Chief Urso."

"Not yet. Not until I've told you what I've learned. I was worried about Anabelle. She's" — Octavia pinched her lips together — "such a babe in the woods."

I didn't have the heart to tell her that Anabelle was creeping up my murder suspect list.

"She needs someone to watch out for her," Octavia continued. "That Vinnie. He's up to no good."

"What have you found out?" I asked. Octavia was one of the best researchers. She had connections that went way back to her law school days. I didn't know how she did it, but she was able to delve into sealed files and get all sorts of dirt on people.

"Did you know he's up to his eyeballs in debt?"

"Because he's a gambler," I said.

"That might be part of the reason, but the other is — wait for it — he's been married four times, and he has eight children to support."

"Are you sure? Jordan said he'd only been married twice and had a couple of kids."

"Your boyfriend is out of the loop. Vinnie's an amoeba. He multiplies. And here's another thing. Vinnie and his brother were staying at Violet's Victoriana Inn. The night they arrived last week, Violet overheard Vinnie and his brother arguing about his brother's last will and testament. She didn't think anything of it. Private conversations are private conversations."

"Why hasn't she told Urso about the argument?"

"The chief scares her. What can I say?"

I waved a hand. "Did Violet glean any details of this *private* conversation?"

"Vinnie ordered his brother to file for divorce without spousal consent and then he tried to convince his brother to rewrite his will. He said Jacky shouldn't be getting half of anything. She should be cut out of the will entirely."

"Did Violet hear who was inheriting the other half?"

"She assumed Vinnie meant himself."

"Vinnie didn't mention a foundation?"

"I don't think so." Octavia tapped her fan to my arm. "For the record, Violet is distraught that she gave them shelter. She had no idea that Giacomo Capriotti was related to Jacky. She adores Jacky. After Giacomo wound up dead, Violet asked Vinnie to skedaddle."

I said, "I've got to tell Urso."

Octavia flipped open her fan and pumped it. "What am I going to do about Anabelle? She doesn't want to leave town and tend to her father. That Vinnie has cast a spell on her."

I wet my lower lip with the tip of my tongue. "I don't know, but whatever you do, don't let on about what you told me. Vinnie could be dangerous. Maybe Urso will agree to arrest Vinnie or at the very least restrain him."

More than fifty people wearing *Stomping the Grapes* T-shirts formed a line down the front steps of the quaint Victorian that housed the Providence Precinct and the Tourist Information Center. Each person carried a purple entry form for the race.

I scooted past them and hurried inside. The race line snaked to the left. I headed right, toward the precinct clerk, who turned out to be Urso's mother.

"Hello, Mrs. Urso. Are you today's temporary assistant?"

She nodded. "It's hard to find competent help on the spur of the moment."

"I need to see the chief."

"He's busy."

"I've got good news," I said, starting for the door. "He'll want to see me."

She didn't try to hinder me. She knew me well enough to know I would wheedle past her anyhow. She pressed an intercom button and said, "Umberto, Charlotte Bessette is here to see you." Getting no response, she offered a warning. "Mind you, he's not in a good mood. He and the deputies just helped put out a barn fire at Emerald Pastures Farm. By the way, do you know who was here for lunch yesterday? Edy Delaney. What's up with that? That young woman gives me the willies."

I shrugged. "To each his own."

Mrs. Urso shook a finger. "Uh-uh. She is not his, and he is definitely not hers. Not if I have anything to say about it." Smiling at her tenacity, I pushed through the door and hustled down the hall to Urso's office. The door hung open. Sunlight streamed through the blinds and outlined Urso in a golden halo.

He looked up from his desk, his gaze steely and cold. "I should've guessed you could slip past Mom. What do you want?"

I contemplated pointing out the soot that smudged his nose and cheeks and thought better of it. He didn't need a keeper. He would peer into the gunmetal-framed mirror by his door before exiting. "Jacky Peterson is innocent."

"Says who?"

"Says my grandfather." I trod across the chocolate brown carpet toward Urso's desk as I filled him in on Pépère's eyewitness account. "You know he wouldn't tell a lie."

"Except when it comes to sneaking cheese."

I sputtered. "Does everyone in town know?"

"Just about."

"Okay, yes, Pépère would lie about that but not about this."

Urso's mouth curled up in a wry grin. "I'll give him the benefit of the doubt."

"So, arrest Vinnie Capriotti."

"On what charge?"

"He's a liar and a cheat. He's got gambling debts, four wives, and eight children."

Urso lifted a pen from his desk and twirled it between his fingers. "Who'd you hear this from?"

"Octavia, who heard from Violet. Vinnie is —"

"Stop right there." Urso stabbed the pen into the leather blotter. "I have the lowdown on Mr. Capriotti. I know how many times he's been married. I know how many children he has, and I know about his gambling debts."

"You do? Of course you do. You're on the ball. You . . ." I ordered myself to stop blathering. "Do you know that Violet heard Vinnie and his brother arguing at the Victoriana Inn about a last will and testament? Vinnie wanted his brother to rewrite the will. He demanded that Giacomo cut out Jacky. We've got to assume that Vinnie stands to inherit half the estate."

"No, we don't," Urso snapped.

"Violet didn't hear Vinnie say anything about a foundation. I think that's bogus."

"You don't know —"

"C'mon, U-ey. Vinnie threatened Jacky. And he threatened me."

"You? When?"

"Yesterday." I shifted feet. Why hadn't I been up front with Urso after Vinnie caught me near his car? Because I didn't want him telling me to back off, that was why. Not wanting to hear a lecture about personal safety now, I crowded his desk. "He said if

255

Jacky wanted to remain anonymous, I should tell her to pay him some hush money."

"Hush — ?"

"Speaking of which . . . the cash that Vinnie said his brother was carrying. What if it didn't exist? What if Vinnie made that up? What if it's a red herring?"

"You and Miss Zook." Urso yanked the pen out of the blotter and clicked its button repeatedly. After a few seconds, he tossed the pen aside and stood up, shoving the chair backward with his thighs. "Why are you always theorizing?"

"Because I care. Because I hate that Providence — yes, Providence — is the victim of yet another crime. At this rate, we'll lose our tourism. Our economy will suffer. Our citizens will struggle." I jabbed his desk with my index finger. "Vinnie Capriotti killed his brother. He came here with a plan, and when it didn't go his way, things got out of hand."

Urso inhaled and let out a long breath. "For your information, I have my own eyewitness at the Victoriana Inn. The dining room manager overheard the brothers arguing, too. He came to the precinct the day after the murder. Why didn't Violet?"

"She's afraid of you."

Urso wiggled his hands. "Oh, yeah, I'm so scary."

"Yes, you are. You're big, you're gruff, and when you get that look in your eyes —"

"What look? This look?" He drew his eyebrows together. An angry grizzly bear couldn't have appeared more foreboding.

"Yes, that one, but you don't scare me because I know you're mush inside."

"Mush?"

"Yes, mush. Back in winter, when you kissed me and said you would always be in love with me —"

"That doesn't make me mush. It makes me honest." He turned toward the window, his neck red with embarrassment.

I wanted to crawl under the desk. How could I taunt him so mercilessly? *Bad, bad Charlotte.*

After a long, quiet moment, Urso turned to me again, his face unreadable, his eyes steady. He retook his seat and in an official tone said, "I'll have a chat with the rest of the staff at the Victoriana Inn. In the meantime, based on the dining room manager's testimony, I have discussed these matters with Vinnie Capriotti. He claims he and his brother argued because he wanted his brother to file for divorce without spousal consent."

"Did the dining room manager mention that they argued about the will? Did Vinnie bring it up?" I aimed a finger. "Think about it, U-ey. The person with the most to gain here is Vinnie. I promise you, if Jacky dies, Vinnie stands to inherit everything."

"Only if that's what the will says."

I gaped. "You still haven't seen it?"

He raked his hair with his fingers, which gave me his answer. Was the vacationing lawyer's failure to respond coincidental or on purpose?

"All I know, Charlotte, is that Vinnie said he had more to gain by trying to work his magic on his brother. Alive. I believe him. I —"

A jolt of energy shot through me. *Magic?* If I was wrong and Urso was right and Vinnie was blameless, then someone else was the murderer. I flashed on Hugo Hunter. Mr. Houdini. The guy with the mother as his alibi.

Urso cleared his throat. "Are you listening?"

"You should reinvestigate Hugo Hunter's alibi."

"That's not what I was saying."

"And don't rule out Anabelle." I offered a quick rehash of my theory about Anabelle duking it out with Giacomo in the Igloo.

"Charlotte, please."

"We have to learn the truth."

"Not we. *Me.* I'm in charge of this investigation. However, I'll give you this. With your grandfather's claim, I am prepared to believe him about Jacky's alibi. Satisfied? You can go now." He flipped open a file on his desk, dismissing me.

"What about Edy?" I blurted even though, given Urso's grumpy mood, now was not the time to throw her name into the suspect ring.

"What about her?" Urso cast a vicious look.

To be honest, he did scare me sometimes. I flinched and backed off. "Um . . . how was your date?"

Urso leaned back in his chair and weaved his hands over his stomach. "We've had two dates. Nothing serious. I'm playing the field. After my mushy mess with you . . ." He grinned, clearly teasing me, the upset of earlier already in the past. "I'm a little gun-shy."

"Gotcha. Well, good luck with that." I headed toward the exit.

As I reached the threshold, Urso said, "How are Rebecca and that boyfriend of hers doing?"

"They're engaged. Why do you ask?" He

couldn't be thinking of dating her, could he? She was aeons too young for him.

"Deputy O'Shea has been querying."

I breathed a huge sigh of relief. Deputy O'Shea, who turned out to be our friendly tavern owner's nephew, was added to the police staff last year. He was cute, young, and dedicated, and from various conversations with him at Fromagerie Bessette, I had deduced that he, like Rebecca, loved the Internet and old TV crime shows. "He'll have to get in line," I said. "Rebecca is madly in love and engaged to our local honeybee farmer. And if that doesn't result in a wedding, don't rule out that quirky reporter who makes a play for her occasionally."

Urso smirked. "That reporter is an odd duck, always traveling in and out of town."

"Which brings us back to Hugo. He travels a lot."

"That doesn't make him a bad guy."

"I think he's lying about his alibi."

Urso moaned.

I twirled a finger. "Do you really believe he was chatting with his mother for three hours? C'mon, really? That's just plain weak."

Urso rose and pointed at the door. "Out."

"But —"

"Go. You're done in here. Jacky Peterson is off my radar. You have no further interest in this case."

"Except it happened in Providence, and I —"

"— care about Providence. Point taken. Now, leave."

I flashed my palms at him. "Okay, fine, I'm leaving. Man, are you touchy."

CHAPTER 19

I exited the precinct, thankful for the waves of October heat that rolled off the pavement. They warmed me after Urso's chilly reception. Remembering my promise to give Octavia an update after talking to our illustrious chief, I headed east across the Village Green toward All Booked Up. Beyond the clock tower, I walked through the area where Grandmère and her crew had turned the park into Renaissance heaven. Four huge posts sporting red flags and dozens of barrels teeming with luscious fall flowers defined the arena. Rows of wooden benches faced the stage, where *Hamlet* would be performed, at the north end of the park.

As I neared the stage, I heard a whistle. Not a coyote whistle — a summons. I searched for the source. Neither Stratton nor the actor with whom he was slashing swords on stage seemed interested in me. The slew of players sitting on the apron of the stage downing sandwiches didn't pay me any heed, either. And Grandmère was oblivious to my presence. She stood in front of the stage and glowered at the actors, her gaze smoldering with frustration.

"Stratton," she yelled. "Both of you. For the last time, come here and sit."

Like chastised kids, Stratton and his buddy hurried forward and plopped down on the apron. Stratton laid his sword across his lap and kicked the front of the stage with his heels. I heard another whistle. I was surprised when I spotted the love of my life perched on a ladder, a leather tool belt looped around his hips. When had he joined the stage crew? The tails of his work shirt hung outside his jeans. Perspiration coated his tanned skin. He and a handful of other guys, also on ladders, were ramming nails into the outer rim of the backdrop, which was a painting of an Italian countryside complete with statues in the foreground and the Mediterranean Sea in the distance.

Jordan beckoned me with his hammer. I jogged up the stairs at the side of the stage, hurried to the ladder, and ran my fingers beneath the hem of his jeans and up his calf. His smile turned into a shameless grin. Man, he was handsome.

"Guys, I'm going to take a short break,"

he said to his coworkers. He descended the ladder, slung his hammer into the tool belt, and planted a kiss on my neck.

"Since when did you become a stage crew member?" I said.

"Since I heard your grandmother needed help." He winked. "I'm not stupid. Volunteering is the way to your grandmother's heart. I know she's not a fan of mine. I thought a little goodwill might go a long way."

My throat choked up. I couldn't remember being more proud. I was going to marry a man who would meet my spirited grandmother halfway. Was I ever lucky. "Did Jacky call you?" I said.

He shook his head.

I told him about Pépère corroborating Jacky's alibi.

Jordan whooped with delight.

"I meant to call, but I got caught up talking to Urso, who believes my grandfather's account."

Jordan clutched me in a bear hug. "Best news ever . . . next to you saying yes." He whispered how much he loved me, and yelled, "Guys, sorry, but I've got to go see my sister." He drew me in for another embrace and said, "Explain to your grandmother, will you?" He sprinted toward the west entrance to the park.

Grandmère stopped lecturing the actors as Jordan whizzed past her. Catching sight of me, she said to her actors, "Take five," and then greeted me. *"Chérie."* She kissed me on both cheeks. "I did not tell him. I wanted to wait until you had the time to speak with Chief Urso." She grinned. "Jordan's delight tells me that Urso believes your grandfather."

"He does."

She slid a hand around my elbow. "Your Jordan is a hard worker. I am enjoying him."

"Really?"

"Oui."

Life was good. I said, "How is the rehearsal going?"

"Pas bien." She sounded weary. "The actors, they are lazy, especially that Stratton. Delilah works with him, but he cannot seem to understand the character. Why she cast him . . ." She fluttered her hand. "I should not speak ill."

"Relax," I said. "I'm sure he'll come around. Delilah has a way of tightening the reins in the last week of rehearsal. You said so yourself." Secretly I wondered if Grandmère was ruing her decision not to direct this particular play. She had such an affinity for Shakespeare. She said the soliloquy "To

265

be or not to be" was one of the greatest ever written. Within those words was the answer to life itself.

"We must continue," she said and kissed my cheek. As I turned to leave, she added, "*Écoutez-moi, chérie,* before you go, take a look at the giant grape press." She pointed.

Off to one side of the stage stood a huge wooden vat, which Grandmère intended to fill with grapes. For a true Renaissance experience, children would be allowed to go barefoot into the vat to stomp the grapes. Parents had been forewarned that clothes would get stained.

"It is beautiful, *non?*" She cupped her hands together. "Oh, to be a child again."

Minutes later, I entered All Booked Up. What a transformation had come over the place since I last visited. The scent of fresh paint hung in the air. Book boxes were gone. The shelves were stuffed with books. Easy chairs and beanbag chairs abounded. Colorful posters welcomed browsers. But the shop wasn't officially opened. It was as quiet as a tomb. Out of respect for Anabelle, Octavia had wanted to wait to have a launch party until Anabelle moved to Chicago.

"Octavia?" I yelled from the front door. No one answered. I moved to the register and called again.

"Charlotte, is that you?" Octavia pushed through the curtain that screened her stockroom from the public. Her face was pinched, and her light coffee skin was ashen. "Oh, thank the lord it is." She drummed her chest with her fingertips.

"What's wrong?" I hurried to her.

"Anabelle," she sputtered.

"Did something happen to her?" I gazed at the checkout counter. A half-eaten round of La Tur cheese, an Italian double-cream with a bloomy rind, sat on a platter with a dozen or so rice crackers. "Did she consume something that disagreed with her?"

"No, that's my lunch. It was scrumptious, but Anabelle is . . ." Octavia waggled her head. Her beaded hair spanked her cheeks. "It's horrible." She gestured for me to follow her.

Pulse pounding, I trotted after her. Had Anabelle fainted? Had she fallen prey beneath a tipped-over stockroom shelf? Had Vinnie Capriotti hurt her?

I reached the office at the rear of the shop and peeked inside. Nothing seemed abnormal. Anabelle was not lying in a pool of blood. In fact, she was nowhere to be seen. "Octavia, calm down and talk to me."

Octavia gestured to her desk, which was a

riot of storage boxes, piles of papers, an ancient desktop computer, and empty soda cans. If Octavia needed to clean up one thing in her life, it was how much soda she imbibed. A glass of burgundy would have been a better pairing choice for the La Tur, although, admittedly, not in the middle of the day. *When in doubt, drink water,* my grandfather would say.

"I did another computer search," Octavia said. "Look what I discovered."

"Sorry, but I don't see anything. Your screensaver is on." The computer screen fizzed with sparkling champagne-like bubbles.

"Oh, my." She scurried to the computer and hit Enter on the keyboard.

The screen came to life with a bright white Google search page. It wasn't registering the first page in a search; it was registering the twenty-ninth. Even though I considered myself a semi-expert investigator when it came to Internet searches, I didn't know what I was looking at. I shook my head.

Octavia clicked on one of the links. A page emerged with *Abilene Reflector-Chronicle* news listed at the top. "I did what you said. I came back to the shop, and while unpacking, I found . . . I found . . ."

"What?"

She jammed a finger at the topmost box in the pile on her desk, which was marked *Anabelle*.

"I can't see inside it," I said.

I started toward the box, but Octavia snagged my elbow and swiveled me to face the computer. "Because of that, I craved to know more about Anabelle," she said, "so I searched, and I found this . . ."

"This what?" I had never seen Octavia so upset. She was an oak; she never wavered. "Let me read." I nudged her out of the way. Bending over, I braced my palms on the desk and scanned the news article. "I don't see anything about Anabelle."

"Lower-left column," Octavia said.

A headline read: *Teacher Found Murdered.* Five introductory lines followed, as well as a link to page six where the rest of the article could be viewed. I clicked on the link. A teacher named George Garrison was found murdered in an Abilene school library. At one time, he had dated Anabelle Fiorossi. The crime was not yet solved.

I said, "Anabelle's last name is Rossi. This isn't about —" Until I had said her name out loud, I hadn't made the connection. "Ooh. Fiorossi: Rossi."

Octavia nodded. "A while back, Anabelle mentioned she had lived in Abilene."

"The article says she was cleared of all suspicion."

"But she moved here and changed her name," Octavia repeated. "Why?"

Maybe for the same reason Jordan and Jacky had — anonymity. Who knew how many reporters had hounded Anabelle after being associated with a murder?

"And explain this to me. I found this box on the top shelf, tucked behind rolls of wrapping paper." Octavia lugged the *Anabelle* box off the stack and set it on the desk beside the others. She rustled through it and pulled out a doll.

I gasped. It wasn't like Anabelle's other dolls, all sweet and babylike, the kind to which she had cooed, "There, there." It was a dark-haired boy doll dressed in brown pants and a brown shirt. In the middle of the shirt was the initial *G* written in marker pen. Someone — Anabelle, no doubt — had stuck dozens of pins into the *G*.

My stomach twisted into a frenzy. "Voodoo." I didn't believe in the practice. Seeing the doll freaked me out.

Clutching the doll in her hands, Octavia shuffled to a stool and sat down. "The teacher killed in Abilene was named George Garrison. G for George. Coincidence? I don't think so. And Jacky's husband's name started with a G."

Giacomo. My upper lip started to perspire. Two coincidences. Yipes.

"Do you think Anabelle killed him?" I whispered.

"I don't know. What do you think?" Octavia said, worry peppering her voice.

I blotted my upper lip with my finger. Was it possible? Maybe. Probable? I couldn't see Anabelle as a psychopath, and yet she practiced voodoo. I eyed the doll again. Something blue squiggled down from the G. "What's that?" I pointed. "A food stain? Giacomo was killed with Brie blueberry ice cream. Do you think it could be blueberries?"

Octavia smelled the squiggle. "It's old, whatever it is. No scent."

I couldn't see a killer taking a voodoo doll to the crime scene. On the other hand, kookier things had occurred.

Octavia added, "Here's another thing. Anabelle wasn't scheduled to leave town until a week from now, but a few days ago, she moved up the date."

A jingle rang out at the front of the bookshop. Octavia leaped to her feet. She scrambled to the curtain.

"Is it Anabelle?" I said, following her.

"No. A customer." Octavia walked into

the front of the store while clearing her throat. "Sorry, sir, we're not open for business yet." I couldn't hear the rest of the conversation, but she handed him a flyer from the sales counter and guided him out of the shop. As she locked the door, she said, "Eek."

"What's wrong?" I hurried to see what had disturbed her.

"There." She pointed out the window.

I peered over her shoulder. Across the street, Anabelle and Vinnie were exiting La Bella Ristorante. In one hand Anabelle carried a to-go bag. With her other hand, she clutched the crook of Vinnie's arm and leaned into him like she was in love.

"Maybe she and Vinnie worked together to kill his brother," Octavia said.

"I hadn't thought of that. You've got to tell Urso what you've found out about Anabelle."

"Are you nuts? He'll think I'm imagining things. You know how he is."

After our recent clash, I didn't want to contemplate what Urso would think of me if I brought the information to him.

"He'll need proof," Octavia continued. "What have we got? Nada, zilch, supposition. I'm going to ask her."

"You're going to what?" I shrieked.

"She won't hurt us. She's our friend. She'll tell us the truth."

I bit back a laugh. Had Octavia been taking Pollyanna lessons from Rebecca? Thinking about my coltish assistant made me realize how long I had been gone from Fromagerie Bessette, and I wondered if I should give the shop a call. On the other hand, something was, as the pundits would say, afoot between Anabelle and Vinnie, and I had an itch to learn the truth.

"We can't ask Anabelle anything with Vinnie around," I said. "He could be dangerous."

"He won't hurt us in broad daylight."

Before I could hold Octavia back, she grabbed a couple of All Booked Up flyers and hustled out of the shop. Like a shadow, I followed.

Rolling one of the flyers into a tube, Octavia handed it to me and said, "Here."

"What's this for?" I kept pace as she stole down the sidewalk after Anabelle and Vinnie.

"To pry, using a trick I learned when I was working at the library," she said. "Kids listen in on other kids' conversations. Very sneaky. Put it up to your ear."

"No."

"Can you hear Vinnie and Anabelle talking from this distance? No, you cannot. And we dare not go closer." She hoisted her tube to her ear and angled the simplistic device forward.

I didn't mirror her because she looked silly . . . and conspicuous. "Stop that. If they look behind, they'll know something is up."

She lowered the tube. "But we can't hear a thing."

"Let's move closer."

"I thought you wanted to hold back."

"I did . . . I do. But you're right. We need more proof, and I don't want to lose this golden opportunity to eavesdrop."

We picked up our pace, craning to hear, but still couldn't catch a word the couple said. Anabelle was running her hand through her long dark hair, pulling out the tangles in a girlie way. By the way Vinnie was gazing at her, I imagined if a fire hydrant jumped out and tripped him, he wouldn't have noticed. To my amazement, he had lost his permanent sneer and was looking at Anabelle with — there was no other word for it — affection. He whispered in Anabelle's ear. She batted him flirtatiously with her fingertips.

Their antics made me wonder if Anabelle had cast some kind of voodoo lover's spell on Vinnie. Was it possible that she had conned him into icing his brother? Was it my duty to warn him?

Whoa. When had I started seeing Vinnie as a victim?

"They're turning onto Hope Street," Octavia said. "I doubt they're going to the diner. Given the restaurant food bag they're carrying, I'm assuming they just ate."

"Keep pace," I said.

We rounded the corner. The couple passed the Silver Trader and La Chic Boutique. Near the Country Kitchen diner, they paused. Neither noticed us. Vinnie cupped Anabelle's face with one hand and rubbed his nose against hers. Now it was her turn to appear entranced. I had to remind myself that Vinnie had been married four times. He was clever and possibly addicted to falling in love.

"He's talking again." Octavia elbowed me. "Put the tube by your ear."

"No."

"We can say we're listening for the sound of the whip-poor-will." Octavia held up a finger. "Not to be confused with the chuck-will's-widow, which has a similar but slower and lower-pitched call."

"Where did you learn that?" I held up a hand. "Wait, don't tell me. Books."

"Lots of learning in them." Octavia moved

the flyer to her ear.

I whipped the tube out of her hand.

At that same moment, the environment went still. With no cars passing and no people, not even cell phone users, talking at loud decibels, I heard Anabelle say as clearly as day, "Will I see you later?"

Vinnie replied, "You bet, babe. Have fun shopping." After giving a sideways glance at A Wheel Good Time, he rounded the corner, heading north on Cherry Orchard Street.

Anabelle swooned against the side of the diner and fanned herself, as if overcome with love.

I turned to Octavia. "That's it? They're splitting up? We missed their entire conversation?"

"Wait. Anabelle is taking her cell phone out of her purse."

I watched with rapt attention as Anabelle stabbed in a series of numbers and then placed the receiver next to her ear. I couldn't make out what she said to whomever she had called.

"Did you catch that?" I asked Octavia.

"No."

Anabelle snapped the phone shut, rounded the corner, and turned north on Cherry Orchard Street, too.

"Did she lie about going shopping?" I said. "Is she following Vinnie?"

"Curiouser and curiouser."

"Let's go," I said. "Let's confront her."

"Aren't you the bold one."

Crazy would be more like it, but I would be the last to say the word out loud.

CHAPTER 20

As Octavia and I approached the corner of the Country Kitchen, a warning light went off in my head. Opting to be cautious rather than rash, I hooked my hand around Octavia's elbow and detained her. "Hold up," I whispered. I released her and inched forward to peek around the edge of the building.

"What do you see?" Octavia whispered.

"Anabelle is going into Under Wraps."

"Thank heavens," she sighed. "She said she was going shopping. She didn't lie."

I retreated to the shadows and leaned against the wall. "Now what?"

"We question her. Follow me." She wrested free of my grasp and marched ahead.

I had often passed by Sylvie's Under Wraps Boutique and Day Spa, but I had only entered once, and not to buy. I had fetched the girls to take them to a singing rehearsal. As always, Sylvie had taken a potshot at what I was wearing and had pressed me to purchase something that might spruce up my wardrobe. Right. Like I would accept the opinion of the woman who preferred ice white hair, faux animal print coats, and skimpy, tasteless clothing. Spare me.

The pungent aroma of patchouli was the first thing to hit me as Octavia and I entered the shop. I don't know why I was surprised. Sylvie often over-doused herself with perfume. I wondered if she had installed a scent recycler in her ventilation system. The next thing that caught my attention was the décor. Sylvie was never content to live with a style for long. Based on what I had seen in the display windows in recent months, summer's color palette had been silver and black. Autumn's had been gold, and though autumn was still in full bloom, today's theme was shades of red. Sylvie had swathed mirrors with strawberry-colored ribbons. Cardinal bows adorned hanging racks. Scarlet beads cascaded from the necks of mannequins, which were dressed in red flapper dresses. Sylvie had worn the same red outfit into Sew Inspired the other day. Maybe she was trying to put everyone in town in the mood to buy early and buy often for Christmas. The stock in her shop was entirely red and glitzy. Even Sylvie's mousy assistant — Sylvie would never hire somebody who might compete with her in the beauty department — wore a red sheath.

The shop didn't lack for customers. Many carried bags from other stores around town.

Octavia pointed. "There's Anabelle."

Beyond a center table filled with sweaters, Anabelle pulled a cocktail dress from a rack. She moved to a mirror, held it in front of herself, and swiveled. The skirt of the dress danced above her knees.

"Aw," Octavia said. "Isn't that sweet? She's buying a party dress."

I whacked her on the arm. "Don't go soft on me now. She could be buying a dress to wear to a funeral she caused."

Octavia winced. "She wouldn't dare wear red."

"Different strokes," I said.

Wearing a knee-length candy apple red kimono with an ultra-long slit up the thigh, Sylvie sauntered through the archway between the shop and the spa at the rear of the store and posed. "Hello, everyone." As she waved like a model on a float, the glossy red sticks holding the twist of her hair bobbled and clicked.

I bit back a giggle. She looked ridiculous.

Sylvie spotted me, and her mouth turned down ever so slightly, but she quickly replaced the frown with a phony smile. "Darlings, come in, come in." She sidled to Anabelle. "Excellent choice, love. Superb. It's just your color."

What else could she say? *Gee, you'd look better in blue, but I don't have any in stock.*

Anabelle caught sight of us, too, and beamed. "Hey, Octavia, Charlotte. Don't you love this dress? Isn't it me? I'm sure it's going to fit."

"Of course it will," Sylvie said. "We do alterations. Charlotte, you could use a new number, too." She twiddled a finger, gesturing from my toes to my head. "By the way, I saw what Meredith has you wearing for the wedding." She tsked. "Not good."

My hands balled into fists. When exactly had she seen my maid of honor dress? At Tyanne's direction, Freckles had locked all the dresses in an antique wardrobe at her shop. Had Sylvie stolen into the stockroom and found the key?

"You're not a pastel girl," Sylvie continued.

I didn't consider gold pastel. Was it?

"Now this . . ." Sylvie snatched a folded red sweater from a display table and snapped it open. Rhinestone beads adorned the front. "This is so you."

"Thanks, Sylvie, but no thanks." Maybe I would wear the glitzy sweater once, I mused, but no more than that. Jordan and I didn't party hearty. We liked our evenings in, with an occasional dinner at La Bella Ristorante or a day trip to Columbus.

"Try it on." She shoved the sweater into my arms.

I had to admit the fabric was incredible, silky yet nubby all at the same time, but I was not there to shop. "Give us a moment with Anabelle, would you?"

"Yoo-hoo, Sylvie," a stout woman across the shop yelled.

As if thankful for the reprieve, Sylvie said, "I must tend to another customer. Think about this, Charlotte. Ta-ta."

I placed the sweater back on the pile and refocused on Anabelle. "That is a pretty dress."

"Do you think so?" She beamed. "Vinnie wants to take me Irish dancing at the pub."

"Vinnie?" I said, acting ignorant.

"We're going on a date. He's the sweetest man."

I coughed my objection. Vinnie was nothing near sweet.

"I was hoping for something in green, but . . ." Anabelle waved a hand at the sea of red. "Octavia, why are you frowning?"

Octavia opened her mouth but nothing came out.

I found the words she couldn't. "Anabelle, we need to talk."

"What about?"

"We've done a little background check."

"Super. Does that mean you found a new clerk for the bookshop?" Anabelle glanced from Octavia and back to me. "Anybody I know? I had lots of applications over the last two years. I can probably fill you in."

"No, Anabelle," I said. "We checked on you."

Anabelle's saucer-shaped eyes widened. "Why me?"

"Octavia found one more box of yours and it contained a voodoo doll."

Anabelle's face flushed the color of the shop's theme. "You don't understand."

"Enlighten us," I said.

She clutched the dress like a coat of armor. "It's . . . You see . . ." She eyeballed the front door.

I moved to block her escape. "Talk to us, Anabelle. Tell us the truth."

Anabelle's shoulders curved inward. She keened and rocked forward on her toes and back on her heels. Forward, back.

I said, "You once lived in Abilene."

Anabelle shot a look at Octavia, who still looked shell-shocked, and then to me. "And Dallas and Louisville," she muttered. "You name it. Daddy was always moving us."

"But your last place of residence was Abilene, Kansas. Your real surname is Fiorossi."

She didn't deny it. With a sigh, she replaced the red dress on the rack.

"You were mentioned in an article about a schoolteacher who died in Abilene," I went on.

"George," she whispered.

"Your voodoo doll had a G on it. And there were lots of pins jabbed into that G," I said. "Did you wish George dead? Did you kill him?"

Anabelle gaped. "Oh, my, no. I would never. I loved him. I . . . I created the doll to . . . It's a long story." She breathed high in her chest.

"We're listening."

"I had a thing for guys whose names started with the letter G. Don't ask me why. It was like a pattern. Maybe because my father's name started with G. Not that I had a Daddy-complex, I didn't." She licked her lips. "But I liked his name, Greg. I dated all these guys with the letter G. George, Galen, Gareth, Gordon, Grady." She ticked the names off on her fingertips. "I even dated somebody named Gaylord — a family name. I was, like, obsessed." She toed the floor. "I started seeing a therapist. She told me to get the voodoo doll and draw a G on it and stick pins into it to break myself of the habit. I wanted to date other guys with names like Adam or Bill or Carl."

"Who are they?" Octavia said, her voice raw with emotion, but at least she had found it.

"Nobody," I answered. "She wanted to. She couldn't."

"That's right." Anabelle pointed at me. "I . . . I told the police that my previous boyfriend, Grady, might have something to do with George's death, but they never caught him. I was a person of interest, but I convinced them I didn't do it, and they let me go."

"Did you have anything to do with Giacomo Capriotti?" I said.

"What? No!" Anabelle swooped her hair over her shoulders. "I mean, yes, I wanted to date him. He was handsome and debonair, and I was immediately under his spell, but when I realized it was another G thing, I backed off. I didn't kill him, if that's what you're implying."

"There are blue stains on the doll," I said.

"Are they from blueberries or jam?"

"No." Anabelle turned pale. "It's ink. I kept the doll under the register at the shop. Seeing it every day kept me on track, you know? I stored a package of pens on top so no one would see the doll. Only I would know it was there. A pen burst and leaked blue ink on the doll. It's not blueberry jam or anything. You've got to believe me."

Octavia thinned her lips. "But I didn't find the box under the register, Anabelle. I found it tucked onto the top shelf in the stockroom, hidden behind wrapping paper."

"No, no," Anabelle opened her hands wide. "I didn't hide it. I must have put it there by mistake. I moved so many boxes, trying to make space for your things."

"On the top shelf?" I said.

"Yes. I know you don't believe me, but" — she shuddered — "it's the truth."

"This former boyfriend of yours," I pressed. "What's he about?"

"Grady?" Anabelle folded her arms over her chest. "He's mean and vindictive, and I think he killed George, but he couldn't have murdered Giacomo. He's in prison for fraud."

"What about Vinnie?" I moved a little closer.

Anabelle's eyebrows knitted together.

"What about him?"

"Do you think he killed his brother?"

She glanced again at Octavia before returning her gaze to me. "No. He couldn't. He simply couldn't."

I paced in front of her and did a hard pivot. Anabelle yelped at the abrupt about-face. Rebecca had shown me the move. She said the surprise shift always threw off a person who was being interrogated. Personally, I thought Colombo's signature line: *One more thing*" was the sneakiest way to catch a culprit in a lie, but what did I know?

"Anabe-e-e-elle." I dragged out her name.

"Wh-wh-what?"

"Do you know if Vinnie will inherit half of his brother's estate?"

"He mentioned he's coming into a lot of money."

Gotcha, Vinnie.

"Gamblers often talk like that," she added.

She was right. Thwarted but not frustrated, I said, "Where were you at the time of the murder?"

"Watching old movies at the back of the shop. I was packing up all the books that Octavia didn't want. I had to strip off the covers before I could send them back to the publishers. It was tedious and painful. I hate removing the covers. Books are living things.

They shouldn't be harmed." She swatted the air to fan herself. "I turned on the television to the American Movie Channel, you know, AMC. You can check. The TV is still set on that channel, unless you changed it, Octavia."

Octavia shook her head. "I don't watch TV."

"It was a Glenn Close retrospective week," Anabelle went on. "Have you ever seen the movie *Garp*?"

"Another G?" Octavia moaned.

"It's with Robin Williams," Anabelle said, her words spilling together, eager to dispel our suspicions. "Glenn Close is Garp's mother, which was odd, to say the least. I think they were almost the same age."

I had seen the movie. It wasn't one of the American Film Institute's top one hundred, but I enjoyed watching anything with Glenn Close.

"Wait a second," I said. "You told Urso you'd witnessed someone running from the scene of the crime. How could you have noticed anyone if you were watching television?"

"I went outside to take a breather. My arms felt like spaghetti from all the packing, and my lungs were clogged with dust. I needed some fresh air." Tears pressed at the corners of Anabelle's eyes. "Around two A.M. I had my hand on the front door, ready to open it, when I saw a shadowy figure racing from the Igloo."

"Man or woman?" I said, knowing Urso had asked the question, but hoping my brusque tone might jog some new insight.

"I don't know."

"Was it Vinnie?"

Anabelle burst into tears. "I. Don't. Know."

CHAPTER 21

Leaving Octavia in charge of the shaky Anabelle, I hurried back to The Cheese Shop. I tore through the store, ignored Rebecca's pleas for assistance, and went to the office. Rags and Rocket didn't budge, which meant Rebecca had recently relieved them and fed them treats. I picked up the telephone and dialed the precinct.

Surprisingly, Urso took my call. "What now?" he snapped. Not a good start.

Rattling off details as fast as I could before he interrupted me, I told him about Anabelle and her history with the dead teacher and other G-named men. "She thinks this Grady guy is in prison. Can you check it out and see if he's at large? If he has it in for guys she dates, maybe he killed Giacomo Capriotti."

Urso sighed. "How long did they date? A nanosecond? It's a stretch."

"But we have to follow all leads, right?"

"Not *we,* Charlotte, *me.* How many times do I — ?"

"Got it. I know. I need to butt out." I held up my hand, as if we were standing in the same room, then added, "Maybe you should consider making me an honorary deputy."

He growled. "Like a title would make you act any differently. By the way, I do feel I owe you one tidbit."

My ears perked up.

"Hugo Hunter has left the building."

"What the heck does that mean?"

"You've heard the phrase: *Elvis has left the building,* haven't you? Oh, never mind. Hugo has split town, and he's not answering his cell phone. And before you ask, yes, I'm following up." He slammed down the receiver.

A new theory caromed through my brain as I hurried out of the office. Hugo could have killed Giacomo to protect Jacky, fashioned an alibi of talking to his mother, and then, realizing the alibi was flimsy as all get out, decided to hightail it out of town. Could he act more culpable?

Rebecca planted her hands on her hips and gave me the evil eye as I slung on an apron. "About time you returned to the fold." She waved a hand, indicating the flock of customers. "Every one of them is hankering for our special."

Recently I had discovered Capriole's Julianna, a lovely raw milk goat cheese, which had an aged white rind enhanced with natural herbs. It was delicious on a cracker smeared with sweet jam. It also melted beautifully and turned grits into something fabulous.

Rebecca said, "Matthew is in the cellar retrieving a dozen rounds for me because you weren't here."

Ignoring her obvious frustration with my tardiness, I said, "I'm back now."

"And . . . ? What did Urso say? What's going on? Where have you been?"

"I'll catch you up once the line peters out."

"But —"

"Promise."

Twenty minutes later, when the shop was free of customers, I perched on one of the ladder-back chairs by the tasting counter. Either standing all day or packing up the twins' things was really taking its toll on me. My lower back ached. I stretched my calves and rotated my head. What I would have given for a shoulder massage or a hug from Jordan. He and Jacky were probably celebrating her good news.

"Dish." Rebecca perched on the other

chair and tugged her pencil skirt and the hem of her apron down a smidge on her thighs.

I started by telling her about Vinnie's money troubles, his possible inheritance, and Anabelle's voodoo-hoodoo history with men.

"I don't think Anabelle's ex-boyfriend did this," Rebecca said.

"You don't? But what if he was jealous about Anabelle dating anyone else?"

"It's a reach."

"And Vinnie's inheritance?"

"Money trumps most motives." She raised an index finger to make her point. "Anything else?"

"Yes. Hugo Hunter is missing."

"Abracadabra, poof." She smacked her hands together. "I told you that a magician could be wily."

I gave her my opinion about his departure then sighed. "I wonder if Jacky knows? She'll be sad. He seemed sweet."

"There are cheeses that smell sweet," Rebecca said, "but they don't taste good."

I smiled. "I think you have that backward. There are cheeses that smell horrible but taste great. Époisses de Bourgogne, for example. If you get the smell of the rind on your hands . . ."

". . . it's super-gross, but the taste is heavenly."

There was an urban legend that the cheese was banned from public transportation in France because it was so pungent at room temperature.

Rebecca drummed her fingers on her thigh. "What does Urso think about Hugo?"

"He's hunting for him."

"Hunting for Hunter. Good. Except for one thing. I don't think he's guilty."

"But you just agreed that —"

"Why would Hugo take the risk?" Rebecca thumped the counter once. "His business is flush, his love life is good, and he doesn't seem like a cause guy."

"What do you mean, *cause* guy?"

"You know, someone who wants to right a wrong. I'm still stuck on the money." Rebecca twisted the tasting platter on the counter, positioning the cheese in front. " 'Show me the money.' Do you know that line?"

"From *Jerry Maguire.*"

"Exactly. Money is a vital force. It makes people do weird things. There was this Amish farmer, a good friend of my grandfather's, who left the fold when he didn't feel he was getting his fair share. He moved to Pennsylvania and started a bank."

I gaped. "You're not telling me he's a killer."

"No. But money was the driving force. He gave up everything — his wife, his life, his religion — to have it. I saw an episode of *The Mentalist* where —"

The front door opened.

Sylvie, still wearing the red kimono, sashayed into the store and trilled, "Charlotte." She moved toward me waving a silver Under Wraps bag. Prudence and Iris followed her in. So did a handsome older man and a pair of thirty-something women — real customers.

I slid off my chair to greet our visitors, but Sylvie cut me off mid-hello. "Charlotte, take this." She shoved the gift bag into my hands.

Inside was the red sweater she had tried to get me to buy earlier. I turned to Rebecca. "Would you help the folks who just entered, please?"

"I'm on it." She sidled behind the cheese counter and flashed a toothy smile.

I turned to Sylvie and gave her a scathing look. "Sylvie, I'm not buying this."

"Aha!" Prudence marched toward us, pointing an accusatory finger. "I told you, Iris. The woman is going around town, hand selling her wares."

"I am not," Sylvie said. "That cow bought it for Charlotte."

"Cow?" I said, not understanding.

"That woman who was in Under Wraps earlier when you were there, love. You know the one." Sylvie drew a curvy form with her hands.

"The greengrocer's wife?" I said.

"That's the one." Sylvie tapped her nose. "She's a cheese hound, and she adores you. I can't imagine why."

The greengrocer's wife was stout, but she wasn't a cow. She had a lovely gamine face, bright eyes, and a buoyant spirit.

"You're despicable, Sylvie Bessette," Prudence said. "Calling someone a cow."

Sylvie whirled on Prudence. "What business is it of yours?"

"You represent Providence. We all do. Every shop owner, every assistant." Prudence stared at us, trying to garner support. "The hideous things you say will get around, and we'll all bear the brunt."

"Tosh." Sylvie fluttered her fingertips. "You're worried because your business is suffering."

"It is not." Prudence thrust her chin in the air.

"Oh, no? I happen to know that Edy Delaney intends to buy you out."

Prudence sputtered, "That's a lie."

"Is it?" Sylvie jutted a hip.

"My shop is not for sale, do you hear me? It is *not for sale.*"

Iris grabbed Prudence by the arm. "Pru, shh. You're always warning me not to rise to the bait. C'mon, Sylvie is not worth it."

"But she's a bully," Prudence whined. "She trashes everyone. Someone has to put her in her place."

Iris nipped Prudence's chin with her fingers and swiveled Prudence's face. "Look over there. See that handsome man by the cracker display? Let's go flirt."

"Flirt?" Sylvie said. "Puh-leeese. Prudence is about as flirtatious as a thorn."

"Don't listen to her, Pru. You've got looks and brains."

Rebecca, who was busy wrapping a wedge of cheese, raised an eyebrow; I stifled a smile. Perhaps Iris was going a little over the top on behalf of her pal. Prudence might be smart, but attractive? Maybe dating Stratton had warped Iris's sense of reality.

Iris steered Prudence to the left. As Prudence passed Sylvie, she snarled; Sylvie made a not-so-subtle gesture of raking her claws.

"Sylvie," I hissed.

"What?" She puffed on her fingernails

then polished them on her kimono. "Cleopatra was a lamb compared to —"

"No," Prudence shouted, causing Sylvie and me to turn.

Iris tugged; Prudence ground her heels into the hardwood floor. I cringed at the scuffmarks her spiky heels made.

"I won't do it," Prudence said. "You can't make me." She shook free of Iris and dashed out of the shop.

Iris followed in hasty pursuit. "Prudence, wait."

"So much for the path of true love." Sylvie smirked.

Rebecca rushed to us. "So, Sylvie, is it true about Edy?"

"Is what true?" Sylvie asked, knowing full well what Rebecca ached to hear.

The thirty-something women, with purchases in hand, were exiting. The handsome older man, unaware of almost being the object of Prudence's desire, seemed oblivious to our conversation and content to browse.

"Is it true that Edy is buying out Prudence?" Rebecca said.

"Of course it's not true," I said. "Where would she get the money?"

Sylvie clucked her tongue and patted my shoulder. "Don't be ignorant, love. Every woman uses her feminine wiles. If a certain man invests —"

"You don't mean . . ." I sputtered. "He couldn't have . . ."

Sylvie waltzed toward the exit and tossed a knowing glance over her shoulder. "Trust me. I know."

As the door swung shut, Rebecca said, "She might be right. What if Edy overheard you and Jacky talking about Jacky's past, and she tracked down Giacomo Capriotti. What if she told him she would reveal where Jacky was, but only if he would back her new venture? Money, money, money."

I gawked at her, wondering why I hadn't thought of that angle. Silly me, I had presumed Sylvie's parting comment implied Urso was Edy's backer. Running with Rebecca's theory, I said, "What if Edy had counted on Giacomo paying her, but he reneged because he knew she would dun him for more, so she killed him and stole the wad of cash he had on him?"

"How much money are we talking about? Enough to buy a business? Enough to buy a house?"

"Good point. A hundred bucks isn't enough to kill for. But if he was carrying thousands or tens of —"

The sound of dishes breaking shattered

the air. Not dishes in the wine annex. Beyond that, at A Wheel Good Time. And then something slammed the wall and a woman screamed.

"Rebecca, call Urso," I yelled as I bolted out the door.

CHAPTER 22

Smoky gray clouds tinged with sherbet streaked the sky as I dashed to A Wheel Good Time. The front door hung open. I paused in the doorway to scan the shop. Jacky sat hunched on a stool by the sales counter, her body heaving with giant sobs as her foot worked Cecily's baby stroller backward and forward. To my right, a mother in a plaid shift and her daughter in a matching dress huddled by an array of white mugs. The mother gaped at me; her daughter was shivering. To my left, shards of white pottery lay scattered on the floor by the wall that abutted Fromagerie Bessette. I peered into the shadowy recesses at the rear of the store for movement. No one seemed to be lurking there ready for a second attack. Whoever had trashed the place had vanished.

"Jacky?" I hurried to her and clutched her shoulder. "Are you all right?"

Her mouth moved, but no words came out.

"Is Cecily okay?" Panicked, I glanced into the stroller. Cecily was asleep, her little mouth open, her chest rising and falling gently. I turned to the mother and child. "What happened?"

"A short man . . . dark-haired . . . bad skin," the mother said. "He came in and started arguing. He threatened Jacky. He said he would tell everyone. What did he mean?"

"I don't know." I knelt in front of Jacky. "Was it Vinnie?"

She nodded. "He . . . He said I ruined his life. I told him I didn't kill Giacomo. He said I was missing the point." She coughed out a near-hysteria laugh.

The mother and child edged nearer. The mother said, "The man swept his arm across the top shelf. He broke everything." She waved at the mess. "Then he picked up a pitcher and shook it at Jacky, and he threw it against the wall. We" — she clutched her daughter tightly — "wanted to go for help, but we were afraid to move."

I said, "You did the right thing."

"Charlotte," Jacky whispered. "There are free pottery session coupons under the counter. Please give her two of them. Tell her I'm sorry."

I did as she asked. After the mother and child shuffled out, I returned my gaze to Jacky. "I told Rebecca to call Urso."

"What can he do?"

"He can arrest Vinnie for vandalism."

"And Vinnie will hire some expensive lawyer to get him off, and he'll come right back. Vinnie wants us dead. Cecily and I have to move. We have to leave Providence. We have to start over."

"No," I blurted, knowing I did so for selfish reasons. I adored Jacky but, more importantly, I didn't want Jordan to move. And he would. Jacky and her baby were blood. Would he want me to go with him? Could I? I pushed the thoughts aside. "Look, Jacky, I don't think he wants to kill you. He wants money. He's desperate. I think he owes a bundle to someone, maybe the Mob. He's operating in panic mode. If he were rational —"

"That's just it. He's not. He's lashing out. He said he wants . . . no, he needs . . . all of the inheritance."

Aha! That sounded like an admission. He knew that *he,* and not some foundation, was an heir.

"He's afraid someone back home will find out about me being alive," Jacky went on. "I

303

assured him I would never reveal myself, and I agreed to sign over all my rights, but he said he didn't believe me. He's insane."

As upset as she was, I decided that now wasn't the time to question her about Hugo's whereabouts.

Deputy Devon O'Shea, a buff, blond man in his late twenties, hiked into the store, his hand hovering over his holster. Deputy Rodham, redheaded and built like Ichabod Crane, followed. His eyes opened wide as he took in the scene.

I rose. "No need for guns, officers. The man responsible for the mess is gone."

O'Shea let his hand fall loosely by his side, but he looked primed and eager.

"Where's Chief Urso?" I asked.

"On his way, ma'am." Rodham sauntered toward us. "Miss Peterson, are you okay?" Jacky nodded. Rodham whipped a palm-sized camera from his pocket and started taking pictures of the destruction. "Want to tell us what happened?" He nodded to O'Shea. "Take notes."

Jacky shakily summarized the situation.

When she finished and the police continued to survey the scene, I said, "Do you want me to call Jordan?"

Jacky shook her head. "He returned to help your grandmother with sets. I don't want to bother him."

"He'll want to know."

"I'll call him. You go back to work. I'm safe with the officers here." She squeezed my forearm. "Thank you."

As I emerged from the pottery shop, I spotted Vinnie climbing into the driver's seat of his Firebird, which was parked across the street. He must have felt my gaze on him. He turned and grinned, and pointed two fingers, from his eyes to mine.

What in the heck did that mean?

Before I could return inside the pottery store and tell Deputies Rodham and O'Shea, he sped away.

Rebecca and I spent the remainder of the afternoon tending to customers who had flocked into town for the *Stomping the Grapes* race. Neither of us had a free moment to theorize about the murder.

By the time I got home, my body felt like it had been put through the ringer. My feet ached and my shoulders were as tight as rubber bands, but I couldn't rest. I had promised Matthew and Meredith a date night. They needed alone time before the out-of-town wedding guests arrived. I had agreed to teach the twins how to make goat cheese grits, as long as their homework was done. It was.

"Wash your hands," I said to the girls.

Clair and Amy climbed atop a pair of stools by the kitchen counter, each squinting to block the late-afternoon sun that filtered through the Roman shade over the sink.

"Rocket looks gloomy," Clair said. "Think we should give him a treat?"

Amy shouted, "I'll get him one." She scrambled off her stool, scurried to the pantry, and returned with a gigantic home-made biscuit — made during our last cooking adventure. Of course, the girls had insisted I add shredded Cheddar to the mix. "Here, boy."

Our sweet Briard lay nestled in his dog bed in the dining nook, his chin resting on the rim of his bed. He gazed at Amy with soulful eyes. She shook the treat in front of his nose. When he didn't snatch it out of her hand, I knew something was up. I sat on the floor beside him. Rags traipsed through the kitchen and climbed into my lap. He let out a yowl, as if speaking for his canine pal and himself: *What's going on? What's with the mess? Explain. Now.*

The foyer was a sea of boxes filled with books and clothes and so much more. Each day the stacks grew taller.

"They'll be moved out in a week," I said.

Neither Matthew nor I thought it was a good idea to move the girls into Meredith's house — their new house — before the wedding. They would wait until the week following Matthew and Meredith's honeymoon. A lot of adjustments were ahead.

"What's Rags saying?" Amy parked herself beside me.

Clair hopped off her stool and sat Indian style beside her sister.

Give us a campfire and we could have told ghost stories.

"Is he mad?" Clair asked.

"Not mad. Confused." I stroked the animals' heads. "Girls, remember when you first moved in here? We had boxes, boxes, everywhere."

Amy rolled her eyes. "I didn't think we would ever get unpacked. Clair was as slow as a snail."

"I was not. You couldn't choose which side of the room you wanted to sleep on."

"Ooh." Amy patted the floor. "Remember when Mum gave us Rocket, and we bought all his toys and his bed, and we couldn't figure out where it would all go?"

"And Rocket ran around in circles?" Clair laughed. "And poor Rags was so angry, he hissed. Remember when he made that face?" She bared her teeth and narrowed her eyes.

We all laughed.

"He sure didn't like Rocket," Clair said.

"That's not true." I clutched Rags's chin and gave a playful shake. "He just wasn't sure what was going on. Remember, he was top dog for such a long time."

"But he's a cat," Amy said.

"It's a saying," Clair said, sticking out her tongue. "Don't you know anything?"

Amy blew her bangs up in frustration.

I said, "Girls, don't get on each other's cases. Not now."

Clair reached out to Amy. "I'm sorry. I'm a little nervous not knowing what the future will bring."

Such an adult phrase from a young girl plucked my heartstrings. "None of us are ever sure, sweetheart. We take it one day at a time. And that's how the move will go. One day at a time. I'll make sure you see Rags, and I'll make sure you spend time with me. We're in the same city. It'll be easy." At least I hoped it would. If Jordan and Jacky left town to rebuild their lives, I wasn't sure what might happen to me . . . to my family. I loved Jordan, but would I give up everything and everyone else I adored to be with him? I clapped my hands and rose to my feet. Like Scarlet O'Hara, I wouldn't think about that now. I would think about it tomorrow. "Amy, give Rags a treat, too. If he doesn't take it right away, leave it on the floor, and let's get back to cooking. What are we making?" I snapped my fingers.

"Goat cheese grits," the girls answered.

"Right. Clair, fetch the Tupperware of cornmeal from the pantry. Amy, wash your hands again, and get the Capriole Julianna goat cheese from the refrigerator." Because we were using the cheese in a cooked dish, it didn't need to come to room temperature. As I assembled the rest of the ingredients, I said, "We're going to add shallots, some fresh thyme and rosemary from the garden, and some finely chopped onions."

"Not onions," Amy said. "They make me cry."

"There are all sorts of ways to avoid tears when you cut onions," I said. "You can remove the skin and soak the onion for a while, but my personal favorite is sticking a small piece of bread between my teeth. It makes me breathe through my mouth, and the bread absorbs the fumes."

"Does gluten-free bread work the same?" Clair set the cornmeal container on the counter.

"I would imagine so."

"I'll cut them." She hurried to the refrigerator, took a piece of homemade gluten-free bread from a plastic bag, clipped it with her teeth, and reclaimed her spot on the stool. "How much?" she mumbled.

"Half an onion," I said.

Clair pulled a cutting board from the stack on top of the toaster and slid a knife from the knife block. Acting like a surgeon ready for a major operation, she held out her hand for an onion. I grabbed one from the basket of fresh vegetables on the counter and presented it to her.

Amy retrieved a cheese shredder from beneath the cabinet. After climbing onto her stool, she unwrapped the goat cheese and handed it to me. "Can you slice this in half for me?"

The Capriole Julianna was a firm round pound of deliciousness with a glorious mushroomy herb-infused rind. Unlike feta, the cheese couldn't be simply mashed. Using a sharp blade, I trimmed off the rind, cut the round in half, and gave Amy a portion.

She shredded quickly, her forearm muscles flexing with the exertion. "Mmm. I love the aroma." She inhaled. "Rosemary and thyme, just like we're adding to the grits."

"Good nose."

She giggled. "Hey, look. The cheese is in jail." She tapped the side of the silver shredder. "Let me out. Let me out."

Clair hooted.

I did, too, and then I paused as I flashed on Vinnie Capriotti. I hadn't heard from Urso. Had he or his deputies arrested Vinnie for vandalism? Would Vinnie get off, like Jacky said, and hurry back to threaten her? I wondered if Urso and the vacationing lawyer were still at an impasse. Wasn't there some court order Urso could issue to seize a copy of the will? Vinnie had implied to Jacky that he stood to gain half of his brother's estate. Rebecca's words replayed in my head: *Money, money, money.*

"What's wrong, Aunt Charlotte?" Clair said.

"Nothing." Except I couldn't erase the memory of Vinnie giving me the evil eye while getting into his car. Why? Because of our run-in the day before? Was there something that I had seen in his car, something that I should remember? Maybe I should have approached him, right then and there, and offered to pay him to go away. I had twenty thousand dollars in my savings. Was it an opportunity missed? I had promised Jordan that I would let him handle the situ-

311

ation, and I had promised Jacky that I would try to come up with a way to keep Vinnie away from her, but so far, I hadn't come up with anything legal.

"I'm in charge of boiling the milk," Clair said.

I raised a finger in warning. "Remember, cornmeal spits, so get the deep stockpot and put on a kitchen mitt."

She pulled out the All-Clad pot and, using a measuring cup, added six cups of milk to the pan. Tiny biceps bulging, she carried the All-Clad to the stove and turned on the heat.

Marveling at how strong both girls were, my thoughts went to Anabelle. She wasn't totally cleared of suspicion. What if she had been lying about dating men whose names started with G? Had Urso learned the truth? What if Anabelle had created the voodoo doll specifically to represent Giacomo Capriotti? She admitted being drawn to him. Had he rejected her?

And what about Hugo Hunter? Why had he split town? Had Urso been able to track him down yet?

Last but not least, I couldn't forget about Edy, who was the most likely suspect to have called Giacomo and told him about Jacky. Sylvie claimed Edy had the funds to buy out Prudence. Had Edy killed Giacomo and robbed him of the cash he was carrying?

Amy clacked the All-Clad with a spoon. "Where did you go, Aunt Charlotte?"

"Huh?"

"Your eyes. They're, like, all glazy."

"I'm here," I said, working hard to focus on the task at hand.

"Remember the first time we cooked?" Amy said. "We were such klutzes."

"That's because Mum hadn't taught us anything," Clair said, a hint of bitterness in her tone.

"That's not true. She taught us how to make sandwiches."

"Ha! With nothing other than bread and mayonnaise."

We hadn't figured out Clair's gluten allergy until a month after Matthew, Amy, and she moved in with me. Prior to that, Sylvie had dismissed the signs — irritable bowel, repeated diarrhea, and weight loss. While dealing with Sylvie's abandonment, Matthew hadn't taken note of Clair's symptoms, either.

"Mum's trying to learn how to cook now," Amy said. "She's taking classes at La Bella Ristorante."

Jordan and I had met taking classes at the

Italian restaurant. Accidentally I had bumped elbows with him and had felt an instant connection. I glanced at the telephone. Had Jacky reached Jordan and told him about Vinnie's raid on the pottery shop? Should I have called him, too? Were they already planning their move out of Providence?

"Mum likes the chef," Amy went on.

"Really?" I said. To my knowledge, Sylvie hadn't shown interest in any men since she had returned to Providence — any except Matthew. Perhaps she was moving on. Maybe she would bring a plus-one to the wedding.

After preparing our goat cheese grits and making a chopped salad, we moved to the patio to barbecue. Rocket and Rags joined us in the backyard. It thrilled me to see them perk up. If they could get past the boxes and the angst of moving, so could I.

Late sun shone down on the bunches of bright blue asters that filled the flower beds. The pumpkins and zucchini tucked into the vegetable garden looked ready for picking. So did the tomatoes. If I let them go too long, they would all spoil. *Tomorrow,* I thought. I would find time tomorrow.

With birds twittering their cheery *good evening* song, we grilled a couple of lime-

and olive-oil-marinated chicken breasts. A short while later, we ate in the kitchen. Clair set the table with mats she had crocheted. Amy took care of the silverware and water glasses. I poured myself a glass of Santa Margherita pinot grigio, a delicious straw-colored Italian wine that Matthew said paired perfectly with goat cheese. He was right.

After dinner, we retreated to the attic. Before ascending the stairs, Rocket and Rags eyed the boxes in the foyer as if they were intruders. The girls and I read for an hour and dined on little gem gluten-free cookies — a sugar cookie decorated with homemade apricot jam. By nine, we were all yawning, and I sent the girls to bed.

As I was washing dishes, setting the knives and other tools on a towel to dry, Rocket growled and bounded to his feet. He raced to the archway leading to the front of the house and barked. "Rocket, hush, it's just Matthew."

But I didn't hear keys in the lock. I didn't hear the door open.

Rocket yapped again. His tail stopped wagging. Hissing low, Rags weaved beneath Rocket's legs and positioned himself in front of the dog.

Pushing down panic, I grabbed a carving

knife and joined my pals. Both seemed afraid to go through the stacks of boxes to the front door. "Fellas, it's nothing." The old Victorian creaked occasionally. I was used to it. And yet there I was, holding a knife.

Bam, bam, bam. Someone pounded on my door.

CHAPTER 23

Baying like a hound, Rocket inched forward between the boxes in the foyer. Rags paced in a circle, eyeing his compatriot in arms for a *pounce* signal.

Shoulders tense, I said, "Hush, you two. Would someone who meant to hurt me announce his arrival? No, he wouldn't." I lowered the knife and moved toward the door. "Matthew probably forgot his keys. Relax."

Bam, bam, bam. Louder. "Open up!" a man yelled.

I didn't recognize the voice. I recoiled, hoisted the knife, and aimed.

Whoever was demanding entry rattled the doorknob. The door shook.

Bam-thwack.

My heart drummed in my ribcage. That wasn't the sound of a fist pounding wood; the intruder was using his shoulder. He seriously wanted inside. He grunted.

I didn't have my cell phone on me. The nearest phone was in the study down the hall.

Another bash. Another groan. The door heaved, the old lock gave way, and the intruder tumbled into the house.

Vinnie scrabbled to a stand. He brandished a black and gray gun in his hand. Was it a Beretta? Was it his brother's gun? "It's all your fault, blondie," he said.

"I didn't kill your brother."

"I didn't say you did." He advanced a step. "Oh, that's right, you killed him so you could inherit half of his estate."

"I'm not his heir."

"I don't believe you." I edged backward. My heels jammed into a box. I was trapped. Mimicking Meredith and her schoolteacher strict voice, I said, "Leave."

"No." He aimed, but he didn't shoot. Was he simply trying to rattle me?

Taking the offensive, I said, "Did you lie about the money your brother was carrying?"

"No."

"How much was it?"

"A hundred Gs."

I sucked in a breath. That was a lot of cash. "Don't move a step closer." I wielded the knife. Yeah, right, like it might stand a chance against a gun. "Matthew," I yelled, pretending he might come running.

In lieu of the missing Matthew, Rocket bolted around the treacherous boxes and lunged. He grabbed Vinnie's trouser leg in his teeth and yanked to the right.

"What the —" Vinnie stumbled; his gun clattered on the floor toward me.

I kicked it behind a stack of boxes.

"Call him off," Vinnie cried.

"Are you nuts?"

Normally Rocket was a pussycat, the furthest thing from an attack dog, and yet there he was, assaulting an intruder.

"Good boy," I egged him on. "Why are you here, Vinnie?" I demanded, feeling more confident now that the gun was out of reach.

"You shouldn't have gotten in the way."

"What are you talking about?"

Rocket yanked Vinnie's pant leg to the left. Still on his feet, Vinnie skidded and swiped a box with his shoulder. The boxes teetered. One marked *Books* crashed to the ground with a thud. Rocket didn't release his hold. His growl intensified.

Clair and Amy's door opened. Dressed in nightgowns, they scampered to the railing. "Aunt Charlotte!" they screamed in unison.

"Go back in your room and call 911," I yelled.

Both girls disappeared.

"You contacted my brother," Vinnie said. "You lured him here. Lured him to his death."

"I did no such thing."

"A woman called him."

"Not I."

"Jacky, then."

"Why would she do that?" I said. "She was scared of him. Look, Jacky doesn't want your brother's money. She doesn't want a dime. All she wants is for you to leave her alone. She said she'd pay you."

"No, she didn't."

"Sure, she did. At the pottery shop. You were too busy tearing up the place to hear. I'll pay you, too," I blurted. The instant the words were out, I heard Jordan's warning that Vinnie would continue to dun me if I paid him one red cent. I pushed his voice to the back of my mind. I would do practically anything to get Vinnie out of my house — now! "You're in debt. That's what this is about, isn't it? Take the money and run."

Rocket yanked Vinnie's pant leg again and, as if he knew what he was doing, released his hold. Vinnie went flying. His feet backpedaled. He landed on his rump. Rocket charged and straddled him. Like a well-trained comrade in arms, Rags paraded up Vinnie's leg, claws bared.

Vinnie yowled. Something rang. A cell phone. In his pocket. His face turned ghost white. "I gotta answer that. Can you leash your animals?"

"No."

"Fine. Be that way." Vinnie chomped his teeth and snarled. "Off me, you beast. Off!"

Rocket's true skittish nature surfaced. Frightened, he recoiled and bumped into Rags. The two tumbled away from Vinnie, giving him time to scramble to his feet.

As he fished in his pocket for his cell phone, he said, "I'll stop by your shop in the morning, blondie. Have the money ready. Fifty thousand. You give me that, and I'll believe Jacky is going to sign away her rights. Got me? Fifty." Without waiting for my response, he pressed Send on his phone and darted from the house.

Breathing in jerky bursts, trying not to think about where I would manage to scrape up fifty thousand dollars, I set the carving knife on the side table, slammed the front door, and slid a stack of moving boxes in front of it. Next, I retrieved the gun. Indeed, it was a Beretta. I searched for markings that would establish it as Giacomo Capriotti's weapon but found none. The safety was on. When I was a teen, Pépère had taken me to an open field and taught me to shoot cans. I hadn't fired a gun since, but I could remember the kickback and the blare of the blast.

The twins' bedroom door opened. I shoved the gun behind my back and scanned the foyer for a place to hide it. Nowhere.

"Aunt Charlotte?" Clair crept toward the balcony. She looked ashen. So did Amy. "The lady at 911 is asking if we need a deputy to stop by."

I stilled my chattering teeth and peered through the window beside the front door. I really didn't feel Vinnie would return. He had bolted off. "Tell her yes. I should give a report. But don't worry. The scary man is gone. Go back to bed. I'll be upstairs in a sec."

I hurried to the study. After I stowed the gun in a wall safe behind a painting of Ohio, my breathing returned to normal. I dialed Jordan. He answered after one ring.

"What's up?"

I told him. "A deputy is on the way, but I don't think Vinnie will be coming back."

"I'll tell Urso," Jordan said.

"You know where he is?"

"I've got a sneaking suspicion."

Was he with Edy? I put the snarky image from my mind, ended the call, and dialed

Matthew. Frantic, he arrived home minutes after Deputy Rodham arrived. He immediately went to the girls' rooms to quell their fears, and I dealt with the deputy.

No matter how confident I was that Vinnie wouldn't return, when Rodham left, I knew I wouldn't be able to climb into bed and focus on a book, so I went to the study and switched on the television. As I channel surfed, I replayed the argument with Vinnie in my mind. Had he been capable of killing his brother? He had brought a gun to tonight's encounter, yet he hadn't fired it. He hadn't even retrieved it. For a quasi-gangster, he was pretty pathetic.

If I ruled him out as a suspect, who else did I have?

I flipped the channel and landed on AMC. *Fatal Attraction* was playing, which made me think of Anabelle. Had she lied about her alibi? Had she really been watching television at the back of the bookshop on the night of the murder? She could have known about the Glenn Close retrospective and used that to establish her whereabouts, but was she that savvy?

Giving her the benefit of the doubt, I focused on Hugo Hunter again. Missing in action. On the run. Why? He was a man of mystery. Had he killed Giacomo Capriotti?

Was there more to his motive than simply a man protecting the woman he loved?

After watching *Fatal Attraction* for two minutes, I flipped channels again and settled for a rerun of an old *Mike Hammer* mystery. I watched with rapt attention as the detective wrote a list of suspects on paper, crossing off each entry because he didn't have enough evidence to convict anyone.

I knew his frustration.

CHAPTER 24

At dawn, Matthew, the ratfink, called my grandparents and told them about Vinnie barging into my house. Early risers, they came straight over. As they delivered oodles of advice about being more cautious, Pépère paced around me, eyeing me from every angle, and Grandmère petted my hair. Before long, I felt like the youngest in a herd of apes. Thankfully, Matthew's announcement that it was time for him to take the girls to school interrupted my grandparents' counsel. Before leaving, he whispered that he was glad I was alive, and he wished me luck with Tarzan and Jane.

However, later, at The Cheese Shop, I couldn't escape my cousin's fretful glances.

"What would I have done without you?" he said, rehashing Vinnie's violent behavior as he followed me from kitchen to cheese counter. "What are you going to do to protect yourself once we move to Meredith's? Will you move in with Jordan? I'm worried, Charlotte."

Though I had pondered similar notions, I hadn't voiced them. I silently willed him to stop. When he didn't, I said, "Matthew, relax. I'll be fine. I'm a big girl." And Providence was a safe town, I kept reminding myself. Like the rest of America, we had occasional bouts of crime, but we could overcome them.

While I made broccolini and pine nut quiches using Marieke Foenegreek Gouda from Wisconsin — the fenugreek seeds providing a zesty, nutty flavor — the rest of the town learned of last night's event. Matthew told Tyanne, who was quick to tell Rebecca, who hurried across the street to inform Delilah.

Around ten A.M., Sylvie stamped into the store wearing a red silk bag of a dress that draped off her shoulders and clutched her knees. With venomous intent she marched toward the cheese counter in her super-high heels. A few feet from me, she posed, right hand fisted at her waist.

I felt like retreating into the kitchen but held my ground. "Hi, Sylvie, what'll it be? We're offering a Tumbleweed cheese today. It's made in Pennsylvania from raw cow's milk and has a buttery aroma and fruity taste. Take a morsel from the tasting platter."

"How dare you put my girlie-girls in harm's way," Sylvie hissed. "You do this all the time, Charlotte. You get in scuffles."

Was that what someone from England called an altercation with a man threatening me with a gun? A scuffle? I bit back a tart response and said, "Sylvie, the twins are fine. They're at school. They were never in harm's way. And just so you know —"

"Sugar." Tyanne, who was manning the counter alongside me, leaned in and whispered, "Remember, bees with honey in their mouths have sting in their tails." She raised an eyebrow, silently asking whether I understood. I did.

I shrugged off the instinct to lash out at Sylvie and, starting where I had left off, said, "Sylvie, I like your dress." I didn't. It didn't suit her or anyone in Ohio, for that matter, but the compliment defused her.

Won over, she whisked her hand along her thoroughly hidden curvaceous torso. "Isn't it fabulous? It's a sari by an up-and-coming Indian designer. Only six hundred dollars."

"You've been hornswoggled," Tyanne giggled. "Saris are skintight."

Sylvie huffed. "As if a New Orleans yokel

like you would know anything about fashion."

"Now wait just a minute, sugar." Tyanne raised a fist. "I'll have you know —"

I grasped her wrist and whispered, " 'Bees . . . honey . . . sting.' Ring a bell? C'mon, take a deep breath. Sylvie loves to goad us. Don't take the bait. Keep focused on work and the wedding, got me?"

She exhaled and nodded.

I returned my gaze to Sylvie. "Thanks so much for your concern about my health and well-being, but I must get back to my customers." A few lingered in a line. "Oh, look, there's Matthew." I waved to him in the wine annex. "Matthew, Sylvie's here."

He shot me a scathing look. Sylvie missed it and left us to chat with him. Though she would hold him accountable for last night's attack, as well, I knew he could handle himself. At least, I hoped he could.

As the minutes of the morning ticked by, I kept wondering when Vinnie would appear demanding payment. Before going to bed, I had reviewed my savings account statement online. It hadn't changed an iota from when I had scanned it two weeks ago. The number still read twenty thousand dollars. I had set the cash aside for my wedding and renovations on my house, but I would gladly give Vinnie the whole bundle if he would go away and keep silent about Jordan and Jacky's whereabouts.

Close to noon, the door to the shop swung open. I looked up, expecting to see Vinnie. My spirits soared when Jordan swaggered in carrying a wicker picnic basket. Working outside on the set for *Hamlet* was making him even that much more handsome. His skin glowed with a fresh tan. His eyes sparkled with sex appeal.

"Forgive me, ladies and gentlemen," he said in a bold, Shakespearean tone as he skirted the line of customers and cut around the register. "Milady," he said, addressing me. He pulled a tablecloth from the hamper, snapped it like a gentleman's cape, and laid it at my feet. He reached for my hand. "Might I dine with you at the Village Green? Thou dost look starved and in need of food and libation."

"What does libation mean?" Tyanne whispered.

"Drink," I answered. Continuing Jordan's playfulness, I said, "And what, pray tell, kind sir, might you have in your basket?"

"For thee, only the best of the best. A wedge of Pace Hill Farm Gouda, a hunk of freshly made sourdough, raw vegetables from the Pace Hill Farm garden, and an herb-and-sour-cream dip that I made myself. It will delight your fancy." Jordan held up a finger. "If this is not enough to satisfy milady, I have purchased a warm chicken pot pie from the purveyor of fine food across the way." He was referring to the Country Kitchen diner. "And if milady needs more sustenance, I have brought caramel goat cheese cookies from the Providence Pâtisserie." He bowed gallantly. "I offer you a feast . . . and me."

I applauded. So did my customers.

Tyanne nudged me with her hip. "Go, sugar. He's too delicious for words. I'll handle the counter."

As I started to untie the strings of my apron, Rebecca tore into the shop. The door hit the cheese-shaped doorstop with a clack. Gasping for breath, she said, "He's dead."

"Who?" I said.

"Vinnie Capriotti."

My mouth fell open.

Jordan whispered, "You're kidding."

"He was found at the Igloo," Rebecca said.

"The Igloo?" I echoed. "Again?"

She nodded. "Someone killed him with an ice pick."

My lungs constricted. Murmurs of concern passed between the customers.

"I would have come back earlier," Rebecca

said, "but everything was happening so fast. Chief Urso is already there, as well as the coroner and a crime scene tech. The Scoops found him."

Those poor teenagers. Finding two dead bodies in the same week. "When did it happen?" I said.

"Sometime between nine and midnight. The Igloo is closed on Mondays and Tuesdays."

"At nine," I murmured. Right after Vinnie stormed from my house. Right after I had called Jordan. Even though I knew he had nothing to do with this, I cut a quick glance in his direction.

Jordan said, "Don't worry. I have an ironclad alibi. I was with our chief of police building sets. Remember I said I had a sneaking suspicion where he might be? We didn't finish until midnight." Jordan swooped up the tablecloth and stuffed it into his food basket. "I'm sorry. I'll have to offer a rain check on the lunch. I've got to track down my sister."

"Sure, fine." Who could eat at a time like this? My appetite was gone with the wind.

A second murder in less than a week was good enough reason to close Fromagerie Bessette for an hour so that we could all get the news firsthand, but Matthew insisted we remain open. He would stay behind. He had so much to do to prepare the annex for the rehearsal dinner.

Rebecca and I flew out of the shop and nearly steamrolled Freckles as she exited Sew Inspired Quilt Shoppe. As a trio, we raced toward the crime scene.

"You heard, obviously," Freckles said. "Isn't it terrible? I left my elder daughter watching the baby at the shop. Do you think that's okay?"

I nodded. "I think the killer wanted both Capriottis dead. This is a family affair. It has nothing to do with the folks in Providence." Saying the words out loud made me feel a whole ton better. I actually believed them.

Rebecca said, "You mean *family* as in *Mafia?*"

"I don't know, but it's too coincidental that both men would wind up dead within a week, hundreds of miles from home."

Rebecca whistled. "I hope Jacky has an alibi."

"She does," Freckles said. "Me. After Cecily went to sleep, I was teaching Jacky how to sew. We worked on feeding the thread through the machine and learning basic stitches like the chain stitch and the zigzag stitch. She's a natural. Which reminds me, Charlotte, I need you for a final fitting. I know now isn't a good time to mention that." She tittered. Her skin flushed pink, and her freckles turned deep brown. "Why don't I shove my foot in my mouth while I'm at it?"

"No, you keep talking," I said. "You're Jacky's alibi. Chief Urso needs to know that."

"Could Hugo have killed him?" Rebecca asked.

"I heard he's out of town," Freckles replied.

"Is he really?" Rebecca's voice climbed an octave. "Or did he magically reappear in time to commit another murder? Maybe Vinnie found out something horrible about Hugo, you know, like why he leaves town all the time. Maybe he's got some super-dark secret."

"Do you think he's a mass murderer?" Freckles gasped.

"I doubt it, but perhaps he's married to someone else," I said, which could be what Iris had alluded to last week when she intimated that Jacky should be wary of Hugo.

But why would Hugo kill to hide such a common secret? And why would he use his own business site to carry out yet another murder? A wiser man would have met his foe in an alley or somewhere far from town. Poor Jacky. Right about now, she had to be questioning her taste in men.

As we approached the Igloo, I spotted Urso exiting through the front door. When he reached the sidewalk, he replaced his hat and addressed the crowd. "Folks, please go back to your homes or jobs or shopping. This crime is solved."

"So quickly?" I said to my pals.

Rebecca elbowed me. "Of course not. The chief simply wants everyone to leave."

I splayed my hands. "But what if the case *is* solved?"

Rebecca folded her arms across her chest. "I'm not leaving until we find out."

It seemed the rest of Providence intended to be just as stubborn. No one budged.

"Folks, really, I mean it," Urso barked. "You will be able to read about this in the morning news. I'm giving an exclusive to a reporter. Go!"

Grumbling, people started to move away. Stratton and other actors from *Hamlet* were among them. Octavia and Anabelle stood in front of All Booked Up. Anabelle was peering through binoculars. Was she an eyewitness to this crime, as well?

Pulling Freckles with me, I weaved through the departing throng to the front of the ice cream shop. Rebecca followed.

Before Urso crossed the threshold and returned inside, I said, "U-ey, hold up."

He turned, his gaze cautious but not unfriendly.

"Jacky didn't do this," I said. "She has an alibi. Tell him, Freckles."

Urso held up a palm. "No need. We know Jacky didn't do it. We've got this one solved."

"Really?" Freckles said. "I'm so relieved. In that case, I have to get back to the store. My girls are alone." She hurried away.

My curiosity wasn't so quickly appeased. "Who did it?" I asked.

Rebecca closed ranks and said, "Yeah, who?"

Urso looked around for gawkers trying to listen in. No one stood within ten feet of us. "Some old colleague of Vinnie's followed him to Ohio to settle a score. He pinned a warning note on Vinnie's chest."

"Are you joshing?" I said.

Urso's mouth quirked up with satisfaction. "Luckily, there are some dumb bad guys. There's even a phone call from the guy on Vinnie's cell phone."

I said, "Last night Vinnie received a call

right before he skedaddled from my place. Was the call from the killer?"

Urso cut me a stern look. "About that. Why didn't you call me first?"

"I called 911 and . . ." Embarrassed, I studied my fingernails. "Jordan said he would tell you."

Urso jammed his hands into his pockets, not happy but apparently resigned to the new pecking order.

"Matthew arrived in seconds," I went on. "And I felt in my gut that Vinnie wouldn't return. Now I know why. He was dead. When he left, he looked scared out of his mind. I think he was worried about owing someone money."

"I'll bet the guy who killed him is a Mafia loan shark," Rebecca said. "Am I right?"

"Have you caught the guy, U-ey?" I asked.

Urso shook his head. "Soon. Delilah saw a suspicious-looking guy driving a red Chevy truck, so she took down the license plate number. It turns out the car belongs to the guy who wrote the note. The state police are searching for him. I wish all cases were this easy to crack."

"I heard Vinnie was stabbed with an ice pick," Rebecca said. "Why didn't the killer just shoot him? A Mafia guy would have done that. And why were they in the Igloo?"

Urso sighed. "Miss Zook, I can't answer all the questions. We found a bullet in the wall. I'm assuming at least one of these guys had a gun."

"Vinnie lost his gun at my house," I blurted.

Urso frowned. "Jordan didn't mention any gun."

"I didn't tell him. I forgot. I stored it in the safe in the study." I gazed at the Igloo and something clicked at the edges of my mind, but I couldn't put my finger on it. "U-ey, how do you think this played out?"

"Based on your news that Vinnie wasn't carrying a weapon, I'm guessing the killer caught up with Vinnie and coerced him into the Igloo."

"Which was unlocked, yet again?" Rebecca looked skeptical.

Urso exhaled. "Vinnie fought him. They struggled. The gun went off, and then Vinnie knocked the gun out of the killer's hand. So the killer grabbed an ice pick."

"Did you find the gun?" I asked.

Urso shook his head. "The killer must have retrieved it."

The thing that I was trying to remember moments before popped into my mind. The two Capriotti murders seemed similar. Both involved a fight; both involved an odd choice of weapon. "Are you sure the bullet hole isn't from the previous crime?"

Urso's eyes widened. "No, I'm not. We weren't looking for a bullet then, but now that you mention it, I guess it's possible, though the bullet was located pretty far away from where we found Giacomo Capriotti's body." He scratched the back of his neck. "I'll have to check out that notion."

"Do you know what kind of gun the bullet came from?" Rebecca asked.

I gaped. "Can you know something like that so quickly?"

"They do on *CSI,*" she said.

Urso grinned. "Actually, we do know, but only because our tech is an expert marksman. He said it came from a Beretta."

"Aha," I said.

"Aha, what?" Urso eyed me.

"According to Jacky, her husband owned a Beretta. Let me offer a couple of theories regarding his murder. One, Giacomo Capriotti did get a phone call from a woman or a man disguising his voice to sound like a woman."

"Hugo," Rebecca inserted.

"A woman, Hugo, somebody," I said. "Based on that call, Giacomo came to town to find Jacky. He had to meet his anonymous caller for more information."

"What kind of information?" Urso asked.

"I'm assuming Giacomo didn't know Jacky lived here. For a fee, the killer was going to be more specific. The killer enticed Giacomo into the Igloo."

"At gunpoint?" Urso looked dubious.

"No, Giacomo had the Beretta. I'm not sure how the killer lured him inside." That was a sticking point in my theory, but I pushed it to the back of my mind.

"It was Hugo," Rebecca repeated. "I think he had his own gun."

"Shh," Urso said and indicated that I should continue.

"Whomever Giacomo met gave him the information and then demanded payment."

Rebecca snorted. "That's sort of backward. Usually you get the money, and then hand over the goods."

"Let's assume the killer isn't a pro," I said. "Anyway, Giacomo reneged. The killer got angry. Giacomo pulled out his gun. The killer fought him; the gun went off."

"No one heard a shot that night," Urso said.

"Did someone hear gunfire tonight?" I asked.

"I haven't canvassed the town, but no one has come forward."

"The freezer —" I hitched my thumb

toward the Igloo. "I'm assuming Vinnie's murder happened in the freezer, too?"

Urso nodded.

"So let's assume the freezer is sound-proof," I continued. "The killer and Giacomo fought, the gun fired, and Giacomo lost control of the weapon. The killer didn't have time to retrieve the gun. He hoisted a container of ice cream, which would explain why that was used as a weapon. Let's face it. Using a vat of ice cream is just odd."

Urso nodded. "Go on."

"An ice pick is an unusual weapon, too. I'll bet Vinnie's killer heard about Giacomo's murder and knew it happened at the ice cream store, so he demanded Vinnie meet him there."

"To frame Hugo," Urso said.

"Exactly. Except the idiot left a note, thus clearing Hugo."

"And he brought his own ice pick."

"If we find the gun used in the murder of Giacomo Capriotti" — Rebecca aimed a finger at Urso — "and we match it to the bullet you found —"

"But we didn't find that gun," Urso said. "The killer must have taken it, if there even was a gun."

I snapped my fingers. "We might find it in my safe."

"Your safe?"

I nodded. "Here's my second theory. Vinnie was the killer. He lied about everything, the woman calling and the wad of money. He said his brother had a hundred thousand on him."

"Where did you hear — ?" Urso cut himself off. "Never mind. Vinnie told you when he barged into your place. Go on."

"I think he lied about the cash. Let's face it. Who travels with that kind of money? Vinnie wanted his brother to change the will. His brother said no. The scene played out as before. After Vinnie bludgeoned Giacomo, he took his brother's Beretta and fled the scene. Said weapon is resting in my safe at home." I pinched my lips together. *Listen to you, Charlotte.* Said weapon, *like you're a prosecutor.*

Urso sighed. "Which you will turn over immediately."

"Of course."

"But what if the bullet doesn't match that gun, either?" Rebecca folded her arms.

"Charlotte's theory about Vinnie doesn't hold up," Urso answered.

"Okay, here's a third theory," Rebecca said. "Someone else brought along a gun . . . like Hugo Hunter." She raised her voice to stress the surname. "He's missing in action.

341

He could have set a meeting with Giacomo to duke it out over Jacky. Hugo ordered Giacomo to leave Jacky alone. Giacomo refused. They struggled, yada, yada. Vinnie figured it out. He threatened to expose Hugo, and our would-be hero split town."

"You still haven't found him?" I said.

Urso shook his head. "The Scoops haven't heard a word. Neither has Jacky. She's very worried."

Rebecca gasped. "Oh, no. What if Hugo's dead, too?"

CHAPTER 25

All that day and the next, news of Vinnie Capriotti's murder buzzed around town. Customers flocked to Fromagerie Bessette to get more of the gossip, but we had nothing new to report. Rebecca was surprisingly tight-lipped — no theories, no insider information, no television references for inspiration. We did hear that Vinnie's murderer was caught on Route 76, east of Akron. He sang like a jailbird, but he didn't croon about killing Giacomo Capriotti. In fact, he swore he didn't. He had his Beretta in his glove compartment. Many customers told us about Urso storming around town. He hadn't been seen dating Edy. He wasn't smiling.

Around noon, when Urso came into the shop to buy a sandwich, I found the courage to ask him whether the bullet in the Igloo's wall matched bullets from Vinnie's Beretta. He grumbled something that sounded like, "Keep out of it," and marched off. I didn't dare shout out a follow-up question about Hugo Hunter's whereabouts.

Bothered by his dismissal, I told Rebecca to watch the store and, to take the edge off, I visited Sew Inspired Quilt Shoppe and tried on my maid of honor dress.

"Oh, yay! It fits like a glove." Freckles did a merry jig. "The gold color is perfect, don't you think?"

"I love it." I twirled on the riser and viewed the dress via the three-way mirror, appreciating the way the A-line shape hugged my curves. Though I wasn't always comfortable in a strapless dress, Freckles had done a marvelous job of making me feel secure. I especially liked the shirred waist with a faux flower at the cinch. So feminine. Jordan would love it.

Freckles propped a pincushion wristband on her arm. "Now, let's fix that hem. I'm assuming the shoes you dropped off are the shoes you'll be wearing?" She pulled a pair of heels from a cubby and handed them to me. "Slip them on."

Back in September, I had purchased the most darling sling sandals with rhinestones dotting the straps. A simple gold choker and drop earrings would finish off the ensemble.

Freckles crouched down. "Stand tall."

I faced the mirror and squared my shoulders. "Where's Edy?"

"Gallivanting."

"What does that mean?"

"She asked for a little time off. She wanted to ponder her future." Freckles peered up at me and winked. "I think she's stopping by the precinct."

"To see Urso?" Judging by Urso's mood, I expected that Edy would wind up disappointed. Urso had bought a single sandwich earlier, not two as he had been doing for the past week. But it wasn't my business.

"Turn," Freckles ordered. "Stop." She weaved a pin into the hem.

Meredith slipped past the curtain and flaunted loose pages from magazines. "Hey, look what I found, Charlotte. All-cheese wedding cakes." She held the pages so I could view them via the mirror without bending. "See the cheeses stacked one on top of each other? Don't they look divinely different and decadent?"

I grinned. "You've been talking to Rebecca."

"So what?" She jutted a hip. "I love them. Now, which is your favorite?"

One photograph was of an all-white, bloomy rind cake made up of three simple rounds of cheese and decorated with long-stemmed peach roses and peach jams. Another was a combination of blue cheese wheels, swirled with strands of grapes and soft yellow roses. The third was fashioned with multicolored cheeses, each with a different rind. Herbs circled the "cake," top to bottom. Elegant, different, and nothing like any wedding cake I had ever seen.

"It sounds like a lot of cheese," I said. "Are you sure that's what you want? I thought we'd settled on cheese and fruit platters, tartlets, and a traditional cake. It's already been ordered."

"Well, how about for the rehearsal dinner? We haven't settled on anything for that."

Was she thinking clearly? The rehearsal dinner was tomorrow.

"My folks would be over the moon for a blue cheese cake. With the grapes and roses? It'll look divine. You wanted something in gold tones, didn't you? Say yes, please?"

How could I say no to my best friend? "It's your night. I'll do whatever you want."

She hugged me hard. "I'm so happy. I wish for you all the happiness I feel. By the way, have you set a date with Jordan?"

"Not yet." Jordan and I hadn't had a moment alone in days. I missed our long chats and his caresses. "Life has been pretty crazy."

"Tell me about it." Meredith tucked the wedding cake photographs into her tote bag. "Do you know if Jacky has heard from Hugo Hunter?"

"She hasn't."

"He'll show up," Freckles said. "You watch. He'll reappear, and he'll have some great story to tell."

"You liked him," I said.

"We all did . . . do," Freckles replied. "He's a nice man. Great with the kids. He loves dishing up ice cream. The Scoops think the world of him. He's talked both of them into attending college."

"And you don't think he had a hand in Jacky's husband's murder?" I said.

"Not a chance. He might have a secret life . . . perhaps another wife . . ."

I had come up with the same theory while talking to Urso. Was it the truth? Was Hugo in some other city playing husband?

". . . but he's not a killer." Freckles stuck more pins into the hem of my dress. "Turn."

I obeyed.

Meredith cleared her throat. "You know, when Vinnie Capriotti was found dead, there was a moment when we were worried for Jordan."

"Why?" I said.

"Matthew and I thought —"

"Jordan would never hurt a soul."

"That's not what I meant. We thought Urso might suspect him. Aren't you relieved that they were working together to help Grandmère? Alibis are so important. Speaking of which, that Iris —"

"— was never a suspect in Vinnie's murder, either."

"No, no." Meredith rapped me on the arm. "Let me finish a sentence. Sheesh. Granted, I'm mangling the English language — I guess I'm a little hyped up — but what I meant to say, though any segue was lacking, was Iris was supposed to show up for a floral review with Matthew, Tyanne, and me last night, but she forgot."

"Forgot?"

Freckles raised an eyebrow. "She told me this is her biggest paycheck to date."

Meredith chuckled. "Don't worry. I'm not angry. I happened to swing by the Village Green and caught her watching the *Hamlet* rehearsal. I think she has a real thing for Stratton. They make quite an unusual-looking couple, don't you think? She's so tall and slender while he's stocky and bald. On the break, she started goofing around with him. I've never seen her that playful.

We had a brief chat. She was chagrined to miss our appointment. Time got away from her, but she assured me she's on top of things." Meredith's words started running together because she was talking so fast.

I said, "Slow down and breathe."

She inhaled and exhaled and then giggled. "Anyway, not to worry. Iris had her display books in her tote bag. All the flowers are ordered and due to arrive Sunday morning. Did you know she makes everything that very morning? Bouquets, everything. I know she cut her prices for us, but I'm thinking of giving her a bonus."

"Charlotte, are you in there?" The curtain parted and Prudence Hart strode through, wearing an electric blue sheath, matching pumps, and a flashy blue hat. Was she trying to out-Sylvie Sylvie? "Aha, I've found you." Mouth grim, she planted her hands on her bony hips — a woman on a mission. "Meredith, I'm glad you're here, too. You won't believe what I learned. Sylvie is going to throw a wrench into your wedding."

"She wouldn't dare," Meredith said.

Prudence bobbed her head. "I happen to know for a fact that she's planning to bring and release a horde of ladybugs. They'll flock to the food."

"No." Meredith clutched my arm.

"Don't worry," I said. "I'll have a chat with Sylvie."

Sylvie bounded through the curtain. "What will you chat with me about, Charlotte?"

Prudence sputtered. "Are you following me?"

"Heavens." Sylvie slapped her chest and widened her eyes. "Why ever would you think that?"

I gaped at Sylvie. Not because of her holier-than-thou act. She had donned yet another eye-popping outfit, this one a skintight, shimmery red sheath. It was the middle of the afternoon in Providence. She wasn't headed to some swank New York cocktail party or to some corner in the red-light district of Cleveland, for that matter.

"It's getting crowded in here," Freckles whispered to me.

"Do you think?" I bit back a snort.

"I know what you're up to, Prudence Hart." Sylvie stabbed a finger at her nemesis. "You're spreading lies, lies, and more lies." She sidled up to the riser, viewed my dress, and let out a slow hiss. "Pastels and you, Charlotte . . ."

I smiled beatifically and counted to ten. I would not let her get to me. No way, no how.

"They're not lies," Prudence said, dragging Sylvie back to the argument.

Like a heat-seeking missile, Sylvie zeroed her focus on her rival. "Yes, they are, you . . . you . . ."

"I heard you talking to Iris," Prudence insisted. "You asked her about ladybugs."

"For my garden."

"Bah!"

"Believe what you will, love, but I wanted to know about ladybugs taking care of the pests in my garden. They eat aphids."

Meredith said, "Actually they do, Prudence. I'm sure —"

"Not in October," Prudence said. "They are predominantly spring and summer creatures."

Meredith threw open her hands. "Perhaps this was an innocent mistake."

"Innocent, my foot. Sylvie is purposeful, if nothing else."

Sylvie leaned forward. "You're mad, Prudence Hart, because Under Wraps is doing better than La Chic Boutique. My business has put a dent in your earnings, and that's why you're selling."

"I am not selling." Prudence's voice thinned to a screech. "How many times do I have to tell you? I will never sell."

"Tosh. Try to explain away Edy Delaney

looking for a loan at the bank. Just try."

Here we go again, I thought. When had every place in Providence turned into Sylvie and Prudence's sparring arena? Well, no more.

"Excuse me, Freckles." I stepped gingerly off the riser and grabbed Sylvie and Prudence by the elbow. "Ladies, you're leaving."

"What?" they sputtered.

"Out, now." I muscled them through the curtain and to the front of the shop.

"You heard her." Meredith followed behind, a hand pressed against each of the women's backs.

"Leave," I said. "I will not have you scaring off Freckles's customers."

"But I came to warn Meredith," Prudence said.

"Consider me warned." Meredith opened the front door and held it wide. "Go."

"Well, I never." Prudence wriggled free. "Mind my words, Meredith Vance. Sylvie will bring evil to the proceedings." As a parting blow, Prudence said as she tramped down the sidewalk, "By the way, Sylvie, my dear, a woman your age should never wear such an ensemble. You don't have the narrow hips and thighs for it. That's why it creeps up. Tastelessly, I might add."

Sylvie blew a raspberry as she, ever so discreetly, shimmied the dress down her legs.

CHAPTER 26

When Meredith and I returned to The Cheese Shop, I assured her that Sylvie would not be able to pull a prank on the wedding day. "Grandmère and Tyanne will be watching her like a hawk," I said as I passed the center display barrel, automatically straightening a stand of cracker boxes. "And hawks have mighty talons."

Meredith grinned. "Matthew's mother will eagle-eye her, too. She doesn't have fond memories of Sylvie, though she does admit that Sylvie is a better mother to the twins than she was before. The girls seem happy."

"They are." I was the one who was unhappy that they were moving, but I would rally. I would. No more tears at two A.M. No more waking up from worrisome dreams. I paused at the archway between the shop and the wine annex. "I'm back," I called to Rebecca and Matthew, who were chatting beside the old oak bar while Matthew jotted notes on a notepad.

Meredith peeked over my shoulder. "How many lists is he keeping?"

"So many, I've lost count. I found three in the office earlier."

Meredith whistled under her breath. "I guess between picking up the folks and getting my hair styled I'll have to help him coordinate."

"A bride's work is never done," I gibed. "By the way, the twins are looking forward to going to Tip to Toe Salon."

"Even Amy?"

"Yes, even Amy. She wants a cute little French braid." I pointed to the side of my head. "You know the kind, where they gather the bangs and weave them into a strand. She saw a long-distance runner sporting it."

"Does she want beads woven in?"

"I was thinking glitter."

Meredith sputtered. "Glitter? No, no, no, not glitter. Never." She burst into laughter.

"Gee, why not?" I grinned, knowing why not. Back in seventh grade, Meredith and I had styled each other's hair for the Sadie Hawkins' Day Sock Hop. I had wanted to ask Meredith's brother to the event, but he was three years older, and it was taboo for a sophomore in high school to return to junior high for a dance. I settled for a gangly seventh-grade boy who adored basketball and had two left feet. Luckily Gangly Guy had been my date. Why? Because Meredith and I thought we needed glue to keep the glitter in our hair. We applied gobs of the stuff, and it didn't come out for weeks. Meredith's brother would have teased me for years. Gangly Guy kept touching the globules and saying, "Cool."

"What's so funny?" Rebecca returned to the register and taped a note to the change drawer. In response to my glance, she said, "Matthew wants me to make sure we have plenty of natural almond soda and nonalcoholic champagne from the Bozzuto Winery. Some of the folks from his side of the family don't drink."

"Done."

"So what's so funny?" Rebecca repeated. "Why were you and Meredith laughing?"

"We were talking about bad hair days."

"Speaking of bad hair days" — Meredith switched her purse to her other shoulder — "what do you think about the rumor?"

"Which rumor?" Rebecca said.

"About Edy."

"That's cruel," Rebecca said. "Edy's hair isn't that bad. In fact, I like it. I've been thinking of cutting off my locks and going spiky. I saw a model in a *Victoria's Secret* catalogue with the same hairdo. What do you think? Would I look good with short hair?" She swooped her hair into an updo. Strands fell loose and framed her face.

"She's not talking about Edy's hair," I said. "She's talking about the bombshell Sylvie just dropped, yet again, about Edy trying to buy out Prudence. She says she saw her at the bank applying for a loan."

"Now, wait a sec." Rebecca released her hair. "Sylvie intimated yesterday — was it yesterday? — that Edy already had the funds. She has a backer. Charlotte, you've got to find out what's the truth and what isn't."

"I have to? Why?"

"Because, you know . . ." Rebecca twirled a hand like that would fill in the end of her sentence. I shook my head, not getting her directive via ESP. "Because we talked about Edy . . . and money . . . and maybe she bribed Giacomo to get a stake for her new enterprise."

Meredith gaped. "You believe Edy could have killed Giacomo? Charlotte, go." She prodded me toward the door. "No one should get away with murder. Especially Edy. Get the scoop."

"Since when am I the designated fact

finder?" I said, grinding to a halt.

Meredith and Rebecca gave me a united all-knowing look. "Duh," they chimed.

Solving a couple of crimes was giving me a reputation as an amateur sleuth that I wasn't certain I enjoyed. I mean, sure, I liked solving puzzles as much as the next person, but I wasn't brave, and I didn't like people thinking I was a snoop.

"You know Mrs. Fletcher would do it," Rebecca said, referring to the fictional character from *Murder, She Wrote* like she was real.

"What will I say?" I asked.

Rebecca cuffed my shoulder. "Wing it!"

For over a hundred years, one family had owned Providence Provincial Savings. Though the bank was located in a newly built mall near the grocery store, the family staunchly maintained its Old World flavor and hometown appeal. The warm browns and ecru décor and the friendly, intelligent faces of the clerks made me feel confident that my money was secure.

I paused as I entered and scanned the throng of people waiting in line to carry out transactions. Edy wasn't among them. I peered into the nooks occupied by loan officers. Edy wasn't sitting in any of them, either. Sylvie had to have been mistaken.

As I turned to go, I spied Iris with her teenage daughter at a teller window. She was handing her daughter keys and giving her instructions, probably warning her not to drive off without her.

Curious beyond curious as to whether Sylvie had been stirring the pot regarding Edy, I approached Iris. Maybe she had seen Edy and knew what was up. "Hello, Iris."

She spotted me, turned back to her daughter and said, "Get the deposit slip," then hurried toward me, her face tinged with excitement. She wore a floral spandex shift that I had to admit made her look almost attractive. "What a surprise to see you."

"Is that a new dress?"

She beamed. "It is. Do you like it?"

"I do."

"It's a little splurge. You know why? You'll never guess who just called me. Meredith. She's giving me a bonus."

"That's great."

"I have Tyanne to thank. She convinced Meredith to hire me. You know what I think I'll do? I'll insert some of my homegrown orchids in Meredith's bouquet. Won't they be beautiful?" She glanced at her watch. "Oops, sorry, but I have to run. I've got so much to do."

"Wait." I didn't want her to leave before I got a few answers about Edy. But how could I ask subtly? Noticing the Band-Aid on her wrist, I said, "How are your burns healing?"

"Oh." She tinged pink. "Fine. I can't believe I was so stupid. I mean, how hard is it to grab a pot holder? See you."

"Wait, Iris, can I ask you a question?"

She glanced at her daughter who was still standing by the teller.

"It'll just take a sec. Have you been here a while?"

"A half hour. The line was long, but —" She bit her lip. "I'm embarrassed to say it. I wanted to deposit the money Meredith advanced me. I've got to keep my business blooming." She patted the *Growing Stronger* slogan on her tote bag. "Why do you ask?"

"Did you see Edy Delaney in the bank?" *So much for being subtle.*

Iris puckered her mouth as if, heaven forbid, she admit she saw someone her gal pal Prudence detested. "Yes, she was here." She jerked her chin toward one of the loan officer nooks. "She was in there with the old biddy. You know the one I mean. Ruffled hair, beaky nose." She wiggled her fingers to paint me a picture. "If you ask me, Edy was giving the gal a pretty hard time."

"Did the loan officer turn her down?"

"That would be my guess."

I lowered my voice. "There's talk that Edy wants to buy Prudence's shop."

"Oh, Charlotte, didn't you hear Prudence the other day? She is not selling."

"Are you sure?"

Iris clucked her tongue. "Prudence talks to me about everything. Now, mind you, that doesn't mean Edy Delaney isn't wishing she could buy Prudence out. Ah, if wishes were horses . . . or college tuitions . . ." She twirled a finger. "And who knows what measures Edy might take to get what she wants? That woman is reckless. What's with all that jewelry piercing her body? Why, I wouldn't put it past her to have killed Giacomo Capriotti and stolen the money right off of him to pay for all that second-rate silver she owns."

"You know about the money Giacomo was carrying?"

"The whole town does." Iris leaned in. "FYI, as Edy left the loan officer's cubicle, I heard her add that she was on her way to Café au Lait. She asked if she could bring the woman back a latte. What do you bet she's hoping a bribe will get her the loan?"

Intrigued by yet another mention of bribery, I hightailed it to Café au Lait Coffee Shop.

The place was decorated in a fanciful manner. Over each lacy antique iron bistro table hovered a miniature papier-mâché hot air balloon. On every wall, the Francophile owner had hung a watercolor that he had painted. He was particularly fond of France's bridges, the Eiffel Tower, Notre Dame Cathedral, and the Arc d'Triomphe. A jazz saxophone rendition of "La Vie en Rose" played through a speaker.

Edy, clad in a black jumper over black tank top, stood out from the rest of the customers, most of whom were wearing *Stomping the Grapes* T-shirts. She hovered by the milk and sugar station while pouring creamer into a single cup of coffee — not two.

I cornered her and flashed a sociable smile. "Hi, Edy."

She arched a wary eyebrow, which made her tooled hoop earrings wiggle.

"How have you been?" I asked.

"We're not friends, Charlotte. Don't pretend." She sidestepped me and headed to an empty table.

I followed her, mumbling, "So much for niceties," and perched on one of the café chairs opposite her.

"Look, if you're going to hound me, be blunt," Edy said. "I don't like beating around the bush. Got me? Is it about Urso? No, we're not dating anymore. Happy? He's all yours."

I gawked. "I don't want him. I'm engaged to Jordan."

"Right. The cheese farmer. Whoop-de-doo."

Her tone was intentionally mean, yet tears pressed at the corners of her eyes, and for some reason, my heart went out to her. Didn't I believe she was a killer? Was she snowing me? She was a cheat and a liar. Given the chance, she could probably act rings around Sandra Bullock.

I steadied myself and sat taller. "You went to the bank for a loan."

"What do you care?"

"Are you planning to buy out Prudence?"

She scowled. "Oh, yeah, like Prudence would ever sell. She may be under water on her loans, but she'll go to her grave to keep that place, the penny-pincher. Do you know she cut my salary in half, for no reason, and expected me to work the same hours? That's why I left. She's a shrew. And that Iris friend of hers. What a piece of work she is."

"Let's stay on topic."

"Fine, what's your point?" She folded her arms.

"What if you had a backer?" I asked, trying to lure her to a confession. "Would you buy out Prudence then?"

"If I did, she still wouldn't sell, and I still wouldn't buy. Too much bad karma."

So much for that angle. A silence fell between us. I drummed my fingers on the bistro table, trying to fashion another question that might get results. Did district attorneys have to work this hard?

"Is something else on your mind, Charlotte, or are you trying to leave an indelible impression in the wrought iron? Good luck with that."

I lifted my gaze to meet hers. Tears still pooled in her eyes, but they hadn't fallen. Was she faking sadness to manipulate me? I urged myself to be more resolute and said, "Did you call Giacomo Capriotti and tell him where Jacky was? Did you ask him to pay you for the information?"

"Oh, man." Edy let out an exasperated sigh. "I already told you I didn't call him. Check my phone records."

"There was a wad of cash on him. Chief Urso didn't find it."

"Whoa. That's enough." She smacked the table. Her coffee cup lurched. She steadied it. "You're implying that I killed the guy and took his money?"

"I'm not implying —"

"You are, too. I did not call him. I did not take his money. Why would I have cause to kill him? What motive?"

"You need money for something. You were in the bank looking for a loan."

She inhaled and blew a harsh breath out her nose. "Why are you always darting around town playing Nancy Drew?"

Nancy Drew? Is that what people thought of me? Not Wonder Woman, out to lasso the truth? I itched to pinch her arm. How high school of me was that?

"Are you bored with running The Cheese Shop? Is that it?" Edy persisted. "Let's end this. I have an alibi for that night, if you care to hear it. I was with my mother."

I pursed my lips. Really? Another mother as an alibi? Really?

"Yeah, yeah, I know. Mothers will lie," Edy continued. "But not my mother. You don't know my mother."

Actually, I did. I had met her a couple of times during high school. Like an aspiring beauty queen, she had been clipped and exacting, every hair in place, every outfit perfect. Was that why Edy had adopted the Goth look?

"She's sick," Edy said.

"I'm so sorry."

"She's in the Providence Nursing Home

west of town, and I —" Tears slipped from her eyes; she swiped them with her knuckles. "I am behind on payments. That's why I need a loan. I was turned down. Not that my mother deserves my help . . ."

". . . but that's what daughters do," I finished.

Edy hung her head for a long moment and then raised her chin, eyes contemplative. She let out a sigh. "Look, I know I've been a pill to you. I'm not one of your cutesy-pie friends. I'm not touchy-feely."

She had seemed pretty touchy-feely with Urso outside the diner the other day, but I put a cap on that memory.

"You're probably mad at me because of that cheating incident years ago," she went on.

Was I that transparent? Yes, I probably was.

"My mother's the reason I cheated. I know that sounds like a cop-out, but let me put it in perspective. She had me when she was forty-five. I was her only child. She had three miscarriages and then me. I was the miracle baby. She expected me to excel at all times, in all things. I couldn't. I was average. I liked to sew and play dress up. I wasn't pretty, I couldn't do a cheerleading yell to save my life, and I didn't like to study. So I cheated." She thumped the table. "I'm not proud of it, but I have turned over a new leaf. I told Freckles everything."

I was surprised when Freckles had revealed Edy's secret to me. Had Edy really changed? I leveled her with my gaze. "You said you were with your mother the night Giacomo Capriotti was killed. Can she corroborate that?"

She bit her lip. "I wasn't *with* her, per se."

"You lied?"

"No. I was at the nursing home, but I wasn't in her room."

"Why not?"

Edy tugged on her left hoop earring. Strawberry blotches popped up on her neck and face. "Because I'm working a second job to pay the bills. At night, I clean the halls and rec rooms. I'm not good at it, I hate it, but I do it. Do you know you can't get the smell of ammonia off your hands? No amount of hand lotion does it."

I felt like a heel for asking, but I said, "Did anyone see you?"

"Nurse Ratched."

A hoot popped from my mouth. "You're kidding."

"No, really. There's a nurse named Rita, but everyone calls her Nurse Ratched. She's nasty, like that nurse in *One Flew Over the Cuckoo's Nest.* Helmet hair, plastic grin." Edy imitated the smile. "She makes my mother look like a saint, which, believe me, is hard to do. You can call her." Edy twisted her cup of coffee but didn't take a sip. "By the way, you're not the only person in town trying to solve this murder. I've been thinking about it, too. It stinks that Providence is suddenly a haven for crime. You know what gets me? How did someone lure Giacomo Capriotti into the Igloo? I mean, the guy was big, right? He could defend himself, and I doubt the guy was hungry for an ice cream cone."

I flashed on the bullet found in the freezer wall. Had the killer forced Giacomo into the Igloo at gunpoint? Should Urso be looking for a second gun?

CHAPTER 27

Not that I didn't believe Edy — would I ever forgive her for getting me in trouble with the science teacher? — but on the way back to Fromagerie Bessette, I dug out my cell phone and called Providence Nursing Home. The cranky nurse that Edy had mentioned answered in an ultra-crisp tone. Though she was outspoken about Edy's shortcomings where mopping floors was concerned, she confirmed Edy's whereabouts at the time of the murder. She had seen Edy at least four times during the night. The nursing home was in lockdown every night; no one entered or left.

Ruling out Edy and Anabelle as suspects and with Vinnie dead, I was back to square one. Hugo Hunter was missing. Was he dead, too, or was Rebecca right and he was the person who had murdered Jacky's husband? Had Urso obtained a warrant to search Hugo's home? Had he found a Beretta with bullets that would match the bullet plucked from the Igloo Ice Cream Parlor's wall? I dialed the precinct to talk to him, but Urso wouldn't take the call.

The rest of the afternoon at The Cheese Shop, Rebecca and I waited on customers. The *Stomping the Grapes* race for the rescue shelter, which was scheduled for tomorrow, and the opening night of *Hamlet,* which was less than two hours away, had drawn swarms of people. The bed-and-breakfasts were full. All spots at the camping ground on the Nature Preserve were rented. By four P.M., we had sold out of every broccolini and pine nut quiche and all of the Slam-Drunk torpedo sandwiches that Rebecca had made. She had combined the mild semi-soft Drunken Goat cheese with Sopresatta, a rustic spicy salami, and Finocchiona salami, which was laced with fennel seeds. To top it all off, she had added a super-spicy red pepper relish. I had teased her that whoever ate the torpedoes would need an iron stomach.

Around five P.M., Grandmère hurried into the shop. "*Chérie,* I am in desperate need of a meal for the crew." She sounded frantic, but I had seen her like this on previous opening nights. "I have prepared the after-party meal, but I completely forgot snacks.

You know that it is *malchance* to run a show on an empty stomach."

"It is not bad luck. You made that up," I teased. "What's wrong?"

She paced in front of the cheese counter, worrying her hands together. "I have not put on a Shakespeare play for years. What if I have missed the tone?"

"What does Delilah think?"

"She loves it, but she is not a good judge. She is too close to the work." Grandmère peered into the cheese counter display. "Please make me a platter, nothing too heavy. Calabrese salami and a couple of those cheeses, sliced thin." She pointed to the gourds hanging over the back counter.

"Caciocavallo," I reminded her. It was a luscious, pliable Provolone-type cheese from Italy, perfect for a cheese platter. In Italian, *cavallo* means horse; the cheese was said to have been made originally with mare's milk. "How about some green Cerignola olives and a couple loaves of sourdough bread, too?"

"*Oui.*" She fetched crackers and jars of spiced mustard.

As she was setting the items by the register, Jordan entered through the rear door, a plaid blanket draped over one arm, the same wicker basket from yesterday in his hand. A warm breeze followed him inside. As he passed me, he ran a finger along the back of my neck. I shivered with delight, which, by his wink, I could tell he had expected. He ogled my grandmother's purchases and licked his lips. "Looks delicious, Bernadette." He joined her at the front of the cheese display. "Am I invited to the party?"

"*Bien sûr,* Jordan." She said his name with the French pronunciation, a soft *J* and accent on the second syllable, which pleased me no end. She really was warming to him. Yay!

He eyed me. "Ready to go to the theater, milady? I have restocked with lemonade, chicken, homemade cole slaw, peppered corn salad, and watermelon."

My stomach did a cartwheel of appreciation. "Who ate our other picnic?"

"Me." He patted his firm abdomen. "And a few of my crew buddies. We —"

The front door flew open, and Iris hurried into the shop. "Charlotte. You'll never guess who I saw."

Prudence followed Iris in, but she didn't utter a word. How the tides had turned, I mused. Iris was becoming a leader. What a little love and a boost to her career had done for her spirit. But then Prudence poked Iris with a finger and said, "Tell her," and I quickly revised my assessment. Maybe Iris wasn't a leader . . . yet.

"Hugo Hunter is back in town," Iris said. "I saw him."

"He's alive?" The relief in my voice surprised me. Didn't I think he was guilty of murder?

"I spotted him sneaking into his house."

Why was he sneaking, and what was Iris doing watching his house? Had everyone in town turned into an amateur sleuth?

"I was taking my daughter back to work, driving a side route, and we spotted him. I told you he wasn't to be trusted." Iris sidled up to the counter and boldly inserted herself between my grandmother and Jordan. "He seemed suspicious, if you ask me."

Grandmère offered an icy glare. "He returned. That shows character." She didn't like to think ill of anyone. She adored the basic premise of American justice: *innocent until proven guilty.*

"Looks can be deceiving," Iris said.

Last week, Iris had implied that Hugo was bad for Jacky. Maybe she knew what Rebecca had called his super-dark secret. "Do you know why he goes out of town?" I asked.

"No."

"You said he had a past."

"All men do."

I exchanged a look with Jordan. Yes, all men did, but that didn't make them bad men.

"Is he married?" I asked.

Prudence lassoed Iris with an arm and steered her toward the exit. "You've said all you need to, Iris. Let's go."

"Wait," I hurried after them. "Iris, did you date Hugo or something? What do you know?"

Iris opened her mouth to speak, but Prudence said, "Hush. Not another word." She glanced over her shoulder and sneered. "Run and tell Chief Urso that Hugo Hunter is back, Charlotte."

"No. I'm leaving to watch the performance of *Hamlet*," I retorted. "Tell him yourself."

"Ah, but Charlotte, dear," Prudence said. "You find such pleasure in solving Providence's crimes. I would hate to deprive you of that."

As the door slammed shut, I caught Grandmère and Jordan stifling smiles. I held up a finger warning them not to say a word.

Despite Prudence's taunt, I refused to change my plans. Urso would be attending the play. He never missed opening night. I would tell him about Hugo when I saw him.

After locking up the shop, Jordan walked with my grandmother and me to the Village Green. The sun hovered low, its waning rays streaking the dusky sky with shades of orange.

Grandmère said, "How I love October. It signifies all that is good about change."

Within the theater arena, Grandmère's crew had hung silver hurricane lanterns on black shepherd hooks. The glow was magical. Close to the stage, a grassy area was sectioned off for picnickers. Behind the picnic section stood rows of rough-hewn benches. People were taking their seats. A line extended from the box office along the west path.

"This way." Grandmère handed Jordan and me plastic passes for the picnicking area to hang around our necks. "Our family receives *carte blanche*."

Jordan squeezed my hand. "Family. I like that."

"Me, too."

We dodged teenage girls in colorful long dresses who were parading through the area carrying banners with the word *Hamlet* emblazoned on them, and we found a spot on the grass. Jordan spread the plaid blanket. As we set out the food from the basket, laughter spiraled through the air.

Across the grass, supervisors were allowing children to enter the wine vat. The kids climbed into the tub of grapes as merrily as if it were a cage filled with plastic balls and instantly started to stomp. Lucy Ricardo couldn't have looked happier. Dark grape juice squirted upward.

"Listen," Jordan said. "Madrigals."

A trio of musicians playing a lute, flute, and fiddle emerged from behind the stage.

"Your grandmother has thought of everything."

The madrigals meandered through the crowd, singing, "Alas my love, ye do me wrong, to cast me off discourteously; and I have loved you so long, delighting in your companie."

To my surprise, Jordan joined in the chorus. "Greensleeves was all my joy; Greensleeves was my delight. Greensleeves was my heart of gold, and who but my Lady Greensleeves."

I elbowed him. "Watch out. Grandmère is looking our way. What do you bet, she'll want you to star in her next musical production?"

"No way."

"Oh, yes, way. Yoo-hoo. Grandmère."

"No." Jordan covered my mouth.

I ducked from his grasp. "Oho, methinks

376

thou doth protest too much. I —"

Jordan stopped me by planting his lips on mine; I melted. We remained in an embrace, kissing longingly until we heard someone clear her throat.

We broke apart and gazed at our visitor. A flush of embarrassment warmed me.

"Am I interrupting?" Rebecca said while twisting the picnicking area pass that hung around her neck.

I patted the picnic blanket. "Not at all."

"Love is in the air . . . everywhere." Rebecca sighed the sigh of a woman missing her boyfriend as she gestured to the right.

Next to the stage in a roped-off area for actors only, Iris and Stratton clung in a passionate embrace. Where was Prudence? I wondered. Had she ditched Iris after their little performance at Fromagerie Bessette? Or had she, on principle, refused to come to the play because of the riffraff? Delilah strode to the lovers and said something that made them break apart and other nearby actors snap to attention. Within seconds, Delilah rounded up all the actors, and they started deep-breathing exercises.

"It's fun, isn't it?" Rebecca nestled onto a blanket she had brought. "Watching the actors prepare."

"The whole event is terrific," I said.

"There's so much going on."

As the actors started droning, Clair and a couple of her young friends pressed up to the rope and chanted with them. Beyond them, Amy chased Tyanne's towheaded son, who had gotten hold of an actor's wig and hat and was strutting like a drum major, the feather on the hat flouncing with abandon. Matthew and Meredith stood nearby, watching with amusement. Matthew had told me that Sylvie wasn't coming within a mile of the play, claiming she couldn't stand to hear the Bard's words garbled by Americans. Lucky us.

"Want a glass of wine, Rebecca?" Jordan said. "Matthew suggested this one." He pulled a bottle and wine opener from the basket.

Rebecca surveyed the bottle. "Kali Hart pinot noir. It's up front and jammy."

"Perfect. I'm the jammy type," Jordan joked and proceeded to open the wine.

"Good evening, everybody." Urso drew alongside us. "Are you enjoying yourselves?"

Deputy O'Shea, the hunky blond, accompanied him. He scrutinized Rebecca with outright desire, which made me grin. Our sweet honeybee farmer had better hurry back to town before some other guy scooped up his fiancée. Because she was busy tasting the wine Jordan had poured for her, Rebecca missed the deputy's adoring gaze.

"Want some wine?" I said to Urso. "You're off duty, right?"

Urso cracked a smile. "Thanks, but no, we're still on the clock." He scratched the nape of his neck. "I came to apologize. Charlotte, I shouldn't have yelled earlier."

"You should have returned my call, too."

He pursed his lips.

"Don't worry. I understand," I said, letting him off the hook. "You want the case solved."

"Are you sure the guy that killed Vinnie didn't kill Giacomo, too?" Jordan said.

"Positive," Urso answered. "He has an alibi in New Jersey the night Capriotti was murdered."

"By the way, Hugo Hunter is back in town," I said. "He was seen sneaking into his house."

Jordan elbowed me, ribbing me for doing Prudence and Iris's bidding. *C'est la vie.* Someone needed to keep our police chief up to date.

"Says who?" Urso asked.

"Iris Isherwood."

"Did I hear someone call my name?" Iris crossed the lawn in front of the stage. She had to have supersonic hearing, or she was waiting for something — anything — to drag her away from where the actors were chanting. One could only tolerate so much droning.

I said, "I told Urso you saw Hugo."

"Oh, that," Iris said. "He seemed pretty suspicious. All in black carrying a small duffel. Chief, do you think it's possible that Hugo is involved with the guy who came after Vinnie Capriotti? I mean, he comes and goes. Maybe he's a hit man."

Urso's eyes narrowed. "Interesting notion. I'm on it. Deputy O'Shea, let's go." Urso headed off.

At the mention of the deputy, Rebecca raised her chin. Her gaze met his and she smiled.

"O'Shea," Urso repeated.

"Yes, sir." Before leaving, O'Shea bent at the waist and said to Rebecca, "By the way, that black hair we found? It might have been fake."

"How interesting." Her eyelashes fluttered at rapid speed.

"O'Shea!" Urso barked.

When O'Shea hustled away, I tapped Rebecca's leg. "What was that about?"

She shrugged. "Urso has been less than forthcoming, don't you think? And Devon

O'Shea has information. So what if I give him an occasional slice of his favorite Cheddar cheese to keep the pipes lubed, know what I mean?"

"You're brazen," I said.

Jordan roared. "And smart as a whip."

Rebecca twirled her ponytail. "I got the idea from watching *Castle*. He was flirting with this snitch, and I thought he was so clever."

I became aware of Iris, lingering. I said, "Care to join us?"

"That's sweet, but no, thanks. I'm going to wander and drink in the local flavor." She gestured with her thumb and walked away.

Rebecca swiveled to face us, knees tucked beneath her. "So . . . did you hear Deputy O'Shea mention the fake hair found at the crime scene? Do you think he meant from a faux fur or hair extensions or something?"

"How about a wig?" Jordan said.

I cut a sharp look at Tyanne's son, who, at present, was tossing the wig back and forth to a buddy, playing keep-away from Amy. It would have been easy for someone to steal one of the actor's wigs. Grandmère wasn't terribly cautious. She hadn't set a guard to watch over the costume closet.

"Ladies, gentlemen, and children." Speak-

ing through a handheld microphone, Grandmère stood in the aisle by the rear row of
seating. "We're about to start. Please take
your seats."

Just beyond her, I caught sight of Hugo
Hunter leaning against one of the flagged
posts, arms folded across his chest. A shiver
cut through me. Dressed entirely in black,
he reminded me of a bad guy in an old
western. And yet he didn't look mean-
spirited or anything close to that. He appeared relaxed and ready to enjoy the
performance. I searched for Urso, but he
and Deputy O'Shea were gone. I dialed his
cell phone, but as was typical in our cellular
phone–challenged county, my call rolled
into voicemail.

Lights dimmed. An actor darted onto
stage and yelled, "Who's there?"

As the scene advanced, I scanned the rear
of the audience for Hugo, but he was
nowhere to be seen. Had I imagined him,
or had he vanished like Houdini? *Poof!* I
remembered Freckles saying she liked
Hugo; everyone did. I know I did . . . had.
Was he capable of murder? I fashioned a
scenario in which Hugo plotted to kill Giacomo Capriotti. Though he had lush dark
hair, he stole a shaggy wig to disguise
himself, then lured Giacomo to the Igloo

and threatened him with a gun. Giacomo fought back; the gun discharged, leaving a bullet in the wall. Hugo hefted the ice cream and beat Giacomo with it. He scattered some of the fake hair at the crime scene to mislead Urso. It all sounded logical, except one point kept sticking in my mind. Why would he kill Giacomo at the Igloo? Why risk exposure? Why not take the fight elsewhere? And if he was smart enough to construct the perfect crime, why hadn't he gone back to Jacky's house to establish his alibi?

When the play concluded — it was wonderful; Grandmère needn't have worried — Jordan and I attended the after party. Within the roped-off area by the stage, Grandmère set out a casual spread of canapés, chips, salsa, vegetables, sliced fruit, and dozens of mini-cupcakes. Actors and their guests loaded up paper plates with goodies. Lively conversation followed, with actors spouting lines from various Shakespearean plays while others broke into song. A full moon might have had something to do with the exuberance.

An hour into the frivolity, I settled onto the edge of the stage, my overworked mind roving from thought to thought. First, I wondered whether Urso had tracked down Hugo and obtained a confession. Next, I contemplated tomorrow's footraces and the rehearsal dinner and Sunday's wedding.

Jordan sidled up to me and ran a finger along the edge of my hand. "Tired?"

I was. Dead on my feet. "Thinking."

"About us?"

"About everything but us. Sorry."

He nuzzled my neck with his lips. "Give it a rest."

"I wish."

He lifted my chin with his fingertips and stared intently into my eyes. "By the way, there was something I wanted to say at our picnic, but we didn't seem to have a moment to ourselves."

I fought off a yawn. "What?"

"I want you to know that you don't have anything to worry about anymore."

"Anything? Ever? Promise?" I teased.

"Us. You don't have to worry about us. With Vinnie and Giacomo dead, neither Jacky nor I have any fear of reprisal. We'll be remaining in Providence. We're safe."

Joy bubbled up my throat. I threw my arms around him and let out a whoop.

And then, as I remained tucked in his embrace, a thought of Hugo invaded my mind again. Had safety been his goal? Had he cared so much about Jacky and protecting her anonymity that he killed Giacomo and sicced the other man on Vinnie? What did we know about Hugo? Was Iris right? Was Hugo a hit man or did he know one? Why was he always leaving town?

CHAPTER 28

Morning arrived before I was ready. My alarm blared, and I awoke bleary-eyed, my head aching from too much theorizing at two A.M. After a quick shower and dressing in jeans, a mock-peasant yellow blouse that was shirred at the waist, and zipper-style tennis shoes, I trotted downstairs to the kitchen.

Matthew was already there, cordless phone wedged between his jaw and shoulder. He was chatting to the driver whom he had hired to fetch family members at the airport. He gestured to the pot of vanilla coffee on the counter. I blew him a kiss of thanks for brewing it. The aroma smelled divine.

"What do you mean they're late?" Matthew said. "Yes, I know what *late* means, sir, it's simply" — he listened — "got it. They're late. But it's not a weather issue, is it? They'll make it to the rehearsal dinner, won't they?"

Our weather was perfect. The sun was shining. The temperature was supposed to reach the mid-seventies. Fabulous.

I whispered, "Want breakfast?"

Matthew nodded. "Something light. Uh, no, sir, I was talking to my cousin."

I fed Rags and Rocket first, otherwise they would have followed me hither and yon. Then I poured two cups of coffee and made quickie meals of pumpkin bread topped with cream cheese. When Matthew ended his conversation, he downed his breakfast.

"Thanks, cuz," he mumbled as he dialed Lavender and Lace B&B to double-check room reservations. Though my aunt and uncle had been invited to stay with my grandparents, they had opted to rent rooms as a family at the bed-and-breakfast.

I ate my breakfast standing by the sink, which according to my grandmother wasn't the best for digestion, but my stomach didn't rebel, and soon, I was able to function like a human being.

As I was setting the table for the twins' breakfast, a gluten-free mascarpone and apple French toast casserole that I had made before going to bed, I heard brakes squeal on the street. Rocket barked and darted through the doggie door into the yard. Rags followed.

"They're here." Amy, who had dressed in running shorts, *Stomping the Grapes* T-shirt, and tennis shoes, jogged into the kitchen. "The movers are here."

Clair, dressed similarly, charged in after her. I was surprised by her enthusiasm, seeing as she wasn't an athlete. Plans to get her hair styled and the impending wedding were infusing her with more verve than she normally had.

The doorbell rang.

As if trained by Pavlov, Rocket and Rags sped back into the kitchen through the doggie door and sprinted toward the foyer. Rocket skidded as he rounded the corner, probably anticipating the sea of boxes that would block his progress.

Amy followed. "I'll get it."

"Me, too," Clair chimed.

"I'm coming." Matthew hustled after them.

I took a deep breath and exhaled while urging myself, at all costs, not to cry. I did pretty well until an hour later when I sat on the front porch steps and watched the last of the boxes being stowed onto the truck. Tears trickled down my cheeks.

"Don't cry, Aunt Charlotte. We aren't going today." Amy sat beside me and patted my shoulder while blinking back her own tears.

"We're living here for another week," Clair said, her eyes moist, as she nestled on the other side of me. "We don't move our clothes and toothbrushes until Daddy and Meredith get back from their honeymoon, remember? Please don't cry."

Rocket and Rags paced the steps below us, whimpering and staring at us in confusion.

That was when the floodgates burst, and I wrapped the twins in a bear hug.

"Let's get going," Matthew shouted from the foyer. "We don't want to be late for the race, do we?" He stopped in the opened doorway and gaped at us. "What the heck?"

I craned my neck and peered up at him, feeling like a fool.

"Uh-uh, no way," he said. "You're not having a sob fest without me." He hurried to the group, squatted down, and said, "Family hug."

Which made us all cry louder.

Even before sounding the popgun for the beginning of the race, *Stomping the Grapes* was a success. Hundreds of people accompanied by pets had shown up for the event. They stood in a huddle at the start line. Children, including Amy and Clair, lined up at the back of the pack so they wouldn't get trampled. Amy had a tight hold on Rocket's leash.

Grandmère, clad in a brown safari-style outfit, stood at the front of the crowd on a makeshift dais constructed of apple boxes. "Thank you for coming." She greeted everyone using a megaphone to broadcast above the crowd's chatter. "We have over three hundred participants. You have no idea how much this means. Tallulah and her furry friends are very grateful."

The town's animal rescuer, Tallulah Barker, a munchkin of a woman, waved from her spot at the foot of the dais where she was managing a knot of dogs on leashes. Tallulah wasn't comfortable with public speaking or leadership, which was why my energetic grandmother had jumped onboard the project.

"As you know," Grandmère said, "Tallulah has been rescuing animals since she was ten years old." As she continued lauding Tallulah for her dedication, Clair broke from the rear of the pack and rushed to me. She clutched me around the waist.

"What is it, sweetheart?" I crouched to her level, unsure whether I could handle another sob fest.

"When I grow up, I want to rescue dogs and cats, too." Passion gushed out of her.

I stroked her hair. "You can do whatever you want to do. A year ago, you wanted to be a librarian or own a knitting store."

"Can't I do both? Like your friend Octavia. She's a Realtor and a librarian, and now she owns the bookstore. And you own a cheese shop and you're a detective."

"I'm not a detective."

"Yes, you are."

Out of the mouths of babes. I rubbed the back of Clair's neck. "We'll discuss what you want to become every year until you decide."

"But I won't be living with you. When will we talk?"

"I'll be less than a mile away. I'm sure you will see me more than you'd like. And Meredith is just as good as me — no, better — at helping young people find their true paths. I promise." I swatted her rear. "Now, get back to the race."

She lingered. "Do you think Rags is lonely at home?"

"He's probably relishing the peace and quiet."

"Where's Daddy?"

"Up ahead with Meredith, holding our spot along the route so we can watch you run." I had asked Rebecca and Tyanne to man the shop. They were more than pleased to get a jump on decorating for the night's rehearsal dinner. "Go, sweetheart," I said to Clair. "Wave when you dash past us."

As she hurried away, I tuned in to the rest of Grandmère's introduction. "Remember, the race winds back and forth through the Bozzuto Winery. Stomp those fallen grapes. They won't mind. And the winner will take home this trophy." She held up a gold-plated urn etched with dogs, cats, and birds. "Don't forget to look for your friends and families among the vines and run like the wind."

Clair dashed to Amy and Rocket, scratched the dog's ears, and screamed, "Yee-haw!"

Amy echoed the shout.

"Ready, set, go." Grandmère fired a pop-gun and then handed it to Tallulah.

The leaders in the race tore ahead. Dust kicked up.

"This way, *mes amis.*" Pépère beckoned Grandmère and me to join him.

Both of my grandparents had worn jeans and tennis shoes, as well. Scuttling ahead of me, they seemed young and sprightly. I hoped, when I grew to their age, I would be as energetic.

"It is an intriguing setting for a race, *non*?" Grandmère said.

In autumn, the winery took on a tired look. The vines were nearly bare, the leaves yellowing, and the twine holding the vines to wire guides was dry. However, the surrounding hills shimmered with burnt orange trees mixed among the evergreens, and the skies were a brilliant blue and awe-inspiring.

"*Oui.* Intriguing." Pépère squeezed her elbow and led her through an arch. I followed.

Minutes after we reached the location that Matthew and Meredith had secured, the first band of racers barreled past. I recognized a few locals who regularly ran along the streets of Providence. Both of Urso's deputies were among them, but not Urso. He was a walker and an occasional bicyclist.

More people rushed by, including the art gallery clerk, the pastor, the cute barista as well as the Francophile owner from Café au Lait, and a few tourists I recognized as customers of Fromagerie Bessette.

Behind them loped a large group of men. Close on their heels was a gaggle of women. Like girls in a fan club, they dashed toward the men, screaming with glee while waving their arms overhead.

One of the joyful females, who reminded

me of a sausage in her snug cocoa running outfit, broke from the pack and jogged up the far side of the men's group. "Yoo-hoo!" she shouted. "Hey, y'all. You with the wavy hair. Slow up a scooch." The woman plunged into the men's group and nabbed someone's shoulder.

The other men didn't slow. The target of the Sausage's attack tried to escape, but more of her friends joined her in corralling him. As the dust settled, I realized they had nabbed Hugo Hunter.

"It know it's you, Mr. Hunter," cried a woman in Day-Glo orange who was as skinny as a carrot stick. "Don't try to deny it." She nudged her sausage-shaped friend for confirmation.

The Sausage nodded. "Please, Mr. Hunter, we love you. Would you sign an autograph?"

I gaped. Why would they want Hugo's autograph, and why had they called him Mister? Who was he? To the annoyance of a few oncoming racers, I spurted toward Hugo. "Out of my way" and "Move aside, lady" came at me in a wave of angry shouts. *So much for a little friendly competition.* I ignored them and cut through the throng like a herding dog organizing droves of cattle.

Grandmère yelled, "*Chérie,* what are you doing?"

The Sausage, Carrot Stick, and friends encircled Hugo near a stand of vines. By the time I reached him, he was signing race entry sheets, which he was pressing against his knee for support. When he stood up, his swoop of bangs fell into his face. He brushed them aside and gazed at me.

"Don't tell me you want one, too," he sighed.

"Hugo, who are you?" I asked. "Why are they asking for your autograph?"

"You don't know?" the Sausage said, her southern drawl as sugary as soda pop. "He's a famous director."

"I'm not famous," he muttered.

"He directs independent films," Carrot Stick said.

"He's an auteur," the Sausage added. "And famous as all get-out. He directed *Evil World* and *The Destruction* and —"

"— *Avoidance,*" Carrot Stick chimed in. "They're classics in the style of Quentin Tarantino. All were shot in the South."

"They're nonlinear," the Sausage added.

"What does that mean?" I asked.

Carrot Stick flailed her hands to describe. "He uses symbols and expressionism to depict violence —"

"— to illustrate how violence is not now, and never should be, okay in our society," Sausage said. "He's incredible with actors because he was an actor before he became a director."

"He pulls a brilliant performance from everyone," her friend said.

Suddenly all my feelings about Hugo started to make sense. I remembered the night Jacky had worried that her husband was prowling around her house. Something about Hugo had struck me as odd. He had said things that had sounded rehearsed and, like an acting coach, he had coaxed answers out of Jacky.

I said to the women, "Did you know Mr. Hunter would be running in the race?"

"Are you kidding?" the Sausage gushed. "We didn't have a clue. He's a sneaky devil. Nobody even knows where he lives. Do you happen to know? Are you just pretending not to know who he is? Are you really his lover?"

They gawked at me, eager for fan club gossip. I pinched my lips together and shook my head. Relief swept across Hugo's face.

"Here, ladies," Hugo handed them their autographed sheets of paper and forced a smile. "Keep buying movie tickets."

"Oh, we will, Hugo, er, Mr. Hunter, we

will," Carrot Stick sang.

The Sausage pulled out a cell phone. "Would you take a picture with all of us?"

Hugo sighed. "Uh, sure."

The Sausage handed me the phone, and the women clustered around him. I snapped a picture, checked it for quality, and handed the phone back.

As the women hustled off, I heard the Sausage say, "I look horrible. My hair."

Carrot Stick said, "Should we ask him to pose in another one?"

"No, it's okay. I'll Photoshop it. Gee, he was nice."

Other racers sped by. More dust kicked up. Not seeing the twins anywhere in sight, I refocused on Hugo.

He shifted feet. "Why are you staring at me?"

"Does Jacky know who you are or what you do?"

"No," Hugo said. "I've kept my life a secret. I like living in Providence. Nobody knows me. I can be myself here."

"You leave town often."

"To shoot films."

"With no forewarning."

"I like anonymity. I get raw footage at all times of the day and night. I don't want people — fans — stalking me. You saw how they act." He jutted a hand at the retreating women. "I need quiet to be creative. I know it's hard to understand."

Actually it wasn't. That was one of the reasons I liked coming into Fromagerie Bessette so early in the morning — for a peaceful solitary moment in my own environment.

"Did Chief Urso talk to you last night?" I asked.

"Nope. Didn't know he wanted to."

"Why didn't you answer your cell phone when he called you over the past two days?"

"I forgot my charger, and the battery died. I wasn't expecting calls. Jacky and I agreed to take a breather from each other."

"You claimed to be talking to your mother on the night of the murder; however, Chief Urso contacted her, and she said she couldn't remember the phone call."

Hugo sighed again. "I did talk to her, but Mama fell asleep. I put on a jazz CD so she could hear I was still around when she woke up. She has this illness. It's a long story. I worry about her."

A guy who worried about his mother couldn't be all bad, could he?

Hugo raked his fingers through his hair. "That night I left the house and went outside to capture a picture of the quarter moon. I came here, to the winery, and got a great shot lying on the ground with the vines in the foreground."

"Did anyone see you?"

"A couple of mice. If it helps, I have footage. It's time-stamped. In case you don't know, the quarter moon comes right before it waxes gibbous. It goes full after that." He frowned. "I needed the shot to show the passing of time. I'm filming the full moon this evening."

Another notion prickled the edges of my memory. "The other night, when Jacky thought someone was outside her house, you said you could protect her. You claimed you were trained in combat fighting. Did you serve in the military?"

"Nah."

"Do you own a gun?"

"You heard my fans. I make movies about nonviolence. Look, I was a stage actor. I learned stage fighting." He mimed a parry and lunge. "I'm pretty good with an épée."

"Why did you lie about being with Jacky that night?"

He swallowed hard. "I thought she might need an alibi."

"You mean you thought she was guilty."

"She'd told me how horrible her husband was. I" — he squirreled a toe into the dirt, popping grapes indiscriminately — "I don't know what I thought."

"Why didn't you simply tell Urso you were shooting a film?"

He shrugged. "Like I said, I wanted anonymity. I was afraid if it got around who I was, my time here was up. People would start flocking to Providence to see me scoop ice cream."

"You're kidding."

"I'm not. Those women? There are thousands more like them." He tilted his head and twirled a finger at me. "I can see those wheels churning in your head. You're thinking more tourists could be good for the town."

I grinned. He had me pegged.

"They're not good for me." He held his hands open, palms up. "I'll take the footage to Urso. Happy?"

"Ecstatic."

"Will you keep my secret?"

"Hugo, I'm pretty sure, thanks to your fan club, that your secret has flown the proverbial coop."

CHAPTER 29

"Aunt Charlotte." Amy charged toward me, her legs splattered with grape skins and grit. Rocket scampered alongside her. "Did you see us?" Amy waved her purple *Stomping the Grapes* ribbon that she had received for finishing. "Halt, Rocket." She pulled up on Rocket's leash. He skidded to a stop and sat. "Good boy." She ruffled his beard. "Did you see us running?"

"Of course I did. We all did." Granted, I had watched from a slightly different angle than the rest of my family. I slung my arm around her shoulder. "Where's Clair?"

"Back there talking to a friend. She'll catch up."

"Let's join the rest."

Grandmère, Pépère, Matthew, and Meredith stood about fifty yards down the aisle of grapevines.

"Heel, boy," Amy said. Rocket leaped to his feet.

When we reached the family, Meredith said. "Amy, you have good running form."

"Grandmère taught me." Amy pumped her arms. Rocket looked befuddled by the command. "She says runners are like ballerinas, only running goes in a straight line." Amy gazed at her great-grandmother. *"Merci."*

"De rien," Grandmère said, then whispered something in Amy's ear and kissed the top of her head. Amy giggled. They were two of a kind, with the same outlook on life. The bond between them made me smile.

Seconds later, Clair ran up. Though a little out of breath, she was beaming, equally proud of her ribbon. She held it out to display to her father.

"Who's the guy?" Amy said.

Clair scrunched up her face. "What guy?"

"You know who. Geek-Face." Amy mimed a pair of round glasses.

Clair tinged red. "Just another racer."

"I'll bet." Singsong, Amy said, "Clair's in love."

"No, I'm not. Take it back."

"Won't."

"Will." Clair made a fist.

Amy dodged behind her father's back and peeked out. "When are we getting our hair done?"

Meredith tapped her watch. "Right now."

"Uh-uh," I said. "Home first to shower. The girls are not going to a salon with grape gook and dirt clinging to their legs."

After showering and switching into play clothes for the girls and work clothes for me — I was bringing a change of clothes for the rehearsal dinner and would don them at The Cheese Shop around five thirty — we headed to the hairdressers. The first order of business was to do a trial run on the hairstyles for tomorrow's wedding. We would leave with our hair styled for the rehearsal dinner. I had even agreed to allow the makeup artist to apply my makeup for the evening. I had never done that before.

Tyanne met us at the door of Tip to Toe Salon. Bubbling with enthusiasm, she said, "Oh, sugar, look at all of you. I can see excitement in those eyes. This way. Follow me." She crooked her finger and motioned us inside. Her pretty blond hair, held off her face with a silver beaded bungee headband, swished to and fro as she marched ahead.

Clair leaned into me. "That's the band I want on my hair." She pointed to Tyanne's.

"Done," I said. While at the salon, I wanted both girls to feel like princesses.

Tip to Toe Salon had undergone a major face-lift in the past six months. Whereas it was once a beige establishment with soft lights and no character, it now bustled with energy and fun. The receptionist's desk was shiny black granite with silver trim. All the stylists' stations were black with silver mirrors. Black and white tiles decorated the floor. The customer chairs were bright yellow. Primary color art deco prints adorned the walls. Vibrant rock music played through the speakers.

The day Tyanne's sister, Lizzie, moved to town, I switched stylists. I was delighted with her skill. I had been trying to grow my hair longer but hadn't been pleased with the look, and so I reverted to my shorter hairstyle. Lizzie had a knack for a sassy cut.

"Tyanne, Lizzie has done a marvelous job with this place," I said.

"Isn't she the best?" She wiggled her fingers. "Lizzie, sugar, they're all here."

Lizzie looked entirely different from her sister. She was a good half-foot shorter, she wore her red hair an inch long, and she dripped with funky jewelry — bracelets, earrings, necklaces, and rings. She wore black shorts and a yellow tank top, and she had jacked up her height with four-inch wedge sandals. A butterfly battling a dragon tattoo graced her right shoulder.

"It's so nice to meet y'all," Lizzie said. She and Tyanne sounded the same, with similar tone and syncopated rhythms. "Aren't you the cutest?" She grabbed the chins of both of the twins and twisted them gently to one side and the other. "Good bone structure, ladies. This is going to be a pleasure."

Clair and Amy ogled each other and shared a silent exchange: *What are we in for?*

"Now, sit yourselves down and get comfy. You're going to be here for a while. And tomorrow" — Lizzie tapped Meredith's shoulder with her forefinger — "you will be the most gorgeous bride on earth."

Tears filled Meredith's eyes.

"Aw, honey, don't do that. I've got a refresher stick with caffeine for puffy eyes, but we don't want to use too much of that, you hear?" Lizzie grinned. "Pre-marriage jitters, huh? I know. I've been there, done that. Three times. But yours, of course, will last for a lifetime. I'm prickly." She chortled. "Charlotte, why don't you have a sit-down, and I'll deal with you last." She rubbed strands of my finger-combed hair and clucked her tongue. "Perhaps a little moisture for you, first. This feels like straw. Did you change shampoos?" She grinned at me.

"Slip on a gown. There are magazines in the reception area."

I stepped into the dressing room and zipped a black robe over my clothes, then exited and found a silver-and-glass coffee table filled with magazines. I scrounged for one that wasn't all about style and was delighted to find a *Food and Wine* magazine beneath the pile. Almost nothing relaxed me more than reading recipes.

"Hi, Charlotte," a woman said.

I pivoted and saw Iris checking out at the reception desk. Although her shaggy hair was refreshed, her face looked wan. The ecru blouse and slacks she wore did nothing to enhance her pallor. Only her peacock blue tote bag added a hint of color. "Are you all right?"

"Fine," she said, though her lackadaisical tone made me certain she was lying.

"Did something happen regarding the flowers for tomorrow?"

"What?" She brightened. "Oh, no, nothing like that. No, everything's fine. I'll be at the ranch raring to go."

"Is it Stratton?"

"No, he's still my plus-one. Don't worry about me." She took her receipt from the receptionist and headed out of the salon.

Lizzie tapped me on the shoulder. "Honey,

the girls and Meredith are picking out the beads and things they want in their hair. In the meantime, let's get you shampooed." She offered me a glass of water with a slice of lemon in it. "I saw you talking to Iris."

"Yes. She seemed a little down."

"She's concerned about her daughter."

"Why?"

"Chief Urso has been asking questions. Iris thinks he might be zeroing in on her daughter as a suspect in that man's murder. Can you believe it? She's a kid. A Scoop, for heaven's sake, and on her way to college." Lizzie guided me to the rear of the shop, sat me in a black leather chair by a shampoo bowl, and draped me with a cape. "And to add insult to injury, Prudence is being a pill to her."

"To the daughter?"

"No, to Iris. I'm afraid poor Prudence can't help herself."

Lizzie wet my hair with warm water, squirted it with a solution that smelled of pineapple, and scrubbed. I closed my eyes and drank in the relaxing feel of her fingers massaging my scalp.

"I guess Prudence is less than thrilled that Iris has been trying to fix her up on a date," Lizzie went on. "I heard them talking on the cell phone."

"I thought we weren't supposed to use cell phones in here."

"You're not, but that's not saying everybody follows the rules. There are those that do, and those that don't."

I was one that did . . . unless, of course, I had to break the rules to deal with an emergency or to investigate a crime.

"Anyway, Prudence was giving Iris lip" — Lizzie's fingers dug into my neck muscles — "telling Iris that she heard Stratton talking about her behind her back."

"When?"

"Last night."

"What could Prudence be referring to? Stratton was doing *Hamlet,* and she wasn't even there."

"I guess she meant afterward. According to her, Stratton went to Timothy O'Shea's Irish Pub. She saw him there."

"Prudence was at the pub? Whatever for?"

"Perhaps she was seeking companionship without Iris's help." Using heavenly warm water, Lizzie rinsed the shampoo from my hair. "So back to my story, you'll never guess what happened next. Iris called that boyfriend and gave him what for. She said she'd see him freeze in hell. I didn't hear his side, of course, but it sounded like he was begging and pleading." Lizzie laughed.

"Ooh-wee, I've got to say, it was like watching a soap opera. I miss those, now that I work days." Back in New Orleans, Lizzie had owned a coffee shop. She had always wanted to switch careers. Moving to Providence to be closer to Tyanne had given her the gumption to try something new. "I record the darned things, but it's not the same, you know? When they're on live, it's like you're in the moment with them."

I didn't have the heart to tell her that soap operas were taped. "I don't think Iris has had the best luck with men."

"That's an understatement." Lizzie leaned down and whispered, "Left at the altar."

"I heard that. So it's true?"

"All is *not* fair in love and war. Oh, and to top it all off, she once had a stalker."

Her words made me tense up. Anabelle came to mind, not because of the stalker angle — I felt sure she was telling the truth about her ex-boyfriend — but because I wondered whether Urso had nailed down the guy's whereabouts.

Lizzie tapped my shoulder. "Honey, where did you go? Relax that forehead before you look like an old lady."

I worked hard to put thoughts of the investigation out of my mind and focused on the soap operas that Lizzie mentioned, wishing I had time to watch one or two, when suddenly my thoughts boomeranged back to Anabelle. She said she had been watching TV at the time of the murder, specifically the Glenn Close retrospective. What if she had taped it? She could have forced Giacomo to the Igloo, killed him, returned to the store, breezed through the recorded programming to glean the story, and cemented her alibi. But how did she gain entrance to the Igloo? Had one of the Scoops left the door open? Was that why Urso was fixated on Iris's daughter?

As Lizzie rubbed in a luscious conditioner that smelled like coconut and cherries, she said, "Honey, this is going to do the trick and get your hair back to silky smooth. Jordan will thank me. Promise." She combed my hair, wrapped a plastic cap around it, and guided me to a hair dryer. "Grab a few winks. You've got twenty minutes."

I needed them. My brainpower was spent.

CHAPTER 30

"How was business today?" I asked Rebecca as I removed a platter of sliced Fontina, Montgomery Clothbound Cheddar, and Green Dirt Farm Bossa from The Cheese Shop's refrigerator and set it on the island counter, ready to spruce it up for the rehearsal dinner. When I had entered the store at three forty-five, the shelves had looked restocked and the cheese case neat and tidy.

"Good but not great," she said as she orbited around me, her gaze moving from my head to my toes. "I think everyone in town was either participating in or attending the race."

I frowned. "What are you doing?"

"Getting style tips. Lizzie did a nice job with your hair. It's flirty. And your makeup is ooh-la-la."

I blushed. The makeup artist had gone a little bit overboard. I rarely wore this much eyeliner and shadow and definitely not this much lipstick. She told me the extra color would make all the difference in photographs. That was when it dawned on me I hadn't arranged for a photographer for the rehearsal dinner. Luckily Tyanne had. She had thought of everything.

"The girls look fabulous, too." I added dried apricots around the rim of the cheese platter and mounded toasted almonds in the center. "You'll see tonight. Neither wanted to remove the glitzy hair jewelry or stretchy headband."

Rebecca checked the clock on the wall. "Only a few minutes until we close up and guests arrive. Are we ready?"

"All I have to do is unwrap these" — I picked up a stack of gold napkins embossed with M&M — "and change clothes." I had hung my cocktail dress in the office and had advised Tyanne and Iris to do the same.

"I almost forgot to tell you." Rebecca fluttered a hand. "Matthew called. The buses have arrived at Lavender and Lace. He's loading up his family. Nobody missed a flight."

"Perfect."

I peeked through the kitchen archway toward the wine annex. Tyanne weaved between tables, straightening chairs and place settings. Iris tweaked the cobalt blue ribbons around the crystal fishbowl-shaped vases that were filled with white roses, asters, and greens. She appeared happier than she had at Tip to Toe Salon. Perhaps all she had needed was to vent to Lizzie. At our initial appointment, Lizzie confided that hairstylists, like bartenders, were often called upon to act as consolers.

At five thirty, the twins raced in with Grandmère and Pépère. "We're here," they chimed.

Rebecca said, "Go change, Charlotte. I'll put up the *Closed for private party* sign."

Amy and Clair skirted the counter in sassy pastel dresses that Meredith had purchased as a surprise for them. They stopped, and Amy said, "On three: one, two, three."

Both posed like budding rock stars, Clair with a right hand on her hip, Amy with her left. After another count of three, each began to bounce her hip while shaking her hair. Amy's single beaded braid flipped merrily. Clair's hair, secured off her face by a bejeweled bungee headband, swayed to and fro. Shop lights flickered in the prism-like jewels.

Clair snapped her fingers and said, "One, two, three, go."

The duo sprang into a chorus of "Single

Ladies," made famous by Beyoncé. "If you liked it, then you shoulda put a ring on it. If you liked it, then you shoulda put a ring on it. Oh, oh, oh."

The girls stopped and burst into giggles.

"Well?" Amy said. "What do you think?"

"About the singing?" I said.

Rebecca elbowed me. "They mean about the whole thing. The getup, the hair."

I winked, letting her know that I wasn't dumber than dumb. "Super," I said. "You look fabulous, dah-lings."

Rebecca shooed me away from the cheese counter. "Go."

"Back in a bit, girls."

As I headed for the office, I heard Clair say, "Grandmère, come this way. I'll show you where you're sitting."

"Charlotte, sugar, wait for us." Tyanne followed me, yelling over her shoulder, "Iris, let's get a move on."

Rocket bounded to his feet when I entered the office. I saw why. He had nabbed Iris's tote bag and was using it as a headrest.

Before she could see, I snatched it from his dog pillow, brushed off his hair, and repositioned the tote bag on the office chair, logo facing out. "Bad dog," I whispered. "No treats."

He whimpered. Rags jumped to his defense and mewled as he threaded through Rocket's legs.

"Fine," I said. "You get one, but only because it's a special night." I reached into the drawer of the desk where I kept their treats, palmed two bacon-flavored biscuits, and kicked the drawer closed with my heel. "Sit."

Rocket and Rags parked their rear ends on the floor. I released their treats and they devoured them.

Tyanne entered. "Sugar, you take the bathroom first. You have to greet your guests."

"They're not my guests. They're Matthew and Meredith's."

Iris waltzed in after her and shut the door. She grabbed a floral dress hanging on a hook behind the door. "Isn't this exciting? I'm so happy for them."

"Hey, Iris," I said. "I'm sorry to hear about the breakup with Stratton."

"We're not . . . we're fine. Ooh."

She shot Tyanne a peeved look. "Your sister Lizzie has a big mouth."

"All of my sisters do, me included." Tyanne freed her simple blue sheath from a hanger. "I'm not proud of it, mind you, but we are who we are."

I stepped into the bathroom, slipped into

my dress, and checked for mascara beneath my eyes. The fine powder the makeup artist had applied was doing the trick. Nothing was smudged.

As I stepped out of the bathroom, Tyanne and Iris grinned.

"Sugar, I like you in silver," Tyanne said. "Very tasteful."

I had donned silver spangled earrings and a pair of silver tooled bracelets.

"I agree. And satin, to boot," Iris added. "Classy."

I had never owned a satin dress in my life. Freckles had insisted that she cook me up a little number for the rehearsal dinner. Heaven forbid I have to choose between buying a dress at Prudence's or Sylvie's shop.

Tyanne said, "If only Iris had brought an orchid to pin in your hair."

"Wouldn't that have been perfect?" Iris gushed. "A little splash of white for health, spirit, and purity. Just like you, Charlotte."

"Gag me," I joked. "Who paid you guys to butter me up?"

Someone knocked on the office door.

"Ready?" Rebecca said. "Guests are arriving." Without waiting for my reply, she opened the door. "Wowie." She winked. "You'd think you were the bride-to-be."

"Is it too much?" I asked, suddenly concerned.

"No, it's perfect. Don't worry. Meredith looks fabulous, too, in a frothy dress the color of blueberries." She pirouetted. "What do you think of this? A Victoria's Secret special."

The cream scoop-necked blouse and pencil skirt fit her like a glove. She had changed in the restroom at the back of the store. Three in the office were all we could manage.

"Nice."

Before leaving the room, I bent down to the animals and said, "I promise to take you on a walk later." I stroked their heads. "And yes, you can beg me for treats. I'm sure I'll oblige."

After we ate a delicious dinner of roast turkey, sweet potato pie, and grilled fall vegetables, I brought out Meredith's pick of the tiered all-cheese cakes, which I had fashioned out of four spicy, pungent cheeses: Rogue Creamery Oregon Blue, Roaring Forties Blue, Gorgonzola Mountain, and Roquefort d'Argental. Rebecca had loved decorating the cake with grapes and baby yellow roses. The result was enchanting. In an aside to Clair, I told her to steer clear of the Roquefort d'Argental. It was one of the few cheeses still cultured on rye bread, which meant gluten could transfer to the cheese.

While we toasted the happy couple with my Uncle Henry telling a funny story about Matthew as a rambunctious, naughty boy, we nibbled on cheese and grapes. After Aunt Alice closed the toasts with praise for Meredith and her beautiful, wondrous, fabulously good heart — Aunt Alice was known to prattle — Matthew rose from his chair in the wine annex and announced that he would give us the long-awaited cellar tour. He led my aunt and uncle, the twins, and our grandparents down first, with a proviso to the rest of us to wait to come down. He wanted to make sure no one felt crowded.

A few minutes later, I opened the door to the cellar, and the lusty aroma of aging cheese wafted out. "After you," I said to Meredith's parents and her brothers.

As they descended single file down the cellar stairs, Meredith sidled up to me. "I'm so excited, aren't you guys? Matthew's been dying to show us this."

"It's quite chilly down here," Meredith's mother said from below.

Tyanne sidled up to me. "I wish I'd thought to provide a few shawls."

"Grandmère brought two," Rebecca said, wiggling a pair of hand-knit oyster white shawls. "She made them herself."

"Give them to both of the moms," I suggested.

Rebecca handed them to Meredith, and she descended the stairs.

Iris joined Tyanne, Rebecca, and me. "If you don't mind, I'll stay above," she said. "I don't like confined spaces. Meanwhile, I'll gather the vases from the tables in the annex."

As she left the kitchen, and Tyanne and Rebecca headed for the cellar, Jordan, who had been quite attentive during dinner, sauntered up. He slipped his arm around my waist and whispered in my ear, "Let's elope."

"We can't."

"Sure, we can."

"No, we can't. What would my grandparents say?" I batted his chest. "Coming down?"

"Been there, done that, remember? I built it."

"You mean, you supervised."

"Same difference." He grinned. "I'm heading out to see Jacky, if that's okay."

"Give her my love."

"Charlotte?" Matthew cried. It wasn't a

distress call. He was growing impatient.

"Coming." I pecked Jordan's cheek and said, "I'll see you tomorrow at the wedding."

"Wouldn't miss it for the world."

I descended the stairs. Matthew and the others were clustered into the alcove in front of the faux window painted with the view of Providence. Tyanne, Rebecca, and I crowded beside them.

"Wait for me," a woman shouted from the top of the stairs.

Recognizing the voice, I moaned. Sylvie was not invited. How had she slipped past Jordan? He must have left through the rear door. Shoot. I glanced at Meredith. She mouthed, "Oh, no."

Sylvie emerged beneath the arch, a triumphant grin on her face. She struggled with the spaghetti strap of her sleek red sheath as she clip-clopped across the tile. "I didn't mind not being invited to dinner, but —" She gazed at her former in-laws. "Hello, Alice and Henry. Don't you both look . . ."

Her hesitation turned my insides into a whirligig. What would she say? Grandmère's hands were rising ever so slowly, ready to snare Sylvie if she dared to make a scene.

". . . lovely," Sylvie finished. "Healthy, glowing." She brazenly pecked each parent on a cheek, then turned to Meredith's folks. "And you must be Meredith's family. Lovely to meet you. I'm Sylvie, the ex. I'm sure you've heard about me, but don't worry. I promise to be on my best behavior." She winked, and Meredith and I breathed a collective, albeit silent, sigh. "Might I stand with my girlie-girls?" She snuggled between the twins. "Don't you both look as pretty as punch?"

Crisis averted, I said, "Matthew, give us the gold-star tour."

He went through his spiel about how long it had taken us to design the cellar. "Jordan, Charlotte's fiancé, was instrumental in bringing this about. He came up with the design."

"Why do you put wine in a cellar?" Aunt Alice asked.

Matthew grinned. "Well, Mom, though most wine today can be consumed young, there is wine that benefits from extra aging. It needs to reach its peak. A sauvignon blanc, for example, is great young and fresh. However, a Bordeaux is a bold wine that has a complex tannin structure and needs more aging."

Meredith tapped Matthew's arm. "You're losing them, champ. Too much information."

"Why is it so dark, Daddy?" Clair asked.

"Because UV rays will cause the degradation of the organic compounds."

Clair nodded, truly understanding his scientific explanation.

"Why is it so cold?" Sylvie asked. Gooseflesh covered her bare arms.

"It's only fifty-five degrees," Matthew answered.

"I repeat, it's cold, love."

"Higher temperatures affect aging."

"Isn't that the truth?" Aunt Alice fanned herself, removed the shawl from her shoulders, and handed it back to Grandmère with a peck to her cheek. "Can you spell hot flash?"

Grandmère laughed.

But I didn't. As the cold cut through me, my mind fixated on Giacomo Capriotti's murder. Why had he and the killer been in the freezer? Who had lured him there? A lover?

"Yoo-hoo, Charlotte." Rebecca leaned in. "Your eyes are blank. What are you thinking?"

"I'm still not certain about Hugo Hunter," I whispered. "No matter what he claimed was his alibi." Earlier I had filled her in about the fracas at the race, Hugo's fan club, and his dismay that his secret would be revealed. "So what if he is a movie director? And so what if he was taking photographs of the moon? He was the only one with reason to go into the freezer of his store."

"He or the Scoops."

"Right."

Iris had been worried about Urso questioning her daughter. Was I missing an important clue?

"Hugo makes weird films, if you ask me," Rebecca said.

"You've seen them?"

"If it's on the Mystery Now channel, I watch. *Avoidance* was so solitary and dark. I didn't "friend" Hugo on any of my social networks because I didn't know it was him, but after you told me, I researched him. In his photo" — she fluttered her fingers — "he's wearing this big pompadour hairstyle, you know, like that Illinois governor who went to jail. I think the picture's super-old."

I recalled Hugo raking his hair off his face when the fan club women nabbed him at the race, and I flashed on Tyanne saying, *Fake is as fake does.* "Might he wear a toupee?" I asked.

"Ooh." Rebecca's mouth formed a round circle. "A hair from a toupee could have been the wig hair the medical examiner identified." She pointed at me. "Hey, what if Hugo is Anabelle's stalker boyfriend in disguise?"

I gaped. "No way. That sounds like a tagline for one of Hugo's movies. Anabelle knows Hugo. I've seen her buy ice cream in the Igloo."

"Just saying," Rebecca added. "You should at least mention it to Chief Urso."

The guests applauded at something Matthew said.

He took a humble bow. "Okay, that's it. We'll bring the wines upstairs and have an after-dinner tasting. I also have nonalcoholic champagne. Who's game?"

Hands rose in the air.

When I returned upstairs, I didn't join the festivities. I slipped into the office. Rocket and Rags greeted me with a yip and meow. After I fed each a treat, I sat at the desk and dialed Urso at home.

He answered on one ring. "Don't tell me. You're recounting the guest list for tomorrow."

"No, that's Tyanne's job."

"What's up?" He sounded relaxed and settled in for the night. In the background, a TV announcer was chatting about the OSU football game.

"What's the score?" I said, being a huge

424

Buckeyes fan.

"Ten all. Why are you calling?"

"Hugo Hunter."

"Thanks to you, I caught up with him, or rather, he caught up with me. He showed me the film. It was time-stamped and dated, which corroborated where he was at the time of the murder."

"So you don't think he could have fabricated that?" I said.

"I'm not an expert, but I doubt it, and to set your mind at ease, I also followed up on Anabelle's ex-boyfriend. He's locked away in Illinois for assault."

I knew Rebecca's theory that Hugo and Anabelle's ex were one and the same was absurd.

The sound on the television decreased. "What's going through that overactive mind of yours?" Urso asked.

"The wig hair."

He paused. "How do you know about that?"

"A birdie," I said, loathe to get either Rebecca or Deputy O'Shea in trouble.

Did Urso growl? "What about the wig hair?"

"Could it have been from a toupee?"

"You're asking because Hugo wears one."

"He does?" I said, the model of innocence.

"You know he does. You think you are so slick." Urso snorted. "The hairs we found were longer, not toupee length. Now, that's all the information I'm giving you. Go back to your party. Relax. I've got this covered. I promise. I haven't ended my investigation."

An hour later, after the party disbanded and Matthew, Meredith, and the twins said good night to the last guest, I leashed Rocket and Rags and closed up the shop. While turning the key in the lock, a question popped into my head — one that I had thought of earlier but had downplayed. How had the killer entered the Igloo at night without a key and without breaking down the door?

Hoping that if I viewed the front of the ice cream parlor the answer might come to me, I steered the dog and cat in that direction. As we strolled along the sidewalk, I ran through possible scenarios.

One: Iris was worried about Urso suspecting her daughter. The girl was too young to have considered a quickie with the rakish Giacomo Capriotti in the freezer. Had someone paid her to leave the door open on purpose?

Two: Giacomo, who had a history of violence against women, muscled his way into the Igloo to accost whoever was closing the store. Again, I thought of Iris's daughter. He forced her at gunpoint into the freezer. She struggled. The gun fired. Iris's daughter got scared and lashed out with a five-gallon container of ice cream, but if that were the case, why hadn't she come forward and explained? Because the incident didn't end in rape or a beating, it ended in murder, and she was scared spitless.

Three: One of the Scoops lent her key to someone. I stayed with Iris's daughter as the perpetrator. Either she lent it to a boyfriend or she lent it to Iris. Since Iris knew about the problem, I considered Iris. She had no reason to have killed Giacomo Capriotti unless she held a grudge against Hugo — which she had intimated days ago — and meant to frame him. Or perhaps Stratton had taken the key from Iris's purse. He was bald. A wig would have disguised him. He had access to wigs. But what would have been his motive to kill the man? Had he taken up the gauntlet to protect Iris's daughter's virtue?

You're reaching, Charlotte. Keep it simple.

As Rocket, Rags, and I neared the Igloo, I peeked inside. Hugo stood at the counter happily serving ice cream. The Scoops were there, too, and neither appeared worried about being arrested.

And then I felt a hand on my shoulder.

CHAPTER 31

I whipped my head around and caught Anabelle leering at me. Her right hand was jammed into the pocket of her overcoat. My pulse skyrocketed. Did she have a gun? Would she shoot me right in front of the store? Why hadn't Rocket barked at her? Why hadn't Rags yowled? Weren't they as scared as I was? I scanned the rest of the street. No one was near. The patrons inside the ice cream parlor seemed oblivious to my dilemma.

Working hard to keep my voice steady, I said, "Hi, Anabelle. What a surprise." Was she crazy? Had she made a voodoo doll in my image? Had she killed that science teacher back in Abilene? Had she killed Giacomo Capriotti?

"I've got . . ." She struggled to pull something from her pocket.

I flinched. I had nothing. No shield. No Harry Potter invisible cloak. I was toast unless I could get her to be reasonable. "Look, Anabelle, I know the stress you're under with your dad sick and moving and . . ." I licked my lower lip. "I'm sure I can talk to Urso."

"Aha, got it." She removed her hand from her pocket.

Being a bigger chicken than I realized I was, I squeezed my eyes shut.

"Charlotte, what are you doing? Why are your eyes closed? Did you get something in one? Can I help?"

Help? Oh, for heaven's sake, had I overreacted? One at a time, I opened my eyes. Anabelle was holding a book tied with ribbon. My gaze went from the book to her face. She wasn't leering; she was grinning.

"I know I wasn't invited to the wedding," she said, "but I wanted to give this to Meredith."

My gaze was drawn back to the gift. *The Prophet,* by Kahlil Gibran.

"Whenever Meredith came into the shop, she browsed through it," Anabelle went on. "It must have special meaning to her."

In high school, Meredith and I had spent hours in the library devouring Gibran's book and dreaming of the kinds of relationships he described. A passage from the poem about marriage and how the married couple should let the winds of the heavens dance between them stuck in my head.

"Would you mind giving it to her tomorrow? I'm" — tears filled Anabelle's eyes — "leaving first thing in the morning. I'm packed and ready to go. I said good-bye to Octavia. This was the last thing I needed to do." She thrust the book at me.

"I'd be glad to," I said. "You'll be missed in Providence."

She threw herself at me and hugged me like I was her long-lost sister. How could I have ever thought she was a killer?

By dawn Sunday morning, I was already moving in high gear. I fixed breakfast for the kids and pets, opened the store, baked a number of three-onion-and-potato quiches for the Sunday brunch set, and last but not least, made sure that Bozz, my teenage Internet guru who was attending the local college and had only put in minimum time at the store of late, felt comfortable running The Cheese Shop on his own. Everyone else who worked at the store was attending the wedding.

Around eleven, Rebecca and I headed to Harvest Moon Ranch. Meredith, her mother, and the twins were already there. Lizzie was fixing their hair in the bridal suite. Rebecca and I planned to review the menu with the caterer and then change our clothes in the guest suite. Matthew would arrive with his parents, Grandmère, and Pépère at noon.

"Isn't the weather glorious?" Rebecca waltzed from one counter to the next, inspecting platter after platter of foods that were being brought to room temperature. "I'm so excited."

"Really? I couldn't tell."

She grinned. "Okay, confession. I'm imagining my own wedding, aren't you? I think we'll get married wearing bee-keeper outfits. They have veils. And we'll play "Flight of the Bumblebee" and serve honey cake." She giggled. "What will yours be like?"

"I want it to be dreamy with butterflies and all of you wearing shimmering gold. I want an Irish prayer to honor my mother, and maybe a French horn will play the wedding march to honor my dad. I've even thought that I should have Jordan come to my grandparents' house and pick me up. That's an old French tradition." Worried that any more talk of my wedding would make my misty eyes turn into waterworks, I said, "Enough about me. Let's focus on one wedding at a time, okay? There's more food in the walk-in. I want to take a look."

"Won't the caterer be upset that we're double-checking everything?"

"She'd better not," I said with a laugh. "I warned her that I was a hands-on person."

Through the kitchen window, I saw Tyanne giving instructions to the caterer, a pleasingly plump woman who reminded me of the popular chef Paula Deen. She had a winning smile, silver hair, and a cheery disposition. Six waiters, each wearing white trousers and crisp white shirts with blue ties, followed Tyanne and the caterer from the buffet table to the dining tables, which were draped in white cloths. Each table was adorned with a floral centerpiece consisting of white and blue flowers. An additional waiter was setting up the wine bar, which would feature Krupp Brothers' Black Bart Bride, a lovely blend of chardonnay and viognier grapes, and the Kali Hart pinot noir that we had drunk while watching *Hamlet*. A thin young man in a white suit attended to the Indigo Buntings in the white rattan birdcage. Iris ambled along the white carpet leading to the gazebo, doing last-minute touches like tightening bows or sprucing up arrays of sprigs of flowers tied to chairs. Stratton, Iris's plus-one, sat on a chair in the shade. Already dressed for the wedding, he looked uncomfortable and rest-less.

"Let's have a peek at the desserts." I entered the refrigerator and eyed the shelves to the right. The mini-cheesecakes and mas-carpone fruit tarts, arranged on trays, looked exactly as I had designed them. The caterer had made three dozen of each. The white chocolate candy shells for the Brie blueberry ice cream were stacked. Each would be set on a white plate lined with a sky blue doily. The ice cream was stowed in a freezer section at the rear of the walk-in.

"Brrrr." Rebecca entered and rubbed her bare arms. "Everything looks good to me. Very organized."

I opened the freezer door, retrieved a container of the Brie blueberry ice cream, and bumped the freezer door closed with my hip. "I think I'll test the texture."

"The Igloo made it. I'm sure it's divine."

I raised an eyebrow.

"Okay, fine," she laughed. "But now you're pushing the hands-on thing. You're being persnickety."

"Me? Never." As I moved toward the refrigerator exit, the container slipped. I caught it between my wrists. The cold scorched my skin. I hefted the container back between my hands and halted.

"What?" Rebecca said.

"I caught it."

"Do you want a prize? There's a lot of blue ribbon around."

"Don't you get it? I caught it with my *wrists,*" I said, emphasizing the word. "Remember when we were here last week for the tasting, and Sylvie asked Iris how her wrists were healing?"

"I didn't come."

"That's right. I forgot. Anyway, we were testing appetizers, and Iris said something to Sylvie that irritated her."

"Big surprise."

"So Sylvie lashed back and asked Iris how the salve she had given her was working on her wrists. Iris explained that she had forgotten to put on oven mitts and burned her wrists on the edges of a pot while boiling eggs for her orchids."

"Ouch."

"But how could she have done that with the pot's handles in the way?"

"I'm not following."

"Pots have at least one handle." I set the ice cream container on a refrigerator shelf and mimed lifting a saucepan. "One or both wrists couldn't have hit the side of the pot unless she was a contortionist." I exposed my already red wrists to Rebecca. "What if she freezer-burned them on a container of Brie blueberry ice cream?"

Rebecca's mouth dropped open. "Are you suggesting that Iris killed Giacomo Capriotti?"

I peeked out of the refrigerator. Iris was still tweaking her floral décor. Stratton was nowhere to be seen. I hurried back to Rebecca. "Iris was with Prudence the day Jacky told me about her husband. I accused Edy of calling him because she overheard us. She swore that Prudence overheard the conversation, too. Prudence tells Iris everything. What if Iris was the one who called Jacky's husband?"

Rebecca opened her hands. "Why would she do that?"

"Her business was suffering. She needed money. She told him that she knew how he could find Jacky. She would give him information for a price."

"But she doesn't need money. She got the wedding gig."

"After Giacomo was found dead," I said. "And it's not enough cash. Her daughter is planning on college. When I saw Iris at the bank, she was gleeful about making a deposit from Meredith. I remember her wistfully saying, 'If wishes were college tuition.'"

Rebecca shook her head. "That's not enough to convict her."

"What if the motive we ascribed to Edy holds true for Iris? Giacomo agreed to pay her, but when they met, he reneged. She got angry and lashed out."

"Iris has light hair," Rebecca said. "Urso found dark hair at the crime scene."

"Iris is dating Stratton. What if she borrowed his wig from *Hamlet*?" I remembered how Rocket had plucked Iris's tote bag from the office chair and wedged it beneath his head as a pillow. Was there a wig in that bag? Stratton was a dog groomer. Did the scent of other dogs linger on the wig?

"How did she get Giacomo to meet her at the Igloo?" Rebecca asked.

"Remember how Iris hinted that she knew something more about Hugo? She said he had a past. What if they had dated?" The other day, I asked Iris, but she didn't answer because Prudence hurried her along. I could have kicked myself for not having asked Hugo later.

Rebecca bobbed her head. "That makes sense. On one of their dates, they shared a flirtatious moment in the freezer."

"What if Iris thought, *Aha, the freezer is the perfect place to meet privately.* She stole her daughter's key to the Igloo." I related the scene at the bank when I spied Iris giving her daughter a key chain. "She had easy access to her daughter's keys."

Rebecca listened, as riveted as a kid hearing a Grimm's Fairy Tale.

"She asked Giacomo to meet her at the shop after it closed," I said. "He came alone. He'd fought with his brother, remember? Giacomo was a ladies' man. He probably thought he could get a kiss or two out of the deal. When they met, however, things got ugly between them. He said he wasn't dumb. He had figured out Jacky lived in Providence, so he didn't need Iris's help any longer and wouldn't pay her. Iris protested. She said she would warn Jacky. That's when Giacomo pulled out his Beretta. He threatened to leave her in the freezer if she said a word to anyone. Iris told me last night that she has a fear of enclosed spaces. What if that's a recent development?"

"She attacked Giacomo; they struggled."

"A shot was fired. Iris grabbed a container of ice cream —"

"— and wham! What about the gun?" Rebecca asked.

"It went flying. Iris retrieved it and the cash Giacomo had on him, and she ran."

"Why wouldn't she tell Urso it was an accident?" Rebecca said.

"She isn't blameless in this. She demanded money for information."

"That's extortion."

"Right. She had no concern about Jacky's welfare. And she kept the money."

"The bank could verify the amount of the deposit," Rebecca said.

"I'll bet she only deposited the check Meredith gave her, and she's sitting on the rest of the cash. I'll bet it's in that tote she carries around." Along with the wig.

Rebecca glanced at her watch. "Golly Moses, we've got to get cracking. Guests will be coming soon. We should change clothes but, first, we have to call Urso."

The screen door leading to the kitchen squeaked open. Iris yelled, "Charlotte, where are you?" She sounded panicked. Her high heels clacked as she crossed the kitchen floor. "My scissors broke." She appeared at the refrigerator doorway, rummaging through her tote bag. "Do you have a pair?" She looked up.

Before I could stop myself, I glanced at my wrists. Then at the ice cream container.

Iris looked between Rebecca and me, and then her face pinched with fear. She knew we knew. She pulled the refrigerator door shut.

"You told us you burned your wrists on a hot pot while boiling eggs for your orchids," I said.

"You don't understand."

"You lied. You killed Giacomo Capriotti with the vat of ice cream."

"It was an accident. He pulled a gun on me. I defended myself."

"You stole the hundred thousand he was carrying."

"He owed me. He promised. But he was a mean, vicious man."

The words to the song "Babylon" came to me: "Sleep with the devil and then you must pay."

"Look, let me leave town," Iris pleaded. "I'll never hurt anyone again. You know I won't."

I shook my head.

"There's so much good I can do with that money, Charlotte. Think about the possibilities. I can donate to the Providence Women's Shelter. I'll give half to Jacky and her baby."

"I'm sorry, Iris. You have to turn yourself in."

"No. I won't do it." She reached into the tote bag and withdrew a gun — an all-black Beretta, not gray and black like Vinnie's; it had to be Giacomo's weapon. She aimed it at me. *Dang.* Why hadn't I searched the darned tote when I had caught Rocket cozying up to it? Because I hadn't suspected Iris, that's why.

"Charlotte, do something," Rebecca cried.

"No, don't do anything, Charlotte," Iris ordered. "Don't move. Do not even breathe or I'll shoot. I won't let you ruin things for my daughter and me."

"Please, Iris, if you turn yourself in, I'm sure the court will be lenient, given the circumstances."

"Stop being so darned optimistic. It's a royal pain." Iris backed toward the exit. "I'm sorry, but I'll have to lock you in." With her left hand, she groped for the refrigerator door handle. She missed it and pivoted to gain focus.

Having a second to act, I lifted the container of Brie blueberry ice cream from the refrigerator shelf, swung it like a bowling ball, and released it. The vat hit the floor and hurtled toward Iris. It nailed her in the back of the legs. She let out an *oof,* pitched forward, and hit the refrigerator door with her forehead. At the same time, the gun flew from her grip; it skidded beneath a refrigerator shelf. I raced forward and threw myself at Iris. We tumbled to the floor. She flailed, but I was stronger. A skinny florist was no match for a cheese monger.

Rebecca dropped to her knees and reached beneath the shelves. She rose triumphantly with the Beretta in hand. "Got it."

"Good," I said. "Now get help."

CHAPTER 32

Urso, looking smart in his brown Sunday suit, entered the ranch through the front door. Rebecca edged in behind him. I met them in the foyer with Iris in tow. Mentally beaten, she wasn't struggling at all. Urso pushed his tongue against the inside of his cheek as if he was trying to figure out what to say. I countered with a glare. How could he fault my actions? Rebecca and I had been trapped in the refrigerator with a killer. If I hadn't launched the ice cream container, Iris would have escaped, and Matthew and Meredith's wedding would have been ruined — not to mention that Rebecca and I might have ended up with frostbite . . . or worse. How long could we have lasted in a locked walk-in refrigerator? The caterer wouldn't have opened the door for at least an hour.

"We've got to keep this hush-hush," I said.

"Miss Isherwood." Urso produced a pair

of handcuffs. "I am placing you under arrest."

Iris thrust her arms forward. "My daughter had nothing to do with it."

"I believe her," I said.

Urso shot me a look.

"Can you take her out the way you came?" I said. "Out of sight from any of the guests or help. If Meredith gets wind of it, she'll freak. She'll cancel the whole affair. Tyanne's reputation will be ruined. Grandmère will be furious with me."

"I'll do my best," Urso said.

"Will you be able to go to the precinct and get back in time for the wedding?" Rebecca asked.

"Miss Zook, I think there are more important matters right now."

"Not to Matthew and Meredith. They'll wonder."

Urso smirked. "I think they'll wonder the moment they don't see their floral consultant."

"I'll cover that end," I said. I couldn't suggest that Iris suffered from food poisoning; the mention of poison would put everyone on edge. Maybe I would take a page from both Edy and Anabelle's lives — Iris needed to visit a sick parent. "By the way, Iris, you did a good job on the flowers."

"Big deal," she said. "I don't think they'll have a need for my skills in jail."

Just when it was time for me to take my seat, I saw Jordan, looking as handsome as ever in a gray pin-striped suit. My gown rustled as I ran to him.

"You look fabulous," he said.

"So do you." I pecked his cheek, grabbed his hand, and we walked down the white carpet to the tune of the Beatles' "Here, There, and Everywhere."

As we sat in the front row beside Grand-mère and Pépère, Jordan leaned in. "Now, are you going to tell me what's going on?"

Channeling Scarlet O'Hara, I batted my eyelashes. "Whatever could you mean?"

"Urso arrived late. Iris is missing. And you have minor burns on your wrists."

"Why, you astound me with your powers of observation, sir."

"Charlotte," he said, dragging out my name.

"Okay, fine." In a hushed voice, I related the whole tale. He whistled. I batted his leg. The moment I finished, the wedding procession began. Talk about timing.

Fifteen minutes later, the pastor held out his hands and said, "By the power vested in

445

me by the state of Ohio, I now pronounce you man and wife. You may kiss the bride."

Matthew and Meredith turned toward each other, kissed tenderly, and faced the crowd.

"Guests and family, I present to you Mr. and Mrs. Matthew Bessette."

The string quartet played "All You Need Is Love," and Tyanne signaled the young man in the white suit to unlatch the birdcage. Indigo Buntings flew from their confinement and spiraled into the air. At the same time, the twins swooped to Matthew and Meredith and threw their arms around them. Guests applauded. I squeezed Jordan's hand and peeked at Sylvie, who sat beyond Jordan and was properly dressed, for once, in a sea blue frock that scooped low in front, but not too low. Mouth pursed, she patted her palms together politely. I was pleased that she had shown restraint — no ladybugs or other surprises — which was a marvel and, no doubt, a challenge worthy of the mighty Hercules.

Matthew and Meredith, each holding one of the twins' hands, strolled down the white carpet. At the end of the rows of chairs, they turned right and headed back to the gazebo where they would receive guests. Grandmère and Pépère followed, and then Meredith's parents and Matthew's parents. All were grinning. None knew what had gone down in the Harvest Moon Ranch's kitchen.

Following the ceremony, Grandmère said, "Charlotte, Jordan, *venez ici.*" She stood with Pépère and the twins at one end of the buffet table.

We joined them, and Jordan openly admired the caterer's bountiful, multilevel display. Atop each high point stood a blue and white floral bouquet set in a hand-blown, handkerchief-shaped crystal vase.

"You have outdone yourself with the menu," Grandmère said.

"Thank you, but the caterer did all the work."

"Ne sois pas si modeste," she said.

"I'm not being modest."

She petted my cheek. "So like your father. Will you dine with us?"

"Please do, Aunt Charlotte," Clair said. "We're sitting at the table near Meredith's and Daddy's table. See our sweaters on the chairs?"

"Closest to the hill," Amy pointed.

Meredith and Matthew sat at the wedding couple's table with their backs to the valley so they could face their guests. Meredith hadn't cared for a formal sit-down dinner.

She wanted everyone to feel free to move about.

"We've taken the whole table. Mum is sitting with us, too."

"Mum particularly liked the heart-shaped corkscrew and wine stopper table gifts," Amy said.

"Only after we told her we picked them out," Clair added.

I eyed my grandmother. She smiled. "We do what we must on a special day, *non?*"

"We do, indeed."

"Lead the way, *mes petites-filles.*" Pépère nudged the twins.

As my grandmother moved along the buffet, filling her plate with Dorset Drum cheese, the goat cheese crostini, and ricotta-stuffed mushrooms, she turned to Jordan and winked. "It is nice to see your sister enjoying herself."

Jacky was already seated at one of the dining tables. Hugo nestled beside her, feeding her tidbits from his plate.

"They are in love, *n'est-ce pas?*" Grandmère asked. "He does not take his eyes off of her."

"I'm not sure about Jacky," Jordan said, "but Hugo has asked Jacky to star in his next film. Right now, I think he's assessing the angles of her face that he likes best."

I tilted my head. "Really?"

Jordan grinned. "Kid you not."

I placed a couple of radicchio marmalade turnovers on my plate, my mouth watering in expectation.

Grandmère said, "She will leave Providence?"

Jordan shrugged. "Her life is her own now that her husband is dead."

Grandmère scanned the rest of the wedding guests. "Our little Rebecca looks delicious."

Rebecca had changed into a dandelion yellow dress with cap sleeves and a pair of buff sandals. Her hunky Hawaiian fiancé had returned from his jaunt with his folks and, to show his devotion, had dressed in a buff suit, white shirt, and dandelion yellow tie. They stood beside the gazebo beaming at one another.

"On the other hand, *chérie,* our Chief Urso looks *très désolé.*"

Urso had delivered Iris to jail and made it back to the wedding in the nick of time, but he did look distressed.

"Hello, Chief Urso." Grandmère waved to him. She nudged me. "Talk to him. Cheer him up."

Far be it from me to tell her I was most likely the reason he was out of sorts.

Urso joined us and nodded greetings to everyone.

I sidled to him and whispered, "So?"

"So, what?"

"Iris?"

"She's remorseful and giving her entire statement to Deputy Rodham."

"And her daughter?"

"She swears that her daughter has no knowledge of anything she did. The girl is innocent."

"Could her mother's plea of guilty affect her chance of getting into college?"

Urso shook his head. "I doubt it. A child should not be measured by the integrity, or lack thereof, of a parent. By the way, I meant to tell you that I heard from Capriotti's estate lawyer. Jacky is sole inheritor. No foundation. No Vinnie. The estate is large."

The string quartet stopped, and Tyanne clicked a spoon against a crystal glass. "Yoohoo, everyone. Welcome. Do you have champagne?"

"I don't," Amy said.

I grinned. "Your father brought some natural almond soda for you. Set your plates on the table and hurry to the wine bar for a glass."

As the twins scurried off, a waiter carrying a tray of wine flutes filled with Veuve Clicquot brut champagne toured through the guests. I selected five glasses, two for my grandparents and the remainder for Jordan, Urso, and me.

When everyone held a glass, Tyanne said, "Charlotte, I believe you have a toast prepared."

My mother had embroidered and framed an old Irish blessing, which hung in my bedroom. The words were etched on my brain. As everyone drew silent, tears pressed at the backs of my eyes. I raised my glass of champagne and said, "May God be with you and bless you. May you see your children's children. May you be poor in misfortune, rich in blessings. May you know nothing but happiness from this day forward."

The guests raised their glasses and yelled, "Hear, hear."

Meredith blew me a kiss. So did Matthew.

"And now," I added, "if you'll join me in singing 'The Irish Blessing.' I believe many of you know the words, since it's sung almost nightly at Timothy O'Shea's Irish Pub." The violin played a middle C note. I eyed Jordan and he nodded. Together we sang, "May the road rise up to meet you, may the wind be ever at your back. May the sun shine warm upon your face, and the rain fall soft upon your fields."

When we finished the verse, the guests let out another cheer.

Grandmère smiled a flinty grin at me. "*Chérie,* you have a secret you've been keeping from me."

My face grew warm. "Um, no. No secret." Had Urso told her what had happened with regard to Iris?

"Your Jordan," she said.

Oh, no. She had found out — from Rebecca or Delilah or someone — about Jordan's past. With all that went on in the last two weeks with Jacky and her husband's murder and the rumors, how could she not? Even so, my stomach twisted into a pretzel. Was she mad at me for not confiding in her?

She eyed Jordan. "You are a man of mystery. You not only know how to build a set, but you have a fine voice."

I breathed easier. "Yes, he does."

Grandmère crooked a finger. "You must be part of my next musical."

Jordan shook his head.

Urso joked, "You're stuck now, buddy."

I nudged Jordan. "I told you so."

"*Mais oui.* You must. I am not taking no for an answer." Grandmère finished loading her plate and headed toward the table, singing "The Irish Blessing."

Jordan chuckled. "She is a pistol."

"Don't I know it."

Urso left us and made his way to the bride and groom.

When Jordan and I finished eating, I asked him to take a stroll. I reached for his hand. "C'mon. I've got something to tell you. You're going to like it."

He slung an arm around my waist.

At the edge of the bluff, I turned into him and walked my fingers up the front of his shirt. I stopped at his neck and ran a fingertip along the hollow of his neck. "I've picked a date for our wedding. You wanted December. I like December, too. December tenth. My mother and father's anniversary. Is that okay?"

He turned silent.

"Oho," I teased. "You don't like that number? Fine. The fifteenth, the twentieth?"

"Charlotte." He swallowed hard then gripped my hand. He held it against his chest.

My stomach plummeted. Had he changed his mind? Had I blown it by delaying? Shoot, shoot, shoot. When would I learn to seize a good opportunity? "Is it because I didn't tell you about Iris the moment I sat down?"

"No." He released me and slipped his

hand into his pocket. "I'm sorry about Iris, and I'm sorry, despite my warnings, that you got involved again but, no, that's not it."

I swallowed the lump in my throat and said in a teasing tone, "Okay, let me guess. Throughout the service, your right hand was fingering something in your pocket. It has something to do with that, doesn't it?" I tapped his arm. "I know it's not an engagement ring because I'm wearing that. It's not your cell phone, because you keep that in your left. So what's in there?" I pawed at his wrist, playing like I might filch whatever he was hiding.

"Don't." He backed away, his voice stern.

I stiffened. "What's in there?"

His mouth turned grim. "It's a slip of paper with a phone number on it."

"Whose phone number?" Suddenly I couldn't breathe. Was there one more secret I needed to learn? Was there another woman?

"It's my WITSEC case officer's phone number. My *new* WITSEC case officer. I have to leave next week."

"For where?"

"New York. The trial has been moved up. The attorney isn't sure how long the trial will last."

RECIPES

BRIE BLUEBERRY ICE CREAM

1 cup half-and-half
1 cup heavy cream
1/2 cup mascarpone cheese
3 egg yolks
1 cup sugar
1 teaspoon vanilla extract
dash of nutmeg
4 ounces Brie or Fromage d'Affinois, trimmed of its rind
1/2 cup blueberries (rinsed and de-stemmed)

Put the half-and-half, cream, and mascarpone cheese into a saucepan. Place over medium heat and stir occasionally until steaming.

In a bowl, whisk the egg yolks, sugar, and vanilla together. Once the cream mixture is hot, begin ladling small amounts into the eggs while whisking.

After adding about 1/2 cup of the hot cream mixture to the eggs, pour the cream-egg mixture back into the saucepan and stir continuously while it thickens. Once the mixture starts steaming gently again, you can turn off the heat. Keep stirring for a few minutes.

Add the Brie in chunks and stir vigorously to melt the cheese into the custard. Add a dash of nutmeg.

Place the creamy mixture into a bowl, cover, and chill thoroughly, about 2 hours.

Freeze in an ice cream maker per its instructions. [Mine requires 30 minutes of automatic stirring action.]

Five minutes before complete, add in the blueberries. Serve with blueberry sauce.

BLUEBERRY SAUCE

1/2 cup blueberries
1 tablespoon lemon juice
1 tablespoon water
3 tablespoons sugar

Place all the ingredients in a saucepan and place over medium heat. Bring to a simmer and cook for 5 minutes. Allow to cool and then refrigerate. Reheat gently if you want a warm sauce.

BROCCOLINI, PINE NUT, AND EDAM CHEESE QUICHE

1 pie shell, unbaked (homemade or frozen)
3/4 cup chopped broccolini (blanched)
2 teaspoons olive oil
1/2 teaspoon chopped garlic
2 tablespoons pine nuts
1/4 cup cream of chicken soup
3/4 cup milk
4 eggs
1/2 teaspoon dried bouquet garni
1/2 teaspoon salt
1/4 teaspoon ground pepper
4 ounces shredded Edam cheese (more, if desired)

Blanch broccolini in boiling hot water for 1 minute then drain and rinse with cold water.

Sauté garlic and pine nuts in olive oil at medium heat.

Take pan off burner, add drained broccolini, and sauté for 1 minute.

Sprinkle 2 ounces of shredded Edam cheese on piecrust.

Put sautéed vegetables and nuts on top of cheese.

Mix soup, milk, eggs, and seasonings together.

Pour into piecrust on top of vegetables.

Sprinkle with remaining cheese.

Bake 35–40 minutes at 375° until quiche is firm and lightly brown on top.

GLUTEN-FREE POPOVERS

3/4 cup tapioca flour
1/4 cup potato flour
1/4 cup sweet rice flour
1 teaspoon whey powder
1/2 teaspoon salt
1 cup half-and-half
2 large eggs, room temperature

Preheat oven to 450°.

Liberally grease a popover pan with vegetable oil.

Combine gluten-free flours, whey powder, and salt in a small mixing bowl.

Combine half-and-half, eggs, and gluten-free flour mixture in a large blender pitcher. [* IMPORTANT: Add the items in that specific order.] Blend at high speed for 30 seconds. Scrape down the sides of the pitcher and pulse briefly, 15 seconds. The batter should look like thin pancake batter.

Place popover pan in preheated oven for 3 minutes. Carefully remove pan and fill each popover cup 1/2 to 2/3 full. Place pan back in preheated 450° oven and bake for about 15–20 minutes. Reduce oven temperature to 300° and bake an additional 5–7 minutes or until the popovers are deep golden brown. Serve warm.

Note: I made a batch using a cupcake tin instead of a popover tin. It doubled the amount of popovers and you need to cut the baking time to a total of 15 minutes. They cook fast!!!

DELILAH'S GRILLED CHEESE WITH GRAPES, ONIONS, AND BACON
(SERVES 2)

4 slices bread
4 tablespoons butter
4 tablespoons cream cheese
4–6 oz. Doux de Montagne or Fromage d'Affinois cheese
6–8 seedless grapes
1/2 yellow onion, chopped
2 tablespoons olive oil
4 slices bacon, cooked crisply and chopped
1 teaspoon pepper
dash of paprika

For each sandwich, butter two slices of bread on one side only. Spread cream cheese on the other side of the bread.

Meanwhile, grill the bacon to crisp and drain on paper towels. When cool, cut or chop the bacon into small bites. [Delilah suggests grilling the bacon in the microwave, on paper towels. No mess. Takes about 3–4 minutes to make them crisp.]

Sauté the chopped onion in a sauté pan with the olive oil for 3–5 minutes until slightly browned. Cool.

Rinse and slice the grapes into "chopped olive" sized slices.

In a bowl, mix the bacon, onion, grapes, pepper, and dash of paprika together like a salsa.

Heat up a flat grilling pan. Place one slice of bread, butter side down, on hot grilling surface. Layer with Doux de Montagne or Fromage d'Affinois (or other favorite soft) cheese. Top with the grape-onion salsa. Top with the other piece of bread (butter side up). [Repeat for the second sandwich.]

Grill the sandwiches on low to medium for 4–5 minutes. Flip the sandwiches and grill for another 4–5 minutes, until a nice golden brown and cheese is oozing.

Remove from heat and serve immediately.

[This can be made on gluten-free bread. It is still amazing.]

RICOTTA-STUFFED MUSHROOMS
6 mushroom caps
4 tablespoons fresh ricotta cheese
2 tablespoons Rice Chex-style cereal, crumbled

1 teaspoon fresh parsley, chopped
1 teaspoon fresh rosemary, chopped
1/2 teaspoon salt
1/2 teaspoon ground pepper
3 dashes Worcestershire sauce
2 tablespoons olive oil
Mixed lettuce
Paprika
Parsley sprigs

Preheat oven to 400°.

Brush a flat baking pan or cookie sheet with 1 tablespoon olive oil.

Wash and scoop out mushroom caps. Drain on paper towels.

Meanwhile, mix ricotta cheese, crumbled Rice Chex-style cereal, parsley, rosemary, salt, pepper, and Worcestershire sauce in a bowl.

Brush mushrooms with remaining olive oil. Spoon a tablespoon-plus of cheese mixture into each mushroom cap. Set the caps on the baking pan or cookie sheet and bake for 15 minutes.

Remove from oven. Sprinkle with paprika. Set a sprig of parsley on each. Place on a serving plate adorned with mixed lettuce.

Serve warm. (Warning: Do not eat right out of the oven or they will burn the inside of your mouth!!)

The employees of Thorndike Press hope you have enjoyed this Large Print book. All our Thorndike, Wheeler, and Kennebec Large Print titles are designed for easy reading, and all our books are made to last. Other Thorndike Press Large Print books are available at your library, through selected bookstores, or directly from us.

For information about titles, please call:
  (800) 223-1244

or visit our Web site at:
  http://gale.cengage.com/thorndike

To share your comments, please write:
  Publisher
  Thorndike Press
  10 Water St., Suite 310
  Waterville, ME 04901

CPSIA information can be obtained
at www.ICGtesting.com
Printed in the USA
BVHW032122300920
590043BV00001B/4